I0676392

Tales of Asculum

Dracona's Rebirth

by
V.J.O. Gardner

Ink Smith Publishing
www.ink-smith.com

Tales of Asculum
Dracona's Rebirth
By V.J.O. Gardner

Copyright © 2013 V.J.O. Gardner
All Rights Reserved
Please visit www.vjogardner.com

Cover Art by Katerina Danailova

All rights reserved. This book or any portion therof may not be reproduced or used in any manner whatsoever without the express written permission of the publisher except for the use of brief quotations in a book review.

The final approval for this literary material is granted by the author.

Printed in the U.S.A, 2014

All characters appearing in this work are fictitious. Any resemblance to real persons, living or dead is purely coincidental.

ISBN: 978-1-939156-54-9

Ink Smith Publishing
710 S. Myrtle Ave Suite 209
Monrovia, CA 91016

www.inksmith.com

Table of Contents

Acknowledgements

The journey of becoming a published author has been quite the adventure. Without the help of others it would not have been possible. I would like to thank my friends and family for putting up with me throughout the process.The adventure began with a story I called *Quest of the King* which developed into what is now *Dracona's Rebirth*. I thank my neighbors for repeatedly reading my manuscripts. Without my husband, Earle, *Dracona's Rebirth* would not be possible. In spite of his initial refusal to read and be a critic of what I wrote, he has become my best content editor. He spots the details that I overlook. He is the other half that makes me whole. I thank the rest of my family for their love and support.

I would also like to thank several authors who have become good friends and allies that helped me to get to this point. Thomas Wright (*The Fisherman's Catch*) for being brave enough to rent a kiosk at a mall for a group of independent authors to sell their own books at. I thank C. David Belt (*The Children of Lilith Series*) for his love of display, costumes and swords along with his beautiful singing that helps both pass the slow times and attract attention. Bryce Anderson (*Singularity Girl*) an author whom I first met as he was learning how to present his book. By mentoring him it opened my eyes to areas that I need to improve in. Also for his enthusiasm and warped sense of humor that is so much like my own. Last, but certainly not least, Stephen Miller (*Captain Justo Series* and *The Santa Claus League*) for teaching me the art of the pitch along with helping me keep my sanity and have the strength to not give up.

I am grateful for all of those who reviewed my first book, Blood of Ancient Kings, pointing out both my strengths and my flaws. As painful as a one star review can be it proved to be the greatest gift I got for I was able to use that criticism to improve my writing. Others pointed out that I accurately depicted medieval peasant life but needed to clarify the world my books are set in is not medieval Europe. Courtney Brooks and Clair Amber both showed me that my characters were believable and even lovable. Finally I want to thank Katerina Danailova for the beautiful and amazing artwork for the cover.

Table of Contents

Acknowledgements

The journey of becoming a published author has been quite the adventure. Without the help of others it would not have been possible. I would like to thank my friends and family for putting up with me throughout the process. The adventure began with a story I called *Quest of the King* which developed into what is now *Dracona's Rebirth*. I thank my neighbors for repeatedly reading my manuscripts. Without my husband, Earle, *Dracona's Rebirth* would not be possible. In spite of his initial refusal to read and be a critic of what I wrote, he has become my best content editor. He spots the details that I overlook. He is the other half that makes me whole. I thank the rest of my family for their love and support.

I would also like to thank several authors who have become good friends and allies that helped me to get to this point. Thomas Wright (*The Fisherman's Catch*) for being brave enough to rent a kiosk at a mall for a group of independent authors to sell their own books at. I thank C. David Belt (*The Children of Lilith Series*) for his love of display, costumes and swords along with his beautiful singing that helps both pass the slow times and attract attention. Bryce Anderson (*Singularity Girl*) an author whom I first met as he was learning how to present his book. By mentoring him it opened my eyes to areas that I need to improve in. Also for his enthusiasm and warped sense of humor that is so much like my own. Last, but certainly not least, Stephen Miller (*Captain Justo Series* and *The Santa Claus League*) for teaching me the art of the pitch along with helping me keep my sanity and have the strength to not give up.

I am grateful for all of those who reviewed my first book, Blood of Ancient Kings, pointing out both my strengths and my flaws. As painful as a one star review can be it proved to be the greatest gift I got for I was able to use that criticism to improve my writing. Others pointed out that I accurately depicted medieval peasant life but needed to clarify the world my books are set in is not medieval Europe. Courtney Brooks and Clair Amber both showed me that my characters were believable and even lovable. Finally I want to thank Katerina Danailova for the beautiful and amazing artwork for the cover.

Prologue

"Why doesn't anyone go into the forest to the east?" Cherie asked Olvan as they walked towards his house.

"It belongs to the lords of Dracona," Olvan said. "Of the few men that dared go in, one came back a babbling idiot. He had to be watched like a child until he died."

"What about the others?" she asked.

"The other two were found laid out next to the forest," Olvan said. "There wasn't a mark on them anywhere, but they were dead just the same. Since then we stay out of their forest and they stay in it. Occasionally we will see one just inside the edge of the forest herding one of our cattle farther into the forest. It's best to just let them do it. If we belonged to a kingdom we would be paying taxes to the king anyway, so we might as well let them take a cow now and then so they will leave us alone."

Cherie considered that as they walked along. She wondered what he would think when she told him who she really was and why she had been travelling.

"I've heard that the villagers once lived in the town around the castle of Dracona, but those that survived to move here would never talk about why they left," Olvan said. "Grandfather said his father had nightmares frequently. He had burn scars on one arm and most of his back."

Cherie shook her head. She would definitely stay out of Dracona's forest.

"You look worried," Olvan said as he stopped. "I didn't mean to frighten you with such talk."

"It's just that I find myself wanting to stay here with you," Cherie said. "I've never met a man quite like you."

Olvan smiled and said, "I would be very happy if you stayed. You are so different from any woman in the village. I find myself dreaming about you and then I wake to find myself alone."

"Oh, Olvan, are you saying?" Cherie asked as her heart started beating faster.

"I've fallen in love with you, Cherie," Olvan said.

She threw her arms around his neck and hugged him. He put his arms around her. She knew what she had to tell him might change his mind. She knew that if she married him it was almost guaranteed that what should be her duty would pass to her sister. She also knew what she was giving up if she married Olvan, but she loved him.

In the silence there were voices. In the darkness there was light. In the stillness there was life. In the cold there was warmth. Yet he was lonely.

Chapter 1 – The Last Lords of Dracona

It was late in the evening when Bryant finished weeding the garden. He was tired and hungry, but not eager to return to the empty castle. His father had been gone for a couple of days to check the forest for trespassers. Bryant had decided to remain at the castle since he and Father had spent a lot of time arguing over the past few weeks. Life at the castle was hard and lonely.

He went inside to fix a cold supper when he heard Haskell's voice in his mind say, 'Eamon's horse fell crossing the creek near the village. He's been injured!'

Bryant felt like his heart had stopped.

"If they find him alone and injured they'll kill him!" he responded out loud as he quickly went back outside and headed for the stables.

His mind went through what else he would need to bring and he went instead towards the armory to get the sword he seldom carried.

He found it and was headed to the stables when Haskell said in a worried tone, 'A villager he doesn't recognize has found him.'

"No!" Bryant cried as he stopped in the center of the courtyard.

He ran to the stables to get his horse saddled. He was nearly finished when Haskell spoke again.

'The villager has offered to help him. He doesn't even have a knife.'

"He's still in grave danger! I've got to get to him now. The horse might not be fast enough!" Bryant responded as he buckled on his sword.

'The villager is stitching the wound shut. Eamon says he is safe and wants you to go find the finest yearling bull and cow from the mountain pasture and mark them with the old mark. Meet him tomorrow at the south clearing midway to the village.'

The images that accompanied Haskell's words told Bryant exactly where he needed to meet his father. Bryant gathered some food and a couple skins of water so he could leave at dawn. He found some rope to make two halters from. He was surprised that Haskell had spoken to him. It was the longest conversation he had ever had with his father's dragon. After a restless night he saddled his horse and was soon on his way to the mountain pasture. It took him some time to find the two cattle. He took them to the castle and found the tool he would heat and use to mark them with. He trapped first the bull, then the cow between the wall and a stall door so he could press the tool he heated in a torch to their left shoulders. When he was finished both were marked with what looked like two mountains with a line between them, but Bryant knew it symbolized a

2

dragon. Like the clasp on his cape it was a reminder of the duty that bound him and his father to remain in the empty castle and town caring for the last two dragons; Haskell and his mate Evelina.

He mounted and started down the trail back to the town. They clattered though the empty streets breaking the silence that hung heavily in the abandoned town. The memories of the awful incident that emptied the town and castle of Dracona were still all too fresh in Bryant's memory. He had run through the chaotic streets filled with people running from burning houses screaming in terror and in pain. When he reached the fields surrounding the town he found his father clutching Uncle Rolf's body in his arms with his sword still in it. Not far away Haskell had Uncle Rolf's dragon, Mackin, by the throat as the dragon fought a losing battle with death. Bryant had sunk to his knees and cried with his father as the smell of smoke, blood and burning flesh filled the air.

Entering the forest broke through his thoughts and brought his mind back to the present. Bryant arrived in the clearing a couple of hours before supper to find his father waiting for him next to a small fire.

"Are you alright?" Bryant asked as he noticed the scabs on father's horse's knees. "What happened?"

"I'm sore, but I'll recover," Father said as he held out his arm to reveal a long gash that was stitched shut. "I didn't expect any help, but a young man who just moved to the village came running into the forest to find me when he heard me fall. He'll soon get married and the cattle are for him. I had you mark them so we would know they belong to him and not keep any."

"When Haskell told me you were injured, I was terrified that you would be killed before I could get to you," Bryant admitted as he sat down.

"The man who helped me is named Langward. He is about your stature with dark curly hair and eyes that are very dark. He understands that we are not evil, but just wish to be left alone. He mentioned he has his own past that he wishes to forget."

"Did he say what it was? Certainly it can't be as shameful as ours."

"He told me enough that I know he understands the pain in my heart," Father said. "His kindness gives me hope that someday you will be free of the shame my brother has brought upon us both. Meet him tomorrow at dusk near where I fell and give him the cattle. He's expecting you. He will need his own cattle if he is to support his new wife and any children she bears him."

Bryant nodded knowing Father would tell him no more.

"Have you eaten?" Bryant asked and Father shook his head.

Bryant opened his saddlebags and gave his father some meat and bread. He was worried about Father. It had been close to a hundred years since Father had to kill Uncle Rolf, but he still carried that shame and guilt. It was long enough that most of the villagers certainly didn't remember what happened, but they still remembered the fear. The villagers only lived about seventy five to a hundred years, but Bryant was far older than that already and would live to be seven hundred to a thousand years old. Although Father was only five hundred and sixty right now he looked much older.

Bryant's mother had fled with the rest of their people across the mountains to establish the village of Merton on a rocky cliff overlooking the ocean, but Bryant and his father were bound to remain in Dracona. They were the last two men in their family and the last to bear the title of Lord Dracona passed down from their ancestor who had founded Dracona. Bryant knew little about where Lord Fanchon came from and even less about the strange language that he had spoken. Bryant missed the days when the villagers had lived in the town and his family lived in the castle, but after that horrible day everything had changed forever. The village and the castle sat abandoned, frozen in the past.

"I know that look," Father said suddenly breaking through Bryant's thoughts. "You can't dwell in the past."

"For us there is no future," Bryant said bitterly. "This is all there will ever be. We will live and die alone. We will be shunned, hated and finally forgotten."

"I know," Father said softly. "Still, I pray that your fate will be different than mine. We should go visit Merton. You need to spend some time with the living instead of being stuck here where reminders of death are ever present."

"When I visit Merton I feel awkward and out of place. Even people I used to be friends with barely speak to me," Bryant said with a sigh.

"Someday you will be their leader, Bryant," Father said. "You can't forget that. They will look to you for leadership and guidance."

Bryant considered his possible responses knowing each one would only start the age old argument that there was no way for either of them to win. They sat in silence watching the fire slowly die. He could tell Father was talking with Haskell from the expression on his face. Without Haskell, Father probably would have taken his own life after burying his brother. Bryant had often wished for a brother, but that was as likely as the town being repaired and repopulated.

"I'd better be heading back to the castle," Father said. "It's a long walk and I don't want my arm to start bleeding again."

"Take some of this food and a skin of water," Bryant said. "You'll get hungry before getting back to the castle. Perhaps you should wait here until dark and get Haskell to take you back to the castle. I'll get your horse and bring it back to the castle for you."

"Perhaps that would be for the best," Father said with a sigh. "I'm going to sleep. I'm still tired from walking."

Father moved over into the shade and lay down. Soon he was snoring. Bryant watched the cattle and horses graze while he wondered what to expect when he delivered the cattle to Langward. The last few contacts they had with any of the villagers hadn't gone well at all. One had gone completely crazy after seeing Haskell. They finally had to give him a sleeping draught and took him to the edge of the forest near the village. Bryant had watched over him until he woke and found his way to the village. Soon his family found him and calmed him. A couple of years later two men were found dead in the armory. The box containing Fanchon's Sword was opened. Bryant had been told to never touch it. The sword lay still in the box, but not cradled in its proper place. He had tapped the side of the box and was relieved when the sword settled back in place so the lid could be shut.

That time instead of returning a live man to his family, Bryant and his father had returned the bodies to be buried by the mourning families. Bryant had made certain that they were laid out so they would fit in the coffins for burial. He didn't want them to appear to have been simply carelessly left there. He knew it would be traumatic enough for the families to find them dead. Again he had watched over the bodies until they were found by their families. He quietly left to join his father as the wails of the women faded in the distance. These were memories that were still painfully fresh in his mind. Equally painful was the aching loneliness and hopelessness that seemed to be his constant companions. Even with his father he felt alone.

The remainder of the day went by slowly and night was welcome relief from the heat. Soon after dark Haskell arrived and he helped Father to mount.

"I'll see you in a couple of days, Bryant," Father said. "You can trust Langward."

"Be careful dismounting," Bryant said before jumping down to the ground.

He walked around to Haskell's head and stood facing the dragon.

Haskell put his head down and Bryant said softly, "Get him home safely."

Haskell nodded slightly and pushed Bryant gently back with his nose. Bryant went over to the animals and watched Haskell launch into the air. Bryant watched towards the castle even after the trees hid the dragon and his father from his sight. When he finally settled down to sleep his dreams were troubled and he woke tired. It would be a long day. He stayed in the clearing until afternoon before heading towards the village. Soon he found the designated meeting place and could see the creek bed had been disturbed where Father's horse had stumbled. After tying the cattle to a tree he tied his horse to another and ate some more bread.

He found a place to sit and wait as he watched the village through the trees. The people worked in the fields as children played and laughed. He saw women bringing water to the men working in the fields. It was a hard life, but they seemed happy. For Bryant it was almost as painful to watch as the memories that had erased all hope for such happiness from his life. He was glad when the people went into their homes to eat. He stood as he saw a lone man with dark hair walking along the edge of the forest coming from the south west. His hair was curly and his shoulders broad as he held his head higher than any of the villagers. He was obviously not accustomed to stooping over to work in the fields. He knew this must be Langward. When the man stopped just outside the forest Bryant stepped forward to be visible to Langward in the shadow of the trees.

"You are Langward?" Bryant asked.

Langward nodded and he gestured Langward forward. Langward followed him to where his horse and the two cattle were tied.

"Thank you for helping my father," Bryant said. "He has been so bitter towards the villagers. He did not expect anyone to help him when he was injured. He thought at first that you would kill him."

"I am a peaceful man," Langward said. "I have heard some about you and your father, but I know that what is seen and said is sometimes not the entire truth. Know that I am willing to be of assistance, you only need to ask."

"Always mark your cattle as these two have been marked," Bryant said as he handed the lead ropes of the two cattle to him. "We will drive them out of the forest and not keep any."

"Thank you," Langward said as Bryant mounted his horse. "I will not tell anyone of meeting you. They probably wouldn't believe me. I'll say that I found these two coming out of the forest."

Bryant nodded and turned his horse deeper into the forest leaving Langward standing there with the cattle. He had been surprised that Langward had volunteered his assistance. It was the first time anyone had made such an offer. Langward had seemed completely unafraid of him. Bryant returned to the clearing where Father's horse waited. The following morning he took a more direct route to the castle in spite of having to pass through the center of town where the most burned buildings stood. The brick structures remained along with some of the charred wood. The dark windows and missing doors made the homes seem like skulls reminding him of the death Rolf's rampage had brought to Dracona.

Once in the castle courtyard he took care of the horses and turned them loose in the tiny pasture inside the castle wall before taking his saddlebags inside. Although the castle was dark, he didn't bother lighting a torch or candle. He went up the stairs to the fourth floor to his room and his bed. His dreams were troubled and he woke to his father shaking his shoulder.

"You were screaming again," Father said. "Same dream?"

"A little different, but pretty much the same," he said with a sigh as he sat up. "This time you were injured too and I was left completely alone."

"A part of me did die that day," Father said softly as a tear ran down his face. "My greatest fear is leaving you alone. You should get married Bryant. You need someone besides me here with you."

"To bring a woman here would be cruel," Bryant replied. "Besides none of the women in Merton will speak to me unless I speak first. It seems they answer only out of politeness and quickly excuse themselves. Only Brenndah is friendly to me and she doesn't speak to anyone. I know she of all women would not want to return to Dracona. There's no sense in even trying to speak to any of the village women and risk repeating the past."

"Try to get some sleep. We'll leave in the morning for Merton. Haskell can take us since I really don't want to ride on horseback with this arm," Father said as he stood up.

Bryant lay down as his father shut the door behind him, but just couldn't sleep with all his emotions jumbled up. He sighed and sat up knowing it was still several long hours to dawn. He lit a lamp and got out his journal. He began to write about what had happened and how he felt about it. Soon tears were pouring down his face as he tried to put his heartache into words. He was startled as a hand was placed on his shoulder. He shut the journal quickly.

"I know, Son," Father said softly. "I know. I couldn't sleep either. Let's get packed and go."

Bryant quickly gathered some fresh clothing together. He was packing the saddlebags when Father returned.

"All black? Why don't you wear something a bit less somber while visiting Merton? At least pretend you still know how to smile."

"It wouldn't change how I feel inside and the moment I say something it is obvious how I feel. What's the use?" Bryant said bitterly.

"At least wear this shirt," Father said as he drew a dark blue shirt out of Bryant's closet. "It's still almost as dark as your mood, yet not black."

Bryant took the shirt and shoved it into the bags before pulling on his boots. He followed Father out to the courtyard where Haskell waited. Once his father was safely mounted, Bryant mounted behind him seated on his saddlebags. He seldom rode with Father on Haskell and really wasn't very comfortable being so far off the ground. It was a cold ride to Merton and Bryant was glad to be safely back on the ground. They were greeted by Bryant's mother who hugged them both tightly warming Bryant's heart. Brenndah stood nearby waiting to check Father's arm.

"I've been so worried," Mother said. "Come in and have some breakfast. I know you two didn't eat before leaving."

They sat around the table eating breakfast while Bryant's parents talked. Bryant answered his mother's questions, but mostly just listened. Once he had finished eating he excused himself and went outside. He was surprised that Brenndah followed him. She pointed to him then traced from her eye down her face.

"Yes, I haven't gotten over that day any more than you have," Bryant said with a sigh. "Father wants me to get married, but I still have nightmares and it would be cruel to take a woman to live in Dracona. So much reminds me of that day, that nothing will ever be the same. Nothing will bring back the lives lost or erase the terror and shame that has emptied the town and the castle. Dracona will die hated, feared and finally forgotten."

He looked down at the ground as he struggled for control over his emotions. She put her hand gently over his heart and he looked up. She motioned for him to follow her and she led him to her home. There she got out some paper, pen and ink.

'It is hard to not be bitter over it,' Brenndah wrote. 'I don't know if I dare let anyone into my heart for fear of losing them, watching them die.'

"I figured you'd understand better than anyone. I try talking to my father, but it just starts the same old argument."

'There are things about me I dare not tell anyone else. Things I feel and things I can do. I think people would not understand, would fear me if they found out,' Brenndah wrote.

"I know that the villagers fear me and I think some of our people do too. I don't want to be hated and feared."

'Someday you will be our leader. Without leadership we would not survive. Eventually you will need an heir to take your place. You need to start thinking about the future.'

"I know, but it's difficult to think about living when surrounded by so many reminders of death," Bryant said as his throat tightened and he tried keep from being overwhelmed by the emotions.

His head hurt and his eyes were losing focus. He felt dizzy as a red glow further clouded his vision and he let his head drop onto his folded arms on the table. He heard footsteps and felt a gentle touch on his head. His head quit throbbing as he felt his back patted. He fell asleep as he heard Brenndah's footsteps fading.

* * * * *

Bryant woke to quiet talking. Brenndah came over with a bowl of soup for him and a questioning look on her face.

"I feel a little better," he replied to her unspoken question. "Perhaps someday we can both find what we need."

Brenndah nodded as his mother and father sat down at the table. Brenndah brought soup over for them and herself as well. They ate in silence since there really wasn't much to say that hadn't been said so many times before.

"Bryant," Mother said as she set down her spoon. "You do need to find a wife."

"I know Mother, but right now I don't know if I can let someone into my heart. I don't know if I am capable of loving a woman in that way yet."

"Don't give up on love, Bryant," she said as she stroked his face. "You deserve to be loved."

Bryant got up and headed for the door.

"Bryant!" Father's voice had a commanding tone to it, but Bryant opened the door anyway and left the house.

He stood at the cliff edge looking out at the ocean. He knew that the surface hid a whole world full of fish, strange plants and creatures just as his somber appearance barely hid the emotions churning within him. He had to find a way to push his emotions down so they wouldn't surface so easily. He didn't respond as a hand was placed on his shoulder.

"Perhaps you should stay here with your mother for a while," Father said.

"Who would take care of you?" Bryant asked. "I don't belong here, I belong in Dracona. Even if I am the last Lord Dracona I belong in Dracona. I'm full of uncertainty about myself and my future, but I know I need to remain in Dracona now. The very thought of marriage terrifies me right now. Somehow I know that if I do get married, I haven't met her yet."

"I know by your tone I can't change your mind," Father said with a sigh and Bryant turned to look at him. "I also know that nothing will convince anyone here in Merton to return to Dracona no matter how difficult life is."

"I want to start repairing the homes in the town," Bryant said. "I know it seems like a waste of my time, but someday someone might want to live there. It would give me something to do that will show progress instead of doing the same things over and over again."

"It would give you something to do to work out your frustrations. I haven't wanted to touch them, but perhaps it would help both of us."

They stayed for another day before returning to Dracona. Bryant began working on one of the houses and found it was hard work that left him exhausted enough to sleep through the night. Father's wound slowly healed to a scar. Sometimes he would help Bryant, but mostly let Bryant work on the buildings. Sometimes they would take a couple of days to camp in the mountains overlooking Dracona.

As the years passed, Bryant sometimes would check the forest and stop to watch the villagers. He noticed Langward with his wife and a small daughter but he suddenly seemed to vanish. About the same time Father started getting sick frequently. Bryant studied what books they had in the library on the healing arts and began making medicines. On one trip to check the forest, Father was bitten by a snake. Bryant was glad he knew how to make the medicine to save Father's life. After that he made some to keep in a vial in the healer's cottage that he had been using to make medicine.

* * * * *

It had been a long harsh winter in Dracona. Bryant's father had fallen ill and just never completely recovered. With the spring Bryant hoped that Father's health would return. He made new medicines with the tender young herbs from the healer's garden, but nothing seemed to be helping. As Bryant watched Father eat some soup and bread, he noticed how frail he looked. The bones of his hands were so prominent that they looked like there was no muscle left. He only finished half the soup.

"I'm tired," Father said as he set down the spoon next to the half eaten bread.

"You need to eat more, Father," Bryant said gently. "You can't heal if you don't eat."

"Help me get to bed Bryant. Maybe I'll have more later."

Bryant helped his father to bed, gently covering him then went down to consult the books on healing again. He found nothing to give him any hope. Slamming the books shut one by one didn't make him feel any better either. All too soon Father would die leaving him completely alone. He went down to the kitchen and dished up a bowl of soup which he ate standing in the kitchen before washing the bowl. Not wanting to return to where his father lay dying, Bryant went out the kitchen door and around the end of the castle along the pasture. He ignored the horses and made his way to the stairs hidden behind the armory along the castle wall. Once at the top he went to the corner of the battlements and stood watching the coming night slowly cloak the valley in darkness. The silver moon rose like a scythe ready to cut the harvest among the velvet night sky sprinkled with stars.

Turning his back on the moon he returned to the dark castle and climbed the stairs to the fourth floor. He stopped at the first window to look at the mountain side and the black openings that dotted its surface. Father's dragon, Haskell, stood motionless as though keeping his own watch. Bryant hurried down the hall to the very end and opened the double doors. The low lamp light revealed Father lying in the bed. Bryant's heart leapt as his hand motioned him forward.

"I'm here Father," Bryant said as he crossed to the bed and took Father's hand in his own. "Do you want to eat more?"

"No," Father said softly. "It's time for me to go Bryant. I wish I could stay and not leave you alone, but it's time. Find a wife. That's more important than anything else."

Bryant shifted and drew Father up into his arms.

"I love you Bryant," Father said. "You've been a good son, but it's time for you be begin to live again."

"How can I live without you?" Bryant whispered as tears poured down his cheeks. "I need you Father."

Father didn't respond. His breathing was slow and shallow as Bryant held him, loosing track of time. As the silvery dawn began to light the room Father quit breathing. The moon had set taking its harvest with it.

"No." Bryant whispered. "Don't leave me alone."

He sat clutching his father's body tightly to him just as his father had clutched his own brother's body. His heart felt torn in half. The sun was fully up before Bryant could lay Father's body down and leave the room. Bryant's footsteps were heavy and slow as he made his way down the long hallway and the even longer staircase to the great hall that sat silently as a tomb. He walked to the carpenter's shop that he had been using and began the grim task of building a coffin for his own father. By the time he was finished building the coffin and lid he was tired and hungry. He carved a wooden plaque to put on the grave before going to hitch up the horses to the wagon. He ate some bread before taking the wagon to get the coffin. It wasn't easy to lift the heavy awkward box by himself but eventually he got it into the wagon.

When he reached the room where his father's body lay he realized he should at least dress him. Bryant didn't know if it really mattered, if there was anything after death but somehow it didn't seem right burying his father in the night shirt he had been wearing for several days. Bryant got Father's best shirt and suit out of the closet and dressed the body. Bryant felt it important to polish the scuffed and worn boots even though he was the only one who would ever see them. Before picking up the body, he combed Father's hair. As he carried Father's body down to the waiting wagon he realized how light it was as though Father's illness had eaten away at him until there was nothing left but skin and bones.

Tears started running down Bryant's face again as he nailed the lid on the coffin. He climbed to the seat of the wagon and flicked the reins. The horses went slowly as though they understood what was in Bryant's heart. When they reached the cemetery he found a spot next to his grandparent's graves and got the shovel out of the wagon. He began by cutting around the outside and rolling up the grass covering the spot before beginning to dig out the dirt. Bryant was angry that he would have to dig the grave on his own, that he would be the sole witness to the burial. There would be no comfort from friends and family, only a silent empty castle surrounded by an empty town. Now he would be surrounded by death and silence until his own death with no one to care for his body or mourn his passing. He chopped at the dirt savagely with the shovel and threw it out of the grave with just as much force until the grave was the proper depth before climbing out only to collapse exhausted and empty next to the grave.

* * * * *

'Bryant,' a deep voice called drawing him out of unconsciousness as something pressed against his shoulder. 'You need to wake up.'

Bryant groaned and turned away from the pressure.

'Wake up!' the familiar voice persisted, breaking through the darkness that surrounded his heart and mind.

'Why should I?' Bryant replied in his dream. 'What is worth waking up for? Leave me alone!'

'Evelina says your life is very important. There are things she sees that only you can do, but you can't do them if you don't wake up!'

Something large pushed against his chest and rolled him back over onto his back. When he tried to push away whatever had pushed him, his hand was met by an unexpected texture that was both smooth and bumpy. He finally opened his eyes to find Haskell's nose on his chest.

"What are you doing here?" Bryant asked out loud.

'You were dying,' Haskell replied. 'If you had rolled over any farther you would have fallen in the grave.'

Bryant sat up and found that he was a lot closer to the grave than he remembered.

"Maybe it would have been," Bryant began but Haskell cut him off.

'No it wouldn't. You need to live. Evelina and I need you. You are Lord Dracona."

"A title that is as empty as the castle and town," Bryant said bitterly.

'A title that has meaning and responsibilities. Eventually you will understand that. Let's get Eamon buried.'

Bryant stood up to find the horses had wandered off, but they suddenly lifted their heads from grazing and returned to bring the wagon beside the open grave. Bryant watched as Haskell carefully slid the coffin out to rest in his curled forefoot. Haskell then spread his wings and lifted the end of the coffin out of the wagon using his wings to help him balance with the extra weight. He then carefully dropped the coffin into the grave. Bryant began shoveling the dirt back into the grave while Haskell scraped dirt in with one forefoot. It still took some time for the grave to be filled. Bryant knelt and put the wooden marker at the head of the grave. He felt the tears start again. Haskell nuzzled his shoulder gently.

'I sent the horses back to the castle,' Haskell said. 'I'll take you back.'

"I'd rather walk."

'I know you've never been comfortable flying, but it's time for you to get used to it. Climb up on my shoulders. You can sleep in the cavern near my den tonight so I can watch over you.'

Bryant stood and began walking away only to have Haskell nudge him back around to where he would mount.

"Alright, I'll let you take me back to the castle," Bryant said realizing it was useless to even try to argue with the dragon.

He mounted without further protest and closed his eyes as Haskell launched into the sky. Haskell landed on the courtyard wall and Bryant carefully dismounted and climbed down to the battlement. As he went down the stairs Haskell left. Bryant took care of the horses and wagon before entering the dark castle. He went up to his room and bathed before taking a quilt and a pillow down to the great hall. At the back of the great hall he turned the mechanism to open the massive doors in the back wall to access the cavern behind the castle. The walls of the great cavern glowed softly allowing him to find the steps to the left of the doors that led to a ledge lined with tunnel openings. After leaving the bedding on a ledge near Haskell's den, he left to get some food. He ate the last of the soup and bread before washing the dishes as darkness began closing in with the coming of night.

As Bryant made his way to the cavern his boot steps echoed in the great hall making him hurry to the soft sands of the cavern. Haskell was laying half out of his den on ledge above the hot sands in the center of the cavern. Bryant fixed himself a bed and lay down before covering himself with the quilt. He laid awake wondering if there would ever be more to his life than repairing the deserted town and maintaining the empty castle until his death. When he finally slept he dreamed of being a tired frail old man who stumbled through the forest only to die in the fields surrounding the village. He watched as the villagers rejoiced at his death then woke crying.

'That won't happen,' Haskell said.

'No, but I will die and won't be found until I am nothing but bones and a tale to scare children with,' he replied bitterly as he cried.

After putting away the bedding, Bryant ate some fruit before going to work on the house he had been repairing. There really wasn't anything else for him to do. His life fell into a routine of repairing the houses and tending the herb garden along with the vegetable garden at the castle. He cooked his own meals, cleaned his own dishes and washed his own clothes. When he visited his mother she tried to get someone to return to Dracona with him, but no one volunteered and he told her he didn't need anyone. He still guarded the forest against trespass, but avoided watching the village. The few times he had found someone in the forest, the mere sight of him had sent them running for the village.

Months passed as did the seasons with Haskell as his only companion and link to life other than when he visited Merton about once a year. Haskell even began helping with the repair work by helping to haul the wood and lift pallets of shingles onto the roof for Bryant to nail into place. At night Bryant collapsed into bed exhausted, but he still had frequent nightmares. He had long ago given up hope that anything would ever change before he finally died alone and forgotten.

Chapter 2 – Problems and Promises

"No," Bryant groaned as Father quit breathing. "Don't leave me alone."

Bryant felt the tears running down his face as he held Father's body tightly in his arms. He knew what had to be done even though he dreaded doing it, but there was no one else to do it.

'Bryant! Wake up!' Haskell's voice intruded into his dream.

Bryant woke with a start to find himself in his own bed. After five years he had hoped the memory would fade, but he still dreamed the same awful dream several times a month. His heart was still just as empty as the town and castle.

A heavy sigh escaped his lips as he stood up next to his empty bed. He dressed in his riding clothes and then stood in front of the polished shield next to the window. As he combed through his sleep tousled hair, he caught a movement in the corner of his eye. A thin column of smoke rose from a small meadow in the forest.

'I'll start there this morning,' he thought as he carefully shaved.

* * * * *

A heavy sigh escaped her lips as she examined the small handful of herbs she carried in a piece of bark. She would need much more than that if she were to have any hope of helping her father. As she turned to continue her search, she heard the sound of hoof-beats approaching. She ran quickly back to the small clearing where she left her father to find the source of the sound.

The tall black horse shook its head defiantly as its rider brought it to a sudden halt. At the sight of the rider, her breath caught in her throat and her heart seemed to freeze in her chest. He was tall and dressed all in black with scarlet trim. For an instant a voluminous black cape floated behind him like an ominous black cloud. Against it his blond hair glinted in the sunlight.

"Keep away from him!" she ordered as she sprinted across the clearing to her father's side. "I'm here, Father."

Father's only response was a low moan.

"What are you doing here?" he asked.

"Trying to save my father's life," she answered defiantly.

15

* * * * *

He dismounted and walked over to where she knelt beside her father.

"What happened?" he asked as he felt for a pulse at the man's neck.

"A snake bit him this morning," she answered.

"What did it look like?"

"Brown, like a stick, with a red stripe down its back."

"How long ago?"

"Just about ten minutes ago."

"Stay here!"

Before she could even respond, he had mounted his horse and galloped off into the trees. His mind raced ahead to the herb garden and the small cottage adjoining it. Although it was now uninhabited, he still used the cottage and its herb garden for when a healer was needed. The empty cottage bespoke of happier times long past. With a sudden turn, his horse leapt from the forest and onto a weed grown field. Soon the dirt path gave way to a cobbled street. He brought his horse to a sliding stop in front of the arched gate of the garden. Quickly he dismounted and ran to the cottage. Blinking in the sudden darkness of the cottage, he found the vial he came for and hoped it was enough to save the man.

On the return trip he wondered what had made him help her instead of chasing them away as he had with previous trespassers. Perhaps it was the look of open defiance on her face as she stood her ground, as though it was he who was trespassing. He vaulted off of his horse as it burst into the clearing and ran to the man's side.

"Drink this, quickly!" he ordered as he pressed the mouth of the vial to the man's lips.

The man swallowed once, then again.

"We wait now," he said.

"Will he live?" she asked with a frightened look on her face.

"I have done all that can be done. All we can do now is wait."

"You are the young Lord Dracona," she stated as she looked up from her father.

"I am the last Lord Dracona," he said looking back into her emerald green eyes. "I usually run trespassers off rather than help them."

"So my sister said in her letters," she answered back as she stared at his chest and the clasp that held his cape.

It was in the shape of a dragon whose wingspread reached from one shoulder to the other.

"Why didn't you run us off?"

"I am the lord of this land and I do as I please."

He noticed that her hair was the color of spun gold and found himself wondering what she would look like with it falling loosely around her shoulders rather than in the tight braid that encircled her head like a crown.

"If your father dies, you can go, but if he lives I will come to get you and you must come to live with me," he said, "forever."

"That is a steep price, but my father is the most important person in my life," she replied. "I agree to your terms."

He was surprised at the quickness of her acceptance, but he didn't let his excitement and surprise show. He had noticed the man's color beginning to return to his face. He would live.

"Gwladys?" the man moaned.

* * * * *

"I'm here, Father," she said as she took his hand in hers.

"You found the herbs?"

"No, Lord Dracona brought the medicine."

"But, Cherie and Olvan said . . ."

"I know what they said. Lord Dracona does as he pleases."

"You will be weak for a day or two. I will return with a wagon. Don't forget your promise, Gwladys."

With that he turned to fetch his horse.

"What promise?" her father asked as he watched Lord Dracona mount and leave.

"That if you lived, I would live with him."

"No daughter of Auberon should be forced to make such a choice."

"Father, the choice was made for me," Gwladys answered, holding her left arm so he could see the glowing band on her wrist.

"I still don't have to like it," he said. "Just be careful. Since your mother was killed, you are our last hope. Cherie has failed already."

"I will continue the quest. It is my sacred duty."

As they waited for Lord Dracona to return they discussed what they should do. Eventually they began to wonder if Lord Dracona would actually return and what they should do if he didn't. It was just past noon when they heard Lord Dracona approach. A matched team of horses pulled the wagon that looked well used and repaired. Gwladys watched as Lord Dracona lifted her father from the ground into his arms and carried him to the wagon. He set Father in the bed of the wagon.

"You'll want to remain lying down for the journey. I brought a quilt to cushion you from the wood," Lord Dracona said as he unfolded the quilt and laid it out in the bed of the wagon.

17

He helped Father to lie down and fastened a gate up across the end of the wagon bed. He then helped her load the saddlebags before climbing up to the wagon seat. She was surprised as he offered her a hand. His hand was strong as he pulled her up until she was able to sit on the seat beside him.

Father and daughter were silent during the trip through the forest, each wondering what the future would bring. The stillness was only broken by the hoof-beats of the matched team of tan horses and the creak of the wagon wheels. It was late afternoon as they came out of the forest and entered the small village. As they passed, the villagers stopped to see who had come, then ran for their homes. Their passage was marked by the slamming shut of doors and shutters.

"The third house on the right past the well," she said dreading what she knew she had promised as she watched the villager's reaction to their arrival.

He drew the horses to a halt in front of the house. Cherie stood in the doorway as her son and daughter peeked from behind her skirt.

"Cherie!" Gwladys cried as she leapt from the seat beside him.

"Where's Father?"

"In the wagon. He was bitten by a snake."

"Is he . . ."

"No, he will be all right. He is just weak."

Lord Dracona gently lifted their father from the wagon and carried him into the house.

"It is a cruel thing to take a man's daughter from him," Father said as Lord Dracona laid him on the bed.

"I will return for her in two weeks," Lord Dracona said as he turned to leave.

"What did he mean by that?" Cherie asked as Gwladys carried in the last of their belongings from the wagon.

"It means that I will be living with Lord Dracona."

"Why?"

"Because he saved Father's life," Gwladys replied as she held up her left arm. "The choice was made for me. I don't know why, but I am meant to go to his castle."

"Do you know what you're dooming yourself to? I've heard that cattle wandering onto his property disappear right out of their tracks leaving only a few spots of blood behind. The only man ever to go to his castle and return alive came back a babbling idiot. Others were found dead, laid out next to the forest."

"If he wanted me dead or crazy, he wouldn't have saved Father and he would have killed me already."

"Daughters! What is done is done, and already a part of fate's tapestry. There is no use arguing about it," Father said before he turned over and went to sleep.

Gwladys and Cherie walked outside and sat on the bench just outside the door.

"You didn't reveal yourself to him, did you?"

"No, he knows me only as Gwladys. Yet, I don't think that he is being completely honest with me either."

"I'm sure of that," Cherie said as she watched her husband walk towards them. "Olvan, tell Gwladys what you know about the Lords of Dracona."

"The legends say that once our people lived in harmony with Dracona, but something tragic happened. Our people that survived settled here. It has been an uneasy stay. We used to see the old Lord Dracona herding off a cow into the woods occasionally, but no one has seen him in the last five years."

"He is dead," Gwladys said. "Young Lord Dracona said that he was the last Lord Dracona."

"Young Lord Dracona?" Olvan asked in surprise. "You spoke with him?"

"He saved Father. Now I must go to live with him. He will come for me in two weeks," she answered.

In the following days they tried to forget the dark cloud hanging over Gwladys' future. It was decided that Auberon would stay with Cherie and Olvan, at least for a while. Soon the dark day came and many sad farewells were exchanged. The entire village turned out to bid her farewell. All of them expressed their concerns for her safety. All heads turned and silence fell as Lord Dracona approached leading a horse that was as white as his mount was black. She stood calmly in the center of the road holding saddlebags containing her belongings.

Her heart leapt as she saw him ride towards her. He was startlingly handsome in spite of his somber clothing and ominous black cape. He stopped his horses and dismounted. He led the white horse before her then turned to offer his clasped hands to her so she could mount the side-saddle. She placed her foot in his offered hands and mounted. Her heart leapt again when his hand touched hers as he handed her the reins. He met her eyes with expressionless, piercing blue eyes briefly before turning to meet her father's eyes. No words were spoken as they stared at each other for a couple of long minutes. She recognized the stern, angry expression on Father's face. Abruptly Lord Dracona turned to mount his own horse.

She noticed that the path they were following was curiously wide and smooth. They stopped for a moment at a stream to let the horses drink. She noticed that the stream passed under the path, flowing through a stone hole. She realized that the path was really a stone-paved road like she had seen in some of the cities that she had visited.

* * * * *

He had been surprised that she had been waiting for him when he had arrived in the village. He hoped she had not noticed the tremor that went though him as her hand brushed his when he had handed her the reins. He glanced over at her and found she appeared very comfortable on the horse.

"You sit well on a horse," he said. "Have you ridden before?"

"Yes. I have ridden quite a bit," she answered.

"Good. I want to reach the castle before dark."

With that, he urged his horse to jump the stream and galloped up the path. To his surprise she had followed him and began riding at his side. He had not expected her to follow without persuasion. It was not the fastest route to the castle, but it was the easiest. They reached the edge of the deserted town just as the sun approached the top of the forest.

* * * * *

"This town looks deserted," she said as they slowed their horses to a trot. "What happened?"

"It is a long story for another day," he replied cryptically.

She noticed chairs left by doorways and toys left in the dusty walks as though their owners would return momentarily. Closer to the castle she noticed several houses with charred remains where their roofs should have been. Here was a mystery to keep her busy in the long days that lay ahead.

The castle appeared just as deserted as the town had as they entered through the porticos. Unlike the other castles that she had visited, this one sat silently. The loud clatter of their horses' hooves seemed to irreverently break the silence that hung over the castle. The castle had four above ground floors. This seemed unusual to her. Most of the castles that she had visited had only two or three floors above the cellars and dungeons. There were no towers or spires either. All of the windows were dark.

They dismounted in silence and led their horses to the stables on the right of the large courtyard. They groomed the horses before turning them loose in a tiny pasture within the castle wall.

She felt very tired as they entered the main castle through a pair of doors that were actually part of a tall pair of doors whose tops were just below the fourth floor of the castle. They paused just inside the doors as he lit a torch. She followed him closely in the darkness for fear of being swallowed up by the enclosing gloom. They climbed what seemed to be an endless staircase broken into three sections and walked a long hall on what had to be the fourth floor. She wished that she could shatter the darkness with light, but knew it was best that she didn't. Finally he opened a door that protested with a loud creak. Once inside the room he lit a torch just inside the door, and then others around the room. She breathed a sigh of relief to be out of the darkness.

"There is a bathing chamber through that door and a closet through the smaller one. Leave the window shuttered at night. There are many things that fly at night in these mountains."

With those instructions he closed the door behind him. She heard the lock turning to lock her in but she was too tired to care tonight. She dropped her saddlebags next to the bed as she fell into it, asleep almost before her head reached the pillow.

* * * * *

He almost unlocked the door as soon as he had locked it. Almost. The memory of her paled face and frightened eyes stuck in his mind. It was cruel to bring her to such a dark and lonely place. He shook the picture and thoughts from his mind as he opened the door to his room and put on the fur lined jacket and gloves that waited for him. Swiftly he returned to the main chamber and walked straight to the unseen doors at the back of the great hall. Putting the torch in a bracket, he began to turn the mechanism that opened the massive doors that were twins to the ones at the front of the hall. Once the doors were open far enough for him to pass through, he covered his torch to put it out and entered the doors. He had entered the large cavern, turned to the left and climbed the stairway that was carved into the rock wall. At the top of the stairway he paused to look over the sandy floor. He counted seven spherical mounds in the sand. He shook his head.

"Eggs!? How am I going to manage?" he muttered to himself. "I barely manage now. If only I could ask Langward, but I haven't even seen him in the village for years. Now with the girl . . ."

'What girl?' Haskell asked from the tunnel he was standing in front of.

'The one I told you about,' he thought back.

'Maybe she can help.'

'How?'

'I can't say, but something will come up.'

'You're an optimist.'

'Are we going?'

Bryant heard Haskell's claws on the stone floor of his den as he shifted impatiently.

'Yes.'

Chapter 3 – More Mysteries

She woke up feeling as if she had not eaten in a week. On the table at the foot of her bed sat a platter with a loaf of bread, cheese, and some fruit. Next to the platter sat a goblet and a pitcher of water. As soon as she had eaten, she turned to the bathing chamber. She opened the door to find a room almost half as large as the bed chamber.

In the corner of the room there was a metal basin large enough for her to submerge herself in if there were water in it. Coming down from the wall near the ceiling was a brass dragon head and neck. The head rested its chin on the edge of the basin with its mouth open as to drink from the basin. The rest of the bathing chamber was surprisingly similar to those from home other than the obvious dragon theme.

She decided to take a bath. As she looked into the basin she found a disk the size of her hand in the bottom of the basin. She noticed holes in the disk. She climbed into the basin by means of the stone steps that curved around the edge of the basin. She turned the disk and found that the holes closed. Then she climbed out and tugged at the dragon's left ear. Just as she thought it would, a stream of water gushed from the dragon's mouth. As the basin filled, she undressed and loosened her hair so that it fell in a golden cascade that nearly reached her knees. As soon as the water neared the top of the basin, she pushed the ear back to its original position and climbed into the basin.

The water was warm. She sat on a bench opposite the dragon's head. As she sat enjoying the water, she wondered why the builders of this castle had chosen such a design for a water spout. The face of the dragon was a gentle face, not fierce and frightening like the pictures she had seen.

She took her time at washing. When she was finished, she turned the drain disk with her foot and climbed out. She found two drying sheets and dried herself and her hair. She wrapped one sheet around herself and went to see what the closet held. She had only brought two dresses with her. Her traveling dress and another that she could not wear here in front of Lord Dracona. Out of the closet, she picked a dress of emerald green to match her eyes and remind her of her forest home. She dressed and began to comb and braid her long hair. She knew he would ask questions if he saw its length. Just as she finished she heard the door unlock before there was a knock.

23

She opened the door to find him standing there.

"Did you rest well?" he asked as he opened the shutters to the window.

"I am much refreshed," she replied.

"I see that you found the bathing chamber adequate," he stated, as he picked up the drying sheet from the foot of the bed.

She watched him glance at her as he took the sheet back into the bathing chamber.

"Are you ready for a tour of my home?" he asked when he returned.

"Yes," she answered.

She followed him out into the hall and noticed the large windows on the opposite side of the hall. She said nothing about the great caves that dotted the hillside and he did not either. He pointed out the door to his bed chamber next to hers and continued down the hall. They reached a staircase at last and went down. She caught her breath as they reached the bottom of the stairs. To the left of the stairs was an immense hall that had balconies for the floor they were on and the floor below. They went down to the second floor. The floor of the hall was worked in tiny tiles of many colors. She blinked her eyes twice before a pattern emerged in the swirling colors. Worked into the tiles were many intertwined creatures with lizard-like bodies and strange wings without feathers. They were dragons.

* * * * *

"That floor is the original floor that was created when the castle was built," he said as he watched her wide-eyed wonderment of it.

In the green dress she was wearing, she was even more beautiful than he remembered. In the morning light she seemed to radiate a shimmering light.

"The library is on the third floor. Would you like to see it?"

He led her down the stairs, across the great hall and up the stairs to a pair of doors. As he opened the doors, it revealed the library that ran the entire length and width of the floor. Besides the shelves of books and reading tables on the third floor, there were more shelves of books on a fourth floor mezzanine.

"It's wonderful!" she said with obvious excitement. "Most places don't have near this many books."

He found that comment odd. What places?

"You may come to read any time during daylight," he said and she nodded.

He then led her down to the next floor. As they walked down the hall, he noticed her looking at the windows that looked over the empty city. He opened the third door to reveal a room with many musical instruments in it.

"May I use these instruments?" she asked him.

"During daylight," he answered.

He shut the door and led her down to the ground floor. He led her through the dining hall to the kitchen.

"You must cook your own meals. I do not keep servants. The pantry is behind that door," he said and indicated the double door across from the large sink and next to the oven.

He led her through the outside door. They stood outside on the cobbled path that led into the generous garden. At the far end of the garden was the large coop of yard fowl.

"Now I have more important things to do. I will return before dark," he said as he turned to walk down the path and around the corner.

He knew she was watching him. He glanced at the castle as he paused for a moment at the horse pasture. He thought he saw a movement through the dining hall. He put Gwladys out of his mind as he turned his thoughts to the work left for him to do on the church in the deserted town. His black horse trotted over to the fence and tossed his head in greeting.

"Not today Llewellyn. I need the team," he said, turning to the stables.

Obediently the black brought the two tan horses to the pasture gate. The black returned to grazing as he harnessed the team and hitched them to a work wagon.

* * * * *

Lord Dracona left her standing there as he walked down the path to her right. As she watched him go, she thought about the library. Quickly she turned and retraced their steps to the library. Gwladys found the library well organized. She easily located what she was looking for. On a stand in the center of the room was a large volume containing the family history of the Lords of Dracona. She turned to the last page that had been written on. On it was a single name and a birth date.

"Bryant Donley," she read aloud then she caught her breath. "He's five years older than I am!"

She turned back a page and checked the dates. She shook her head in disbelief.

'I wonder if he knows the legends,' she thought to herself.

She knew that she must learn more before she confronted him with the quest. She first looked for the castle's history. She found a very old and dusty book that was not written in the local language. It was written in her own language. She took the book to a window seat and settled down to read.

Her stomach suddenly rumbled and she realized that it was late afternoon. She set the book on a table near her seat. She headed for the kitchen to fix herself a meal. As she was going down the stairs she thought she heard a woman's voice. She stopped to listen.

'I am too exhausted to cover these,' the voice said. 'Please come help me.'

"Cover what?" she asked. "Where are you?"

Her voice echoed in the vastness of the great hall. She realized that the voice had not echoed. She decided that she did not want to stay around in case there really was someone there.

Once in the kitchen she began to prepare the first meal she had prepared in months that was from her homeland. Just as she was looking for plates and goblets, she heard footsteps on the path outside.

"What smells so good?" he asked as he opened the door.

"If you show me where to find the plates and goblets, I will share my meal with you," she answered.

"What is this?" he asked as she poured the golden fluid from the pitcher into his goblet. "And that?"

She picked up the bowl of food and dished some of the food onto his plate.

"Just eat!" she laughed. "You probably couldn't pronounce their names anyway."

"Why?"

"Because they are from my homeland, Bryant."

He nearly choked on what he was eating.

"How!?" he sputtered. "How did you find out my name?"

"In the library," she answered. "I can read after all. Just eat."

She watched him as he began to eat again. He appeared as dirty as she must have been on the day of their first meeting. She found that she enjoyed watching him eat as much as she enjoyed eating the traditional meal that she had prepared.

"This is delicious," he said as he finished his second plateful.

"You mean was," she said with a smile.

She began to clear up the dishes. Silently he began to help her. Together they washed the dishes. As she dried them, he quietly slipped out of the room.

She turned to find him gone. She left the kitchen alone and noticed that the sun was going down. She hurried her steps towards her bedchamber before the castle darkened. In the fourth floor hall she began to run as the darkness began to close in. When she reached the room, she shut the door behind herself.

* * * * *

Bryant quickly went to the library to see if he could find out what she had been reading. He saw the family record open on its stand. It was open to his page.

"Oh!" he groaned as he saw the date. "What will I say if she asks about my birth date?"

'Maybe she won't ask,' Haskell's voice came clearly into his mind.

'She will ask, Haskell,' he replied. 'I know she will ask.'

'Worry about it when the time comes. You have other things to worry about.'

'I'm not worried about anything else.'

'You should be.' Haskell said. 'She heard Evelina today.'

'She what!?' Bryant asked, shocked by the thought.

'She heard Evelina today,' Haskell repeated.

'Now I'm really worried,' he replied as he began walking towards his room. 'We have a lot to do tonight. We can talk about it later.'

As he approached his bedchamber he noticed a light showing under Gwladys' door. He looked again because the light was not the yellow-orange of a torch, but a blue-green light. He rushed to her door and flung it open.

She stood in the middle of the room holding a lit torch that bathed the room in a yellow-orange light. He froze in his footsteps for a full minute. She stood frozen like a beautiful statue that looked at him, but did not see him.

"Goodnight," he said and closed the door before she could respond.

He locked the door and breathed a sigh of relief.

He gathered his gloves and jacket before lighting a torch and leaving his room.

* * * * *

She breathed a sigh of relief. She knew that he had seen her light from the hall. She hoped he would not question her about it. She was not prepared to explain it, not yet. There was still so very much to learn about this place before she could reveal herself. For the first time since they had first met she knew why she was meant to come to this place. She put the torch in an empty wall bracket after lighting the rest of the torches in the room. She hoped that the light from the torches would be enough to cover her own light. She opened the saddle bags and drew out her belongings and laid them on the bed. She next unwound her braids and shook her hair out so it cascaded down her back. She picked up the flat square wooden box and opened it. As she opened the box a blue-green light streamed out of it.

She allowed her own light to grow to its equal. She reached in the box and withdrew a circlet of silver. She placed it on her head.

She stood in front of the polished shield and concentrated. Soon the shield surface seemed to dissolve and behind it there stood her father's sister.

'Gwladys,' the woman said.

'It is good to see you, Aunt,' she replied. 'I am making progress on the quest. However, it will take some time.'

'We heard from Auberon. Who is this Lord Dracona?'

'Bryant Donley. He is five years older than I am.'

'Older!? Are you certain?'

'Yes, I think that the legends must be true.'

'You said it will take some time.'

'There is some mystery about this place. I don't think he will tell me what I need to know. I will have to find my answers in his library, and then confront him with them.'

'When will you contact me again?'

'In a week unless something comes up.'

'Take care, Sonje.'

'I will.'

As the surface of the shield returned she slowly crumpled to the floor.

* * * * *

Haskell and Bryant had almost reached the church when Evelina called to Haskell.

'The girl! Something's wrong.'

Haskell flinched at the sudden urgent tone of her voice.

'What's wrong?' Bryant asked.

'Come quickly!' Evelina urged Haskell.

'Evelina says something is wrong with the girl!' Haskell said as he turned around sharply, nearly unseating Bryant.

'In the courtyard! It's faster!' Bryant ordered.

He dismounted on the run and only paused long enough to open the doors. He flung himself to his knees beside her unconscious form. Gently he put his fingers to her neck and found a faint pulse. He loosened the lacings on her dress. He felt her breath on his hand as he felt her cheeks and forehead.

'Is she alright?' Haskell asked from the courtyard.

'I don't know. There is no fever and she is still breathing,' he answered.

He went to the bed and found her belongings lying there. He carefully examined each as he removed them from the bed, but he could not determine anything from them. After setting the items on the dressing table he pulled down the covers on the bed. Gently he lifted her in his arms and laid her down on the bed. Tenderly he drew the covers up over her. He found his hands trembling as he returned to Haskell who was waiting anxiously in the courtyard.

'No work tonight,' he told Haskell as he removed the work harness.

'Evelina said she was talking to someone before she passed out.'

'How? The room was locked. There's no one else here.'

'In her mind, somewhat like we do.'

'What else did Evelina tell you?'

'The woman called her first Gwladys, then Sonje. They were talking about legends and quests. The man you saved is named Auberon.'

'I must return and watch over her. Take this harness with you.'

He went back into the castle as Haskell took the harness and left the courtyard. He stopped at his bedchamber to toss his jacket and gloves on a chair and pull a quilt from the bed. He closed the door behind him as he entered her room.

She still lay just as he had left her but her face was less pale than before. He dropped the quilt on the floor and sat in the chair next to the door. He pulled off his boots and put his feet on the cushioned stool in front of the chair. Then he covered himself with the quilt and settled down to watch over her.

* * * * *

At dawn she awoke feeling strangely. As she remembered the previous evening's events she sat up suddenly. She found herself in bed instead of on the floor as she remembered. She looked around and breathed a sigh of relief as she noticed her belongings on the dressing table. Then she saw Bryant asleep in the chair. His face was less mysterious than she remembered and more vulnerable. His features were strong and handsome. She found herself wanting to reach out and stroke his cheek

She tightened the laces that he must have loosened the night before. Quietly she got out of bed and walked over to the door. She found it to be unlocked. Silently she left the room. She went to the kitchen and prepared a hearty porridge. Carefully she carried the breakfast tray that she had loaded with enough for both of them back to her room.

* * * * *

When he awoke to find her missing, he leapt from his chair and opened the door. She stood before him holding a large tray.

"Where were you?" he demanded.

"Fixing breakfast," she answered.

"Why didn't you wake me?"

"I didn't have the heart to. You looked so peaceful," she said as she set down the tray. "Are you going to just stand there staring at me or are you going to come and eat?"

Bryant was glad that her back was to him as he felt his cheeks turn red. He couldn't take his eyes off of her hair. To him it looked like a golden bridal veil crowned by a circlet of silver. He shook his head. He had to quit thinking like that. He remembered the tragedy wrought by his uncle's foolish actions. He went over to the table to eat. As he ate he realized how much he had missed having someone to talk to.

"How did you know I had passed out?" she asked as she finished her breakfast.

"Uh," he hesitated.

He certainly couldn't tell her about Evelina.

"I just had a feeling I should check on you."

"I do appreciate your concern for me."

She piled the dirty dishes on the tray and carried it out of the room. He left the room and watched her walk down the hall. He went into his room to take a bath. As Bryant settled down into the bath water all he could think about was her, Sonje. He wondered why her father called her Gwladys and yet the woman had called her Sonje.

"That girl is a mystery!" he said aloud in frustration.

'What do you mean?' Haskell responded sleepily.

'When I found her, she was dressed plainly and traveling on foot like a common peasant. Yet, she can read and speaks as though her family does not speak the local language. From her comments, she must have done some traveling.'

'So?'

'She is educated. Most of the villagers can't even write their own names. She was not born in this area either.'

'What does that matter?'

'I can't get her off my mind. Her face, her eyes, her long golden hair, it's all I see when I close my eyes. And why is she suddenly wearing a silver circlet as though she were royalty? I can't afford to get attached to her.'

'Because of Rolfe?'

'Yes, I am still repairing the damage done to the town. I was crazy to have brought her here.'

'You are lonely.'

'Yes. Once I had family and friends. Now all are gone but you and Evelina. I didn't know how lonely I had been until she got here.'

'You have to be strong. Evelina said there will be at least thirty to care for.'

Bryant groaned and began to wash. He knew that there would be much more work than what one man alone could do.

As he passed the library, he noticed the library doors open. As he entered the room he saw her seated at a table in the back of the room. She had a large stack of books on the table and several large parchments. As he walked closer, he noticed that she was busily writing. To his surprise she was reading from books that were the oldest in the library. He knew that they were written in his great-grandfather's native language, but he had never learned more than a few words.

"What are you reading, Sonje?" he asked, using the name Evelina had given Haskell.

"Where did your family come from?" Sonje asked, ignoring both his question and his use of her name.

"From the north, I think," he answered.

"Your great-grandfather, Fanchon, and eleven others traveled south from Glynis," she said answering her own question. "Here they met Malvin and his family. It is still unclear why Fanchon declared himself as the first Lord Dracona."

He sat down across the table from her. He knew it was only a matter of time before she uncovered all of his carefully hidden secrets.

"Apparently Fanchon and Malvin designed this castle together. What is strange is that there are no dungeons or cellars in this castle other than a small cellar off the kitchen."

Sonje looked up at him as if looking for an answer.

"What is so strange about that?" he asked, confused.

"I have visited dozens of castles and all of them have cellars, dungeons and towers as well. But then there is the attached maze of caves in the mountainside behind the castle."

He knew he had made a big mistake in showing her the library.

"Let's take a lunch and go for a ride," he suggested, trying to change the subject.

"Good idea. I need time to think about all of this anyway."

He breathed a sigh of relief as she got up from the table.

"I'll pack the lunch and meet you at the stables," he said as he got up.

As she left the room he looked at the parchments that were beside the books on the table. Several were floor plans of the castle and another was a map of the deserted town.

"I wonder what she wants with these?" he asked himself aloud.

'Evelina can't tell yet. She doesn't think in your language all of the time,' Haskell answered, interrupting his thoughts. 'Apparently something to do with the legends and quest that she was discussing with someone last night.'

'Now I'm even more worried.'

* * * * *

Sonje broke into a run as she neared her room. She shut the door behind her and leaned against it, breathing hard.

"How did he find out my name?" she wondered out loud. "There's got to be someone else here besides him."

As she caught her breath, she braided her hair into one thick braid. Then she went to the closet to find a suitable riding outfit. After dressing in a dark brown riding habit, she headed for the stables.

He was not at the stables when she got there, so she went to the horse pasture. The black raised his head from grazing to look at her.

"Hello," she said. "Bryant and I want to go for a ride."

The black whinnied once and trotted to the gate. The white followed him to the gate. She let them through into the stables. Quickly she brushed and saddled both horses. As she was finishing she heard footsteps.

"I see that Llewellyn and Guen are ready for an outing," he said as he checked her work.

Quickly, she mounted before Bryant had a chance to help her. He secured the saddlebags that were packed with their lunch in place and mounted up. Together they rode out of the castle gates. She noticed that they were taking a different route through town than the one they had taken when she first arrived here.

As they passed what appeared to be a church, she noticed that someone had been repairing the burned-out roof. Cautiously she glanced at Bryant. As she looked at him she caught a glimpse of a well tended herb garden behind a stone wall. Curious.

Soon they were out of the town and in the forest. He took the lead as the trail narrowed. As she rode behind him, she could not take her eyes off his back. His shoulders were broad and strong.

Soon they reached a tiny meadow that was split by a gurgling stream fed by a waterfall. They dismounted and turned the horses loose to graze. They settled down on the grass next to the stream and ate slices of meat and cheese on bread. The water from the stream was some of the sweetest water Sonje had ever tasted.

* * * * *

"This is very beautiful," Sonje told him. "It reminds me of my home."

"Where is your home?"

"To the north," she answered mysteriously.

She picked up a stick that lay in the edge of the stream. Then she took the knife that they had used to cut their meat and cheese and began to carve the stick into a small flute. When she finished, she began to play a soft, sweet melody.

Bryant found her melody to blend with the sound of the brook. He had never heard such beautiful music. As he watched her play he caught a movement out of the corner of his eye. Slowly he turned his head to see several deer step cautiously into the meadow. Behind the deer came other forest creatures. Several birds landed near where she was sitting.

He didn't dare move for fear of breaking the spell. In all the years he had been coming to this meadow, he had never seen a single creature in the meadow. He desperately wanted to know more about her, yet he knew that the difference between their ages would prevent anything more than a friendship working between them. He did not want to duplicate his uncle's experience. He swallowed hard and tried to forget the painful images that were in his mind.

"What's wrong?" she asked, looking genuinely concerned.

He jumped as though he had been hit.

"No," he said. "Nothing is wrong."

After putting down her flute, she began to unbraid her hair. She separated three hairs from the rest and plucked them. Quickly she wove the hairs together. One of the birds hopped up on her knee and turned its head to watch her work more closely. Soon her hands were moving too fast for the bird or Bryant to follow. Suddenly she stopped weaving. In her fingers, she held a golden strap as fine as a spider's web.

"Hold out your wrist," she commanded as she reached for his left arm.

Placing the strap around his wrist, she began weaving again. As she wove she hummed a quiet tune. When she had finished, the strap had disappeared entirely.

"Where did it go?" he asked as he examined his wrist.

"It is still there," she said as she smiled. "Think of me."

He closed his eyes and thought of Sonje. He opened his eyes in surprise as his wrist became suddenly warm. A warm golden glow was coming from his wrist where the strap had been placed.

"How does it do that?" he asked as he tried to feel the strap with his other hand.

"I can't explain that to you. It can give you guidance if you will trust it," she told him.

"It's time that we go," he said as he stood up.

The bird on her knee hopped to the ground and she rose to her feet. He reached down and picked up her flute. Their hands brushed as he handed her the flute. His heart leapt as she smiled at his touch. She turned towards the horses. He sighed deeply and shook his head. She was even more mysterious now than before.

As they rode back to the castle, a scream split the air. They halted their horses. Suddenly the largest eagle that Bryant had ever seen landed on a tree branch next to him. The eagle clicked its beak before it screamed again.

"Yes, Ernest, I will expect you at the castle," Sonje answered the eagle.

"What was that all about?" Bryant asked as the eagle launched itself into the air.

"Ernest asked to hunt for me."

"He what?"

"He desired the privilege of being my hunter."

'She speaks the truth,' Haskell's voice said to him. 'That is the first time I have heard an eagle show respect for anyone. He practically groveled.'

They continued in silence to the castle. As they entered the courtyard, they were greeted by an eagle's scream. Sonje dismounted. The eagle swooped down and delivered a rabbit at her feet. Then he landed on the cobblestones next to the rabbit. Bryant could not believe his eyes as he watched the eagle bow, beak on the ground, to her.

"Thank you for the fine rabbit, Ernest. I will call for you when I need you," Sonje told the eagle as she picked up the rabbit.

The eagle screamed a farewell and launched itself into the sky.

"If you will take care of the horses, I can have dinner ready before nightfall," Sonje said as she turned towards Bryant.

"Sounds like a fair deal," he said as he dismounted. "Come on Guen."

He led the horses into the stable and began to strip their gear off.

"I just don't understand her. How can she get an eagle to bow to her as though she was royalty?" Bryant asked aloud.

'Maybe she is,' answered Haskell. 'Are we going tonight?'

'Yes, the moon is nearly full. We need to finish before the rains come.'

* * * * *

For six days Sonje barely saw Bryant. She studied in the library during the daytime while he slept. He worked all night while she slept. Again it was time for her to report home.

She stood in front of the shield with her hair loose. She allowed her light to increase until even the torches were extinguished. The shield surface dissolved and her aunt stood in place of her reflection.

'The preparations are being made, Gwladys,' said her aunt without a greeting.

'I will ask him for a week,' answered Sonje.

'How are you coming on the quest?'

'The facility is sufficient for our needs. However, there is still a mystery about the place. Why does he only work at night now? Whose voice do I hear occasionally?'

'A voice?'

'Yes, a woman I think. She is very concerned about something that is increasing in numbers. She seems to labor hard and tire easily.'

'Have you seen anyone besides Bryant?'

'Never.'

'Curious. Tell me when you are coming. Take care.'

'I will.'

As the shield reappeared, Sonje turned towards the bed. She fell to the floor before she reached the bed.

* * * * *

'She's done it again,' Haskell told Bryant.

'Done what?'

'Passed out.'

'Let's get back to the castle then,' Bryant said as he mounted up.

'Evelina says that she spoke with the same woman. Apparently some important event is going to happen and she plans to attend it.'

Haskell left Bryant in the courtyard. He hurried up to her room. The hall was dark except a faint blue-green glow coming from under her door. Quickly he unlocked and opened her door. The room was dark except for a faint blue-green light that seemed to center around her.

Gently he lifted her into his arms. She moaned and turned her head to rest her cheek against his shoulder. He was suddenly acutely aware of how much he had wanted her in his arms. He found his heart beating more swiftly. Slowly he crossed the room to the bed and laid her on top of the quilt. She moaned again. With his hand he gently bushed the hair from her face. His hand trembled as he realized how much he wanted to kiss her. He pulled his hand away and turned his back to the bed. He went to the closet and brought out the spare quilt stored there. Gently he covered her with it. Quietly he left the room and went to his own bedchamber. He lit a torch and then sat on the edge of his bed. He felt as though a very heavy weight rested on his shoulders.

"Haskell?" Bryant said quietly.

'Yes?'

'I had finally adjusted to being alone. It never occurred to me that having her here would force me to remember how alone I was.'

'But, we are here.'

'As I stood there holding her in my arms, I knew why I have been avoiding her.'

'Why?'

'Because I knew that I could not take her in my arms. I can't let myself love her. I want her so badly I ache inside, yet I can't have her.'

'You think you would go insane like Rolfe did?'

'All my family has fled the shame of his wreckage. I could never join them if I were to behave so dishonorably.'

'Have you confronted her with this?'

'No, it would only frighten her and I would lose her even sooner. How should I explain to her why I was not growing older; why my life will be ten times as long as hers?'

'She is intelligent.'

'I don't even know for certain why I will live so long.'

'Evelina suggests you confront her tomorrow about it. She says you may learn some answers.'

'I was going to be gone tomorrow.'

'Why?'

'Because it will be my birthday. I didn't want her asking how old I really am.'

'If she saw your family record, she already knows.'

'But, what if,' Bryant began in futile protest.

'Just get some sleep and worry about it in the morning.'

Bryant sighed. Haskell was right. There was no use in avoiding it any longer. He got undressed and got into bed. He lay there awake until nearly dawn.

* * * * *

Sonje awoke suddenly to the sound of screaming. Quickly she rose to her feet and ran into the hall. She paused to find the screams were coming from Bryant's room. She flung open the door and ran to his bedside. He was screaming and fighting the quilt.

"Bryant!" she cried. "Bryant, it's just a nightmare!"

She put her hands on his shoulders and he began to quiet down.

"Wake up, Bryant."

"What, what happened?" he asked when he opened his eyes.

"You were screaming. What were you dreaming about?"

"I was dreaming about Uncle Rolfe."

"Who is that?"

"Was. It's a long story."

"You can tell me at the meadow. Get up and get dressed. I'll meet you in front of the stables in a half an hour."

"Alright," he said as he sat up.

She drew in her breath sharply as the quilts fell to expose his bare chest. She hadn't imagined his chest to be so broad and strong. She couldn't take her eyes off of him. The morning sunlight streaming through the doorway highlighted his blond hair. She hadn't realized how attracted to him she was. She saw the mischievous smile as it crept across his face.

"Are you going to just stand there staring at me or are you going to get ready?" he said, laughing at her.

She turned and ran from the room as she felt the blood rush to her cheeks. She hurried to change her dress. She left her hair unbraided because she knew he liked it that way. She hoped he liked the birthday lunch that she had prepared and packed the previous day. She hurried to the kitchen for the lunch and then went to the stables.

* * * * *

By the time Bryant arrived at the stables, Sonje had the horses saddled and ready to go. In spite of it being a pleasant day, he was wearing his black cape with the dragon clasp. The sun caught her hair as she led the horses into the sunlight. He tried to keep his hand steady as she handed him Llewellyn's reins. As she turned to mount, he drew his cape closer about him, not for warmth, but for comfort. Llewellyn nuzzled his cheek and whickered softly. He rubbed Llewellyn's neck in thanks and then mounted.

They rode in silence to the meadow. They dismounted and turned the horses loose. She unpacked their lunch. When she was finished, there was a small package left unopened.

"Another traditional family recipe?" Bryant asked.

"Yes. I've tried a lot of food from many areas, but I still like the foods from my home best," she said and began to eat.

After they had finished eating, she handed him the package.

"What's this?" he asked.

"A birthday present," she answered. "Open it."

He opened it carefully. Inside was a signet ring. It was made of gold with a green stone. In the stone was carved a dragon with a crown over its head.

"Where did you get this?" he asked.

"I made it for you. Now tell me about Uncle Rolfe."

"My family is longer lived than the people of the town. My Uncle Rolfe fell in love with a young girl from the town. We had all told Uncle Rolfe that it was not wise to marry someone who could never live as long as he would. She was beautiful and he married her anyway. For fifty years they were very happy, but they never had any children. She grew old, he remained young. She died and his happiness shattered into pain and resentment."

"Then what happened?" asked Sonje.

"He went insane. He burned the town. Those that survived fled. Even my family left. Only my father stayed behind with me. He died about five years ago."

"Why did you stay behind?"

"In hope that the town could be repaired and that things could return to the way they were," he replied as he felt the loneliness even more acutely than usual.

Sonje smiled.

"Perhaps things can return to as they were," she told him.

'Tell her how old you are,' Haskell ordered.

"I must tell you how old I am," Bryant began reluctantly.

"You are two hundred and seventy-one today," Sonje finished for him. "And next month I will be two hundred and sixty-six."

"You're joking!" he said in disbelief.

"I am from Glynis," she stated calmly. "I must return there soon for a week's time."

"Why must you go?" Bryant asked, expecting her request.

"To claim what is rightfully mine. Then I will return," Sonje told him as she put her hand in his. "My place is here."

"What are you claiming?" he asked, confused by her gesture.

"I will explain when the time is right. There are still things for me to learn about this place that will decide our future in it."

Bryant didn't know what to say. He rose to his knees and took her other hand. Gently he pulled her to her knees in front of him. As he gazed into her emerald eyes, she returned the gaze steadily. He could resist no longer. The reasons for holding back were gone. As he drew her nearer, she closed her eyes. Tenderly he kissed her lips. He released her hands. As he put his arms around her, her arms closed around him and drew him even closer. He kissed her again with more passion as he drew her body against his own. She turned her head away and laid it on his shoulder. He kissed her hair.

"I have found my home," she said softly. "My quest is nearly complete."

Reluctantly he released her from his arms. He rose to his feet and drew her up as well.

"You may make your journey on two conditions. The first is that you will return in one week's time. The second is that you take this cape and wear it," he said as he unclasped the cape.

He removed the cape from his shoulders and placed it on hers. He kissed her once more after clasping the cape.

"As you wish, My Lord," she said solemnly. "You are doing the right thing."

He found the band on his wrist to be glowing brightly.

"Evening is coming. We must leave now," he told her, reluctant to leave the meadow. "When must you leave?"

"A week from tonight. I must leave after dark," Sonje answered.

"Why after dark?" Bryant asked as he stood ready to mount Llewellyn.

"I must arrive at the first light of dawn." she said, then mounted Guen.

He mounted and headed towards the castle. She followed behind him. In silence, they cared for the horses and went to their rooms.

'What should I tell her? I can't let her leave at night,' Bryant asked Haskell.

'She will have to know eventually,' Haskell replied.

'Not yet, I don't know how she'll take it. I don't want to lose her.'

'She will need to know before much longer. We can wait for her to leave before coming out.'

'Thank you, my friend.'

V.J.O. Gardner

Chapter 4 – She's Gone

Sonje was up with the dawn. On her way to the kitchen, she paused in the great hall. She walked to the center of the room and stood facing the doors at the rear of the hall.

'Why would someone want such huge doors going to a mountain cavern?' she asked herself.

She looked from the doors to the mosaic floor at her feet. Under her feet was an enormous dragon. It was mostly gold except for black striping on its face, neck, and legs. The other dragons in the mosaic were smaller and of many patterns and colors.

"It almost makes me wish these beautiful creatures were real," Sonje said quietly to herself.

"I'm glad you find them beautiful," Bryant's voice said loudly.

She turned to find him on the balcony. He descended the steps to join her on the mosaic. He took her hand in his and drew it to his lips. He looked up from her hand to find her smiling at him.

"May I have this dance, My Lady?" he asked, bowing formally.

"With pleasure, My Lord."

Her heart leapt as he drew her closer and put his right arm around her waist. Slowly they began to dance. In the back of her mind she could almost hear the music as they danced in ever widening circles. She looked into his eyes as they danced. She wanted the memory of his face etched into her mind before she had to leave for Glynis. Their dance slowed and he drew her even closer. A sigh escaped her lips as he released her hand and put his hand behind her head. She felt as though she had melted as he kissed her.

Sonje laid her head on his shoulder as she tried to catch both her breath and her balance. Gently he stroked her hair that fell down her back. Her heart raced wildly as he drew back and put his hand under her chin to raise her face to his again. He kissed her tenderly and then released her from his arms. She felt as though the room was spinning.

* * * * *

Gently he placed her hand on his arm and led her to the kitchen. His pulse was still racing as they reached the kitchen. He wished that they

40

could hold a ball like he remembered from his childhood. He could dance the night away with her in his arms.

As the week progressed, she doubled her efforts in solving the mystery of the castle and he doubled his efforts in repairing the church. Somehow they found more time to spend with each other.

On the afternoon of her last day, he found her in the music room playing a beautiful, yet hauntingly sad melody. Her back was turned towards the door as he entered quietly. The sound of her flute was like the sad sigh of wind through the leafless trees of winter. He finally recognized the song as a long, sad ballad of farewell. As she played the last few lines, the music brightened, bespeaking of the hope of reunion.

He knelt before her and took her hands in his.

"Swear to me that you will return," he pleaded. "I could not live if you did not return."

There were tears in her eyes as she looked down into his tear filled eyes.

"The journey is very dangerous. If I arrive safely in Glynis, I will return easily," she answered. "When I leave, you may watch, but do not interfere. To do so could be deadly for both of us."

"I do not understand, but I know I must trust you."

"The time has come," she said as the room began to darken with the setting of the sun. "You will witness many strange things tonight. When I return I will explain those that I can."

Together, hand in hand, they left the room. As the shadows deepened and darkness fell, she allowed her light to shine in the darkness. They first went to her bedchamber. Lying on the bed was his cape and next to it a pair of saddlebags. Bryant picked up the cape and placed it about her shoulders. Sonje picked up the saddlebags and took one last look at the room. When they reached the courtyard, she stopped.

"Remain here. Do not move or say anything until I am gone," she ordered. "Remember, I love you."

For the first time she had spoken the words his heart longed to hear.

"I love you too much to risk harming you. I will do as you ask," he replied.

Sonje walked to the center of the courtyard alone. Her light glowed in a blue-green sphere around her. The deepest shadows seemed to expand in a cloud that stopped a short distance before reaching her.

"You have summoned?" it asked in a wheezing whisper.

"I request passage to Glynis," she replied.

"What is your purpose there?"

"To claim my birthright."

"Are you prepared to face my challenge?"

"Yes."

"Do you know the consequence for failing?"

"Death."

"Are you ready to face your deepest hopes and fears?"

"Yes."

Bryant stood silently and helplessly watching as her battle began. Although he could see no physical contact, her body swayed with the effort. Suddenly the cloud exploded in size and gained substance and form. Before Sonje a huge dragon stood on its haunches. Into the air it spewed a jet of flames. Many colors swirled on its body. When the colors quit swirling, the dragon looked identical to the mosaic dragon in the great hall.

"With time and practice, I can become as strong as or stronger than my mother was," Sonje said, then paused. "Yes."

The dragon lowered itself so she could mount. She climbed up the foreleg that it offered. She placed the saddlebags across its neck. Then she straddled the neck on top of the bags. The dragon reared up and then launched into the night sky.

Bryant let out his breath and collapsed against the door. He hadn't realized that he had been paralyzed by the scene, unable to move or speak, until it was over. He ran to the place where she had stood.

"No," he groaned.

He sank to his knees and put his hands over his eyes. He knew that he had not wanted her to leave, that he could not live without her. He wanted her forever in his arms as she was when they had danced in the great hall. It was like losing his father all over again.

'Bryant!' Haskell's voice broke through his despair. 'We saw what happened. She was still mounted while she was within our vision.'

'She's gone.'

'She promised to return if she still lived.'

'What will I do?'

'What you would do if you knew beyond doubt that she was returning. Don't consider for a single moment that she isn't returning.'

"I want her to return. I need her. I love her.'

'Come sleep in the cavern so you will be near us. We will watch over you as you sleep.'

Bryant slowly returned to the dark castle. He lit a torch and went to his room. Once there he gathered up a quilt and a pillow. On the way down the hall he noticed that his wristband was glowing softly. It eased the pain a little. He felt as though it meant she was still alive. When he reached the cavern, he doused the torch and put it in a wall bracket.

He climbed up the stairs to the ledge and spread his quilt on the cool sand and placed the pillow near one corner. He lay down and drew the other half of the quilt over himself. As he closed his eyes, he heard the soft humming of Haskell's lullaby.

Towards dawn he began screaming. Haskell heard his horror filled thoughts and cringed.

'Bryant!' Haskell called as he nudged Bryant's shoulder. 'Wake up, Bryant! It's only a dream!'

Bryant sat up suddenly and then began to cry. Haskell nudged Bryant's shoulder in reassurance.

'Just let it out,' Haskell told him softly.

After a while the tears slowed and Bryant began to calm down.

'Tell me what you will do this week.'

'I want to finish the church.'

'Working in the daylight, we can finish it in three days. What else will you do?'

'I want to go through some things in the jewel chamber.'

'What else?'

'I want to visit her father in town.'

'Good. Is that all?'

'No. I want to reopen my parent's apartment. I want to have it ready for her when she returns.'

'Why don't you go and open it up so it can air out while we work today?'

'I will. I will meet you in the courtyard at dawn,' Bryant said as he stood up.

He shook the sand from the quilt and folded it carefully. He returned the quilt and the pillow to his room then he went to the end of the hall.

He unlocked the double doors and opened them wide. He took a deep breath before entering the spacious room and opened the shuttered windows. He did the same in the bathing chamber. He opened the closet door also.

He returned to his room to bathe and change his clothes. Next he went to the kitchen to pack a lunch. It was difficult not to think about her. The kitchen reminded him of the delicious meals that she had prepared for him. He hurried out of the kitchen as the sun came peeking out from behind the mountains.

'Let's go,' he said as he mounted Haskell.

They worked all day on the church. By nightfall it was nearly ready for the shingles that he had split all last winter. As the sun began to settle over the forest, a scream split the air. The great eagle flew towards them from the forest. Dangling from his talons was a rabbit. He dropped it at Bryant's feet and then landed. Bryant looked at Haskell and then back to the eagle.

"Thank you, Ernest," he told the eagle.

The eagle clicked its beak and almost whistled before it screamed once and then flew off. Bryant picked up the rabbit and turned to Haskell.

'The eagle said, 'you're welcome' and that he would bring another the day after tomorrow,' Haskell told him.

Bryant shook his head and then mounted Haskell. They returned to the castle for night. Bryant gratefully cooked and ate the rabbit that the eagle had brought. That night he slept in his own room. Haskell kept watch over his dreams, nudging Bryant's mind gently away from unpleasant thoughts.

As dawn arrived, Bryant woke. He immediately missed having Sonje around. Even on the days that he hadn't seen her, he had known that she was there, just as he now knew that she was absent.

Slowly he got out of bed and prepared for the day. On the way to the kitchen, he paused at the edge of the great hall. The memory of their dance burned in his heart. He turned from the pain of it and hurried to the kitchen. After eating and preparing lunch, he left the kitchen through the garden and the stable to avoid the great hall and its memories.

"Are you ready?" he asked Haskell as he stood in the courtyard.

"Yes," Haskell answered.

They worked hard all day. Bryant hammered his despair away as he hammered each board and shingle in place. Haskell was silently pleased as he watched Bryant work out his frustrations.

At nightfall, Bryant was exhausted, but felt better. They returned to the castle in the dark. Bryant went directly to bed. Haskell watched over him again, but his sleep was deep and without disturbance. As he woke the next morning, Bryant felt better but still lonely.

'Haskell.'

'Yes, Bryant?'

'I think that I will work on Sonje's new apartment today.'

'Good. I need to sleep.'

'I want it ready for her when she returns.'

'You have other reasons for wanting it ready. It is much larger than just one person would need or you would have moved in a long time ago.'

Bryant just laughed. It was the first time that he had felt cheerful since she had left. He dressed quickly and went down the hall to Sonje's new apartment.

He found everything to be covered with dust. As he worked to clean the rooms, it felt good that he was preparing for her return. At lunch time he found that the dust was so thick in the air that he did more sneezing than cleaning. He rolled up the rugs, dragged them down the hall and down the stairs to the great hall.

He sneezed one last time and then went to the kitchen. As he prepared his lunch he sighed.

"I hope she is alright," he said aloud.

He froze as the band on his wrist began to glow. He felt his heart swell with joy at this revelation. He ate his lunch quickly and then returned to the great hall. Instead of taking the rugs outside, he entered the doors opposite the dining hall.

The large, formal sitting room smelled stale from being shut for so many years. Bryant lit a candle, both to provide light and to help sweeten the stale air. At the other end of the room, he paused to unlock the door to his father's office. Once inside he lit the lamp on the desk.

Bryant stood behind the large, hand carved, wooden desk. He faced the wall behind the desk where a huge dragon's head, skillfully carved of wood, seemed to spring from the wall as though it would come to life and swallow any who faced it. He plunged his arm down its throat and found the lever he was looking for.

Silently the bookcase to Bryant's right swung into the room. He took the lamp from the desk and entered the opening left by the shelves. Silently the shelves swung back in place. Bryant had to blink several times to adjust to the brilliant lights that reflected from his single lamp. He placed the lamp on the table in the center of the room. First he turned to a shelf opposite the door. From among the many glittering jewels, he drew a brass dragon clasp. He placed it on the table near the lamp. It was smaller than his own that Sonje now wore. It was jeweled delicately to match the mosaic dragon in the great hall.

He took a cloth from a shallow drawer in the table and polished the clasp until it glowed in the lamplight. Next he turned back to the same shelf. After a few moments of looking, he found a tiny wooden box that looked out of place among the sparkle of the many gems. Tenderly he brought the box to the table and opened it. The interior of the box seemed to explode with light. He caught his breath as he viewed the contents of the box. One of the two rings was a tiny jeweled dragon whose tail would wrap around the wearer's finger and curl in a tiny loop at its tip. The second ring was plain in comparison except for the single large, round diamond that reflected the light back multiplied. He gently removed the rings from the box. He fit them together so that the single stone was surrounded by the tip of the dragon's tail. He tried to imagine the rings on

Sonje's hand and the band on his wrist began to glow brightly. He separated the rings and put them back in their box.

With the box and clasp firmly in hand he checked the outer room through a peep-hole and then released the catch lever. As the shelves slipped silently in place behind him, he blinked in the darkness of the office. He extinguished the lamp and carried the candle out with him. He locked the door and left the sitting room as it was before. Bryant blew out the candle and left it on the small table that stood next to the sitting room doors.

He returned to Sonje's new apartment and began looking through the closet. He soon found what he had been looking for, a white cape.

'Ernest approaches,' Haskell warned him.

Bryant left the cape, clasp and box on the bed and hurried to the courtyard. Just as he stepped through the door, the great eagle appeared over the courtyard wall. He dropped a plump pheasant at Bryant's feet and then landed.

"Thank you, Ernest. Do you know where Sonje's father is staying in the village?" Bryant asked and the eagle bobbed its head in acknowledgment.

'Ernest knows where you mean,' Haskell said.

"That is where I will expect you the day after tomorrow," Bryant told the eagle.

Ernest screamed once and flew back to the forest.

'He will do as you wish,' Haskell informed Bryant. 'What will you do tomorrow?'

'I will make preparations to go to the village. I wish to find gifts for Sonje's father, Cherie, Olvan, and their children.'

'And get enough courage to go and talk with Sonje's father?'

'I cannot hide that from you.'

Bryant returned to Sonje's new rooms and to his labors after leaving the pheasant in the kitchen. He picked up the white cape. He removed the plain clasp from the cape and replaced it with the dragon clasp. He then took the box, the cape and extra clasp to his bedchamber. Being nightfall, he went to the kitchen and prepared the pheasant for his dinner. As he ate, he realized how much he missed her being around. He knew that it had only been a few days, yet it seemed like forever.

That night, Bryant tossed and turned all night. He was too nervous the next morning to eat more than a piece of fruit for breakfast. His mind kept turning to what he would say to Sonje's father. He knew that to make friends would be a difficult task. Just getting through the village to the home would be difficult. Past contacts with the villagers had gone very badly. The only contact that had been good was the time that Langward had helped Father when he was injured near the village. Father mentioned he didn't ask for anything in return and understood their desire for privacy. Also he had shown no fear or aggression.

Bryant paused as he passed the library. He turned towards the doors and the band on his wrist began to glow. He opened the door and went to Sonje's reading table. The band glowed brighter. A book lay open on the table. He could not read the text, but the man in the picture looked familiar and the woman almost looked like Sonje. As he looked at the picture he realized that it must be of someone related to Sonje. The band glowed even brighter.

Bryant said quietly aloud, "I don't know what this book is, but I will give it to Sonje's father."

Bryant felt better having selected Auberon's gift. Next he went to the second floor on the other side of the great hall. He went to the end of the hall and opened the doors. Inside was a children's nursery. He quickly found what he was looking for. For the girl there was a beautiful porcelain doll with moving arms and a fine lady's dress. For the boy there was a tiny farm wagon complete with horses and driver. Bryant took the toys and the book to his bedchamber and left them there. Next he went to the room next to his and looked through the closet. He found a dress that was the bright blue of a summer sky. He also found two shawls. He went back to his room and began to carefully wrap the doll and the wagon each in a shawl. He carefully folded the dress. From his own closet, he got a grey cape with a plain clasp. He bundled the gifts in the cape and went to the kitchen. He packed bread, meat, cheese and a flask of water. At the stables he packed everything carefully in the largest saddlebags he could find.

Llewellyn was waiting for him at the gate as he came to saddle him for the journey. Bryant got two halters from the tack room and mounted Llewellyn. They took a narrow road that led into the mountains above the castle. Soon they entered a mountain pasture in which cattle were grazing. They looked up as Bryant dismounted and took the smaller halter and a lead rope in his hand. The cattle were unafraid as Bryant walked among them. He finally found a yearling cow that suited his purpose. He placed the rope around its neck until he had the halter in place. The cow followed willingly as he led it from the herd.

'The cow knows that it will live longer if it goes with you,' Haskell told Bryant. 'Travel safely.'

'I will miss your companionship,' Bryant answered as he mounted Llewellyn.

They turned down the path towards the castle. They clattered through the cobbled streets of the town. Halfway through the forest, Bryant noticed the sun was going down. He found a grassy clearing to camp in for the night. He staked out the young cow and unsaddled Llewellyn. He put the halter on in place of the bridle and staked the stallion to graze. He placed the saddle and saddlebags out of the animals' reach and then laid down using the saddle as a headrest and folding his cape over him for a quilt. The sweet smell of the grass made him dream pleasant dreams of being with Sonje in the meadow.

Chapter 5 – Visiting the Village

Llewellyn whinnied softly to wake Bryant at dawn. He woke to find everything covered with dew. He stood up and shook the dew from his cape. He then sat back down and took his food from the saddlebags. As he ate, the sun came up and began burning the dew off. After he had eaten, Bryant packed his food back away before he saddled and bridled Llewellyn. He took up the lead rope for the yearling cow and then mounted. He reached the village just before lunch time. As he approached the first houses, a young man with a pitchfork blocked the road.

"What do you want here, Dracona?" he challenged.

"I come not as Lord Dracona, but as Bryant Donley. I come in peace to seek audience with Auberon, father of Cherie who is the wife of Olvan," Bryant answered the challenge calmly.

"How can I know you are telling the truth?"

"I carry no weapons," he answered as he opened his cape so the young man could see.

"Dismount and walk beside me. I will lead your horse," the man commanded and Bryant complied.

As they passed, people stared at the strange procession. As they neared the house, the sound of a child crying caught Bryant's ears. He turned to see a small boy reaching for a kitten who was in a tree.

"Bring my horse under this branch," Bryant told the young man.

When Llewellyn was in place Bryant mounted, then stood on the saddle. Gently he petted and calmed the kitten then he lifted it down from the branch. He carefully dismounted holding the kitten against his chest. He dropped to one knee in front of the child and handed him the kitten. A smile broke through the boy's tears and then he turned and ran to his home.

Bryant dusted off his knee and returned to the young man. They soon arrived at Bryant's destination. The young man greeted Olvan who stood in the doorway.

"Bryant Donley wishes audience with Auberon," the young man announced.

Bryant bowed to Olvan.

"I come bearing gifts and seeking peace," Bryant said noticing the two children peeking around their father's legs at his mention of gifts.

He untied the cow and led it forward.

"This is my finest yearling cow. It is now yours," he said placing the lead rope in Olvan's hand.

Bryant returned to Llewellyn and removed the saddlebags before returning to where Olvan stood in front of the house. He knelt and drew the children's gifts from the saddlebags.

"I have something here for a boy and something for a girl," Bryant said so that the children could hear.

They looked hesitantly from Bryant, then to their father who nodded silently. The girl walked slowly and cautiously to Bryant who held out the appropriate package to her. She unwrapped the doll and then hugged it tightly to her chest.

"That was my aunt's favorite doll," Bryant told her. "I'm sure that she would like you to take care of her."

The little girl nodded and smiled. Her brother had quietly tip-toed out to see what his sister had gotten. Bryant held the second package out to him. Carefully the boy took the package and unwrapped his gift. His eyes gleamed as he held up the wagon for his father to see.

"That was my favorite toy when I was your age." Bryant told him. "I thought that you might like it too."

The boy nodded shyly and then ran inside the house.

"You may come in. I will care for your horse," Olvan finally spoke.

"Thank you," Bryant responded, trying not to show how relieved he was to make it this far.

He gathered up the discarded shawls and the saddlebags then followed the girl into the house. He was glad to be out of sight of the curious eyes of the villagers. He knew that he still faced the most difficult task, talking to Auberon. Olvan entered and signaled him to sit at the table where a meal was laid for lunch.

"You must wait until nightfall to talk to Auberon," Olvan said as he set a fourth plate in front of Bryant. "He and Cherie are not to be disturbed until then. You may stay here tonight."

"Thank you for your hospitality," Bryant told him.

The two men and the two children ate in silence. Bryant wondered what was going on. He knew that it would be a very long afternoon. When they had finished eating, Bryant helped clear the table.

"I am going out to work in the fields," Olvan told Bryant.

"Could I help you?" Bryant asked.

"I suppose," Olvan said.

Together with the children they left the house. When they reached the field, Bryant spread his cape out below a tree for the children to play on and hung his sleeveless jacket on a low branch. All afternoon Bryant worked beside Olvan in the field. Passing villagers paused to watch the pair work before going on.

"They are very suspicious of my presence," Bryant commented.

"Do you blame them?" Olvan returned.

"No, but I wish that I could somehow regain their trust in my family."

"They have grown up distrusting your family. What happened so many years ago to cause their distrust?"

"It was the act of a man in deep despair, a mark of shame on my family and the source of my nightmares."

"You know what happened?"

"I was still young when my Uncle Rolfe's wife died and sent him insane from grief. She was from the town's people and could never live as long as he would. My father had to kill Uncle Rolfe to end his rampage, but not before the townspeople had fled in horror of the destruction he had wrought."

"Is that why he was so bitter towards the villagers?"

"Not exactly, he was afraid that I would fall in love with a girl from the village and repeat the tragedy."

"I am of the village. Cherie and I waited three years before marrying. We decided it would be best to have children so the time of my death could come easier."

"I wish Uncle Rolfe had been so wise."

"Is Sonje happy at Castle Dracona?"

"I think she is. There are still things that she does not know about the castle."

"The stories are true?"

"Yes, Lord Dracona is not an empty title."

"Does she know?"

"Not yet. I have been trying to let her come to that conclusion herself before meeting them."

"You are wise."

"Unfortunately, time is running out. I will need to tell her when she returns."

The band on Bryant's wrist began to glow.

"You have a band like hers," Olvan commented, noticing the glow.

"She wove it from her own hair."

Olvan smiled. He quit working and motioned Bryant to follow him to the tree where the children played. Bryant put his jacket back on and picked up his cape as the children scampered ahead.

"Where is your black cape with the dragon clasp?" Olvan asked.

"I sent it with Sonje," Bryant replied.

When they reached the house, Olvan began preparing the evening meal with the large rabbit that they found on the doorstep. Bryant helped in the kitchen. Soon the meal was ready and the sun had set. The door that had been closed all day opened. The children ran to their mother as she stepped into the room. They hugged and kissed her, then pulled her to where they had left their new toys. Bryant drew the last two presents from his saddlebags.

"This is for you," he said as she turned towards him.

She unfolded the dress and held it up.

"It's beautiful, Cherie," Auberon said as he entered the room.

Bryant turned and held the book out to him.

"This is for you," Bryant said and then bowed once Auberon had taken the book.

"Do you know what this is?"

"No."

"It is a history of Glynis," Auberon told him. "Can you read it?"

"No."

"Let's eat," Cherie broke in. "Then you two can talk all you want."

They sat down and ate the meal that Bryant and Olvan had prepared. After the dishes had been cleared and cleaned, the children were sent upstairs to bed. Cherie and Olvan went back into their bedroom leaving Bryant and Auberon alone.

"My daughter appears happy with her promise," Auberon told Bryant.

"I try to give her no reason to regret it," Bryant answered. "She has been a ray of sunlight through the darkness that had hung over me."

"Has she given you anything?"

"She wove a band of her hair and placed it on my wrist. She also gave me this," Bryant said as he held out his hand so that Auberon could see the ring.

Auberon examined it closely in the candle light.

"She made this with her own hand," Auberon commented.

Although Auberon seemed less forbidding Bryant was still very nervous.

"I didn't come to see you just to bring gifts," Bryant said, then swallowed hard. "I came to ask for your daughter's hand in marriage. I love Sonje and wish to make her my wife."

"I can see that you will take care of my Gwladys and make her happy," Auberon answered.

Bryant was so relieved that he almost fell off his chair. Auberon didn't seem to notice.

"Kneel before me," Auberon commanded.

Bryant obeyed. A bright white light began to shine around Auberon engulfing both of them. He placed his hands on Bryant's head and spoke words that Bryant did not understand. When Auberon had finished and removed his hands, Bryant felt strangely. Auberon's light faded leaving the room dark except for a soft orange glow that centered around Bryant.

"May you always walk in light, My Lord," Auberon said solemnly and bowed.

"May your days be long and prosperous in this world," Cherie spoke from where she and Olvan stood in a violet glow.

She bowed to him. Bryant stood up, confused. Olvan left his wife's light and stood before Bryant.

"May your happiness grow with each passing day, My Lord," Olvan said and then bowed low.

"Sit down and rest, My Lord," Auberon suggested.

Bryant was glad to sit down. He felt tired. Cherie and Olvan sat down also.

"Did you watch Sonje leave Castle Dracona?" Cherie asked.

"Yes. What was that creature?" Bryant answered.

"It is known only as the Travelor. Only a woman with the birthright may face it. The woman must have the strength, confidence, and courage to face and overcome its challenge in order to remain alive," Auberon answered.

"It assumes the form that the woman must overcome her fear of in order to claim her birthright," Cherie added.

"She arrived in Glynis on a magnificent dragon and wearing a pitch black cape with a dragon for a clasp. Was that the way she left your castle?" Auberon asked.

"Yes. She told me that I could not interfere and that if she arrived in Glynis safely that she would return in a week's time," Bryant looked at Olvan who nodded to him. "The Travelor is not the only dragon Sonje will face."

"The legends tell us that the quest will be dangerous and the foretold one will not be alone in facing her challenges," Auberon said as he stood up. "Come, the hour grows late and we all must have our sleep tonight."

Bryant followed Auberon up the stairs while Cherie and Olvan returned to their room. Upstairs the two children lay asleep in their beds. A soft green glow surrounded the boy and a soft blue glow surrounded the girl. Bryant noticed that Auberon's light had taken on a yellow tint.

Bryant sat on the edge of the bed that had been prepared for him and removed his boots. He was almost asleep as he lay down and covered himself. He had so many questions that he needed answers to. He slept fitfully, dreaming strange dreams.

* * * * *

After sunup, Bryant began to wake up to the sound of children giggling. Carefully he opened his eye just enough to catch a glimpse of the two children whispering to each other. He decided to let them play their game. Suddenly they leapt on him.

"I'm up, I'm up already!" he exclaimed as they regrouped for another attack.

"Mayetta! Alleyn!" Olvan shouted. "Just tell him that breakfast is ready, don't kill him."

The children laughed.

"Breakfast is ready, Uncle Bryant," the children said in unison.

Bryant sat up and began to pull on his boots.

"Come here and sit by me."

Obediently they sat one on each side of him.

"You know that I'm not your uncle yet."

"You will be," Mayetta said.

"Will you take us for a ride?" asked Alleyn, no longer shy.

"On my horse, Llewellyn?"

"No, but he will do today," Mayetta answered.

"You two weren't sleeping last night, were you?"

The children giggled.

"I will introduce you to Haskell when you come to the castle. If you ask nicely, I think he will give you a ride."

The children threw their arms around him and kissed his cheeks. Bryant hoped that they would come to the castle soon. He would miss this sort of attention almost as much as he missed Sonje.

"Come on. Let's eat breakfast so that we can go for a ride."

After breakfast, Bryant saddled and bridled Llewellyn. Bryant mounted and then Olvan handed up Mayetta to sit in front of him and Alleyn to sit behind him. They rode up and down the street and then to Olvan's field. They dismounted and sat together in the grass beneath the tree.

"Do you know why I am not liked here in the village?" Bryant asked them.

"They're afraid of you," Mayetta answered.

"They are afraid of your dragon," Alleyn added.

"I wish there was some way to make them not afraid," Bryant said. "Where are your mother and grandfather?"

"They are attending the Grand Council in Glynis," Mayetta said.

"How are they traveling that far and still be here at night?"

"Not their bodies, just their minds," she answered. "Mother says that tomorrow will be the last day of the Grand Council."

"Then I must return home. I still have things to do to prepare for Sonje's return," Bryant said as he stood up.

He walked out to where Olvan was working in the field. The children followed.

"I must leave, my friend. I hope that you and your family will come to visit soon."

"We will see you again soon. Take care in your travels," Olvan answered.

Bryant mounted Llewellyn and returned to the house. He put on his grey cape and got his empty saddlebags. After securing the saddlebags, he mounted again and rode out of town. He was met with many stares, but few of the villagers hid from him as they had at first. When he left the outskirts of the village, he turned off the road and urged Llewellyn into the forest. As they galloped directly towards the castle, Bryant felt happy.

Night began to fall before they reached the castle. Bryant slowed Llewellyn to a trot. He wished he could use the orange glow that he had the night before. Softly he began to glow. He thought harder about glowing. The glow grew. He noticed that the glow was not quite as orange as it had been before. By much concentration, Bryant made the light large enough to make the path between the trees clear. Llewellyn began to gallop and soon they were home.

After taking care of Llewellyn, Bryant ate a simple supper and then went to the cavern behind the great hall. Bryant climbed the stairs and counted the mounds in the sand.

"Haskell," Bryant said out loud. "There are fifty-two!"

'I know,' Haskell answered. 'Welcome home. How was your trip?'

'Everything went well. No one threw anything and I wasn't run off with a pitchfork. Auberon will allow me to marry Sonje. I have friends now.'

'Who?'

'Olvan and his two children.'

'That's great.'

'The boy, Alleyn, wants a ride.'

'You told him about us?'

'No, Olvan figured it out. Although he is a villager, he showed no fear of the idea.'

'Cherie married a villager?' Haskell sounded alarmed.

'Yes. I told him about Uncle Rolfe. He and Cherie decided that children would give her comfort when he dies long before she begins to grow old.'

'You should invite them to live here. I would like to meet them.'

'I invited them to come visit. Olvan said that they would see me again soon,' Bryant said as he wondered how soon. 'Where is Evelina?'

'She is sleeping,' Haskell answered as he came to the entrance of his den. 'She is growing weaker every day. I don't think she will live to see the hatch.'

They stood together in silence, each knowing that they needed help. Bryant wished that the villagers were not so afraid, but he knew that it would take too long to expect any aid from them. He wished he knew what happened to Langward, but he hadn't seen him among the villagers.

'I learned something on my trip,' Bryant said trying to get his mind off of the sand covered mounds. 'Sonje is not the only one who can make her own light. All of her people can. Each person appears to have their own color of light.'

'That is interesting,' Haskell said, sounding curious.

Bryant concentrated and the glow of orange light returned to surround him.

'I have a light now also.'

'I can see that.'

Bryant could see his reflection in Haskell's large eye as Haskell lowered his head for a better view.

'You look tired,' Haskell told him. 'Go to bed.'

'I am tired. Good night.'

Bryant wearily made his way out of the warm cavern and into the coolness of the great hall. He was glad for his new-found light. He went upstairs and to his bedchamber. He collapsed into bed and slept soundly.

Chapter 6 – New Friends and New Responsibilities

Bryant woke up just after dawn feeling refreshed. He bathed, shaved and dressed then went towards the kitchen. As he was passing through the great hall, he heard a clatter in the courtyard. Quickly he ran to the doors and flung them open.

Riders quickly dismounted their horses and assembled before him. Six men bowed on bended knee. Five women curtsied low.

"All hail, Lord Dracona!" they said as one. "We are sent from Glynis to serve you. Your wish is our command."

Bryant stood frozen in shock for a moment. He had not expected anything like this. He made up his mind quickly as he remembered the conversation with Haskell last night.

"Rise," he ordered. "I keep no servants. I cannot force you to stay or do anything. You may stay of your own free will. There is much to do here. I welcome any help that is offered."

Bryant was relieved to see the smiles that spread among the group.

"You may choose houses in the town for you and your families. When you ask for work, I will show you what needs to be done."

The oldest of the women stepped forward and curtseyed again.

"Lord, may I prepare breakfast for you?" she asked.

He decided that it would be nice to have someone else cook. Especially if she cooked like Sonje had.

"You may prepare breakfast for me and anyone else who desires breakfast," Bryant answered.

He led the woman to the kitchen as the others took the horses and went to choose their new homes. As he waited for the others to return, he wondered if there would be more coming from Glynis.

'It is a possibility,' Haskell's voice rang in his mind.

'I think our problem will be solved,' Bryant responded.

'When will you tell them?'

'As soon as Sonje knows. I will tell her as soon as she returns.'

'Evelina says she is pleased.'

The rest of the group began to enter the dining hall. The woman began to bring plates and goblets out of the kitchen. With everyone's help, the place settings were soon set. They stood silently by their seats and waited for him to take his seat at the head table. He felt a little strange sitting there alone. Bryant ate in silence listening to their cheerful chatter in a strange, musical sounding language. He wondered if someday he would learn to speak in that language. He suddenly felt very lonely. He wished that Sonje could be sitting beside him. He was relieved when everyone seemed to be finished eating. He stood up and they all stood up as well. They assembled in front of his table. The oldest man stepped forward and bowed.

"My name is Hoyt. I have been sent to instruct you on the history and language of Glynis," Hoyt said then indicated the man beside him. "This is Philip. He will care for the horses, gardens, and any other duties that you choose."

Philip bowed.

"Absalon, Keith, and Stanislaus are carpenters and stone masons. They will repair any building needing repair. They will also perform any labors you ask of them."

Each man bowed as he was introduced.

"Edgard will instruct you in swordsmanship and the other battle arts."

Edgard bowed. Hoyt stepped back and the woman who had prepared their breakfast stepped forward.

"My name is Agatha. I will cook and maintain the kitchen. Daryl and Aurora are seamstresses. They will need to take your measurements before beginning their duties. Aloysia and Florene will clean any room or building that you specify."

Each woman curtseyed as she was introduced. Agatha stepped back. Bryant surveyed the small group. In his mind he heard Haskell chuckling.

'What's so funny?' he thought to Haskell.

'You spend years wanting inhabitants for the deserted town. Now that you have them, you don't know what to do with them. You've lived alone too long,' Haskell replied, still laughing.

"Agatha, you already know where the kitchen is and just outside you can find the garden and yard fowl pens," he said.

Agatha curtseyed and began clearing the tables.

"Everyone else follow me."

Bryant led them out into the great hall. He halted in the center of the room.

"The library is on the third floor over the dining hall," he said as he turned to Hoyt. "I will meet you there in an hour."

Hoyt bowed and went to go to the library. Bryant led the group to the front of the great hall.

"These rugs need the dust beat out of them. I will return to show you where they belong."

Aloysia and Florene each picked up a rug and took them out to the courtyard. Bryant led his dwindling group to the stables.

"These are the stables. At the other end is a pasture. The black, Llewellyn, is my mount. The white, Guen, will be Sonje's mount. The two tan horses are a harness team. There is a work wagon for the carpenters to use."

Bryant crossed the courtyard and unlocked a set of double doors. All followed, except Philip who entered the stables.

"This is the armory."

Edgard bowed and then entered. Bryant led the remaining group to the church.

"This needs to be finished as soon as possible. You should find all the tools and shingles you need here."

The three men bowed and then began inspecting the tools. Bryant led the two women to the tailor's shop.

"You may work here. You may use anything here that you find useful," Bryant said as he turned to leave.

"My Lord," Aurora interrupted his exit. "We need to take your measurements before we can begin our work."

Bryant made a sour face before turning around. Haskell chuckled again. Bryant stood as patently as possible while the two women measured him. At last they released him from their measuring tapes. Bryant was glad to be finished with that unpleasantness. When he returned to the courtyard, Aloysia and Florene were rolling the rugs up. Bryant picked up one of the rugs and led the women up to the fourth floor.

"This apartment must be clean when Sonje returns. She will need the clothes from her old room down the hall," Bryant told them after setting the rug down. "I will leave the door wide open."

Bryant opened Sonje's door before he hurried back to the library where Hoyt was waiting for him.

"Before beginning with language studies, I want to tell you the legend and about the quest," Hoyt said and motioned Bryant to a seat.

As he sat, Bryant knew that Haskell was as intently interested in what Hoyt was about to say as he was.

"Glynis is a land protected from the surrounding bitter North land by a ring of volcanoes. Glynis is a green valley of eternal summer. When the first of our people stumbled out of the snow into the lush green valley of Glynis, our leader was dying. Before she died, she had a vision. She told of a time when the volcanoes that protected the valley would begin to destroy the paradise that they had created. She left us with a riddle."

"A riddle?" Bryant was even more curious than before.

"Yes. We have been trying to solve this riddle ever since."

"What does the riddle say?"

"Out of division will come union, out of death will come life, out of destruction will come salvation, that which was lost will be found. One man, who has forgotten yet who has not been entirely forgotten, will claim one woman who has quested for the sake of all. Thus shall the nation be reborn."

"And the quest?"

"Each gwladys or princess takes up the quest on her hundredth birth date and continues until her death. The quest is to find the answer to the riddle, to find the man."

"Do the princesses marry?"

"Yes. In order to become reginas or queens, they must marry and the ruling power must be passed from the previous king and queen to the new rulers."

"Do all of the people have a glow of colored light which they can control?"

"Yes," Hoyt answered, with a confused look on his face.

"When I visited with Auberon, I discovered that I had this glow," Bryant said as he allowed his glow to show.

Hoyt looked shocked.

"What color was Regis Auberon's glow?" Hoyt asked.

"Regis Auberon? You are saying he is King Auberon?" Bryant asked and Hoyt nodded. "At first it was white. Then after giving me his consent to marry Sonje and having me kneel before him, it began to turn yellow in the center."

"My companions and I traveled for two weeks to arrive here. We were unable to attend the Grand Council. Do you know what form the Travelor took to transport Gwladys Sonje to Glynis?"

"It took the form of a dragon," Bryant said with the realization that he must show the caverns to Hoyt.

"I wonder why a dragon," Hoyt said in a puzzled tone.

'Haskell,' Bryant called silently. 'I am bringing Hoyt to the cavern. Our secret has been kept long enough.'

'I am ready,' Haskell answered.

"I have something to show you that will make things clearer," Bryant told Hoyt as he stood up. "Come with me."

Hoyt followed Bryant to the rear doors of the great hall. Hoyt stood gazing at the enormous doors. Bryant opened them just enough for them to enter. Hoyt stood frozen in his tracks at the sight of the cavern. He stood there for several minutes before looking down as he lifted first one foot, then the other.

"Come. It is cooler on the steps here," Bryant said as he led Hoyt off the hot sand.

"What are those lumps in the sand?" Hoyt asked.

"Eggs," Bryant explained. "Dragon eggs."

"No wonder they are so large. Where are the dragons?"

"I will introduce you. Haskell is expecting us."

Bryant led Hoyt to Haskell's den. Haskell was waiting at the entrance. Hoyt seemed nervous at Haskell's immense size. Haskell placed his chin on the floor. As they approached, Bryant noticed Hoyt looking from Haskell's chin to the top of his head and back with an alarmed expression on his face.

"Haskell, this is Hoyt," Bryant said aloud. "Hoyt, this is my dear friend Haskell."

"It is good to meet you, Haskell," Hoyt said with a slight tremor in his voice.

'Thank you for coming, Hoyt,' Haskell replied, speaking in both men's minds. 'I was very fascinated to hear the riddle of your people. I feel it is very appropriate here. Evelina says that Bryant was right to bring Sonje here. It is time for Dracona to be reborn.'

"Sonje discovered that my family originated in Glynis. My ancestor, Lord Fanchon, led a small group of people to settle here. They found the dragons living here and built the castle with their assistance," Bryant said. "It is my duty as Lord Dracona to remain here to care for the dragons, the castle and the surrounding town with or without people."

Hoyt turned to face him.

"Haskell is very old and Evelina is dying. I cannot care for fifty-two baby dragons alone. Without help they will all die. Dragons have helped and protected my family since they settled here. I must help and protect this new generation."

The band on Bryant's wrist radiated a sudden light.

"It is clear that the riddle has more meaning than originally assumed. The legend is true. I see that you, My Lord, are the man in the riddle. You are this legend!"

Hoyt bowed to him on bended knee. Haskell chuckled quietly to Bryant. Bryant felt as though his heart had stopped. It suddenly became apparent to him that his life would never be the same.

"Hoyt," Bryant said quietly.

"Yes, My Lord," Hoyt said as he looked up.

"I must speak with Sonje before any of this is told to the others."

"As you command, My Lord."

"Please stand," Bryant said at last.

He was not used to such treatment. Haskell chuckled again.

"I must be certain that Sonje loves me as Bryant Donley, not because of her duty to the quest."

"Gwladys Sonje will be honest with you. She hides no emotion for sake of diplomacy. She would never marry just to assume her birthright," Hoyt assured Bryant.

'He believes what he says,' Haskell told Bryant without Hoyt hearing him.

As the two men stood in silence, Bryant realized that it was near lunch time. Hoyt followed him as he left the cavern.

"Why is the sand so hot?" Hoyt asked as they crossed the sand.

"There is a dormant volcano in this mountain," Bryant answered as he closed the doors.

"We've been looking for you two," Agatha's voice echoed through the great hall. "Come now or we will eat without you."

Bryant and Hoyt hurried into the dining hall and took their places. Bryant's mind was filled with what Hoyt had told him. He knew that Sonje would marry him, but he needed to know that it was not just for the sake of her people. Although she had seemed to run from her responsibilities as princess, she had actually served them best by agreeing to live at Castle Dracona.

He had lived so long hiding from the fear and hatred that he needed to know beyond any doubt that she loved him as himself, not as the savior of her people. He wondered if he should greet her by sweeping her into his arms as he truly wanted to or if he should pretend a gracious, dignified greeting. Haskell snickered at him in his head.

'And then you can sweep her into your arms as soon as you are out of sight of the others,' Haskell snidely suggested.

That snapped Bryant back to reality. Edgard was standing patiently before his table. Everyone else had finished and left.

"Yes?" Bryant asked.

"Hoyt suggested that you might be interested in a practice dual rather than book study this afternoon."

"Hoyt is a very observant and thoughtful man," Bryant said as he stood up. "And he is right."

At the armory, they selected dull practice swords and entered the practice arena. They started slowly. Edgard gradually increased the speed of the battle as Bryant's mind and muscles remembered forgotten skills.

Bryant put everything out of his mind except for Edgard's blade. Time was forgotten as the two men dueled. They fought until their blades drooped and their breaths came in ragged gasps. Finally they stood motionless in the arena.

"I am impressed," Edgard gasped between breaths.

"My father was unbeaten," Bryant gasped.

"He taught you well," Edgard said as he dropped his sword and sat down.

Bryant sat beside him.

"It has been at least a hundred years since my father and I last dueled. I'm surprised that I remember anything at all," Bryant said when his breathing returned to almost normal.

"I had to work hard to keep you from breaking through my defense. You will be a challenge for me. You can probably teach me as much as I can teach you."

"I will enjoy having a dueling partner again."

"I noticed that you do not carry a sword."

"It was cumbersome. I have had little need of more than a hunting knife."

"Would you mind showing me your favorite sword?"

"Come," Bryant said as he stood up.

He walked back to the sword racks. Edgard stood and brought the practice blades with him. Bryant stood before a plain wooden box that lay on a shelf under the racks. With reverence, Bryant knelt before the box and opened it. Edgard had to shield his eyes from the unexpected blaze of light that sprung from the exposed sword. Nestled in the velvet lining was an exquisite sword. The steel was so highly polished that it shone like silver. The handgrip and guard were of polished brass that shone like gold. The handgrip was in the form of a dragon's body. The tail of the dragon bent back around to join the mouth that spewed a silver flame that joined with the tail to start the blade. The dragon's wings were curved open to form the hand guard. Beginning at the dragon's mouth and running down the center of the blade were tiny letters.

"Do you know what it says?" Edgard asked when his eyes had adjusted to the brilliance of the blade.

"No," Bryant replied. "It was forged by Lord Fanchon in dragon's fire. It will serve only one master. Great pain or even death can come to those who touch it. That is all that I know about it. Two men even died after touching it."

"The lettering is not quite the same as what we now use. I can make out a word or two, but Hoyt should be able to read it," Edgard suggested.

Bryant gently closed the case and picked it up. He carried it with great respect. Edgard opened the doors for him. Hoyt climbed down from the ladder where he had been looking at the books on one of the top shelves. Bryant gently placed the case on the table nearest to the ladder. He opened the case to reveal the sword to Hoyt.

"Can you read the inscription?" Bryant asked.

Hoyt moved closer and reached towards the sword.

"Don't touch it!" Bryant warned as he grabbed Hoyt's wrist before he could complete the action. "It could be fatal."

Hoyt placed both hands on the table before the box once Bryant had released his wrist.

"Lord of Dragons, Protector of Men, pure of heart, strong of body and mind," Hoyt read. "Impostors beware!"

"What does it mean?" Edgard asked.

"I'm not sure," Hoyt said in a puzzled tone.

"Another riddle," Bryant answered. "Only one man may be its master. To touch it could cause great pain or even death to those not its master."

The three men stood staring at the sword.

"Perhaps the answer will come to us when the time is right," Bryant suggested.

* * * * *

Hoyt noticed the band on Lord Dracona's wrist glowing again. He glanced at Edgard. There was a subtle changed to his expression making it clear to Hoyt that Edgard had also seen the glowing band.

"I think that you are right," Hoyt observed. "Do you have a safe place to keep this?"

"Yes," Lord Dracona replied as he closed the case. "In my father's, my office."

"I think that he will be the master of that sword," Hoyt said to Edgard once Lord Bryant had left the room.

'I am certain that you are right,' Haskell said just to Hoyt.

"He is very adept with a sword. I could learn from him," Edgard said, apparently not noticing Hoyt had been surprised by Haskell speaking to him.

"He will make a good leader," Hoyt commented.

'He needs friendship and confidence,' Haskell spoke again to Hoyt.

"I think that you are right," Edgard said.

"We need to help him feel more confident about our loyalty to him," Hoyt told Edgard. "He needs to know that we are his friends."

"We should try to involve him in the conversation at dinner tonight," Edgard suggested. "He looked very uncomfortable and confused at breakfast. During lunch he looked almost like he was in shock."

"I agree. Make sure that the others are told," Hoyt said.

'I agree as well,' Haskell told Hoyt. 'He should be more himself when Sonje returns. He misses her terribly.'

Lord Bryant returned to the doorway.

"I'm going for a ride," he told them. "I should be back in time for supper."

* * * * *

Bryant thought about the sword that he had placed on the desk in what was once his father's office. When he reached his room, he put on his sleeveless jacket and the grey cape. As he left his room, he heard the two women talking as they cleaned. He entered Sonje's apartment to find it much cleaner than he had last seen it.

"My Lord," one of the women said as she noticed him.

Both women paused in their work and curtsied to him.

"It is looking good," Bryant told them. "I am pleased."

"Pardon our asking, but Florene and I were just saying that some flowers would brighten the room up," Aloysia said.

"I think that is a good idea," Bryant replied. "I will gather some while I am out riding."

"We thank you, Lord," Florene said as they curtsied again.

Bryant left the women to their work. He went through the kitchen to find a large basket with shoulder straps on it to gather flowers in.

"My Lord," Agatha greeted him from where she was scrubbing the floor.

"Lunch was delicious," Bryant told her.

"You looked as though you hardly tasted what you were eating."

"You are too observant."

"You were thinking of Gwladys Sonje returning."

"How did you know?" Bryant asked, startled.

"By that far-away look in your eye," Agatha replied. "You miss her."

"Very much."

"She will return."

"Yes, but to her duties or to me?" Bryant asked trusting her to answer truthfully.

"Only she can tell you that," Agatha said. "But she will not lie to you. If she loves you, she will tell you so."

Bryant sighed.

"I will just have to ask her then," Bryant said almost to himself. "Thank you Agatha. I should go now so that I will be back for supper."

Bryant left to get Llewellyn. Philip was in the stables working on a white carriage. Llewellyn met Bryant at the pasture gate.

"I can saddle him for you, My Lord," Philip told him.

"Thank you," Bryant replied. "I will be right back."

Bryant left the basket in the stable and crossed the courtyard to the armory. He took the sword he used to carry from the racks. Drawing the sword from its worn, black scabbard, he checked the edge. Satisfied with its condition, he replaced the sword and belted on the scabbard. Philip was waiting for him with Llewellyn and the basket when he returned to the stables. Bryant placed one arm and his head through the shoulder straps of the basket and then mounted Llewellyn.

* * * * *

As Lord Bryant rode out of the gates, Edgard came out of the castle. Agatha followed. Philip met them in the center of the courtyard.

"The poor man seems very lonely," Agatha spoke first. "And confused."

"We need to include him in the conversation at supper," Edgard told them.

"We should get together after supper to sing and dance," Agatha suggested.

Philip and Edgard nodded their agreement.

"Tell the others," Edgard ordered them.

Agatha left to find Aurora and Daryl. Philip left to find Absalon, Keith, and Stanislaus. Edgard returned to the armory.

* * * * *

Bryant galloped to the northern boundary to a field of flowers. He let Llewellyn graze while he filled the basket with many different types and colors of flowers. Just as he was finishing, he heard a scuffle and some voices in the trees to the north of the field. Quickly he hooked the straps of the basket over Llewellyn's saddle horn and then he ran to the source of the sounds. Two men had pinned another man up against a tree.

"What's going on here?" Bryant demanded.

The two men turned away from the man against the tree.

"He looks like better pickings than this farmer," one growled to the other.

"You're right," returned his companion.

Bryant drew his sword and faced the two squarely.

"Looks like this one wants to try to resist," the first man said.

"Let's teach him a lesson," the second said and leapt towards Bryant.

The first man joined his companion's attack. Bryant knew that this was no practice duel and that he must win. He put everything out of his mind and concentrated only on the swords of his two attackers. He managed to slice the chest and arm of the smaller of the two men and the man soon began to tire. The larger man cut Bryant's left shoulder and left it bleeding.

Bryant only fought harder. The smaller man dropped to his knees soon after Bryant's blade sliced his flesh for the second time, this time more deeply. Bryant circled his remaining opponent to place the fallen man behind his companion. Bryant drove the larger man back over his fallen friend. He stumbled and was cut on the other's sword. Bryant's sword cut a great gash in the man's sword arm and ribs as the man stumbled and in his other shoulder as he attempted to rise. Bryant leapt back as the man fell forward onto his face.

Bryant left the men lying in the growing pool of their own blood and found the farmer lying against the tree. The man was bleeding from a wound in his ribs. Bryant ran to the field, but found that Llewellyn had left. He wiped his sword clean on a handful of grass and sheathed it. He searched for a moment and found some herbs for a poultice. He returned to the farmer and bound the poultice to the man's wound. The man regained consciousness.

"Did they steal anything from you?" Bryant asked.

The man shook his head slowly.

"Are you from the village south of here?"

The man nodded once.

"I will get you home. Just rest now."

Bryant was glad that the sun was beginning to go down.

'Haskell!' he shouted in his mind.

'Bryant?' Haskell's voice said faintly.

'I need you to come to the flower field to the north,' Bryant shouted back.

'As soon as it is dark.'

'No. Now!'

'They will see me.'

'Tell Hoyt you must leave and he will take care of them.'

Bryant paced impatiently as he waited for Haskell. Finally he heard the familiar flap of Haskell's wings. Bryant ran to where the farmer lay.

"What is out there?" the farmer asked in a frightened tone.

"A friend who will take us to the village more quickly than any horse could travel."

Bryant gently lifted the man into his arms, wincing at the pain in his arm.

'You are injured,' Haskell said.

'This man is worse off than me. Lay as flat as you can so I can mount,' Bryant answered.

As he reached the edge of the trees, Bryant paused.

"Close your eyes," he told the injured man. "I will allow no harm to come to you, but you must trust me and my friend."

"Who is your friend?" the man asked.

"It is not important. Just trust us."

"I trust you," the man said and closed his eyes.

Bryant let his light glow softly to light his way. Awkwardly he mounted Haskell, tightly holding the farmer in front of him. When both men were safely astride, Haskell rose.

'Gently, Haskell,' Bryant asked.

Smoothly Haskell leapt into the night sky and caught the wind beneath his wings. Almost silently they traversed the night sky to the village.

'There is a stand of trees behind Olvan's house,' Bryant said as he tried to picture where he meant.

'I understand,' Haskell replied. 'There it is.'

Haskell circled, gracefully descending to the intended spot. He landed gently without a bump and lay flat again on the ground. Bryant helped the man dismount and then lifted him into his arms again. Bryant felt very tired as he carried the man through the trees.

"You can open your eyes now," he said, quickly dimming his light.

When they had almost reached the house, Bryant shouted Olvan's name. Olvan opened the back door and looked into the darkness. He disappeared and then returned with a lantern. When he saw Bryant he ran out to meet them. Olvan set down the lantern and took the farmer from Bryant. Bryant picked up the lantern and followed Olvan into the house. Cherie and Auberon met them at the door. Olvan laid the man on the floor and cushioned his head with the pillow that Cherie handed him. Bryant set the lantern on the table and sat down in a chair. He suddenly felt dizzy.

'Bryant!'

* * * * *

Olvan turned to see Lord Bryant slide off the chair onto the floor.

"He's wounded too!" Auberon exclaimed.

He removed Lord Bryant's cape and sword. He tore the shirt away from the wound. Cherie brought him a box with various herbs and salves in it. Olvan brought a basin of water and a cloth to Lord Bryant's side. Auberon cleaned and dressed the wound.

"I'm glad you saw him fall and shouted his name," Olvan told Auberon.

"I didn't shout his name," Auberon replied in a puzzled tone. "I thought you did."

"I'll be right back," Olvan said as he picked up the lantern.

He went out the back door and through the trees.

"I thought it must have been you," Olvan told Haskell out loud.

'Is he alright?' Haskell asked with concern.

"He lost a lot of blood, but I think he will be okay," Olvan reassured Haskell. "Do you know what happened?"

'No. Apparently his horse returned for supper with a basket of flowers and no Bryant. They are very worried about him at the castle.'

Olvan frowned.

"We must get him back to the castle tonight, but he is too weak to ride alone," Olvan said. "Would you let me ride with him and then return me here afterwards?"

'Yes. That would be best,' Haskell agreed with Olvan's suggestion.

Olvan returned to the house. Lord Bryant stirred as Olvan entered the room.

"Haskell?" Lord Bryant asked.

"He is outside," Olvan told Bryant. "He is waiting to take us to the castle."

"Us?"

"He will bring me back here as soon as you are safely in bed," Olvan answered. "What happened?"

"I was gathering flowers for Sonje and I heard a scuffle," Lord Bryant began. "Two men were ganged up on the farmer that I brought. They decided to try to rob me instead."

"So you tried to convince them otherwise," Olvan said.

"I'm glad I wore my sword. If I hadn't, I would be dead instead of them."

"And so would the man you saved."

"Is he alright?"

"He will be just fine," Auberon told Lord Bryant. "Thanks to you."

"You saved his life," Cherie told him as she brought the sleeping draught she had been warming. "Drink this."

Lord Bryant guided her hands with his right hand. When he had drunk the last of it, they helped him up. Olvan replaced Lord Bryant's sword and cape. Auberon and Olvan helped Lord Bryant walk out to Haskell. Olvan mounted where Lord Bryant indicated. Auberon helped Lord Bryant to mount in front of Olvan.

Very gently, Haskell launched himself into the air after Auberon had moved back to the trees. Haskell flew straight to the castle. As they approached the castle, Haskell told Hoyt they would land in the courtyard. As Haskell descended, Olvan saw eleven colored lights forming a large circle. Haskell landed ever so gently in the middle of the circle. All of the men and women ran to Haskell as he lay down.

Gentle hands lifted Lord Bryant from Haskell's shoulders. Olvan dismounted and followed them into the castle. They carried Lord Bryant upstairs to a bedchamber. After they laid him on the bed, one by one they went into the hall until only Olvan, Hoyt and Edgard remained.

"What happened?" Hoyt asked as he checked the dressing.

While they undressed Lord Bryant, Olvan related what had happened.

"We gave him a sleeping drought after dressing the wound. He should sleep until tomorrow afternoon. I'm afraid he will miss seeing Gwladys Sonje's return," Olvan answered.

"You had better return home so Haskell can return before dawn," Hoyt said. "Thank you for helping him and bringing him here. Thank Regis Auberon and Gwladys Cherie for all of us."

"I will," Olvan promised. "We will come soon for a visit."

Olvan left the room and returned to where Haskell was waiting in the courtyard. He mounted and they flew back to the village. Auberon and Cherie met Olvan and Haskell as they landed. Haskell left as soon as Olvan was safely dismounted and clear.

"How is he doing?" Olvan asked.

"He woke for a few minutes and asked about Lord Bryant," Auberon answered.

"What did you tell him?"

"That he had been saved by Lord Dracona and brought here safely on dragon back."

"How did he take it?"

"Better than we expected. He pledged his undying loyalty to Lord Bryant before the sleeping drought took effect."

Chapter 7 – Return and Introductions

As dawn approached, Lord Bryant still slept. Edgard kept watch as Hoyt slept. A movement out the window caught his eye. Haskell stretched and refolded his wings. He had kept his own watch on Lord Bryant. Both were suddenly drawn from their watch by the sound of flapping wings.

"Hoyt, she's here," Edgard said as he woke Hoyt.

Hoyt stretched and then stood.

"Stay with Lord Dracona. I will bring Gwladys Sonje here."

Hoyt left the room to go to the courtyard to meet Gwladys Sonje. He joined the rest who were waiting for the Travelor to land. As Sonje dismounted, the men bowed and the women curtsied. Hoyt stepped forward to receive the two saddle bags that she handed down.

"Where is Bryant?" Sonje asked. "Where did that dragon come from?"

"May I introduce Haskell," Hoyt said, avoiding the first question. "Haskell, this is Gwladys Sonje."

* * * * *

'I am honored to finally meet you,' Haskell said to Sonje alone. 'Bryant needs you. Go to him.'

Sonje ran into the castle and up to Bryant's room. The black cape swirled around her as she stopped suddenly in the doorway.

"Bryant!" she cried and crossed to his bedside.

"Olvan said he should sleep until afternoon," Edgard told her. "Olvan brought him on Haskell after Lord Bryant delivered the man he rescued from two bandits."

"Tell me what happened, from the beginning."

Edgard related what had happened the day before.

"Will he be alright?"

"He lost a lot of blood even though he only sustained one small wound. He should be fine when he wakes up."

"I will watch over him. Go tell Agatha to have food sent up before he awakens."

"As you command, Gwladys," Edgard said reluctantly.

He knew that she was tired from her long trip and needed to sleep. He met Hoyt in the hall.

"Gwladys Sonje insists on keeping watch herself," he told Hoyt.

"I will check on them occasionally. Haskell can keep watch from the courtyard wall," Hoyt said.

'I will inform both of you if anything happens or if he is beginning to wake up,' Haskell told the two men. 'She has taken off her cape and pulled a footstool over to the bed to sit on.'

"It's settled then," Hoyt said. "We might as well work on other things until he wakes up."

"I'll help Philip with that carriage," Edgard said.

"I'll look over the town maps I found yesterday so I can help coordinate the move from this end."

Each man went to his work. The day seemed to crawl. Gwladys Sonje fell asleep while she sat at Lord Bryant's bedside. When Haskell informed Hoyt and Edgard that Lord Bryant was sleeping less heavily, Hoyt carried the tray that Agatha had prepared up to Lord Bryant's room. As he set the tray on the table at the foot of the bed, Lord Bryant stirred and opened his eyes. Hoyt put a finger to his lips and pointed at Gwladys Sonje.

* * * * *

Bryant looked where Hoyt pointed to see Sonje at his bedside. Carefully, Bryant moved away from where she was half laying on the bed. Hoyt helped Bryant to sit on the edge of the bed before bringing him a goblet of milk and some fruit. As soon as he had eaten, Bryant felt strong enough to stand. With Hoyt's help, he walked into the bathing chamber. While Bryant sat on a stool, Hoyt went to the closet for some fresh clothes for Bryant.

"Turn the disk in the bottom of the basin and then pull the ear on the dragon's head," Bryant instructed Hoyt. "I want to take a bath."

Hoyt helped Bryant into the basin. He began washing Bryant.

"How did I get here?" Bryant asked.

"Olvan and Haskell brought you."

"When did Sonje arrive? Why didn't you wake me?"

"Regis Auberon gave you a sleeping drought. Gwladys Sonje arrived at dawn. When she arrived, she noticed your absence and demanded to keep watch over you once we told her what had happened," Hoyt explained.

Bryant finished bathing and got out. He was glad for Hoyt's help getting dried and dressed because his arm and shoulder hurt every time he moved them. Bryant sat impatiently while Hoyt shaved him.

'Sonje is waking up.' Haskell told Bryant and Hoyt.

Bryant was steady enough on his feet to walk back to the bed without Hoyt's support. Sonje lifted her head.

"Bryant!" Sonje cried when she found him to be gone from the bed.

"Here, Sonje," Bryant answered from the foot of the bed.

He staggered backward as Sonje flung herself into his arms and began to cry. Hoyt bowed to Bryant and silently left.

'Haskell?' Bryant asked.

'Yes?' Haskell answered.

'Tell Hoyt thank you for everything,'

He stood holding her in his arms while she cried. When her tears finally subsided and her sobs became fewer, he brushed her hair back and raised her face up from his chest.

"I'm here," Bryant told her. "Why are you crying?"

"I don't want you to die. I love you too much to live without you."

Her tears started anew. He held her shuddering body tightly against him. He kissed her golden hair.

"It just about killed me to see you leave. I couldn't live without you. I love you too much to go on without you near me," Bryant told her in a shaky voice.

She looked up to find the tears he could not stop. Slowly he leaned down until their lips met. His head began to buzz as he kissed her.

"I need to sit down," he told her.

Sonje helped him over to the edge of the bed. As soon as his head cleared, he reached over to pick up the small wooden box on the table next to the bed. He put the box in his jacket pocket. He moved from the bed to kneel at her feet. He took her hands in his and looked into her eyes.

"Sonje, will you marry me?"

"Yes, Bryant, I will marry you," she answered without hesitation.

He drew the box from his pocket and opened it. From it he took the dragon ring.

"Will you wear this ring as a symbol of our intent to marry?"

"I will wear it proudly."

Bryant found his hands trembling as he placed the ring on the third finger of her left hand. Slowly he rose to his feet. Taking her hands, he drew her up. He put his arm around her and led her over to the window.

"You will reign over all that you can see," Bryant told Sonje.

"And you will be my king," she added.

"I have something for you."

Bryant left her side and brought the white cape with the jeweled dragon clasp back to the window. He ignored the pain in his arm as he placed it about her shoulders.

'Hoyt says that supper is in an hour,' Haskell told them.

"Thank you, Haskell," Sonje said aloud.

Haskell bowed from his perch on the courtyard wall.

"I should hurry and get cleaned up," Sonje said.

"I'll walk you to your room."

Bryant led her past her old room to the end of the hall.

"Why are we here?" she asked in a puzzled tone.

Bryant opened the door and motioned her in. The apartment was clean and filled with the fresh fragrance of the flowers Bryant had cut.

"Is this for me?" she asked.

"I will move in after we marry," he answered.

Sonje turned, threw her arms around him and kissed him. When she released him, he was glad for the support of the nearby wall. As she explored the apartment, he found his way to the nearest chair and sat down. She returned with a dress over her arm.

"I will hurry," she said as she headed for the bathing chamber.

"I'll be right here."

After a while, Hoyt came and knocked quietly on the open door.

"Come in," Bryant said.

"Everything work out alright, My Lord?" Hoyt asked as he bowed.

"Will you help me with the wedding arrangements?" Bryant responded.

"I'll take that for a yes," Hoyt said. "Some of the preparations have been started already."

"I am somehow not surprised."

"How does your shoulder feel?"

"Sore," Bryant responded. "And my whole arm hurts when I move it."

"It will heal quickly. It was a clean cut."

"I get dizzy easily."

"You lost a lot of blood. If you take it easy, you should feel better in a couple of days."

"I'm not use to taking it easy."

"It is a good thing too. Your body was strong enough to survive such a loss of blood. You are a remarkable man, My Lord."

Sonje came out of the bathing chamber. She had braided her hair into a golden crown.

"Hoyt," she said, looking surprised to see him.

"You are looking beautiful, Gwladys," Hoyt said as he bowed low.

She extended her left hand to him.

"My congratulations. It is a beautiful ring."

"Is supper ready?" Sonje asked.

"Yes."

Bryant slowly rose to his feet. Sonje took his right side and Hoyt his left and they led him down to the great hall. They paused and Bryant motioned Hoyt on ahead. He didn't want anyone else to know how badly his head was spinning. Together Sonje and Bryant entered the dining hall. After they had taken their seats, everyone else sat down.

As they ate, Bryant was surprised to find that the conversation of the others was not in their native language, but in his. He was a lot more comfortable with Sonje at his side and being able to understand the others' conversation. After everyone had finished eating Bryant rose to his feet, glad for the support of the table.

"I would like to make an announcement," he began. "I have asked Gwladys Sonje to be my wife, and she has accepted."

Sonje rose to stand beside him.

"All hail Lord Dracona and Gwladys Sonje!"

The room rang with their voices as they leapt to their feet.

"Long live Lord Dracona and Gwladys Sonje!"

Bryant was glad for Sonje's support as they walked the length of the dining hall.

"Sonje, you have met Haskell. There is something I must show you and someone else for you to meet."

Bryant paused at the mechanism to open the tall doors at the back of the great hall. Sonje helped Bryant as soon as she saw what he was trying to do. Before they entered, Bryant turned to face Sonje.

"Please trust me. I cannot explain how important this is. When I have gone to bed, you can talk to Hoyt about it. He can tell you what we have discovered."

* * * * *

Sonje nodded, not knowing quite what to think. She was apprehensive about what lay behind those enormous doors because she could see that he was worried about her reaction to what he would show her. Bryant led her through the doors into the fluorescent green light of the great cavern. She could not take her eyes off of the large lumps in the sand. Bryant led her up the steps to the second level of caverns.

"What are those lumps?" Sonje finally asked.

"Dragon eggs," Bryant answered, watching her intently as if expecting a reaction.

"Haskell didn't," she began.

"No," he interrupted. "This is Haskell's den here."

He turned her to face the black opening behind them. She willed her light to shine in the darkness. Her blue-green light was encircled by a halo of white. She was surprised when an orange glow haloed in white joined her own light.

"You've been to see Father!" she exclaimed. "When?"

"While you were gone, I went to the village to ask something of your father."

"Ask what?"

"For permission to marry you."

"I see that he gave his permission."

"Yes, that was when I discovered that I could produce my own light."

"Do you see anything different about my light in comparison to before I left?" she asked him.

"I notice that there has been a white halo added around the color of your light. Does that mean something?" he answered in a puzzled tone.

"Yes, just as the white halo around the color of your light means something." Sonje answered. "Sit down. This could take some time to explain."

They found a place to sit. Haskell joined them from the darkness of his cave.

"The people of Glynis possess the ability to produce their own sphere of light. Each person has their own color which remains unchanged throughout their life," Sonje began.

"Then why has yours changed?" Bryant asked, confused.

"Yours has changed too," she answered. "No one is born with a white light."

"Auberon had a white light," Bryant protested.

"My father, Regis Auberon, has a white light. Regis Bryant will have a white light. Regina Sonje will have a white light," Sonje explained.

"Then you will become Queen Sonje, and I will become King Bryant?" Bryant asked, as it seemed he was beginning to understand what she was saying.

"Actually will become is not quite the right term. We are becoming king and queen," she corrected.

"While I was there, he had me kneel before him. He placed his hands on my head and spoke in a language that I didn't understand. When he finished, I discovered myself glowing. His white glow began to have hints of yellow," Bryant said.

"That's what I thought. He has passed to you the mantle of kingship."

"What do you mean by mantle?" Bryant asked.

"The powers and responsibilities," she answered. "The transfer will be completed at the coronation after our wedding. At that time we will officially take over the responsibilities of ruling the people of Glynis."

"Is that why you had to go to Glynis?"

"Yes, among other things."

'Evelina is waiting,' Haskell interrupted.

"Who is Evelina?" Sonje asked.

"Come," Bryant said as he stood up and took her hand in his.

Bryant led Sonje deeper into Haskell's cave. They came to a large side tunnel leading downward. He led her down the new tunnel to an enormous tunnel. He led her deeper into the mountain. The tunnel widened into a cave. Sonje felt her heart leap as something large moved in the center of the cave.

"Evelina, this is Sonje," Bryant said aloud as he bowed low to Evelina. "Sonje, this is Evelina."

A faint glow began around Evelina. Slowly it increased until it lit the entire cave. Sonje curtsied low to Evelina. Evelina bowed her head to Sonje and Bryant.

"You were the woman's voice I heard and the model for the mosaic in the great hall," Sonje said.

'No, one of my predecessors was the inspiration for the mosaic, but it was my voice you heard,' Evelina answered in Sonje's mind.

"Those eggs belong to you and Haskell," Sonje said.

'Yes,' Evelina acknowledged. 'I need your help. I am concerned for the safety of my eggs.'

"Why?"

'I am dying. When they hatch, the dragons will need food and care before being able to care for themselves. Haskell will not be able to do it alone, even with Bryant's help.'

"Sister Queen, I will help you." Sonje said with conviction. "I see that our destinies lie together. My people will insure the future of dragon kind. This I pledge to you."

'And dragons will insure the future of your people,' Evelina said in agreement. 'My heart is at peace. Leave me to my rest.'

As Evelina's light faded, Haskell finished relaying the conversation to Bryant. Bryant put his arm around Sonje and led her down the tunnel away from Evelina. They came out of the cave onto the sandy floor of the great cavern. They walked around the edge of the cavern to the doors. Hoyt and Edgard were waiting for them in the great hall by the door mechanism. Sonje let Hoyt and Edgard help Bryant up to his bedchamber.

"Let's check that wound," Hoyt suggested.

With help, Bryant removed his sleeveless jacket and his shirt. Hoyt gently lifted the dressing from the wound.

"It will heal nicely," Hoyt told him as he replaced the dressing.

"Wait for me in the hall, Hoyt," Sonje said. "Thank you for your help."

Both men bowed and left the room. Sonje turned back to Bryant. Her pulse quickened at the sight of his bare torso. She could see that he was too used to being active to be easily kept quiet while he healed. She sat on the bed beside him. He put his arm around her waist. She turned towards him. Her heart leapt as he turned towards her and kissed her. Her hand found its way to his chest. Her breath came in gasps as he broke off the kiss. She felt his chest heaving under her hand. As she laid her head on his shoulder, she heard his heart beating as wildly as her own. They sat holding each other until Sonje felt like she could stand unsupported.

"I love you, Bryant," she told him. "I must go so you can sleep and get better. I will see you in the morning."

"I will see you in my dreams."

He kissed her forehead then let her stand. She left the room quickly, fearing that if she didn't that she would just turn back and stay. Sonje led Hoyt to the library to discuss legends, riddles, swords, and dragons.

* * * * *

Bryant slowly finished undressing and got into bed. He closed his eyes and tried to sleep. All he could see in his mind was her sparkling green eyes, her golden hair, and her beautiful figure. Instead of the bedding, all he could feel was her body pressed against him and the print of her hand where it pressed against his chest. He smiled as he thought of her kiss. When he finally slept, his dreams were of Sonje.

Chapter 8 – Malvin's Heart

Sonje stood up and began to pace in front of the table where she and Hoyt had been studying from the books she had brought from Glynis.

"So you are certain that the most difficult still lies ahead," Sonje asked Hoyt as she paused in her pacing.

"I wish I could see it any differently, Gwladys," Hoyt replied. "These are times of great change. We have lived too long a life of solitude in Glynis. It is time to burst forth out of our protective shelter to live in this world, not apart from it."

"I know that Glynis supports the move every man, woman, and child. I also know that Bryant has lived a life of solitude, longing for the company of others. He remembers when the streets of the town bustled with life and activity. He will welcome its return."

"I am relieved to know that. However, the move will be dangerous. It will take an entire month for everyone to complete the move. We must insure the protection of the people of Glynis."

"Our greatest threat will come towards the end of the journey," Sonje said. "King Gustave killed my mother because she would not submit the people of Glynis to slavery. He certainly would not hesitate to capture any from Glynis moving along his border."

"Avoiding his kingdom would certainly lengthen the journey as well."

"Let's talk to Bryant in the morning. Perhaps he will have some suggestions."

"It is late," Hoyt agreed. "We will continue after breakfast, Gwladys."

They both left the library to retire for the night. Sonje paused before Bryant's door before continuing down the hall to her own apartment. She lay awake for a time in her new bed thinking of everything that Hoyt had told her. No matter what others had previously deduced, it was clear that beyond finding Bryant to be the man of the legends, she would have little to do with the completion of the quest. All paths turned to Bryant. Bryant, Lord Dracona, master and protector of the enormous and intelligent dragons. Bryant, steward of an empty town waiting to be populated. Bryant, wishing reconciliation with a people who had fled from Dracona over a century ago. Bryant, protector of a stranger in need.

Bryant, master swordsman, who killed two men while only sustaining one small wound. Bryant, next Regis of the citizens of Glynis. Bryant, the man she loved.

She knew that he loved her. Hoyt had told her of his questions concerning her loyalties. Sonje knew that, like Cherie had done for Olvan, she would give up everything to be Bryant's wife. She opened her eyes to look at the dragon ring that encircled her finger. The tiny dragon looked as though it was meant to be there on her finger. As her thoughts turned to the time she had spent with Bryant that day, she drifted off to sleep. Her dreams were of pleasant, sunlit days spent with Bryant.

Sonje felt happy and refreshed when she awoke shortly after dawn. She dressed quickly and went straight to Bryant's room. She knocked quietly on his door. There was no answer. Silently she opened the door and stepped in. He was still sleeping. She shut the door and sat down to wait for him to awaken. She smiled as she noticed that his right hand was resting on his chest just where hers had been the night before.

* * * * *

Bryant stirred and then opened his eyes. His heart leapt when he saw her sitting there watching him.

"Sonje," he said. "Good morning."

"Good morning," she replied with a smile. "Were your dreams pleasant?"

"All my dreams were of you."

"I dreamed of you. I wanted to be the first person that you saw this morning."

"I am looking forward to seeing you beside me as I awaken every morning."

Sonje stood and walked to the side of the bed. She bent over and kissed his forehead.

"I will see you at breakfast. Afterwards, we need to meet with Hoyt in the library."

Sonje left the room. Bryant sat up in bed. He felt better, but still a little weak. He got up and carefully dressed. His arm and shoulder felt stiff and sore. If he moved his arm too quickly, his wound hurt. He very carefully shaved, trying to ignore the pain. Bryant had to sit for a moment so his head could clear before going down to breakfast. He still didn't quite understand why he had gone to so much trouble for someone he didn't even know.

As soon as the dizziness had gone, he stood and left the room. As he passed the library, he noticed Sonje was sitting at a table reading something. He smiled at her beauty in the morning light. He walked over to see what she was reading. She looked up at him as his shadow fell across the book she was reading from. He took her hand in his and bowed to kiss it. Then he gently pulled her to her feet. She stood before him smiling. Tenderly, he cupped her chin in his hand and tilted her face up towards his. He kissed her lips as he had dreamed of doing all night. He reluctantly released her when his dizziness began to return. He sat on the edge of the table and she put her arms around him and pressed herself close.

"I've got to get better, so I can kiss you without getting dizzy," Bryant told her softly.

"I'm just fine and I still get dizzy kissing you," Sonje replied.

"Let's see if it is time for breakfast yet," Bryant said as soon as his head cleared.

Sonje took the arm that Bryant offered and they walked down to the dining hall where the others were assembling. Bryant enjoyed eating with Sonje seated by his side. As soon as they had finished breakfast, their attention was drawn by the sound of hooves in the courtyard. Bryant stood and walked to the door. Edgard followed closely behind at Bryant's nodded command. Sonje and Hoyt watched from the doorway.

To Bryant's surprise, there was a small group of people in the courtyard along with a horse drawn wagon. At his appearance the men bowed and the women curtsied.

"Please rise and state your business here," Bryant said.

He recognized the young man who stepped forward as the same who had escorted him into the village. The young man bowed again before speaking.

"Lord Dracona, we come in gratitude. You saved my father. He was concerned for your health. He said that you had also received a wound in the fight. He also insisted that we bring this fine bull for your dragon."

Another young man led forward a large, young bull. Bryant took the lead rope from the young man and led the bull away from the group.

'Haskell!' Bryant called in his mind. 'Some villagers have brought you a meal compliments of the farmer we saved. Come; take it out of the courtyard. Try to keep the blood to a minimum.'

'I am coming,' Haskell replied.

All eyes turned to the mountain behind the castle as the sound of Haskell's wings was heard. The bull stood frozen in terror as Haskell approached from above. When Haskell had neatly grasped the bull in his front feet, Bryant released the rope. Haskell carried the bull over the first ridge, out of sight.

'Thank you for leaving no blood,' Bryant said silently.

'Thank them for this delicious meal,' Haskell replied.

"Haskell thanks you for the bull. He says it is delicious," Bryant told the group.

Some of the villagers still appeared a bit unnerved by the sight of a dragon. The son of the farmer bowed again.

"I will convey that message to my father," he said. "He will be pleased. He also sent some other gifts as well."

The young man gestured to the wagon. Bryant walked over to the wagon and examined its contents. There were fine leathers, beautiful furs, colorful materials, exquisite laces, fat poultry, and several wood carvings.

"This is really too much," Bryant said, awed at the man's generosity.

"These are from the entire village," the young man said. "Yesterday morning, my father spoke to the other village elders, and they spoke to the rest of the village. It was decided that even though we don't remember why we have lived in fear of you for all these years, you have demonstrated your desire for peace and friendship. Olvan recommended that we invite you to speak at our village fair in two days."

Bryant turned to Edgard and said, "Tell Sonje and Hoyt to come out. The others can come also."

Bryant then turned back to the young man.

"What is your name, my friend?" Bryant asked.

"Wyman, My Lord," the young man answered. "As is my father's name."

"You and any other villagers are welcome here. I will come to your fair."

"What is going on, Bryant?" Sonje asked as she approached the wagon.

"This is Wyman. I saved his father. These gifts are sent by Wyman's father and the whole village," Bryant explained. "We will be going to a fair in two days."

Wyman bowed to Sonje.

"Wyman, this is Gwladys Sonje, daughter of Auberon, sister of Cherie, and my chosen bride."

"I am honored to meet you, My Lady," Wyman said.

After introductions were made, the gifts were taken inside and laid out on a table in the dining hall. The villagers began their journey home after making certain that everyone was coming to the fair. Aurora and Daryl spoke rapidly in their native language to each other about some of the items brought by the villagers. Sonje listened to their conversation.

"I trust your judgment with that," she told them. "I know that you do beautiful work."

"What were they saying?" Bryant asked.

"These gifts gave them some new ideas for our wedding clothes," Sonje answered. "I can hardly wait to see what they come up with."

Hoyt joined them after inspecting the gifts.

"We have much to discuss today," Hoyt said.

"Let's adjourn to the library then," Bryant replied.

The three left the others to take care of the gifts and went to the library. They sat at the table in the far corner.

"Last night, Gwladys Sonje and I discussed the move of the people of Glynis to Dracona," Hoyt began.

"It will be wonderful to have people living in the town again," Bryant said excited about the idea.

"Unfortunately, there is a problem," Hoyt said and then looked to Sonje.

"Just to the north is a kingdom ruled by an evil man," Sonje began. "It was King Gustave that killed my mother. He found out about the Quest and that the people of Glynis would move when the man in the riddle had been found. He planned to enslave the people of Glynis. When my mother refused to surrender the people of Glynis to slavery, he killed her. Father and I escaped with our lives. We were hiding in your forest from his men when you found us."

"We are afraid it will be difficult to get around the kingdom of Burton without attracting King Gustave's attention and his army," Hoyt continued. "Unfortunately there seems to be no other way around."

Bryant looked at Hoyt and then Sonje. He stood and walked to a chest that contained large flat drawers. He pulled open the bottom drawer and removed the bottom map. This he brought back to the table after closing the drawer.

"This map is more complete to the east of this castle," Bryant said as he laid the map on the table. "I think it may offer some solutions to our problem."

As Sonje and Hoyt studied the new map, they seemed amazed to discover that there was a coastline beyond the mountains as Hoyt ran his finger along the coast.

"Where did you get this map?" Hoyt asked.

"When my family left this castle, they traveled through the mountains and settled here on the shore of this bay," Bryant said as he pointed to the dot labeled Merton. "I visit them about once a year and they give me more information for this map."

"There appears to be only a narrow strand between sea and mountains. Will there be enough to allow wagons to pass?" Hoyt asked.

"No, but there is another way," Bryant answered. "My family has learned to build ships to travel the sea."

"So the people of Glynis could travel by sea," Sonje said.

"It is still dangerous, but it will get them around Burton out of King Gustave's reach," Bryant told them.

"I think it is worth trying," Hoyt commented.

"As soon as we return from the fair, I will travel to Merton and make the arrangements," Bryant said. "How far north is Glynis?"

Hoyt pointed out a spot in the mountains that ran across the top of the map.

"We traveled safely to this point here," Sonje said as she traced her path with her finger and stopped near a low point in the eastern mountain range. "The people of these villages had curious shells that they said came from the sea."

"My family has explored the coast line almost to that point," Bryant said.

"Good. It looks as though Glynis can journey by land to these villages and then by sea from there," Hoyt said with a smile.

Things were looking better than they had before. Bryant, Sonje and Hoyt spent the remainder of the morning making plans for the move of the people of Glynis. After the noon meal, Sonje went to the great cavern to be instructed on the care of hatchling dragons. Bryant unlocked all of the doors to the bed chambers and the nursery. He instructed Aloysia and Florene to work on cleaning these rooms so they could be occupied soon. Then he had Philip hitch Llewellyn to a light carriage so he could go inspect the work that was being done on the church.

* * * * *

'The first thing that you will need to know is that the hatchlings will be clumsy and extremely hungry,' Haskell told Sonje, who wrote it down. 'They will each eat a half of a mature cow at each feeding for three months. They will need to be fed cut up meat once a week for the first three months and one whole cow once a month after that. As soon as they master flight, they will be capable of feeding themselves.'

'How long will that be?' Sonje asked.

'When they are four or five months old. They will grow rapidly during that time and will shed their skins twice. They will need their skin oiled after each shed to avoid cracking and scarring. Their wings especially will need to be oiled.'

'Where can I get that much oil?'

'Bryant has been collecting and storing the oil in a lower cavern.'

'I will have to study the maps of the caverns more closely.'

'Yes, there will be many things that you will need to learn from the maps. You will need to make den assignments also. The young dragons will enjoy bathing in the lake that is above these caverns.'

'It looks as though I will need help with this.'

'Ideally, each dragon should have a family chosen to care for it.'

'That will be possible once Glynis is moved. How will I know which family should care for which dragon?'

'The dragons will help choose. Those who can most easily hear each dragon will be best suited to care for it. It will be difficult for you because you will probably hear all of them until they learn to limit their speech and focus it on just one or two people. You will be the only one who will be able to hear the new queen dragon. Bryant will hear the new queen's mate.'

'What about you and Evelina?'

'Evelina has been weakened by laying these eggs. She may die before they hatch,' Haskell said with a sad note in his voice. 'I am no longer young. My days are also short.'

'I will miss you when you are gone,' Sonje told him.

'When a dragon dies, the body is given to the volcano that lies within this mountain. You will find its location in the maps of this mountain,' Haskell paused. 'Bryant says that Aurora and Daryl need you to come and let them measure you.'

'Thank you, Haskell,' Sonje said as she stood up. 'I will study the maps and then we will talk some more later.'

Sonje made her way back to the great hall and then to the library to drop off her notes. She hurried back down the stairs and out of the castle. Recalling in her mind the map of the town that she had studied, she soon found her way to the tailor's shop. She stopped to stroke Llewellyn's nose before entering.

"Sonje!" Bryant exclaimed as he drew her into his arms and quickly kissed her. "Come see what they are doing!"

He led her to a frame that held a piece of white velvet. Sonje gasped at the dazzling beauty of the embroidery that was worked on it. Worked in shiny, silk-like thread, was a graceful dragon with outspread wings. The work was nearly half finished.

"It is to be a short cape for me," Bryant told her.

"I have never seen anything so beautiful," Sonje told him.

"Thank you," Aurora said as she and Daryl came out of the back room. "Come, we must get your measurements."

* * * * *

The women left Bryant alone in the front of the shop.

'Haskell,' Bryant said silently. 'This reminds me of you on a bright spring morning.'

'When I was still young,' Haskell replied.

'You will always seem that way to me, my friend,' Bryant replied as the women returned. "What thread are you using for this embroidery?"

"We have used the hair of the women of Glynis," Daryl answered.

"No wonder it is so shiny and alive looking," Bryant commented.

"We sewed these for you to wear to the fair the day after tomorrow," Aurora said. "Gwladys Sonje's will be ready before we leave."

Bryant took the neatly folded stack of clothes from her and thanked them. The women curtsied. He offered his arm to Sonje and they left the tailor's shop. Bryant helped Sonje into the carriage and then sat beside her.

"Can we stop at the church before returning for supper?" Sonje asked. "I would like to see the inside of it."

"Of course," Bryant said with a smile.

Llewellyn trotted proudly through the streets and they soon arrived at the church. Bryant smiled in spite of the pain as he helped Sonje down from the carriage. Sonje smiled back. Arm in arm they entered the church. The bright sunlight shone in colored patterns through the stained glass windows. The great arched ceiling was supported by finely carved pillars of dark hardwood. The pews were of a lighter wood with matching carvings. A single pulpit rose before the choir seats.

"You have an organ!" Sonje exclaimed as she looked at the great pipes rise behind the choir seats.

She left his side and seated herself at the organ. After a moment of adjustment, she began to play a soft melody. Bryant sat down in the front row to listen. The melody grew as she added alto, tenor and base. Bryant closed his eyes and listened to the song. He heard the rippling and burbling of a lively stream, the chirping of birds and the rustle of leaves in the breeze. He visualized these things and knew that this song belonged to Glynis. He had only felt such peace when he and Sonje had visited the meadow.

Suddenly something brushed his arm gently and the vision left. The music had stopped and he opened his eyes to find Sonje smiling down on him.

"I think I saw Glynis," he told her. "It is beautiful."

"That music is of Glynis."

Sonje looked happy. They walked slowly, arm in arm, out to the carriage. As they travelled through the streets back to the castle, Bryant noticed that several more of the damaged buildings were showing signs of recent repair work.

As they entered the courtyard, Philip came out of the stables. He held Llewellyn's bridle while Bryant and Sonje got out of the carriage then led Llewellyn into the stables.

"There is something that I want to give you," Bryant told Sonje.

He unlocked the sitting room doors and led her to the office doors. He unlocked the doors and entered the room. Sonje followed behind him.

"This was my father's office. I guess now it will be mine," Bryant said quietly.

He paused at the desk where the box containing the sword sat. He stroked the wooden surface gently. He felt strongly about what he was about to do, but didn't understand why.

"This box contains Fanchon's Sword. Keep it safely away from curious hands," Bryant told her as he opened the box.

The sword's glow joined their own in lighting the room. Sonje drew in her breath sharply at the sight.

"Do not touch it. It is very powerful and can kill those who touch it."

Sonje nodded. Satisfied, Bryant closed the box gently. He noticed that his wristband was glowing almost as brightly as the sword had. He began to realize that there must be a good reason for his compulsive need to complete what he had started. He walked around the desk to the dragon's head. He reached in and released the lever to open the door. Bryant paused as he reached towards Sonje. She took his hand and together they entered the jewel room.

Sonje gasped at the explosion of reflected light. Bryant squeezed her hand and then released it. He searched among the glittering treasures for a box made of dark stone. Cradling the rough box in his right arm, Bryant led Sonje back into the office and shut the bookcase behind them. Before leaving the office, Bryant removed a set of keys from a desk drawer.

He was glad that the great hall was quiet, so that no one would witness their passing. He led Sonje through the doors to the great cavern. They moved quickly along the edge of the cavern to a large tunnel opposite the doors and past the side tunnel where he stored the large jars of oil. He felt the heat of the volcano as they walked deeper into the mountain. It was as hot as a mid-summer day when they reached their destination; a great open cavern that was lit by the red glow from the enormous pit in the center. Bryant stopped and turned to face Sonje.

"Centuries ago, Fanchon's dragon, Malvin, was dying," Bryant began in a solemn tone. "He had helped and advised in the building of Castle Dracona and was a beloved friend of Fanchon and his wife. They were much grieved to know his death was imminent. Malvin knew this and it concerned him. On a moonless night, Malvin flew across the mountains to an island on the sea. There he told his problem to a woman who lived there. She said something he did not understand, placed a strap around his neck that bore a large pendant, then told him to return to Dracona. On the night of the full moon, he was to commit himself to the volcano with Fanchon and Aloysia standing here."

Bryant paused. He knew that continuing this meant that he must part with Sonje again before they could be married, but something compelled him to finish.

"When the fateful day came, there were many tears. Fanchon trusted Malvin although he didn't know why the dragon insisted on going before his time. As Malvin was consumed by the volcano, a white sphere of light appeared over the volcano. In the midst of the light was the woman of the island. She was holding this."

Bryant held the rough hewn stone box in both hands.

"The woman told Fanchon that Malvin had given his life that Dracona's fate might be secure. In turn Fanchon and his heirs must serve to protect Dracona and its inhabitants, both man and beast. To facilitate this she titled Fanchon Lord Dracona, and gave him the family name Donley."

"That is why you and your father were bound by duty to remain when the rest of the family fled," Sonje said softly.

"Yes. This box contains Malvin's Heart. It is to be opened only when the need is great and only to preserve Dracona. It has never been opened," Bryant paused again.

He stepped back a step and then knelt on the uneven floor of the cavern. Sonje knelt before him. Bryant gently set the box between them. He looked into Sonje's eyes and found comfort and reassurance in their green depths. He reached out and took her hands in his. He spoke the strange words that had been passed from father to son. A white sphere hovered over the volcano. The woman appeared in its center.

"You have done well young Lord Dracona. I had hoped you would yield to my calls," she said. "A dark cloud gathers to the north. You must leave Dracona in the hands of your chosen Lady and ride forth into the darkness. We have waited long for your coming. Malvin's Heart will protect you both and bind you together with Dracona."

The woman and her light faded. The box lay open between them. Inside each half was a diamond in the shape of a heart on a serpentine chain. The centers of the diamonds were lit by a fiery red glow. Bryant lifted one gently by its chain and placed it around Sonje's neck. Sonje lifted the other and placed it about his neck.

In silence they rose and left the cavern of the volcano. Haskell bowed his head to them from his den entrance as they passed through the great cavern. As they entered the great hall, they were met by the men and women who had made Dracona their new home. Bryant knew from the heavy silence and the looks in their eyes that they knew what had transpired. He turned to Sonje and handed her the keys he had taken from the desk.

"These keys are to Dracona. Protect them and use them wisely," Bryant told her.

"I will, My Lord," she answered him.

"There are many things to be done in preparation for the coming of Glynis. You all know what to do. I trust you to be ready for them when they come," Bryant told them. "For now I want everyone to get ready to go to the village fair first thing in the morning. We will camp tomorrow night just outside the village."

"Tonight after supper, we will meet here to dance and sing," Sonje told them.

Bryant smiled at the idea. The others seemed to be cheering up also.

"Lunch is ready," Agatha announced.

Everyone filed into the dining hall and took their seats. Lunch was served and eaten in silence. Bryant felt more uncomfortable than he had during their first meal at Dracona. As the meal was over he motioned Hoyt and Edgard over to the head table.

"I want to see both of you in the library in a half an hour," he told them.

The two men bowed then left. Bryant went to the kitchen to find Agatha.

"I want to see you in the library in a half an hour," he told her.

Agatha curtsied then went about her work. Bryant put his arm around Sonje and led her upstairs to his bedchamber. He opened the small drawer in the bedside table and removed the small black bound book. Bryant sat next to Sonje on the edge of the bed.

"I had originally planned to visit my family myself. However, it appears that I will be needed elsewhere. In that case it is important that you take this book to my mother. It is my journal. This afternoon I will try to write an explanation of why you were sent in my place," Bryant told her.

"I will take that book if I am sent to your family," Sonje promised. "I will prepare for the journey just in case it is necessary. I trust your judgment and intuitions. Just promise me that you will return. I don't think that I could live without you."

"I don't think I could live without you either," Bryant said as he set the book back in the drawer.

He turned back to her and put his arm around her. She moved closer to him. He kissed her gently. She began to stand and he followed her. She put her arms around his neck and gazed into his eyes. He drew her closer until her body was pressed against his before kissing her again. He felt his heart leap as he realized that she was crying. Gently he stroked her hair as she laid her head on his shoulder and wept.

"I will always love you, Sonje. In my heart, we will always be together," Bryant said softly. "Malvin's heart will protect us and bring us back safely to Dracona. We are needed here for Glynis and for Dracona."

"The week that I was in Glynis, I missed you very much. I was homesick for the first time in my life. I was homesick for Dracona, not Glynis," Sonje confessed. "Bryant, I love you more than I thought possible. I want you to always be with me."

"In your heart, we can always be together," Bryant said as he dried her tears. "Come on. They are probably waiting for us."

They walked in silence down to the library where Hoyt, Agatha, and Edgard were waiting for them. Bryant led them to where the maps were laid out on the table.

"It has become apparent that we need to prepare for the possibility of my absence," Bryant began. "Sonje will be in charge in my absence. In the case that she is also gone, the three of you will form a council to govern Dracona. I have noticed that the others respect your opinions and I feel that they would accept such an arrangement.

Our primary objective is to prepare for the coming of Glynis. The repairs on the town are progressing beautifully. When they are complete, there are places that need to be cleared of unwanted vegetation or my family may welcome additional hands to prepare their ships for the move of Glynis. All of the castle rooms and halls need to be cleaned. The only room that is to remain undisturbed is my office."

Bryant shifted the maps of the castle to the top.

"Here is my office," he said as he pointed out the appropriate room. "Our second priority is the care and well-being of the dragons."

Bryant shifted another map to the top of the stack.

"There is a large field here where the cattle are kept. This lake was once a volcano vent. It drains underground to a river leading to the sea. This passage connects to the cavern system on the other side of the volcano and to the river's passage. There is enough room for horses and wagons next to the river."

Bryant turned to the next map.

"This diagrams the cavern system. It is difficult to follow because the tunnels are not level and may intertwine in places. The most important paths are here to Evelina's cavern and here to the oil storage."

Bryant traced out both paths with his finger. Sonje nodded.

"I wish to give each of you a special assignment. Hoyt, you are to coordinate the move of Glynis. Edgard, you are to prepare the defense of Dracona. The maps in the armory of the castle, town, and forest will help you. Agatha, you are to coordinate housing assignments for the people of Glynis and those of my family who choose to return to Dracona. I will give you a duplicate map to use. Sonje, you are to prepare to educate the people on the care of dragons."

Bryant left them standing around the table while he located the duplicate map of the town for Agatha. He also brought her some paper, ink and a pen. Bryant smiled as he watched them begin their assignments. Quietly he left the library. Bryant went to the kitchen to see if Agatha needed help cleaning up the lunch dishes. To his surprise, the kitchen was spotlessly clean. He knew that he had made the right decision in giving Agatha her assignment.

Bryant left the kitchen and went to the armory. He was glad to see Edgard already working at sharpening the swords. He would need some help.

"I always think better when I'm sharpening swords," Edgard said and Bryant laughed.

"I need to find a chain-mail shirt to fit me," Bryant told Edgard.

Edgard put down the sword that he was working on and followed Bryant into the next room.

"I'm glad that you are taking your personal safety more seriously although I wish that it was not necessary," Edgard said as they sorted through the body armor.

"I agree, but I feel better that you believe my intuitions," Bryant answered. "Here is one that may fit Sonje."

Bryant held up the small chain-mail shirt and leather undershirt that indeed appeared fitted for a woman.

"It might be wise for her to carry a blade also," Edgard suggested. "She has been schooled in swordsmanship."

"I will have her choose a blade before we leave tomorrow morning."

Bryant was somehow not surprised at Edgard's revelation. He was certain that there were many things that he did not yet know about his chosen lady. After more searching, they found a chain-mail shirt and leather undershirt that fit Bryant as though they had been made just for him. Etched on the collar of the shirt were dragons with outspread wings.

"Thank you for your help and your faith," Bryant told Edgard. "I will take these for Sonje to try on."

"The thanks belong to you, My Lord, for not turning us away and for taking on the responsibilities of being our lord and king," Edgard said as he knelt and bowed his head.

"Rise," Bryant responded. "A king needs subjects that he can trust, to whom he can assign tasks knowing that they will be completed. A king's wealth can never truly be judged by gold, silver, jewels, or land. It can only be judged by the loyalty, happiness, and faith of his subjects. A king is a servant of his people, not a tyrant over an enslaved kingdom."

"Glynis has truly found her king," Edgard said.

Bryant smiled. Many of his worries had been laid to rest. Edgard was a larger and stronger man than he. Edgard was a man who could easily kill Bryant if he truly wished to do so, yet he pledged his loyalties entirely to Bryant. He knew he could trust Edgard with defending Dracona and Glynis.

Bryant took the two chain mail shirts and the leather undershirts up to his bed chamber. After laying them on the bed, he took up a pen and began to write in his journal that he had shown Sonje earlier. Bryant described the day's events carefully, hoping his mother would understand and believe. He needed her to understand the urgency of his requests. Bryant knew that Sonje might be met with hostility and suspicion when she approached Merton and its inhabitants.

Chapter 9 – Fanchon's Sword

Bryant was startled by a quiet knock at his door. A glance at the window told him that he had been writing for several hours.

"Enter," he responded.

Sonje opened the door and entered the room.

"Edgard said you had something for me," she said.

"Yes," he said as he put down his pen. "See if these fit you."

Bryant handed her first the leather undershirt and then the chain-mail shirt. She put them on easily as though she had worn those very shirts before.

"They fit even better than my own did," she commented.

"Come," Bryant said. "We should go find you a sword."

They walked down to the armory after dropping her shirts off at her apartment. After examining and trying several swords, Sonje made her selection. Edgard nodded his approval of her choice to Bryant as she swung the sword accustoming herself to its weight and balance. Edgard found a sheath and cut its belt down to fit her small waist.

"Edgard, I would like to have a practice duel," Sonje said. "It has been a while."

Edgard bowed to her and followed her to the practice ring. Bryant watched the dual from the gate. He was impressed with her skill and agility. He was amazed to see that her skirt didn't seem to hamper her efforts. In fact it quickly became obvious that by swinging and swirling her skirt, she was distracting Edgard's attention away from her sword. Without warning, she disarmed him. The duel was finished as Edgard stood motionless with her sword poised at his throat and his sword lying in the dirt beside her. Bryant had no doubt that she was deadly in a real duel and he felt better knowing this.

"You have forgotten nothing, Gwladys," Edgard said as he gasped for breath.

With a quick movement, she withdrew her sword from his throat, lifted his sword off the ground and into the air. Edgard caught the sword in mid-air and placed it flat across his palms. He dropped to one knee, bowing before her. She sheathed her sword.

"Rise, faithful one," Sonje bade him. "You have taught me well."

"Thank you, Gwladys."

Bryant opened the gate for them to exit the practice arena.

"It is nearly time for supper," Bryant commented.

"Thank you for thinking of finding me a sword and a chain-mail shirt," Sonje told Bryant.

"Actually I came across the shirt while I was looking for one to fit me," Bryant replied. "Edgard suggested the sword. I feel better knowing that you can defend yourself if necessary. My family will not greet your unexpected arrival with open arms. You must tell the first person that you see that you have a message for Lady Miranda, widow of Lord Eamon. Tell them that the message is for her alone. If they ask for your oath, tell them you swear by Lady Aloysia."

"Fanchon's wife," Sonje said.

"Yes," Bryant acknowledged. "By that they will know that you speak the truth. When you speak to Lady Miranda, tell her I send my love, then ask her to read beginning at the marker and give her my journal."

"I will do just as you have said, My Lord," Sonje replied as they entered the dining hall.

There was little talk during the meal. Bryant sensed that they were still apprehensive about the future predicted by the day's events. He hoped their mood would improve with the evening's planned activities. As soon as everyone had finished eating, Bryant stood.

"Meet in the great hall in one hour," Bryant announced.

He and Sonje left the dining hall to go to the music room. With her help, Bryant selected several instruments and carried them down to the great hall. As soon as they had finished, they went upstairs to change clothes.

Bryant wondered what Sonje would wear as he considered his own choices. He finally selected a pair of pale blue pants with a matching sleeveless jacket that had silver trim. He found a silver-grey shirt and then selected a pair of light grey boots. He was soon dressed and ran a comb through his hair before he went down the hall to see if Sonje was ready. He knocked quietly on her door.

"Come in, Bryant," she called.

She was sitting in front of the polished shield, tying a ribbon in the end of her hair. She stood up and turned to face him. Her hair was twisted into a glistening cord that hung down over her shoulder. Her dress was rose colored with gold trim. Her shoulders were nearly white above the gathered straps that joined in front with a gold rose. Bryant found himself speechless at the sight of her beauty.

"You look even more handsome than usual tonight, My Lord," Sonje broke the silence between them.

"Your beauty would make the flowers bow their heads in shame of their plainness, My Lady," Bryant said as he finally found his tongue.

"I would be honored if you would consent to wear this, My Lord," Sonje said as she held up a circlet of gold like the silver one that encircled her own brow.

He took it gently from her hands and examined it. In tiny detail, dragons were etched in its surface.

"I would be pleased to do so," he replied.

She took the circlet from him and settled it on his head. He was surprised as it shaped itself to his head.

"There is still much for you to learn about Glynis," she said as she noticed his reaction. "Come, we will be late."

Bryant offered her his arm and led her down to the great hall. As they started down the stairs, the quiet chatter of voices stopped. Everyone stood frozen where they were at the sight of Bryant and Sonje. It was Stanislaus who first stepped forward and bowed before Sonje and Bryant. One by one, the others followed.

"Rise," Bryant commanded. "Let the music begin."

Daryl, Aurora, and Absalon took up instruments and began to play. Bryant turned to Sonje and bowed. Sonje curtsied then placed her right hand on the hand he held out to her. Gracefully, they began to dance.

"When you left to visit Glynis, I was afraid that I would never see you again," Bryant told her softly. "Then when the others arrived, I was afraid that you would return only out of duty to them and not love for me."

"I returned for both reasons," she answered. "Yet if returning meant forsaking Glynis entirely, I still would have returned."

"When I first saw you in the forest, you caught me off guard. Besides my family, you and your father were the first people that I had seen since I buried my father. Your father appearing almost dead and you so fiercely protecting him," Bryant paused. "For a split second, I saw myself trying vainly to fight off my own father's death. It was then that I knew that I could not chase you off without trying to save your father."

"What made you tell me that you would save my father only if I promised to return to Dracona to live forever?" Sonje asked.

"I don't really know," Bryant replied slowly as he searched his feelings for an answer. "When my father died, he took with him the last glimmer of light in my life."

"You had Haskell."

"I owe a lot to Haskell. When I buried my father, it was his voice that pulled me back into living. Yet there had been something still missing. There was a great emptiness that hung over Dracona. A silence that hung heavily in the halls and made the great hall seem an enormous tomb."

"You lacked company of your own kind."

"Yes, and love," Bryant said as he pulled her closer so she would not see the tears that were filling his eyes. "My father had spent so many years trying to keep the outside world away from me to save me from Rolfe's fate that when you came to Dracona, I was afraid of you."

"Afraid of loving me?"

"Yes, and afraid of you. I was only one hundred and fifty when everyone left. After being alone for so long strangers were frightening for me."

"For whatever reasons, I am glad to be with you now," she told him softly as she moved even closer to him. "I have grown to love you and I don't want to be gone from your side for very long."

Bryant heard the tremor in her voice and looked down into her face. There he found the glistening trails of her tears on her face to match the ones on his own. He leaned down and gently kissed her on her lips.

"I have grown to love you more with each passing day. I wish that our thoughts could be together even when we must be apart," Bryant told her.

"Then we would never be truly separated," Sonje agreed. "I wish that could be true."

Bryant kissed Sonje again.

* * * * *

As she played, Daryl had been watching the royal pair dance. She stopped suddenly as she saw a red glow envelope them. The others stopped playing as she rose to her feet. Soon everyone had gathered in a circle around the red glow.

"Join hands," Hoyt commanded.

One by one they began to glow as they joined hands. The colors of their glows combined in a white dome over the red glow that enveloped Lord Bryant and Gwladys Sonje. The red began to take the form of a dragon and then suddenly disappeared. Gwladys Sonje and Lord Bryant began to go limp and fall. Edgard and Agatha broke the circle and rushed forward to catch the two before they fell to the floor. With help, they were laid gently on the floor. Hoyt checked their pulses and breathing.

"They seem to be alright. We can only wait," Hoyt announced. "Let's take them up to bed. They will be more comfortable there."

The men stepped forward and gently lifted Lord Bryant and Gwladys Sonje from the floor. They carried them gently up the stairs to their rooms. Hoyt and Edgard prepared Lord Bryant for bed.

"I will take the first watch," Edgard told Hoyt.

"I will relieve you in two hours," replied Hoyt.

Agatha tapped on the door, and then peeked in.

"Gwladys Sonje is in bed. Daryl will take the first watch," she reported.

"The dragons will keep watch over their dreams," Hoyt told her as he stepped out of Lord Bryant's room and into the hall. "Haskell will wake us if we are needed."

"Do you know what happened?"

"I suspect that it has to do with Malvin's Heart," Hoyt said as they walked slowly down the hall. "I really don't know much about it. The records that I have read mentioned only its origin, not its powers."

"Maybe Haskell knows more," Agatha suggested.

"Haskell," Hoyt asked aloud, "Can you tell Agatha and me anything more about Malvin's Heart and what it has done to Gwladys Sonje and Lord Bryant?"

'Only that the last thing that they said before the event in the great hall is that they wished their thoughts could be together even when they were apart,' Haskell answered.

"Are they dreaming?" Agatha asked. "Or are their minds without thought now?"

There was a pause before Haskell answered.

'Their minds are full of identical pictures flashing by with incredible speed. I catch glimpses of events from Bryant's past and others I don't recognize at all,' Haskell's voice said with a tremor. 'There is a green valley with a city of many people. There are volcanoes spewing smoke into the sky. There is snow and ice. There are many villages and castles. There is a beautiful woman who is killed in a fight in a castle and a man in fine clothes whose sword hand is cut off. I don't understand.'

"Those must be Gwladys Sonje's memories. The green valley is Glynis," Hoyt answered. "The power of Malvin's Heart must be that the thoughts of the two who possess the pendants will be as one."

"Perhaps it gives them a dragon's power of speech through thoughts," Agatha suggested.

"All we can do is wait and see," Hoyt said. "I wonder if distance will impair it."

Hoyt and Agatha retired to their quarters to get some sleep. Haskell kept his own silent watch over Lord Bryant and Gladys Sonje. As Hoyt entered Lord Bryant's room to take his turn at watch, Lord Bryant sat up in bed and began to speak in the language of Glynis.

"Where am I? What happened? Where is Sonje?" he asked in rapid succession.

"Slow down, My Lord," Hoyt replied in the language of Glynis. "You are in your own room and Gwladys Sonje is in hers. The two of you were dancing and then suddenly a red glow surrounded you. When it left, you were both unconscious."

"How can you understand and speak our language so suddenly?" Edgard asked with surprise.

"Sonje must have taught me," Lord Bryant said. "I don't understand how."

"Malvin's Heart," Hoyt said. "Is Gwladys Sonje awake yet?"

"Yes," Lord Bryant said after a moment. "She believes that you are right."

* * * * *

'Your wish must have been granted,' Haskell told Bryant.

"Morning will come early. Let's all get some sleep," Bryant said.

Edgard and Hoyt bowed and then left the room.

'Bryant?' Sonje's voice spoke quietly in his mind.

'Yes?' he replied.

'You now know exactly what happened in Burton.'

'It confirms that King Gustave is a very dangerous man and he must be dealt with before Glynis can dwell safely in Dracona.'

'I fear for your safety in Burton,' Bryant heard the tremor of emotion behind her thoughts. 'He is not an ordinary man.'

'I doubt that this is written in the records, but there was a thirteenth member of Fanchon's group. When they passed through Burton, this brash young man encountered a young woman in a garden. Before the evening was over, the two had become enchanted with each other. He promised to meet her in the garden at midnight. At the appointed hour, the two met and proceeded to enjoy what most people reserve for their marriage bed.'

'What happened after that and what does it have to do with King Gustave?' Sonje asked.

'The young woman was the wife of the king's eldest son. The prince woke to find himself alone and went looking for his wife with sword in hand. When he reached the garden, he was too late to stop his wife's unfaithfulness. He immediately slew the young man and then turned to find Fanchon standing between him and his wife. Fanchon told the prince that he would have killed the young man for such a misdeed if the prince had not. He then convinced the prince to take his wife with him as if nothing had happened. The young man was buried in a field of flowers on the northern border of Dracona a few days later. To this day, nothing grows on that grave.'

'You think that King Gustave is of that lineage?' Sonje asked.

'He must be,' Bryant answered not liking the implications that this previously unimportant incident put into place.

'We had better get some sleep,' Sonje said after a long pause.

Bryant rose with the sun and quickly dressed. He put on the chain mail shirt before the clothing that Daryl and Aurora had made for him. The black pants and red shirt were trimmed with gold cording. The sleeves of the shirt had pleats that opened to reveal black panels. The sleeveless jacket was red and black with gold trim. He also put on black boots and his sword before clasping his black cape about his shoulders.

He wasn't waiting long before Sonje came out of her room wearing a dress with a full skirt and puffed sleeves. It was red with black and gold trim. A shawl of gathered white settled about the top of the skirt. Her hair was braided creating a crown around her head. After closing the door she clasped the white cape around her shoulders. Bryant smiled at her beauty, then drew her close and kissed her good morning. He was feeling stronger and his left arm and shoulder did not hurt at every motion.

"The others are probably waiting for us," Sonje said and then returned his kiss.

"Come, My Lady," Bryant said as he released her from his arms and led her down to the courtyard.

Agatha handed them each a slice of bread with butter and fruit preserves. As soon as they had eaten, the others began to get in the wagon. As Bryant strode towards Llewellyn, he realized that he was leaving something important behind. He stopped short of the horse.

"What is it, Lord Bryant?" Hoyt asked as he noticed Bryant's actions.

"Fanchon's Sword," Bryant replied. "I feel that it should not be left here."

Bryant returned to the castle at Hoyt's nod. He quickly crossed the sitting room and unlocked the office door. The glow of the band on his wrist matched the fierce glow emanating between the lid and base of the sword box. Bryant gently placed his hands on the box as though it were going to cut him. He pulled his hands back quickly when he discovered that the box was warm to the touch instead of cool as he had expected it to be. The box flung open suddenly and Bryant stepped quickly back away from the desk.

"Bryant!" Sonje's alarmed voice rang both in his ears and his mind.

Hoyt and Edgard followed Sonje into the room. Bryant was barely conscious of their presence. The sword seemed to beckon to him. Slowly he reached forward with his right hand. All that he knew was the sword. As his hand came within a palm's width of the sword, it leapt from its resting place in the box and into Bryant's grasp. As Bryant brought the sword to an upright position, the blade seemed to turn to flame.

"I swear by this blade to protect Dracona, its inhabitants, and all those who are in need of its services," Bryant said aloud.

The blade returned to its original form and the room became suddenly dark. Bryant blinked then willed his glow to light the room. His light was followed first by Sonje's then by the two men's.

Chapter 10 – Confessions and New Enemies

Bryant watched the dancing flames of the campfire lick the wood that fueled it. They had stopped for the night in a small meadow within an hour's ride from the village. Sonje crossed between him and the fire then sat next to him.

'I knew that the inscription on the sword referred to you from the first time that Hoyt recited it for me,' Sonje's voice broke into his thoughts.

'Yet, I do not understand,' Bryant replied. 'Why now? Other than a natural attraction to it as a fine blade, I had no desire to possess it as my personal sword until this morning. I have witnessed several men try to take it up. Some lost the use of their arms and a couple even died.'

'With time, it will make sense,' Sonje said. 'I trust your instincts. You are Lord Dracona. I'm certain that you have been guided all along so that Dracona would be preserved for the coming of Glynis.'

'From what I remember, Fanchon forged the blade in Malvin's flame the night before the full moon. He never used the sword himself. After placing the blade in the box he had prepared for it, he never touched it again.'

'The blade has waited through the centuries for the right time and the right man. The time is now. You are the man.' Sonje said.

'I have a feeling that tomorrow holds much in store for us,' Bryant said. 'We should get some sleep.'

He turned and kissed her lips tenderly before standing up. Bryant walked around the camp checking the others and the horses. As he completed his rounds, he heard a familiar flapping of wings.

'Haskell?' Bryant asked silently.

'Yes,' Haskell answered. 'I felt it would be good for me to be close to the village in case you might need me.'

'That would make me feel better, my friend,' Bryant told him. 'I will meet you in a clearing to the south in a few minutes.'

Bryant made his way to the clearing by using his light. Haskell arrived shortly after Bryant. Bryant approached the dragon who put his chin on the ground so that Bryant could look him in his eye.

V.J.O. Gardner

'You have changed. Your light is much less orange than before,' Haskell observed. 'Do you have the sword with you?'

Bryant slowly drew the sword from its scabbard. He held the blade across his open palm for Haskell to see.

'It is beautiful,' Haskell remarked. 'It was forged before I was hatched.'

Bryant returned the blade to its scabbard.

'I don't understand what is happening,' Bryant said quietly. 'It is all going so fast.'

'I understand,' Haskell said sympathetically. 'First Sonje, the eggs, Hoyt and the others, then Glynis, legends, and Fanchon's Sword.'

'And trouble from the north,' Bryant finished the list. 'I wish I could take a day to be alone and sort this all out.'

'I'm afraid you may not get the chance until this is all over,' Haskell replied. 'Go get some sleep so that you can enjoy the fair. I will keep watch.'

Bryant placed his hand on Haskell's enormous cheek for a moment before turning to leave. Haskell wished that Eamon had not died. He could see that Bryant was in need of a father's guidance.

Bryant returned to the camp and sat down against a tree. After wrapping himself in his cape, he watched the fire until sleep overcame him.

* * * * *

Sonje was the first to wake in the early morning. The sun had not yet risen over the mountains and there was a chill in the air. She slowly rose to her feet and looked around. Guen whickered softly as Sonje turned in the mare's direction. Sonje put a few sticks and some dry grass on the embers of last night's fire to rekindle it. Soon the fire was going and the sun began to peek above the mountains.

The others were beginning to stir and wake. Sonje quietly made her way to where Bryant slept against the tree. She knelt on the ground beside him. As she looked at his face it seemed so young and so vulnerable.

'Sonje,' Haskell's voice broke quietly into her thoughts.

'Haskell?'

'He needs a father's council. He has been thrust into manhood by his father's death and then from solitude into leadership just as abruptly,' Haskell told her. 'The speed of events in the last month has left him feeling he needs time to sort it out.'

'I understand,' Sonje replied. 'Perhaps my father may be able to help him.'

'Thank you,' Haskell said gratefully. 'I can only do so much for him. His father's dying wish was that I watch over him for as long as I can. He knew that Bryant would need guidance.'

'Lord Eamon was a wise man and a caring father.'

Their conversation was interrupted by Bryant waking. Sonje smiled as he stirred and then opened his eyes.

"After seeing your beautiful face, I feel that it was worth waking up," Bryant said.

"I am glad that you feel that way, My Lord."

* * * * *

Bryant unwrapped his cape and then put his arms out to her. Sonje shifted closer until she was leaning against him. He gently put his arms around her. Feeling her body enclosed in his arms somehow made him feel stronger. He knew that in spite of her having traveled so far and done so many things on her own she still needed and trusted him. Tenderly he kissed her forehead. In the clearing to the south, Haskell was pleased.

Once everyone had eaten breakfast, they continued their journey. Bryant and Sonje led the way on Llewellyn and Guen. They rode in silence in spite of the light conversation that was going on amongst those in the wagon. Edgard urged his horse up even with Bryant and Sonje.

"I will stay near you and Gwladys Sonje today, My Lord." Edgard said.

"I appreciate your concern," Bryant said. "Keep an eye out for the others also. I would rather be prepared than caught unaware."

"As you wish, My Lord."

At the fork in the road, a lone man approached on horseback. He carried no sword, but a mandolin was strapped to his back.

"Hail travelers!" the man called in greeting. "Are you going to the fair?"

"Yes, we are going there," Bryant responded.

"My name is Gale," the man said. "If I might travel with your party, I will sing or give you news from the north."

Bryant glanced to Sonje, then to Edgard before answering.

"Travel with us and give us your news," Bryant said, aware the man's offer had interested Haskell as well.

Edgard dropped back at Bryant's nod and Gale took his place at Bryant's side.

"King Gustave has made his first appearance since his mysterious accident. He is still clumsy at eating with his left hand," Gale began.

Bryant heard Haskell's soft chuckle in his mind. He noticed a grim, but mischievous smile play across Sonje's face.

"He is also still plagued by rumors that his nephew, rightful heir to the throne of Burton, still lives in spite of the fact that no one has seen him since his supposed death at the same time as King Reginald's unexpected death nine years ago," Gale continued. "Burton's army has had little success expanding the northern boundary. King Gustave is furious, claiming that the taxes he collects are not enough to support the kingdom."

"How long were you in Burton?" Bryant asked.

"Nearly a year," Gale answered.

"Why did you leave?" Bryant pressed.

"King Gustave was getting tired of my songs and threatened to throw me in the dungeon if I couldn't sing some fresh songs. So I decided to leave last night after hearing news of the fair."

"And you decided to travel with us in case Gustave sent someone after the horse you borrowed," Sonje finished for him.

"How did you know, My Lady?" Gale asked with a trembling voice.

"Lucky guess," Sonje replied cryptically.

Bryant glanced at her.

'He did not even have a bed to call his own when I was in Burton,' Sonje told Bryant silently.

"Give us a song, Gale," Bryant ordered.

"Yes, My Lord," Gale answered, seeming glad for the change of subject.

While Gale sang, Haskell relayed the information about King Gustave to Hoyt and Edgard. Soon the forest thinned and gave way to the fields surrounding the village. The fair was being held in a grassy meadow on the edge of the village. As the group approached, young Wyman recognized them and waved.

"Hail, Lord Dracona and his Chosen Lady!" Wyman called as he came to meet them.

Wyman bowed low before Bryant and Sonje.

"Rise, Wyman," Bryant ordered.

Philip came forward to take the horses as Bryant, Sonje and Gale dismounted.

"Welcome to our humble fair, Lord," Wyman said. "Come with me please."

Bryant and Sonje followed the young man through the fair. The villagers bowed as they passed. At the far end of the fair was a stand. Wyman led Bryant and Sonje up onto the stand where some men waited for them. The men bowed low on bended knee as they reached the top of the stand.

"Rise," Bryant ordered.

"Hail, Lord Dracona and his Chosen Lady!" the men said and the villagers echoed.

One man, whom Bryant recognized as the farmer he had saved, stepped forward and bowed.

"Long ago our ancestors fled Dracona for reasons no one clearly remembers," Wyman began. "It is time for us to rekindle our friendship with Dracona. You, My Lord, have shown yourself to be a kind and good man. We now pledge our loyalty to Dracona."

Bryant held up his hand.

"I feel that the truth which has remained forgotten for so many years should be brought to light. The event which prompted your ancestors to leave Dracona has been a mark of shame on my family that must be cleared before I can truly be worthy of your loyalty."

Bryant paused and drew a deep breath. He knew that this would not be easy. He felt approval from Sonje's thoughts and Haskell's as well. He told them about the fateful day that Uncle Rolfe burned the town and had to be killed. Bryant paused to view the solemn faces of the crowd as he struggled with his emotions.

"My father feared that I would repeat Uncle Rolfe's mistake if I were to have any contact with you of the village. That is why he drove trespassers from the forest. When he died, all I knew was what he had taught me. What I had learned was to fear contact with you and all others not of my family."

"Fortunately, Gwladys Sonje and her father came to find refuge in the forest. Through her I learned that Dracona need not die feared and finally forgotten. Sonje's people are of the same heritage as my family. Soon they will be coming to live in Dracona's town. I want you of the village to live in peace and friendship with Dracona."

Bryant felt a heavy weight beginning to lift from him.

"It is up to you. If you still want to pledge your loyalty to Dracona, it is of your own free will. I will not force my rule over unwilling subjects. Mostly, I want to be your friend."

As he finished speaking, Bryant felt free of the weight that he had carried for over one hundred years. He hoped that no one would notice that his hands were trembling.

'You have done the right thing,' Haskell's voice broke into his thoughts. 'The truth needed to come to light.'

'They had the right to know,' Sonje added.

The villagers murmured amongst themselves. The village elders waited patiently for the result. One of the elders stepped forward and raised both hands as the crowd became still.

"Have you reached a decision?" the man asked.

"Long live Lord Bryant and Gwladys Sonje!" the crowd replied.

A small boy broke away from the crowd and scampered up the stairs of the stand. When he reached Bryant, he flung his arms around Bryant's legs then tipped his head up.

"I am your friend," the boy said.

Bryant recognized him as the boy who had the kitten that Bryant had rescued from the tree.

Bryant picked the boy up and said, "I am glad to be your friend."

"Long live Lord Bryant and Gwladys Sonje!" the crowd repeated. "Long live Dracona!"

Bryant noticed that even Gale had joined the cheer. Bryant held up his left hand while still holding the boy in his right arm. When the crowd stilled, he spoke.

"The village council will still function as it has in the past. They may bring any problems or questions to me that they see fit," Bryant announced. "Enough business for now, on with the fair!"

As the crowd dissipated among the booths, Bryant gently set the boy back on his feet.

"I know which booth has the best fruit pies," the boy said.

"Which one is that?" Sonje asked.

"My mother's booth!" the boy exclaimed. "Follow me!"

Bryant and Sonje followed the boy through the fair to the booth that indeed served delicious fruit pies. Regis Auberon found them just as they were finishing their pies. He hugged his daughter in greeting before bowing to Bryant. Gale, the minstrel, burst from the crowd behind Regis Auberon. He bowed quickly before Bryant and Sonje.

"A word with you, My Lord," he said nervously glancing right and left.

Sonje and her father nodded at Bryant's glance and went together to view the rest of the fair.

"What is on your mind?" Bryant asked.

"Not here," Gale responded. "Somewhere more private."

"Come," Bryant ordered.

Bryant led Gale to the stand and around behind it. Edgard rose from his vantage point on the wagon as if to follow, then sat back down as Bryant shook his head. As Bryant turned to face Gale, he allowed his cape to briefly expose the two swords hanging at his side. The minstrel's eyes widened and his face paled at the sight.

"Now speak," Bryant ordered as he sat on a nearby stump.

"The woman you called your chosen lady," Gale began, "She traveled through Burton recently. I didn't recognize her at first, but now I know she is the same."

"The same?" Bryant pressed at the minstrel's pause.

"The same who was traveling with a man and a woman when they were detained by King Gustave."

"What of it?"

Bryant knew what Gale was getting at. Gale licked his lips nervously and swallowed as though his life were in danger.

"I was just outside the castle window when Gustave's 'accident' happened," Gale continued. "I heard him arguing with the woman. He told her that he would kill her if she did not bring her people to his kingdom. She replied that she would die for the freedom of her people. I turned and looked in the window just as he ran her through with his sword. As she fell, your lady and the man burst through the door. Your lady grabbed the knife off of the cheese platter on the table and swung at Gustave. It must have surprised him to see his hand drop from his sleeve to the floor. Your lady and the man grabbed some saddlebags, leapt out the window and disappeared into the garden behind the castle without looking back. King Gustave recovered enough to run into the hall screaming and trailing blood behind him."

"I climbed in through the window. The woman moaned. As I leaned over her, she told me to take her ring and keep it safe for Glynis sake," Gale paused and glanced around again. "Then she closed her eyes and died. I felt that Gustave should not have her body, so I drug her over to the window and hid her in the bushes. Then I wiped away the blood from the window and floor with a table cloth. I put Gustave's hand, still clinging to its sword, on the cheese tray. I then waited in the bushes until the search for Gustave's attacker had left the garden."

"What did you do then?" Bryant asked.

"I washed up in the well before visiting a carpenter nearby. He and I built her a coffin that night. I put her in a cave south of town to the east of the town gate."

"Is she still there?" Bryant asked.

"Yes. I returned the next night and covered her coffin with rocks to keep it safe. I slept last night in the mouth of that cave. Everything was as I left it, almost."

"What do you mean almost?" Bryant's curiosity prompted him to ask.

"Around midnight, a red and white glow filled the cave. The red glow centered on the coffin. Then a woman's voice told me to seek the dragon and to bring its Lord to the garden well," Gale paused. "When I saw the clasp on your cape, I thought you must be the man she spoke of. When you gave your speech, I knew I had found the right man."

Bryant rose from his seat and paced back and forth before the nervous minstrel. Gale leapt back a pace when Bryant finally turned to face him.

"Have you told anyone else what you just told me?" Bryant demanded.

"N-no, My Lord," Gale stuttered.

"What about the carpenter?"

"He didn't want to know. He helped build the coffin then gave me a large sack to fetch the body in. He met me outside the town gate with the coffin. He did not see the body, or where it came from. He loaned me his wagon, which I returned after I had left the coffin in the cave."

"Good," Bryant replied. "You and I will visit the cave and retrieve the woman's body for a proper burial at Castle Dracona."

Gale swallowed nervously.

"Once that is complete you are free to do as you wish. You may remain as my court minstrel or you may continue your travels. The choice will be yours." Bryant paused as Gale seemed calmer. "Now, where is the ring that you spoke of?"

The minstrel knelt and folded down the top of his boot to reveal a small pocket in the boot lining. He then drew out a small packet of cloth and handed it to Bryant.

"Go enjoy the fair. Meet at my wagon at sundown. If you need me sooner, tell the man waiting with the wagon." Bryant said before he left the minstrel.

* * * * *

"It is good to see you again Gwladys," Father said. "I have missed you terribly."

"I have missed you too, Father," Sonje responded as she walked beside him. "I was surprised, but happy to find that you and Bryant had made friends while I was away."

"I trusted your judgment, Daughter. I decided to give him a chance when he came to visit us here in the village. I knew it was a brave thing to walk unarmed and alone through the village after what Olvan and the other villagers told me. You look happier now than at the Grand Council."

"I am happier. When I returned to Glynis, I realized that Dracona was now my home. I also knew that I loved Bryant as Cherie loves Olvan."

"Enough to give up everything?"

"Everything," Sonje acknowledged without hesitation.

"It is good to know that you love Bryant for himself. It will make the completion of the quest easier for you."

"Except that we will be separated again before the quest is complete."

"How do you know?" Father asked in a puzzled tone.

She drew her half of Malvin's Heart from her bodice.

"This is half of Malvin's Heart," she began. "Bryant wears the other half. The legend of Malvin's Heart says that it would be used in time of danger to Dracona. It is to bind its wearers together and to Dracona for Dracona's protection. With it I can speak into Bryant's mind like the dragons do."

They paused in front of a wood-carver's booth before continuing. Sonje saw the worried look on her father's face.

"I will have to travel to the sea to gain Bryant's family's aid in the move of Glynis. I think Bryant's fate will draw him northward before he returns to Dracona."

"And the wedding?" Father asked.

"Will have to wait until Dracona is secure and Glynis is moved," Sonje responded with a heavy heart. "Haskell told me that Bryant has need of you."

* * * * *

"Need of me?" Auberon asked in surprise.

"Yes, the death of his father not only left him alone in a deserted castle, but also thrust him into manhood. My arrival thrust the responsibility of leadership on to him. He was not expecting to fall in love either," Sonje explained. "Haskell feels Bryant is in need of some fatherly advice. Haskell swore to Lord Eamon that he would care for the dying lord's son, but this is beyond his capabilities."

They walked in silence for a time. He had seen Bryant's eyes when he came to the village to pick up Sonje. Bryant's face was of a man, but his eyes betrayed the frightened child inside. He knew that Bryant needed someone then.

"I will see what I can do," Auberon said at last.

* * * * *

Bryant paused before entering the milling crowd of villagers. He glimpsed Sonje and Regis Auberon. Her face looked anxious, his looked solemn. As he reached the pair, Sonje kissed Auberon on the cheek. Bryant smiled. He did not know what the conflict had been; only that it was resolved.

"I have something for you," he told Sonje. "Hold out your hand."

Sonje obeyed, giving him a curious look. Bryant placed the packet in her hand. She gasped as the ring was revealed.

"Do you know what this is?" she asked.

"Where did you get it?" Regis Auberon demanded.

"The woman you were traveling with gave it to the minstrel before she died. He has hidden her body from Burton's king." Bryant answered.

Olvan, Cherie and their children came out of the crowd.

"Go with them Gwladys," Regis Auberon ordered. "We must talk, My Lord."

Bryant nodded and led Regis Auberon back to where he had spoken with the minstrel. After Bryant related the minstrel's story, Regis Auberon finally spoke.

"Sonje said your fate lies to the north. She is right. The ring is my wife's signet ring. When we were first taken to Burton's castle, we had some things we did not want in King Gustave's hands. We sealed them in a box and sunk it in the well in the garden. You can retrieve the box by lowering a rope with a hook on it. There was one kitchen boy that helped us escape. He was trying to tell us something else, but he was mute and we did not understand what he tried to tell us. He took a basket of food out of the kitchen every night. No one knew who it was for. He always returned within an hour with an empty basket."

* * * * *

"I will check into it," Lord Bryant promised.

Auberon was pleased that he was prepared to aid a lowly kitchen boy.

"I am worried at sending Sonje alone to enlist the help of my family," Lord Bryant said. "She will be met with hostility."

"It will not be the first time she has faced such a challenge," Auberon responded. "Your task will not be easy either."

"I will not go unprepared," Lord Bryant responded as he held his cape open to reveal the two swords at his side.

Auberon's eyes widened at the sight. Lord Bryant carefully drew out the beautiful dragon gripped sword and raised the blade on his open palm. Auberon gave a low whistle as he read the inscription. Lord Bryant sheathed the sword.

"I have seen men killed in their attempt to grasp the handgrip, yet yesterday it leapt into my hand," Lord Bryant spoke first. "While I held it the blade turned to flame until I had sworn an oath to use it to protect Dracona and those in need."

"And the other sword?" Auberon asked.

"I will continue to carry it also. I will not use Fanchon's sword except to defend others."

"Have you given Gwladys a sword to carry on her journey?"

"Yes and a shirt of chain mail also."

"You have done well," Auberon said, satisfied.

"So much has happened in such a short period of time," Lord Bryant said with a sigh. "It has been difficult."

"You have gone from being alone to being a ruler over many people," Auberon said with understanding. "I at least had fair warning of what was in store for me. You are getting it all at once. I'm afraid that things won't slow down until Glynis is safely moved and Dracona is secure."

* * * * *

Bryant was surprised by Regis Auberon's comments.

'He is right, Bryant,' Haskell's voice came to him.

"I am at your service, Lord Dracona," Regis Auberon said with a bow.

Bryant had not expected this.

"I should be bowing to you. You are King Auberon of Glynis," Bryant said.

"Remember when you knelt before me in Olvan's home?"

"Yes," Bryant responded.

"That had nothing to do with your intentions to marry my daughter. I was giving the kingship to you."

"I thought that I would be king after the wedding when the coronation takes place."

Regis Auberon chuckled and said, "No. The coronation is simply a symbol of your kingship, a mere formality. You became king when I lifted my hands from your head. It was then up to you to earn the loyalty of your subjects. You have done well so far."

"Sonje told me that I would become king after I described what you had done," Bryant said slowly. "But, I didn't believe that the process had already begun."

"I have spoken to Hoyt and the others. They are completely loyal to you. They feel confident with your leadership," Regis Auberon said with a smile as Bryant felt very relieved.

"I am confident in your leadership also. Today you faced a great challenge. You told the villagers the truth today and allowed them to make their own decision of loyalty. You could have hid the truth, but didn't. You could have forced your rule on them, but didn't."

"My father hid the truth for so long that I felt that I had to bring it to light. Perhaps now my nightmares will stop."

"They will, My Lord," Regis Auberon said with a smile. "Come enjoy the fair."

As Regis Auberon and Bryant walked around the end of the stand, they were greeted by Cherie and Sonje. Bryant caught a sudden movement out of the corner of his eye. Edgard stood facing north on the seat of the wagon.

"Soldiers," Edgard said grimly as the little group approached him.

Bryant and Sonje exchanged a quick glance before they went to their mounts. Llewellyn and Guen seemed to sense the urgency and broke into a trot as soon as their riders were mounted. Bryant urged his mount into a gallop as he heard Edgard raising the alarm behind him. Sonje followed him to the northern edge of the village. They stopped on the road waiting for the approaching soldiers. Bryant did not turn as he heard the villagers assemble behind them. Edgard took his place beside Bryant. Regis Auberon stepped forward beside Sonje. Silence fell as the approaching army came around the bend of the road. Bryant recognized the uniforms as the same ones worn by the men whom he had killed in the northern forest.

'Haskell?' Bryant thought silently.

'I am here,' was Haskell's reply.

'We may need you.'

'I will await your command.'

The man leading the soldiers was ornately dressed with a gold crown on his helmet. The arm he held up to signal his men to halt had a bandage where his hand should have been. Bryant knew he was King Gustave of Burton.

"Surrender or be conquered!" King Gustave ordered.

"These people are free to choose their own destinies," Bryant countered. "I will serve as leader to all those who will stand by me."

"Then choose!" King Gustave demanded. "Swear you loyalties to me, King Gustave of Burton, or to this man."

'Be ready, Haskell,' Bryant thought.

"Long live Lord Dracona!" the villagers shouted as one.

'Now!' Bryant ordered Haskell as he saw the soldiers draw their swords and lift their bows in response to the villager's decision.

Gustave lifted his arm to signal his men to charge, but his words were drowned out by the shouts of the men and the screams of the horses as Haskell rose out of the forest. Gustave's horse reared and plunged. The would-be conqueror was dumped in the dirt as his mount turned and fled with most of his soldiers. Bryant glanced to see the villagers stand their ground in spite of Haskell's sudden appearance as he dismounted. Llewellyn stood calmly where Bryant left him.

'Stay put,' Bryant thought to Sonje when she caught his eye.

She nodded ever so slightly.

"Retreat while you can, King of Burton," Bryant ordered as he stopped before the man.

The few remaining soldiers gathered around their leader as he got to his feet.

"Take your soldiers with you," Bryant continued. "Those wishing to surrender in peace are invited to lay down their arms. Those who wish to fight can expect the same fate as your two scouts who decided to rob one of these villagers."

"We found them dead to the north of here," one of Burton's soldiers said. "My cousin was one of the best swordsmen in the kingdom. How many of you did it take to kill him?"

"I met him and his companion and defeated them both," Bryant responded to the man's challenge. "Alone."

"I am the villager they tried to rob," the elder Wyman said as he stepped forward. "I was alone and unarmed. He fought them both by himself. I stand here armed, prepared to fight at the side of the man who saved me."

"We will meet again, Dracona, and it will not be under such fortunate circumstances for you," King Gustave growled breaking his silence.

Bryant watched in silence as King Gustave and his men followed the others in their retreat.

'Thank you, Haskell,' Bryant thought to the circling dragon.

'Take care,' Haskell replied. 'That was no idle threat.'

'I know,' Bryant thought as he turned to face the villagers.

"Long live, Lord Dracona! Long live the dragon!" cheered those of the village and those of Glynis.

Bryant raised his hands to silence them.

"We have been warned," Bryant told them. "We must now guard our borders against attack. Those not guarding the borders must be prepared to fight or run for cover at any time."

Bryant signaled for Edgard to step forward. The man knelt before Bryant. Bryant drew his old sword and placed the flat of the blade on Edgard's left shoulder.

"I proclaim you General of Dracona's army and Minister of Defense," Bryant said before lifting his sword from Edgard's shoulder.

"I pledge my loyalty to Dracona and its Lord," Edgard said as he drew his sword. "I commit this blade to the protection of Dracona and its citizens."

"Rise, General Edgard," Bryant commanded.

Edgard rose and stood beside Bryant.

Bryant signaled to Hoyt. He laid his sword blade on Hoyt's shoulder.

"I proclaim you Minister of State," Bryant began. "You will be my advisor and will form a council to aid in the governing of the citizens of Dracona."

"I pledge my services to Dracona and its citizens," Hoyt responded before taking his place beside Edgard.

Bryant signaled to Agatha. Bryant laid his sword blade on her shoulder as she knelt before him.

"I proclaim you Minister of the Interior," Bryant decreed. "You will find duties and housing for the coming citizens and all citizens unhappy with their current situations."

"I pledge my services to Dracona and its citizens," Agatha said before taking her place beside Hoyt.

"These three with the assistance of Regis Auberon will govern Dracona in the event of the absence of myself and Gwladys Sonje," Bryant told the people. "To achieve peace, we will all have to work together. The fields of those acting as soldiers must be cared for by those remaining behind. If the work is divided equally it will be easier for everyone."

Sonje dismounted and took her place by Bryant. Philip led the horses away.

"We will meet in half an hour at the stand with the village council to co-ordinate our defense plans," Bryant said, finishing his announcements.

The crowd slowly returned to the fair booths.

'You did well,' Sonje thought to Bryant. 'Let's find something to eat before the meeting.'

Chapter 11 – Raising an Army

Bryant and Sonje hardly spoke while they ate. They both knew that their time of parting was imminent. With heavy hearts they walked slowly to the stand where the two councils were waiting for them. One of the village councilmen bowed low to the couple.

"My house is nearby. We can meet there in privacy," he offered.

With a quick nod, he thought to Haskell, 'Notify us if Philip spots any more soldiers.'

'I will,' was Haskell's reply.

As they took their places around the table, Wyman introduced the other members of the village council. Barnarr, Sebastian, and Kyle each bowed in their turn. Silence fell as Bryant studied each council member. Edgard sat immediately to his left. The large muscular man shifted as he felt Bryant's gaze on him. He was a good three hundred years or more older than Bryant. Agatha sat next to him. Her graying hair drew attention to her surprisingly youthful face. Her carefully folded hands bore calluses that told of many years of labor. Hoyt's face displayed great patience born of many years of teaching. His graying hair told of the hundreds of years he had seen. Wyman's weather beaten face spoke of his years in the sun, wind and rain. His gnarled hands spoke of the hard labors that had exposed him to the elements. Sebastian's face was younger than those beside him, yet he seemed comfortable with his position. Barnarr's upper body seemed to crowd his neighbors. The singed hairs and scarring on his hands and arms told of many years spent thrusting metal into the forge before shaping it on an anvil. Kyle's slim build contrasted with Barnarr's muscular one. His expression was of determination. Regis Auberon sat looking around the table as though he too was analyzing each in turn. Sonje sat quietly as though she knew that this was something he must take sole charge of. Bryant swallowed before beginning.

"Although the move of Glynis to Dracona is urgent due to the impending destruction of their valley by volcanoes, the threat of invasion from Burton is more immediate. Gwladys Sonje will travel alone through the mountains behind Dracona to enlist the help of my family in the move. That will free the rest of us to deal with Burton. It has become clear to me that I must travel to Burton to see if I can stop this invasion."

"I will go with you," Edgard stated.

"No," Bryant said with appreciation for his loyalty and obvious concern. "I will travel alone. I will ride through the north forest along the mountains so I can approach from the north-east. I will need some clothes that make me appear to be a farmer. I will also need a horse more befitting a farmer."

"Will you take both swords?" Hoyt asked.

The villagers glanced at each other in puzzlement. Bryant caught this with amusement. He flipped his cape over his left shoulder to expose the swords.

"I will need a different cape for my journey. A hooded cape should sufficiently disguise the swords. I will strap them to my back," Bryant responded. "I will only use Fanchon's Sword in defense of others."

"May I examine your dragon grip sword?" Barnarr asked.

Bryant drew the sword carefully from its sheath and laid it across his open palm.

"Don't touch it," Bryant warned. "It will only serve one man and it will kill or injure all others that touch it."

"That is fine work," Barnarr said with an appreciative tone. "Who forged it?"

"My great-grandfather, Fanchon, forged it in dragon fire. I am the first to bear it." Bryant answered.

Bryant sheathed his sword and returned to his seat. He could see by their faces that all were finally satisfied with his decision.

"When all is safe, I will send for the minstrel," Bryant said. "He and I have some unfinished business in Burton. Now for the problem at hand, we need to raise enough of an army to defend our border."

"Our men are willing to protect the village, but we don't have any weapons," Sebastian said.

"There are plenty of swords at the castle," Bryant offered. "The men can come to the castle in groups so that the village is not completely unprotected. Edgard will help coordinate defense of the village and the castle."

Bryant stood and put his hand on Sonje's shoulder.

"Gwladys Sonje and I must make preparations for our journeys," Bryant announced.

"Fare well, Lord and Lady," Kyle said as he stood and bowed.

The others followed suite, each in turn. Sonje stood and followed Bryant out. They were greeted by the questioning looks of the four women who gathered near the house. The women curtsied to them before one stepped forward.

"I am Hellene, wife of Sebastian," the woman said. "Is the meeting over?"

"No," Bryant replied. "We must make preparations for our journeys."

"You are leaving?" Hellene asked, as if hoping for more information. "We are at your service if there is anything we can do to help in your preparations."

"I don't think I need anything for my journey," Sonje began. "But, Lord Dracona is traveling to Burton and will need a disguise."

"Yes," Hellene agreed. "It would be very dangerous for Our Lord to go to Burton dressed as Lord Dracona."

"Your horse is too fine also, My Lord," said the tallest woman. "Barnarr just delivered a new wagon and received a horse and small cart in trade. We were not going to keep the cart and the horse is too old to pull a cart much longer. You may take them for your journey."

"That will help, Barbara," Hellene said. "Now for the clothes."

"Kyle has a pair of pants that are too large," said the youngest of the women. "I think that they would fit you, My Lord."

"What color are they, Raye?" Barbara asked. "Barnarr has a brown shirt that is too small."

"The pants are a dull green," Raye responded.

"Wyman has a dark brown, hooded cape," the last woman spoke up. "And we have some squash and some grain that could be put in the cart."

"That will help a lot, Erta," Hellene said. "Sebastian has an old pair of boots that might fit."

"Meet us at the blacksmith's shop in an hour," Bryant said, seeing that the women had things well in hand.

"We will, My Lord," Hellene replied as she and the others curtsied.

Bryant and Sonje walked slowly down the street. Somehow, they were just not in the mood to rejoin the fair. They walked in silence until they found a secluded bench next to a tree in the churchyard. Bryant cautiously let his glow shine softly around them after checking to see if anyone would see it. Sonje allowed her glow to join his.

"Your father explained to me what really happened when I visited him," Bryant said, avoiding speaking of their parting. "You didn't tell me that I am already king."

"I was afraid you wouldn't believe me," Sonje replied, looking at the ground.

"I would believe you," Bryant assured her. "I am wondering if your people will accept me as their leader."

"At the Grand Council, I presented that to them. Each princess must present her intended husband for the people of Glynis to accept or refuse as their king. Cherie knew Olvan would be refused before she presented him."

"She knew that she would have to give up her claim to the throne if she married him," Bryant said, understanding where Sonje was leading. "Did you know what would happen when you presented me?"

"Actually, no," Sonje answered. "When I found out the form the Travelor took, I knew that Lord Dracona was not just a title, but a duty. I knew that every picture and sculpture of a dragon was not just an artist's idle fantasy. I did not know how the people of Glynis would take the idea of living with dragons. The only thing that kept me going was the legend."

"How did they take it?" Bryant asked.

"I think the appearance of the Travelor prepared them for what I had to say," Sonje responded. "I was still surprised at their response."

"Oh?" Bryant said with curiosity.

"They responded, 'Long live Regis Bryant!' So that night Father transferred his kingship to you," Sonje explained. "I wish that we could just go home to the castle. I don't want to say goodbye to you."

Bryant drew her closer until her body was pressed against his side. Then he gently put his hand under her chin and lifted her face towards his own. He saw the tears glistening on her cheeks.

"I don't want to go either," Bryant said with a tremor in his voice. "A lot of people are depending on us. We have done everything we can to make our journeys safer. You know that I will think of you every moment I am away from you."

"I will think of you, too," Sonje responded with a quivering voice as tears began to run down her cheeks.

"I love you, Sonje. I think I have loved you from the moment I first saw you. The more time I spend with you, the more I love you. I am looking forward to spending the rest of my life with you. I don't know how I survived so long without you."

Bryant could feel the tears on his own cheeks.

"All my life, I knew that I would have to marry the man of the riddle if I found him, even if I didn't love him. I had met many men in my search, but I had been careful not to love any of them. When I saw you in that clearing, you were terrifying. Yet I was drawn to you like I had never been drawn to anyone before. When the time drew near for you to take me to your castle, I was almost afraid you wouldn't come for me. Until I found your family history in the library, I was still trying not to get attracted to you. But even if you hadn't been the man we had quested after for so many centuries, it was still too late, I had already fallen in love," Sonje paused to take a deep breath before continuing. "I don't care if you are King of Glynis and Lord Dracona. I love you, Bryant Donley, with all my heart."

Bryant's heart leapt as he saw the fierce determination in her eyes. He leaned closer until their lips met. His heart began to race as she kissed back. All time was lost to him and his awareness narrowed down to her lips on his own. When he finally lifted his lips from hers, his heart felt as though it would burst. His lungs burned as he gasped for air. He was suddenly aware of how closely her body pressed against his own and of how she also gasped for each breath. He kissed her again.

* * * * *

Her heart wouldn't stop pounding after that first kiss. She had not much chance to catch her breath before he kissed her again. A tingle went up her spine as his hand moved up her side to press her even closer. As he broke off the kiss, she felt his hands lifting and turning her. She did not argue as he guided her until she sat on his lap. He leaned back against the tree. She felt her feet leave the ground as he turned her more and drew her against him. She glimpsed his flashing blue eyes before his lips found hers again. Her heart leapt as his kiss grew harder and more demanding. She felt her head spinning as their lips finally parted. With a gasp and a sigh she let her head fall against his shoulder.

* * * * *

Bryant leaned his head back against the tree. He felt Sonje slowly relax against him. He wished that the moment would never end. Ideas of what they could do if they were married and had more time flashed through his mind. He sighed softly as he turned his thoughts from what he knew must wait until Glynis was safely moved.

'We should be getting to the blacksmith's shop now,' Bryant thought softly to Sonje.

Slowly she got to her feet and doused her glow. She smiled as he rose to stand at her side.

'We will never be truly alone again,' she thought to him.

'Of that I am grateful,' Bryant thought in return.

Arm in arm, they walked in silence to the blacksmith's shop. Darkness had fallen over the village. Torchlight from the fair booths lit the road. Light spilled from the window of the house behind the shop. The door opened as they left the road.

"Come in and eat before changing," Barbara said as she stepped back from the doorway.

The four women bowed as Bryant and Sonje entered the room. The table was burdened with a large, delicious smelling meal.

"Thank you," Bryant said as they sat down to the table. "We had not expected such hospitality."

"We knew that you would not get such a meal while you travel," Erta replied. "We have also prepared food for your journey."

'I am glad someone is looking out for you,' Haskell thought to Bryant. 'I am happy that you have made amends with the villagers.'

'I'm glad, too,' Bryant thought back as he ate. 'I'm not looking forward to this journey. It will be the first time I have traveled so far alone.'

'And into such danger,' Haskell finished. 'You are strong and a skilled swordsman, but you will have to rely on your wits as much as your sword.'

'Yes. I hope I can pass as a farmer,' Bryant thought with a worried tone.

'Let these women take care of that,' Haskell replied. 'They have thought of everything.'

'I'll miss you, Haskell,' Bryant thought to the dragon. 'You must stay to protect Evelina and the eggs.'

'I shall miss you, also,' Haskell replied.

"What is the matter, My Lord?" Raye asked, noticing Bryant's sad expression.

"I just realized that I would be leaving behind everyone including Haskell," Bryant explained. "I will miss Sonje and Haskell very much."

"I understand how you feel," Barbara said quietly. "It has been fifteen years since I left my homeland to marry Barnarr. I am happy here, but I still miss my family."

In silence they finished their meal. Barbara and Erta quickly cleared the table. Bryant stood and removed his cape. He carefully folded the cape so the dragon clasp lay on top of the cape. He gently caressed the clasp after placing the folded cape on the table.

"The clasp must be very dear to your heart," Barbara's voice said and he looked up to see her fingering a pendant made from a shell. "It reminds you of who you are."

"The memory is one that is both bitter and sweet," Bryant replied. "I remember my father's words as he handed me the clasp. 'As my father gave this to me on my hundredth birthday, I now give it to you.' Father said. 'He told me to wear it proudly as a symbol of our responsibilities. Now it is time for you as my son to take on the responsibilities that must be borne as Lord Dracona.' It was only fifty years after that when Uncle Rolf's grief drove both the villagers and my family from Dracona, leaving my father and me alone in the castle."

Bryant was startled by a touch on his arm. He turned to find Sonje at his side.

"I'll put it in your office at the castle. It will be safe there until you return," she reassured him. "You must put aside Lord Dracona and become simply Bryant Donley."

She gently put her hands to his head and lifted the circlet from his brow.

"Give me the ring also," she said as she held out her right hand. "I will change these so you might wear them around your neck. You must take care not to show them."

Sonje returned to her seat at the table. She placed the circlet on the table before her and the ring below it.

"Good women," she said to get the villagers' attention. "Do not be alarmed at what I am going to do. It is a talent that is held by some of my people. Do not be afraid of the light that will be around me as I work these."

"We trust you, Lady," Hellene assured Sonje.

Sonje allowed her glow to join the lamplight in the room. Sonje lifted the circlet and held it between the thumb and forefinger of her left hand. With her right hand, she traced the circlet with her finger. As her finger passed along the surface, the solid band turned into a chain. She laid the finished chain on the table and picked up the ring. Holding it in both hands, she separated the band and laid it flat on either side of the stone. She curved the ends up and placed the ring back on the table. She separated the chain and moved the ends to the ends of the ring band. As soon as the circlet and ring had become a pendant on a chain, her light began to fade. Bryant rushed to catch her as she began to tip off her chair.

"Are you alright?" he asked with alarm.

"I will be fine in a moment," she answered.

"That is quite a talent, My Lady," Barbara said.

"Thank you," Sonje answered as she straightened up in the chair. "Let's get Bryant ready to go on his journey."

"The clothes are in the bedroom," Hellene said.

Bryant shut the door behind him. He carefully folded each article of clothing as he removed it. The rough weave of the pants rubbed unfamiliarly on his legs as he bent to pick up the shirt. He pulled the shirt on over the chain mail then tightened the laces to hide the shining metal. He sat on the edge of the bed and pulled on the worn leather boots before turning to the swords.

He removed the belt from the scabbard of his old sword and threaded the belt of the other scabbard in its place. Then he buckled the belts together crossing to form two loops. He stood before slipping an arm through each loop. After settling the swords on his back, he placed the cape around his shoulders over the swords. He picked up his clothes and boots and returned to the other room.

"Bryant?" Sonje asked in surprise at his appearance.

"Yes, My Lady," Bryant bowed low to hide the smile that played across his face.

"With the dust of a few days travel, no one will recognize you as Lord Dracona," Erta said in a pleased tone.

Sonje placed the pendant around his neck after he placed his clothes next to his cape. Bryant slipped the pendant down the neck of his shirt and tightened the laces again. Everyone turned in surprise as the door opened and Barnarr cast a puzzled look around the room.

"Do you know where Lord Dracona is, My Lady?" Barnarr asked as he bowed to Sonje. "Hoyt is looking for him."

"I am here, Barnarr," Bryant said with amusement.

Barnarr looked closer with a confused look on his face before he suddenly looked very surprised.

"My Lord!" he exclaimed as he dropped to one knee. "I didn't recognize you."

"Rise," Bryant said with pleasure. "Your wife and her companions have done well then. I am now Bryant Donley, poor farmer."

"Hoyt wants to meet you at your wagon and horses," Barnarr said after he had returned to his feet.

"Everything is loaded in the cart for you," Barbara said. "Follow me."

Bryant gathered up his clothing and boots before he and Sonje followed her out the back door. The horse whickered softly at the light. Sonje took his clothing from him and Bryant untied the lead rope from the hitching post. They led the horse into the street and walked quickly down the street to the fair. The horse Bryant followed closely with its cart creaking along behind.

'Ask what its name is,' he thought to Haskell.

'She says her name is Dusty,' Haskell responded. 'She is happy to be pulling a cart again.'

'Thank you,' Bryant said.

He wondered if the disguise would work well enough that he wouldn't be recognized.

'Go on ahead,' he thought to Sonje. 'I want to see if Hoyt recognizes me.'

'I hardly recognize you,' Sonje responded as she hurried on ahead.

Bryant slowed down as he approached the appointed place. He tried to hunch over a bit to appear more like one of the villagers.

"He should be here by now," Hoyt said as he looked past Bryant. "He told you he was coming straight here?"

"Yes," Sonje answered. "He was right behind me."

"Beg your pardon, Sir," Bryant began in a nasal tone. "Would you care to buy one of my fine melons?"

"Come back later," Hoyt responded. "We are waiting for someone to meet us here."

"You must be waiting for Lord Dracona," Bryant countered in his normal voice as he straightened up.

"My Lord!" Hoyt exclaimed as he bowed. "Forgive me."

Bryant was pleased.

"Now, with a few days of road dust, my own mother would not recognize me in broad daylight," Bryant said. "I can now travel into Burton without being recognized."

"I still fear for your safety, My Lord."

"It is a necessary risk, Hoyt," Bryant responded. "Burton is more skilled at waging war. The minstrel's words gave me hope of gaining peace without doing battle. Haskell will remain at Dracona to help protect Dracona, Glynis and this village. Sonje will travel though the mountains to Merton to enlist my family's help. I will journey to Burton in hopes of putting its rightful king on the throne and forging an alliance with Burton."

"And Gustave?" Hoyt asked.

"I think the rightful king of Burton should determine his fate," Bryant answered. "If he survives being dethroned."

Regis Auberon approached the group. He cast a questioning glance towards Bryant before speaking.

"We will be ready to leave soon, Hoyt." he glanced again at Bryant. "Has Lord Dracona shown up yet?"

"I will simply be Bryant Donley, poor farmer, until I return from Burton," Bryant answered for Hoyt.

Regis Auberon looked closer at him then nodded as the rest of those traveling to the castle began to assemble around the wagon.

"I will start out now." Bryant said reluctantly. "I should not be traveling with you in case Gustave's men still lurk in the forest."

"Safe journey, Bryant," Regis Auberon said, placing his hand on Bryant's shoulder. "Return soon in safety."

"Watch over things for me," Bryant responded. "Especially your daughter."

Regis Auberon nodded.

"Be careful, My Love," Bryant said to Sonje. "Your journey may be as difficult as mine. I will contact you each sunset."

"You be careful also," Sonje replied. "If I don't hear from you, I will come after you."

"I love you." Bryant said as he felt his throat tighten.

"I love you, too." Sonje said as she stepped closer.

Bryant lifted her chin and kissed her. As he turned to hide the tears he felt coming, he saw the tears glistening in her eyes. He fumbled with the catch on the lead rope as he unfastened it and patted the mare's neck before checking the wick in the lamp and climbing to the seat. He took up the reins and urged the mare forward. When he was out of sight of the village, he wiped his tears on his sleeve.

'I wish I could go in your place,' Haskell's words came softly. 'I will miss you.'

'You know that is not possible,' Bryant responded. 'I will miss you too. Take care, My Friend.'

Bryant turned the horse off the road on to a half hidden trail between the trees. After about an hour they came to a small clearing.

"We'll stay here for the night, Dusty," he told the horse as he unhitched her.

After caring for the mare, Bryant tied her to a tree. He carefully removed the swords from his back and propped them against a tree. He blew out the lantern then settled down next to his swords. Bryant listened to the forest sounds until he fell asleep. He woke suddenly to a scream. He grabbed the swords as he leapt to his feet. He had half drawn his old sword before he noticed the eagle in the center of the clearing.

"You startled me, Ernest," Bryant said as he sheathed his sword.

The eagle clicked its beak and nudged the mound of feathers at its feet.

"Thank you," Bryant said as he understood what the eagle wanted. "Don't let anyone else see you deliver prey to me. It might make them suspicious."

The eagle bobbed its head before launching itself into the sky. Bryant shook his head as he watched the eagle leave. The pile of feathers turned out to be a small dove. Bryant made a small fire and cooked the bird. He watched the mare graze as he ate the dove and some bread and cheese he found in the cart. The mare was smaller than Llewellyn and more angular. She shook her uneven mane and swished her brushy tail. She was the color of road dust with dark stockings.

Bryant scratched at the stubble on his chin and considered shaving with his hunting knife, then decided against it. A beard might help complete his disguise. He got up as he noticed that the dew was beginning to burn off the grass in the clearing. He put out the fire and carefully hid all evidence of it. Then he hitched Dusty to the cart.

"It's just you and me now, Dusty," Bryant told the mare as they followed the trail back into the forest.

Chapter 12 – Choosing a Path and a Gift

Sonje felt her father's arm across her shoulders as she turned from Bryant. She gladly accepted the handkerchief that she felt pressed into her hand. With it she wiped the tears from her eyes. She drew a deep breath and let it out slowly. She turned to hand back the handkerchief and Hoyt shook his head.

"Keep it, Gwladys," Hoyt said.

"Thank you," she replied gratefully. "We should be leaving soon also."

"We will stay the night where we did last night," Hoyt said. "In the morning you can ride on ahead and make preparations for your journey. Agatha has borrowed a horse from the village and will go with you to help you prepare."

"I want to stay with my father and sister tonight," Sonje told Hoyt. "I will meet you in the clearing shortly after sunrise."

"As you wish, Gwladys," Hoyt said. "Philip is about the same height as Lord Bryant. Perhaps he should stay here with you tonight then ride Lord Bryant's horse wearing his cape back to the castle in case soldiers lurk in the forest."

"He's good with a sword Gwladys and can protect you," Edgard added.

Sonje nodded and Edgard unbuckled his sword, handing it to Philip. She gathered her things from the wagon. Father picked up Bryant's clothes as Philip led Guen over. Sonje and Father stood and watched as the group departed. Some of the villagers had joined the group in a wagon of their own. Sonje stood watching them slip into the darkness of the forest as she thought of the day's events.

* * * * *

Auberon stood quietly, studying his daughter's face. She had matured much in the past weeks. He had observed how comfortable she had appeared to be with her position as the intended wife of Lord Dracona as the two had faced the villagers on the stand. She had once confided in him about how intimidated she was to know that one day she could become the ruler of Glynis. During their travels, she had matured a lot, but she still occasionally mentioned her reluctance to assume her birthright.

Auberon pondered that perhaps she was afraid that they would find the man of the legends and that she would be required to marry him whether she loved him or not. He smiled quietly to himself. She had fallen in love with Bryant before she knew he was the man of the legends.

Auberon's thoughts were interrupted as Guen nuzzled his shoulder.

"The hour grows late, Gwladys," he said softly as he placed his hand on her shoulder.

* * * * *

Sonje's mind felt numb and her heart ached. Silently she allowed her father to lead her to Cherie and Olvan's home. Cherie sat alone at the table as they entered. Sonje heard her father say something about the horse and Philip.

"Are you alright, Sonje?" Cherie asked in a concerned tone of voice. "Come sit down."

"I feel numb," Sonje responded as Cherie led her to a chair.

"You've had a long, busy day," Cherie said as she poured Sonje a drink of cider. "I would not want to have a day like you've had."

"I'm afraid," Sonje said.

"Afraid for Bryant?" Cherie responded as she watched her sister's face for a reaction.

"Yes," Sonje began, "And for myself. He said that his family does not like strangers. He found a sword and a chain mail shirt for me."

"You are an excellent swords-woman," Cherie responded. "Edgard told me you disarmed him without any trouble. He came because he is Glynis' best swordsman."

"I'm worried that they will not approve of my engagement to Bryant."

"That is something you will have to deal with when you reach Merton," Cherie responded. "All things considered, they will probably be glad you are as long lived as they are. There is no use worrying about that tonight. Just deal with things as they present themselves."

"You're right," Sonje admitted. "I wish Mother was still with us."

"She is with us in our hearts," Cherie reassured her. "When you have a problem, think of her and what she would do."

"She would be telling us to go to bed," Sonje said.

"That's right," Father said as he quietly shut the door behind him.

Sonje finished the last sip of cider before she stood up. She said goodnight and went upstairs. She smiled at the sight of the two sleeping children. She sighed as she realized that the only way for her to relive the innocence of childhood was to have her own children. With that thought in her mind, she laid down.

Sonje woke to her father gently shaking her shoulder. The grey light of dawn told her she had slept even though it seemed like only moments since she had closed her eyes. She quietly followed him past the sleeping children and down the stairs. Philip was rolling up some blankets near the fireplace and Cherie was setting a pot of porridge on the table as they reached the bottom of the stairs. Philip and Sonje ate while Cherie packed the saddlebags with Sonje's things. Olvan entered the front door as she finished eating. Sonje rose and picked up the saddlebags.

"Journey safely, Daughter," Father bade her. "Long live, Gwladys Sonje."

"May your path be smooth and your way clear, Sister," Cherie spoke next. "Long live, Gwladys Sonje."

"May all strangers turn to friends and all dawns herald a fortunate day," Olvan said in turn. "Long live, Gwladys Sonje."

"I'll miss you all," Sonje said as she hugged each of them.

Olvan opened the door for her. Guen and Llewellyn were waiting for them at the front tie post. Sonje secured the saddlebags behind the saddle before untying the reins. She placed her foot in Olvan's cupped hands and mounted. She waved to the three standing in the pale morning light before turning Guen northward. Just after passing the empty booths from the fair, they turned their mounts into the forest and urged them to a gallop.

Soon they had reached the clearing where the others had spent the night. They were just finishing breakfast as she dismounted and tied Guen to a tree. She realized how chilly it was when Agatha offered her a cup of hot tea. She pulled her cape tighter around her as she sipped the tea. She felt calmer than she had last night. She also knew there was no turning back.

"I'm ready when you are, Gwladys," Agatha said as she curtsied.

"I'm ready also," Sonje said as she handed Agatha the empty cup.

Sonje nodded to Philip as she walked to where she had tied Guen. Philip bowed before going to fetch Agatha's mount. Edgard helped her mount as Hoyt held her mount's reins. Sonje smiled. She knew that they were showing their loyalty to her. It was something she would never quite get used to.

The rest of the group gathered around as Agatha halted her mount next to Guen. Sonje surveyed the faces of those gathered around her; the villagers' faces beside the familiar faces of those from Glynis.

"Take care, my friends," Sonje said. "I pray for your safety and strength as I pray for Lord Dracona's safe return. Guard well our homes and our freedom."

Wyman, Jr., stepped forward and bowed.

"We pray for your safe journey and return. We also pray for the safe journey and return of Lord Dracona," Wyman Jr. said for the group. "Long live Lord Dracona and Gwladys Sonje!"

"Long live Lord Dracona and Gwladys Sonje!" echoed the others.

Hoyt smiled and nodded to Sonje as he released Guen's reins. Sonje did not have to be able to read his thoughts to know he was pleased by such show of loyalty from all present alike. She returned Hoyt's nod before urging Guen forward.

Sonje held Guen to a slow gallop so that Agatha's shorter mount could keep up the pace. They paused to let the horses drink in the stream as they crossed it at mid morning. They continued at a walk for a while to let the horses catch their breath. Soon they were galloping again. By noon the trail broke free of the forest and found its way through the fields surrounding the abandoned town.

Sonje slowed Guen to a walk. She could see the sweat on Guen's neck. Agatha brought her mount beside Sonje's. The horse's nostrils were flared and its neck was shiny with sweat. Sonje knew that the horses would be nearly cooled by the time they reached the castle if they were allowed to walk.

"I didn't realize the fields around the town were so extensive," Agatha commented.

"It appears that the town and castle can be self supporting," Sonje replied. "Haskell told me that there is a large herd of cattle grazing on mountain pastures above the castle. We should separate out some breeding stock before the dragons hatch."

"And some for milking," Agatha agreed.

No more was said until they reached the castle gates.

"I will care for the horses while you prepare some lunch," Sonje said.

Agatha curtsied and hurried up the path to the kitchen. Sonje removed the saddle bags and saddles from the horses. She then led the horses in circles around the courtyard until their backs were dry. She checked each horse carefully before tying them to the hitching post. She drew a bucket of water from the well beside the stable door and began to wash the horses. Soon they were clean and she turned them loose in the pasture. Sonje quickly put away the tack before taking the saddle bags inside.

Her stomach growled as she encountered the delicious smell of the lunch Agatha was setting in the dining hall. Sonje left the bags on the end of the table as she hurried to her seat. Without a word the two women began to eat.

"Thank you, Agatha," Sonje said after she had finished eating.

"It is a pleasure to serve you, Gwladys," Agatha answered with a smile.

"When we were traveling, my parents and I had no servants. I liked it that way. I have always felt guilty having someone waiting on me," Sonje confessed.

"Don't feel guilty!" Agatha responded. "It is a pleasure to serve you because you are so good to your servants. You respect our feelings and opinions. We know that you never ask us to do what you would not do yourself. Your duties as a ruler of Glynis are important. You have found the answer to the riddle and the solution to the quest. You have found Glynis a new home and a new regis. That makes you a servant of all from Glynis. We are grateful to be able to repay you through our service to you."

Sonje sat silent for a moment after Agatha had finished. She felt a burden lift from her shoulders.

"Thank you, Agatha," Sonje said. "You have suddenly made clear something that had troubled me nearly all my life. I will strive to continue to be a ruler you will be proud to serve."

"Go now and clean up," Agatha ordered. "I will meet you in the library in an hour."

Sonje nodded and rose from the table. She picked up her saddlebags and hurried upstairs. She paused at Bryant's door, almost hoping he would be there. After letting out a deep sigh, she continued down the hall to her chambers. She dropped her saddlebags on the table at the foot of the bed before heading for the bathing chamber. Soon she was immersed in a basin of warm water. She loosened her braids and allowed her long hair to float freely in the water. As her muscles began to relax, she began to wash. Soon she was clean and refreshed. She opened the drain disk as she stepped out of the basin. Her hair fell down her back like a stream of liquid gold. Carefully, she wrung the water out of her hair and wrapped a drying sheet around it. She dried herself and wrapped another drying sheet around her body before heading to the closet.

After choosing a dark brown dress, she dressed and braided her hair. As she sat at the dresser, she looked at the polished shield hung above it. Tiny dragons had been embossed around its edge. As she traced the entwined bodies around the shield she realized how entwined her own life had become. She sighed and turned as she realized that Agatha must be waiting for her already.

Agatha glanced up from the maps to see Sonje enter the library. When Sonje reached the table, Agatha gave her a look of understanding.

"Here is the map showing the road to Merton. There also appears to be a horse path that would be quicker," Agatha began. "They both join here at the entrance to the caves on the other side of the lake."

After studying the maps, Sonje replied, "I should have no trouble finding Merton. I can only hope that the rest of my mission is as easy."

"You will find a way, Gwladys," Agatha reassured her. "Come. Let's get your bags packed."

The two women worked together and soon had the saddlebags packed. Sonje took Bryant's clothes down to his office as she had promised him. On the way back to her room, she stopped in his room and took his journal from the night-stand. She returned to her room and carefully tucked it into the left pouch of the saddlebags.

As she turned to leave, her eyes fell on the chain mail shirt that lay next to the saddlebags. Slowly she caressed the smooth links before picking it up. She took it over to the chair next to the door and sat down. Her glow reflected off the bright metal as she traced the collar with her fingertip. Tiny dragons with outspread wings appeared as her finger passed over the metal.

She smiled as she leaned back into the chair and her glow faded. Perhaps things would work out after all. She would have to take a gift for Bryant's mother.

'Haskell,' she called in her mind.

'Come to my den,' Haskell replied. 'I will show you where to find what you seek.'

'Thank you, my friend,' Sonje replied as she rose.

She left the shirt on the table before leaving the room. Sonje hurried down to the great hall and opened the doors enough to slip through. She let her glow show her way up the stairs and into Haskell's den.

'It is a long walk. Would you like a ride?' Haskell asked as she approached him.

'Yes, thank you,' Sonje replied as she climbed up on the offered foreleg.

Once she was safely mounted, Haskell began walking to the outer entrance to his tunnel. The lengthening shadows at the cave entrance told Sonje that evening was swiftly falling. She could see why Haskell had brought her here. Around the tunnel, just inside the entrance, were bands of colored stones. On the slope below the entrance was a band of gold.

"Thank you, Haskell!" Sonje exclaimed as she dismounted. "Now if I only knew what to make for her."

'She used to collect carved figurines that the villagers would make,' Haskell suggested.

'I know now what to make,' Sonje said with excitement.

Carefully, she climbed down to the band of gold. Her glow brightened as she scooped a quantity of the soft metal from the surrounding rock. She climbed back up and placed the lump next to Haskell's clawed foot. Next she turned to the stones. She brushed across the bands of color with one hand and caught the stones in her other hand. The stones stuck together as they landed in her hand.

'Take me back to the great cavern, please,' Sonje said as she picked up the lump of gold. 'I had better have something to eat before I do any more with this.'

'The others are returning and Agatha is preparing a meal,' Haskell told her as she carefully mounted.

Soon Haskell and Sonje arrived at the inner entrance of his tunnel. She thanked him as she dismounted. Quickly, she left the caverns, climbed the stairs and hurried to her room. After placing the stones and gold on a table, she washed her hands before heading back downstairs.

As she entered the dining hall, Sonje saw that Agatha had begun to set the tables. Just as she reached the kitchen doorway, Agatha turned away from the pot she had been stirring.

"You look pale, Gwladys!" she exclaimed. "What is the matter?"

"I am making a gift for Lady Miranda," Sonje replied as she leaned on the door frame for support.

Agatha quickly ladled out a small bowl of soup from the pot and gave it to Sonje with a spoon.

"Sit down and eat this. The others will not mind," Agatha said as she turned Sonje towards the tables.

Sonje gratefully took her seat and began eating. Soon she felt her strength returning. Philip entered the room just as she set her spoon down. He approached her table and bowed.

"I have cleaned Guen's hooves and checked her shoes for your journey tomorrow," Philip reported.

"Thank you," Sonje replied. "I will be leaving at dawn."

"I will have her ready for you," he responded.

Philip bowed before turning to find a seat. The others were beginning to arrive and several women had begun helping Agatha set the place settings and food on the tables. Soon everyone was seated. Sonje rose from her chair.

"Lord Dracona and I want you to know how grateful we are for your support," she began. "It is our desire to bring peace and prosperity to the people of Dracona and Glynis. Times will be trying these first months. Lord Dracona and I will be very busy with the move of Glynis and settling the conflict with Burton. Until these objectives are settled, we are asking that you accept the rule of the councils we have appointed. We trust them to lead you wisely in our absence. It is our hope that our travels bring us safely back to Dracona."

A wave of relief swept over her as she saw the response on their faces. Haskell spoke to her as she took her seat.

'They are all very pleased with your speech,' Haskell began. 'I am pleased at the loyalties expressed by the villagers.'

'Thank you, Haskell,' Sonje returned as she began to eat.

As she ate, Sonje looked up and down the tables before her. The faces of the villagers showed curiosity and wonderment at what they saw. She knew that they must feel the same apprehension that she felt her first day at the castle. She realized that it must have taken a lot of courage and trust for them to even enter the forest around the castle.

As soon as the meal was over, Sonje hurried out to the great hall. She stood studying the dragons in the mosaic floor for several minutes before she felt ready to return to her room. As she turned towards the stairs, Agatha joined her.

"Have Haskell call me if you need anything," she said. "Remember you need your sleep for your journey."

"I will," Sonje responded with a smile. "I have a design in mind, so I shouldn't be long creating the gift."

"Good night then, Gwladys," Agatha said.

"Good night," Sonje said as she started up the stairs.

Once in her room, she checked her packed saddlebags and placed them on the table at the foot of the bed. Next she laid out a dress to wear in the morning. She prepared for bed before turning her attention to the gold and stones she had gathered earlier.

She sat on the edge of the bed and picked up the stones. Her glow brightened as she separated the stones by size and color. Next, she took the gold in her hands. As she worked the gold, the figure of a dragon emerged. It stood with wings outspread and neck arched gracefully. She set the dragon on the bedside table and stroked its neck, body, legs, and tail. Under the gentle touch of her fingers, scales appeared. When she was finished, she turned her attention to the stones again. She chose two brilliant blue stones and shaped them to make the eyes. As she set the blue stones in place, the gold formed around them to hold the stones. Next, she formed and placed tiny stones in stripes on the face, neck and legs. Soon she had finished.

Her head was spinning as she allowed her glow to fade. As she lay down on the bed she called to Haskell.

'Tell Agatha I am going to bed now.'

'I will,' Haskell replied. 'Good night.'

* * * * *

As he relayed Sonje's message, he heard Bryant calling.

'Haskell, where is Sonje?' Bryant's words came softly to Haskell.

'She is asleep,' Haskell replied noting the alarm in Bryant's tone. 'She made a gift for your mother.'

'A gift?' Bryant asked in a puzzled tone.

'A tiny jeweled gold dragon,' Haskell replied.

'That will please my mother,' Bryant replied sounding pleased. 'Tell her I tried to contact her tonight.'

'I will,' Haskell reassured him. 'How is your journey progressing?'

'Lonely,' Bryant replied. 'I haven't seen anything but trees and grass. The day after tomorrow I will turn west towards Burton.'

'Good,' Haskell responded.

'I am growing a beard and mustache to complete my disguise.'

'Good idea. You would be in grave danger if you were recognized.'

'Tell Sonje that I miss her and that I will try again tomorrow night.'

'I will tell her,' Haskell promised. 'Be careful and take care of yourself.'

'I will, My Friend,' Bryant replied.

* * * * *

Sonje woke as the sky turned from black to grey. She brushed through her hair and braided it. She wrapped the braid around her head and fastened it down before putting on the leather undershirt and chain mail. She put on the dress she had laid out the night before over the chain mail shirt. The dress was forest green and cut for riding. Next she settled the white cape around her shoulders and fastened the clasp. She pulled on the leather riding boots that were in the closet.

'Sonje?' Haskell asked sleepily.

'Yes, Haskell,' she replied as she picked up the small golden dragon.

'I spoke with Bryant last night. He was concerned when he couldn't contact you.'

'I should have made this figurine after talking to Bryant,' Sonje replied. 'Is he doing alright?'

'Yes, he says he is lonely and misses you. He is growing a beard and a mustache.'

'That is a good idea. Will he try to contact me tonight?'

'Yes.'

'Thank you, Haskell,' Sonje said as she tucked the dragon carefully into the saddle bags.

She took one last look around the room before she picked up the saddlebags with a rolled quilt and left the room. Philip and Agatha were waiting in the courtyard with Guen. Philip bowed before taking the saddlebags and quilt from her. As he secured the saddlebags and quilt, Agatha handed Sonje a slice of bread and cheese.

"Thank you, Agatha," Sonje said. "I will miss you."

"I will miss you also," Agatha replied. "I hope I have packed enough food and water for your journey."

"I have faith in you. I should reach Merton by tomorrow noon," Sonje reassured her.

Sonje placed her foot in Philip's hands and mounted.

"Safe journey, Gwladys," Agatha said.

"A speedy return, Gwladys," Philip said.

'Success in your negotiations,' Haskell added to their farewell wishes.

Sonje nodded to them before turning Guen towards the castle gate. Once out of the castle courtyard, she urged Guen to a trot. Soon they were headed up the horse-path that Agatha had found on the map.

* * * * *

"I have misgivings about her going," Agatha told Philip as Guen's hoof-beats faded.

"She knows how to take care of herself," Philip reassured her.

"Somehow I feel that something is going to go wrong."

"All we can do is make certain that nothing goes wrong here," Philip replied. "There is nothing more that we can do for Gwladys and Lord Dracona. They will have to take care of themselves until they return."

"You are right, Philip," Agatha agreed. "It is time to start our day."

As the sun crept down the courtyard walls, they parted ways. Agatha headed towards the kitchen and Philip headed towards the armory. By noon all of the villagers had been outfitted with weapons that suited their abilities. Edgard was supervising some practice fights when Florene called them to lunch.

"How is the army coming?" Florene asked Edgard and Philip as they followed the villagers to the dining hall.

"Some of them show some promise," Edgard replied. "Most of the others could probably do alright on strength alone. We must pray that Lord Bryant is successful in his mission before much blood is spilled."

After lunch, the villagers left to return to the village. Agatha, Hoyt and Edgard met in the library to work on their assigned responsibilities.

"The castle and surrounding town appear to be easily defendable," Edgard told Hoyt as they looked over a map of the area. "However, there is not enough information about the village to even suggest a plan of defense."

"Perhaps we could ask Haskell to fly one of us over the area to help fill in the details on this map," Hoyt suggested.

"If we could fly over at dawn, perhaps we could escape notice," Edgard agreed. "Haskell?"

'I have been listening and am willing to help,' Haskell replied to both men. 'I will land in the courtyard before dawn.'

"Thank you," Edgard said. "I will meet you there."

Chapter 13 – Dangers of the Journey

Bryant wiped his sweaty brow with his sleeve as he pulled Dusty to a stop. They were in a small clearing that was bordered on one side by a small creek. On the other side of the creek was a dirt road. He climbed down off the wagon and unhitched Dusty. As soon as the horse was staked out, he built a small fire. He watched the creek while he prepared his supper.

After eating, he walked over to the edge of the creek. The stream bed appeared to be smooth enough to afford an easy crossing. As he shifted his weight, the fading sunlight made the surface of a calm side-pool reflect his image. The face that was staring back at him was unfamiliar. His short beard and mustache along with his uncombed hair gave him a rough appearance. He smiled at the knowledge that his present appearance bore little resemblance to the Lord Dracona that had appeared before Burton's army. He returned to his fire and settled back against a tree.

'Sonje?' he called out in his mind.

'Bryant?' Sonje's voice inquired in his mind.

'Yes,' Bryant responded. 'I missed talking to you last night.'

'I missed you, too,' she replied. 'I didn't think that making your mother's gift would drain me so.'

'How is your journey?'

'These mountains are beautiful, but I wish you were here with me.' Sonje sighed. 'How is your journey?'

'Progressing,' Bryant replied. 'I have come across a road. Tomorrow I will follow it west towards Burton. My disguise is complete. I don't think anyone will recognize me.'

'Good. If I read the map right, I should arrive in Merton by tomorrow noon.'

'If you took the horse path, you are right. I will contact you again tomorrow night.'

'I will look forward to hearing from you again. I love you.'

'I love you, too,' Bryant responded. 'Sleep well'

'Sleep well.'

Sonje sighed again as she wrapped the quilt over her cape and settled back against a tree. She grew sleepy as she watched the stars appear one by one.

* * * * *

She was awakened the next morning by the sound of Guen stirring. Her small fire had gone out during the night. She ate her breakfast without rebuilding it. Soon she had saddled Guen and fastened the saddlebags and quilt to the saddle. As soon as everything was secured, Sonje mounted up.

The road had overgrown with grass from disuse. Sonje slowed Guen as the road turned away from the edge of the lake and straight into the black maw of the mountain. There was a torch in a bracket just inside the opening. She realized that it would be wise to use the torch instead of her own light so she would not alarm Bryant's family. Soon she had lit the torch and remounted. Carefully she urged Guen forward as she held the torch high to light the way. Sonje found the road beside the river to be surprisingly smooth for being the floor of a cave. She kept Guen at a swift walk so the horse would not slip. Time seemed to creep by slowly as they descended toward the sea.

Sonje was relieved to at last glimpse a light other than her torch. She breathed a sigh of relief to find the torch bracket near the mouth of the cave. She extinguished the torch in a sand filled ledge and placed it in the bracket without dismounting. Guen seemed nervous and reluctant to leave the cave. Sonje gently urged her mount forward into the sunlight. Several feet out of the cave entrance, Sonje realized she should have Bryant's journal in her hand as she approached Merton. She drew Guen to a stop before taking her foot out of the stirrup and turning in the saddle. As her hand closed around the journal, Sonje heard a growl from above the cave entrance. As Guen reared up, she tried to regain the stirrup and posts, but it was too late. The world turned topsy-turvy as she fell from Guen's back. As Sonje hit the ground, everything went black.

* * * * *

Bryant wiped the sweat from his brow with his sleeve. The mid-day sun was still warm in spite of the approaching cold season. As they rounded a bend in the road, the sounds of Dusty's hoof beats were drowned out by shouts and laughter.

Bryant felt his muscles tense as he saw the group of soldiers lounging by the side of the road. He hoped they would pay no attention to him as he passed by.

"Hey, farmer!" one of the soldiers called out. "Got anything to eat in that cow cart?"

Dusty's ears flicked down at the insult and laughter that followed. Bryant drew her to a stop and climbed off the cart. He laid his hand on her rump before going to the back of the cart.

"I have some fine squash and grains," he answered in a nasal tone. "I'd be glad to sell some to you."

"You'd be glad to give us some or it might cost you your life!" another said as he strode towards the cart.

Bryant tried to circle around the cart to where he had tucked the swords and cape under the seat, but he was surrounded before he could get that far. He was grabbed by two men and drug away from the cart. As he struggled to get away, he felt a sharp pain on the back of his head and everything went black.

* * * * *

"Who do you think she is?" one of the men asked as they stood over the young woman.

"She wears a dragon clasp," commented another as he gently rolled her onto her back.

"And a sword," another commented as her cape fell open.

"Look at the circlet of silver on her head and the book she was laying on," said the fourth man as he led the limping horse to where the other men stood. "We will take her to the lady."

The other men nodded then knelt to lift her.

* * * * *

The captain laughed as he watched the farmer go limp under his blow. He sheathed his dagger as the men dumped the farmer by the side of the road. Before he could reach the cart to examine the contents, the captain heard a howl from the surrounding forest that sent chills up his spine. He spun around just in time to see several wolves step out of the trees. The wolves snarled with bared teeth as they stepped around the farmer and approached the soldiers. They ignored the frightened horse as they drove the soldiers away from the cart.

"Let's get out of here," the captain ordered as he ran to his frightened mount.

As the soldiers beat a hasty retreat, the wolves turned to the unconscious farmer. A scream split the air as an eagle swooped out of the sky and landed on the man's chest. The eagle chattered and screamed again. The wolves whined and lay down with their heads down.

"This is no ordinary farmer, sister," said a woman's voice in the trees.

"But who is he?" came the reply. "Only a king may fly an eagle in the hunt."

A whine of acknowledgment came from the large black wolf that lay nearest to the fallen man. The two women emerged slowly from the trees followed by a horse drawn wagon. The younger woman guided the older woman as she walked. The eagle turned towards the man's face and nudged his cheek with its beak. Then it turned back towards the women.

"I think the eagle seeks aid for the man, sister," the young woman commented with amazement.

The eagle bobbed its head, then leapt and fluttered to a position near the man's head.

"Take me to his horse," the older woman said. "The poor thing sounds frightened."

The young woman led her to the mare before returning to their own wagon. As the older woman clucked and crooned to the frightened mare, the younger woman brought a box out of the wagon. As she made her way to the fallen man, the wolves moved aside to leave her a path.

She set the box down near him and laid a cloth on the ground. On the cloth, she laid a smaller cloth and began measuring herbs. She ground them with a mortar and pestle before pouring them on to the smaller cloth. She added a few drops of a pungent oil and quickly folded the cloth with the herbs inside. She took a strip of cloth from the box and lifted his head to tie the packet in place over the swelling bruise. As she gently laid his head back down, something caught her eye under the collar of his shirt. She pulled it out to see what it was. She was surprised to find a curious gold pendant with a crowned dragon etched on the stone.

"This is no farmer, sister," she said as she pulled open the lacings to reveal a chain mail shirt with dragons etched on the collar. "And certainly more than a fine gentleman."

"What tells you this?"

"A chain mail shirt and a dragon with a crown."

"We must get him to cover before the soldiers return."

The young woman tucked the pendant back under his shirt and tightened the shirt laces before passing the open bottle of oil near his nose. He coughed and sputtered before opening his eyes.

* * * * *

Bryant found a young woman looking down on him with a bottle in her hand.

"Who are you?" he asked the young woman as he sat up.

"There is no time now," she replied as she returned the bottle to the box beside her.

He groaned from the pain in his head as she helped him to stand. As he looked around he was met by a curious sight. An old woman held Dusty's bridle and he was surrounded by wolves that lay with their tails wagging. There was a flutter behind him as Ernest flew up and landed on his shoulder. He glanced at the women wondering how much they had figured out. He turned to the great black wolf beside him.

"Come my friend," he said to it.

The wolf stood and followed Bryant as he walked to where his cart was. Bryant lifted the old woman onto the seat of the cart and waited as the younger woman turned the wagon around. Bryant led Dusty as he followed the wagon into the forest. As they entered the forest, he glanced back to see the wolves pacing and rolling to cover the tracks leaving the road.

After a distance, the trees opened up into a meadow. Bryant noticed signs that the women had been camping in the meadow for some time. Bryant stopped and lifted the woman down. The black wolf nuzzled her hand and led her to where the camp fire had been.

"Ernest, see if you can find a rabbit for tonight's meal," Bryant said, "and notify the wolves if there are soldiers approaching."

The eagle bobbed its head once before launching into the air.

"We should be safe here tonight," the young woman said. "But we should move on tomorrow."

"I probably won't be safe wearing these clothes." Bryant commented. "I need to change them somehow."

"I think we can work something out." the young woman responded. "But first we would like to know a little more about you."

Bryant's heart sunk. He had hoped that they wouldn't ask. He felt Dusty nuzzle his arm in reassurance.

"Let's get these horses unhitched and then we can talk," Bryant said, hoping he would have time to figure out what to tell them.

As he began to unhitch Dusty, the young woman nodded and went to unhitch her team. Bryant decided he should try to contact Haskell.

'Haskell!' Bryant called in his mind. 'I need your advice.'

'Yes, Bryant?' Haskell's reply was faint but clear.

'I was attacked by soldiers wanting a free meal. Two women and their wolves rescued me. They seem willing to help me further, but are asking about my true identity. They have figured out that I am not just a farmer.' Bryant told Haskell quickly. 'What should I tell them?'

'Do you feel you can trust them?'

'Yes.'

'Then tell them the truth,' Haskell advised. 'Notify me if you need further help.'

'Thank you, my friend.'

Bryant jumped as someone placed their hand on his shoulder.

"Are you alright?" the young woman asked with concern.

"Yes," Bryant answered as he finished removing Dusty's bridle and turned her loose. "Let's sit down. This will take a while to explain."

He laid the harness and bridle across the cart seat and drew his cape wrapped swords from under the seat. Bryant and the woman walked to where the old woman was sitting and sat down.

"I know that you have realized that I am not the simple farmer that I would like everyone to believe me to be," Bryant began. "I am in grave danger if Burton's soldiers discover my true identity. I must tell you that by knowing my identity you could be in danger as well."

"We live our life constantly on the move from place to place," the old woman responded. "It will not be the first time we have faced danger."

"Nor the last," the younger woman stated. "Tell us your tale and we will tell you ours. Then we will decide if our paths lie together or apart."

"And if we part, we shall keep your secrets as our own," finished the older woman.

Bryant felt his left wrist grow warm as he looked first to one woman, then the other as he searched for a way to begin.

"To the southeast of Burton lies a great mountain that is the remains of a volcano. In the mountain is a maze of caverns and tunnels. At the foot of the mountain lay a castle and a town. The castle is my home. The caverns are the homes of dragons. The castle is called Dracona and I, Bryant Donley, am its lord."

"Why do you travel to Burton alone and disguised as a farmer?" the young woman asked.

"Far to the north lies a narrow valley in the great snows. This valley is warmed by an encircling ring of volcanoes to a lush green eternal summer. This valley is called Glynis. It is home to a people that live ten times longer than most. From the time that they first settled there, they knew that their paradise could not last forever. They were given a riddle to solve that would give them their key to survival," Bryant began.

He told the two women about the riddle and finding Sonje and her father in the forest. Soon he had told them most of the story of Dracona and Glynis.

"So are you the man foretold by the riddle?" the old woman asked.

"Yes," Bryant replied before continuing. "My ancestors traveled out of Glynis and settled in Dracona. They built the castle with the help and guidance of the dragons. By the time Sonje realized that I am the man of the riddle we had already fallen in love. We are engaged to be married, but there are a few things left to clear up."

"In Burton?" the young woman asked.

"Yes. After I had made amends to the villagers, King Gustave and his soldiers came intending to conquer the village. The villagers swore loyalty to Dracona instead of Burton, and so did the dragons. Gustave swore to return before making a hasty retreat," Bryant replied.

"So why go to Burton in disguise?" the old woman asked.

"And alone?" the other added.

"None of the villagers know how to defend their land against a trained army. The Queen of Glynis was killed because she refused to submit Glynis to Gustave's rule. In an effort to escape, Sonje cut off Gustave's hand. He knows she is now in Dracona."

"So you come alone to invade and conquer Burton?" the young woman asked incredulously.

"Not exactly," Bryant replied. "I have information that Gustave may not be the rightful king of Burton. I hope to place the rightful king on the throne and forge an alliance with him. I wish for Dracona to live in peace with its neighbors."

"Are you armed with more than a hunting knife?" the old woman asked.

Bryant unwrapped the swords.

"Two swords?" the young woman asked.

"Yes," Bryant responded as he drew the dragon grip sword from its scabbard. "This sword was forged by the first Lord Dracona in his dragon's fire. I am the first to bear it. It is only to be used to protect others. The other is the sword I have always carried."

"The writing on that sword is like the writing on the things my father had," the young woman said. "Our mother kept them and gave them to me before she died. I will get them."

As the young woman rose, Bryant looked from her to the old woman in disbelief.

"You two are sisters?" he asked.

"Riva's father died in an accident soon after she was born. Our mother was traveling back to her parent's home when she met my father in the forest outside the village. He was a woodcutter and provided well for us until a tree he was cutting fell and killed Mother. He dug two graves and buried her in one. He died the next morning of a broken heart."

"We stayed for a while but we soon noticed that while I stayed young, Xylia was growing older," the young woman said as she placed the box she was carrying down in front of Bryant.

The box contained a few items of clothing, a couple of books and a few unusual objects. Bryant lifted one of the books out that looked similar to the older ones in his library. He opened it and began to read out loud.

"Left Glynis this morning before sunrise. Perhaps I'll die tonight, frozen in the ice and snow, but my dreams promise more for me than that.

Mother's dreams told her of a granddaughter bearing her name living in a forest south of Glynis. I know I must go on."

"Glynis is a reoccurring name in my dreams," Riva said. "Now I know why."

"And we know why you remain young while I grow old." Xylia added.

"There's more," Bryant said before continuing to read. "Brought along great Grandfather's journal and the things he and great Grandmother brought into Glynis. I have read the journal several times, but I still can't make any sense out of it. Perhaps someday someone will understand. Mother said perhaps the man in great Grandmother's last words will understand. Great Grandfather said that the journal and the things with it would be needed someday. He died after giving them to Grandfather. I leave Glynis to find the mysterious man in Great Grandmother's last words."

"Then these are for you to decipher," Riva said.

"I would like to send them straight to Dracona and not risk their safety in Burton," Bryant said as he looked over the objects in the box.

"We will think of something," Xylia said. "Let's eat and get some rest first."

* * * * *

Sonje's efforts to turn her head were met with blinding pain. She paused to catch her breath and remembered falling. What she was laying on was too soft to be the rocky cave entrance. Slowly she opened her eyes just enough to see if it was dark or light. As her eyes began to focus she found herself looking at a rough stone wall. Shadows danced dimly across the wall as if from a fire or torch. Slowly and carefully she moved her left arm. She was relieved to find it was not bound.

Sonje lay very still and listened. She heard the hissing and popping of a fire. Suddenly there was a metallic click and footsteps. She heard a strange rhythmic whooshing before the door clicked shut.

"Is she awake yet?" a woman's voice asked. "Well, she should wake soon. Let's put this soup on the fire to warm it. She'll be hungry when she does wake."

Sonje heard some shuffling.

"Yes, her head will hurt for some time," the woman said. "She took a nasty fall."

Sonje wondered who the woman was talking to and it made her head hurt worse. Her stomach pinched and growled as the smell of the soup reached her.

"Now remember to treat her respectfully," the woman admonished her mysteriously silent companion. "I must return to the meeting now. Send me word if she awakens."

Sonje heard the door open and shut again. She slowly let out her breath with relief. She now knew that she was not being held prisoner. She still did not know if the woman was Lady Miranda or even if she was in Merton. Her stomach growled again and she groaned softly as she tried again to move her head to the right. The throbbing pain took her breath away. When the throbbing subsided, she opened her eyes again to find a young woman standing over her. The woman held out a small leaf to Sonje and then motioned from the leaf to her mouth.

"You want me to eat the leaf?"

The woman nodded. Sonje took the leaf and sniffed it. She smiled as she recognized the bitter scent of it. She chewed it gratefully knowing that it would soon relieve the throbbing in her head. While she waited for the herb to do its work, Sonje watched the young woman carefully dish up a bowl of soup. She cut a thick slice of bread to set on a tray with the bowl.

The woman approached Sonje and motioned to the table, then the bed. Sonje slowly sat up. As her head began throbbing again, she put her hand to her forehead above her left eye. In place of the familiar silver circlet, she found a poultice tied with a strip of cloth.

"I think I'll stay here to eat," Sonje replied to the unspoken question.

The young woman nodded and helped her lean upright against the head of the bed before bringing the tray of food. Sonje ate slowly and studied the young woman as she sat in a chair next to the bed. The young woman's skin had strange rough patches on her face and arms. Her red hair hung loosely down around her shoulders and nearly to her waist. Her eyes were not quite brown and not quite green. She would briefly meet Sonje's gaze, but quickly glanced away. Sonje felt stronger when she had finished eating.

"Thank you, that was delicious," Sonje said as she placed the spoon back on the tray.

The young woman stood and took the tray over to the table. She then opened the door and went out. Before Sonje had a chance to identify the rhythmic whooshing sound, the young woman was back.

Sonje leaned back and looked around the small room. It was simply furnished with rough wood furniture. It seemed crowded, yet tidy. Next to the bed was a small dresser. She spotted her silver circlet lying on top of the dresser. It was slightly dented and scratched in places. She thought about fixing it, but realized that it would not be wise considering her present circumstances.

Suddenly the door opened. A tall figure in a cape entered the room. Sonje caught her breath as the woman's face was revealed. Her strong resemblance to Bryant left no doubt in Sonje's mind that the woman must be Lady Miranda. The young woman curtsied before taking her cape and motioning to Sonje.

"I am glad to see you awake, Gwladys," the woman said as she approached the bed. "Brenndah will care for you while you are healing."

"She has been most kind," Sonje replied.

"Haskell told me Bryant was sending someone to Merton, but wouldn't say who or why. When the men brought you to me, I knew that Bryant had sent you. I have read his journal and understand your purpose in coming to Merton."

"Bryant was worried that I might be greeted with hostility, My Lady," Sonje replied. "That is why he insisted that I seek out you, Lady Miranda, and that I should speak the name of Lady Aloysia."

"There is still much shame felt by the people of Merton," Lady Miranda responded. "Brenndah was rescued from her burning home after seeing her parents die. She has not spoken since."

The burned and missing roofs of the town flashed in Sonje's mind.

"The body heals faster than the heart and mind," Sonje said with understanding.

"You must rest now," Lady Miranda said. "In the morning we need you to show us your plan on our map. Brenndah will get you what you need."

"Thank you," Sonje replied as Brenndah placed Lady Miranda's cape about her shoulders.

As the door clicked shut, Brenndah turned back to Sonje.

"I am sad to hear of your ordeal," Sonje told her. "I saw my mother killed and could do nothing to save her. It must have been even worse for you."

Brenndah nodded and met Sonje's gaze for the first time. She gently helped Sonje to lie back down and arranged her comfortably. She was too tired to try to call out to Bryant, but sensed his thoughts in the back of her mind and that he was talking to someone. As she tried to listen to his thoughts Sonje soon drifted off to sleep.

Chapter 14 – New Allies and New Plans

Bryant's head was still sore when he woke in the morning. The women were still sleeping as he stood up and surveyed the meadow. Several of the wolves stirred, but laid their heads back down as he passed. Soon he located the herbs that he was looking for. He winced at the bitter flavor, but knew that it would relieve the pain.

As Bryant got the fire started, Riva and Xylia awoke. Riva began to make breakfast. Xylia sat by the fire with one of the wolves. They ate in silence as each was involved in their own thoughts. As the dishes were being packed back in the wagon, Riva was the first to break the silence.

"There is a way to dye your hair brown and some of Father's clothes might fit you," she began. "I think it would be best if you had a different wagon also. Yours might be recognized."

"Riva, I feel that you should travel with Bryant," Xylia suggested. "Perhaps I could make it to Dracona with the horse and cart if it is not too far."

"Dracona is about two and a half days' travel from here," Bryant replied. "You should take a couple of the wolves with you for protection. The eagle could lead you to the castle. I can contact Haskell and tell him you are coming."

"Then it is settled," Riva said. "I'll pack some food for you now so that you can start your journey before noon."

As the women prepared for Xylia to travel, Bryant began to hitch Dusty to the cart.

'Haskell!' Bryant called out in his mind.

'Yes, Bryant?' Haskell answered.

'One of the women will be bringing Dusty and the cart to Dracona. Her name is Xylia. She will be bringing a box of important items concerning the origins of the people of Glynis. She is blind and will be guided by Ernest and some wolves.'

'I understand. I will notify Hoyt, Edgard, and Agatha immediately.'

'Thank you, My Friend.'

'They will send Philip to meet her and guide her to Dracona,' Haskell said after a moment.

Ernest landed on the side of the cart as Bryant finished harnessing Dusty to the cart.

"I'm glad to see you," Bryant said. "Xylia needs to be taken to the castle at Dracona. You two will have to get her there safely. She will bring along a couple of wolves for additional protection."

Ernest and Dusty both bobbed their heads in acknowledgment. Bryant pulled the cart up next to the wagon so it could be packed for the trip. Soon Xylia was on her way. Riva collected bark while Bryant filled a pot with water and put it on the fire to heat. Soon the bark was in the boiling water.

"How long will this last?" Bryant asked, suddenly realizing that he was not certain about having brown hair at his wedding.

"It should grow out quickly," Riva replied. "And it will fade after you wash your hair a few times."

"Good," Bryant said.

Riva wrapped the end of a small stick with strips torn from Bryant's shirt. Then she dipped it carefully in the pot. Slowly and carefully she dabbed the cloth end on Bryant's hair.

"With this darker hair you may want to shave off the beard and mustache. It would be hard to treat it every day to keep it the same color as your hair," Riva suggested.

"Do you have something polished so I can see what I'm shaving?" Bryant asked.

Riva nodded and brought a silver platter from her wagon. Bryant carefully shaved with his hunting knife. His hair had dried and was almost curly.

"This is definitely a change," Bryant said.

"Go in the wagon and try these on," Riva said as she handed him some clothes.

Bryant climbed into the wagon and put on the dark grey pants and blue shirt.

"These fit well," Bryant said as he climbed out of the wagon.

"Then we should bury your old clothes."

Several of the wolves dug a hole while Bryant placed his swords under the wagon seat and hitched up the horses. Soon the old clothes were buried and they began their journey to Burton.

* * * * *

Sonje slept deeply and awoke refreshed but still sore. Brenndah was already awake and preparing breakfast. She brought Sonje another leaf to ease her pain and a basin of water to wash in. The two ate in silence at the small table. Sonje felt much better after eating.

Brenndah removed the poultice and offered Sonje a brush. Sonje smiled and began to unbraid her hair and brush it as Brenndah washed the dishes. Soon Sonje's hair was brushed out and she braided it. She picked up the silver circlet from the dresser. Its condition told her just how hard she had fallen. Brenndah looked at the circlet then to Sonje with a questioning look.

"I think I can repair it without expending too much energy, but I do not want to frighten you," Sonje said. "Do you trust me?"

Brenndah nodded. Sonje slowly let her light glow. She smoothed the metal between her fingers before placing the circlet on her head. She allowed her light to fade. Brenndah smiled at Sonje.

"All of the people of Glynis can glow," Sonje told her. "But not all can shape metal and stone as I can."

Brenndah nodded and closed her eyes. Faintly at first, she began to glow. Her glow was a fiery red as it encircled her. She opened her eyes and smiled. She held out her arm and stroked it with her other hand. The skin became smooth at her touch then she stroked her arm again, returning the scarring. Sonje gasped in surprise.

"Does anyone else know about this?" Sonje asked.

Brenndah shook her head.

"There will be a time when you do not need to hide your talent anymore."

Brenndah smiled as her glow faded. The door opened and Lady Miranda stepped into the room.

"You are looking much better," she said.

"Brenndah has taken good care of me," Sonje answered.

"Are you strong enough to attend the meeting?"

"Yes"

Brenndah brought her cape to her and helped her put it on. Sonje followed Lady Miranda out the door. She was amazed to realize that the town was built on a cliff top above the ocean. The houses were built of stones roughly shaped to fit together. Some were built on several levels to accommodate the uneven surface of the cliff. Others were built in wide crevices of an upper cliff.

Sonje followed Lady Miranda to what appeared to be double doors set into the face of the cliff. They were met by other people at the end of a rough, torch-lit tunnel. Lady Miranda led her down to the far end of a large spherical chamber in the rock. Opposite the tunnel, was a large map carved into the wall. Silence fell over the cavern as Lady Miranda stood before the map.

"For over a hundred years, we have lived in Merton. We fled our family's shame and came to this rocky perch above the ocean. Our fields abandoned for the rolling ocean. We also left behind our duties and responsibilities. We left my husband, Lord Eamon, and our son, Lord Bryant," Lady Miranda said. "Two nights ago I dreamed of Lord Eamon. He told me that a new day was dawning and that our heads need not bow in shame any longer. He said that the dragon shall wear a crown."

She paused, waiting for the murmuring of the people to stop.

"I awoke with a feeling of urgency as though the day would bring change to our family. That day Gwladys Sonje was brought to us."

She motioned Sonje to her side. She held up Bryant's journal.

"Gwladys Sonje brought Lord Bryant's journal. Written in his own hand is an accounting of his meeting her and her father. It tells of her knowledge of Lord Fanchon's origins. And of their plans to marry," Lady Miranda smiled for the first time. "It also tells of the saving of a farmer from the village. Perhaps Gwladys Sonje can help us understand the importance of these things."

Sonje had not expected such a large group. Her mind raced through what she knew must be said.

"My father and I come from Glynis, as did Lord Fanchon and the original settlers of Dracona. Glynis is a verdant green valley that is protected from the northern snows by a ring of volcanoes. Recently the volcanoes have become more active, threatening our valley. Our leader foretold of this as our people stumbled out of the snow generations ago. She also gave a riddle holding the key to our salvation."

Sonje paused. The intent expressions of the people encouraged her to continue.

She began to tell them about the riddle and what it now meant. As she explained what had happened in Burton, she could not stop the image of her mother lying on the floor as they left through the window from flashing through her mind. Then she told them about meeting Bryant and that her sister lived in the village with her husband and children.

"King Gustave wanted the inhabitants of Glynis to be his slaves. He has also threatened the village. One of the village elders was attacked by Gustave's scouts. He was saved by Lord Bryant and Haskell. Since then the villagers have been told the truth about Dracona's past and have forgiven Rolf and all of Dracona."

Sonje heard the murmuring among the people. A quick glance at Lady Miranda's smile gave her the strength to continue.

"Lord Bryant and I gained some news that Gustave is not the rightful king of Burton. He has gone in disguise to try to find the rightful king and place him on the throne. We hope that we can make peace with Burton so that the people of Glynis might be safely moved to Dracona."

Sonje saw the alarm in the people's eyes and in their murmurings.

"Bryant felt that since the villagers were no match for Burton's army that a more discreet attack on Burton's throne would be better. I am here to ask your help so that the people of Glynis can be moved by ocean."

Sonje waited as her proposal was discussed in hushed tones. She glanced in Lady Miranda's direction. As their eyes met, she smiled. Lady Miranda stepped forward and raised her hands for silence.

"There is more that Gwladys Sonje can tell us, but it can wait until tomorrow," she said. "She can rest while we discuss the move of Glynis by ocean."

At Lady Miranda's nod, a young girl came forward and bowed before Sonje. As she rose, she smiled and extended her hand. Sonje smiled and took the girl's hand. The girl led Sonje back to Brenndah's house and left when she was safely inside. Brenndah offered her more of the soup which she gratefully accepted. Soon she was back in bed and asleep.

* * * * *

The journey to Burton was uneventful for Bryant and Riva. As they approached the city, the road became more crowded. There were many soldiers among the other travelers, but none gave them more than a precursory glance.

"How are we to find the rightful heir?" Riva asked as they entered the city gates.

"As a young boy, I learned that the castle staff members usually know more than the residents," Bryant replied. "Also, Sonje told me of a scullery boy that had been trying to tell them something."

"Then we will set up near the castle. Xylia and I have been doing fortune telling to earn a living. Perhaps we can find out a few things and find that boy."

"Good idea," Bryant said in agreement.

They traveled in silence through the crowded streets. Bryant noticed that the people didn't seem very happy. Even the soldiers seemed to be less than cheerful. Soon they came to a plaza at the castle gate. Riva went into the wagon and brought out a bundle and some poles. Bryant tied the horses to a hitching post as Riva set up a small tent. As Riva climbed back into the wagon, some soldiers approached.

"What do you think you are doing here?" one asked with an authoritative tone.

"Madame Riva will foretell the future and give personal fortune readings for a small fee," Bryant announced in answer. "Come back this evening and learn your future."

"We will return," the soldier responded. "Her fortune telling had better be real or you will both lose your heads."

Riva emerged again with a small table and two chairs as the soldiers disappeared into the crowd. Bryant helped her set the table and the chairs into the tent.

"That was close," Bryant said. "I thought we were going to be thrown out or in the dungeon."

"You covered well," Riva replied. "Let's have something to eat before we finish setting up. We will take our first customer at dusk."

After a cold meal, they finished setting up. In the tent a multicolored cloth covered the table to the dirt below it. On the center of the table was a stand made of greenish metal. Four clawed feet rested on the table and supported a small horizontal ring and a large vertical ring. On the top of the large ring rested a circular lamp. On the small ring rested a sphere of crystal. Outside the tent, they placed two lamps on tall poles. Riva gave Bryant a wide red sash to tie about his waist. She then went back into the wagon. Bryant lit the lamps. Soon a curious crowd began to gather.

"The spirits have guided us to this fair city. Madame Riva will reveal to you your futures for only a small silver coin," Bryant announced as he strutted before the tent.

A hush fell on the murmuring crowd as Riva exited the wagon. She was dressed in a crimson dress and her dark hair fell to below her waist. She seemed not to notice the crowd as she approached the tent. Bryant bowed low before her as she entered the tent.

"Who will be the first to learn of the future?" Bryant asked.

The first to enter the tent was the soldier who had spoken to Bryant earlier that day. Bryant searched the crowd anxiously as he brought each new customer from the crowd. Near midnight the crowd thinned. Bryant thought he saw something move in the shadow of the castle gate. A hunched figure stepped cautiously out of the shadows. Soon the two stood alone in the plaza. Bryant knew that this was the boy he had been looking for.

"Tonight your fortune will be told for free," Bryant told him.

A crooked smile spread across the boy's face as he finally met Bryant's gaze. He led the boy into the tent. Riva sat with her eyes closed and her hands on the table in front of her. Bryant motioned for the boy to sit. Riva opened her eyes and stared at the sphere.

"You come not in your true form," Riva said softly. "The time for change is here. A dragon's breath will bring the moment you have waited for. The spirit of the city will be cleansed with blood. The way will be made clear for you to assume your birthright."

Bryant was amazed at Riva's prediction. As Riva's eyes closed, the boy took Bryant's hand and kissed it.

"Gwladys Sonje and Regis Auberon asked that I find you and help you," Bryant confessed to the boy. "Are you the rightful king of Burton?"

The boy smiled and nodded. Riva opened her eyes and stood.

"We will watch for you at the castle gate tomorrow morning," Bryant said. "We will follow you to a meeting place of your choosing."

The boy nodded and left the tent. Riva smiled.

"How did you know?" Bryant asked.

"It is not by accident that I came by this trade," Riva confessed. "I can truly see into the future if I so will it. It doesn't make accepting misfortune easier, just less surprising."

"Let's get some sleep," Bryant said. "Tomorrow will be a long day."

* * * * *

Sonje awoke feeling refreshed and free of pain. Brenndah smiled as she dished up hot porridge. As they finished breakfast, Lady Miranda opened the door.

"Good morning, My Lady," Sonje said in greeting.

"Good morning, Gwladys," Lady Miranda replied. "And to you also, Brenndah. How do you feel this morning?"

"Much better, thank you."

"I have some questions for you if you are up to it."

"Yes, I would be happy to answer any questions that you may have," Sonje replied. "I would also like to update your map."

"Good. Let's go to the cavern first. I have some questions about the location of the villages you spoke of. Brenndah can fetch the stone carver to update the map."

"That will be unnecessary," Sonje said. "I am able to do it myself."

Lady Miranda's face showed surprise. Brenndah smiled and nodded reassuringly. Sonje followed Lady Miranda to the doors in the cliff.

"We will not need that," Sonje said as Lady Miranda reached for a torch to light. "I do not know how much Bryant put in his journal. There are many things about Glynis that Dracona has forgotten. This is one of those things."

Sonje shut the door behind them and let her light shine. Lady Miranda gasped in surprise.

"You and the others have this ability also. You have just never learned to use it."

"And Bryant?"

"Yes. His light is orange, but like mine, it is changing to white as he becomes regis or king. My father has already passed the mantle of leadership to him."

The women walked in silence to the map.

"Each of our people possesses certain talents. Some have the ability to heal the body, others see the future. Some can form metal and stone to their will, others can talk to animals and some can even understand when they speak back. There are many talents and many combinations of talents."

Sonje placed her hands flat on the rock wall before her. As her light increased, new lines began to form until the map was completed to include Glynis and all the lands visited in Sonje's journeys. Her light faded and she sank to her knees.

"Are you alright?" Lady Miranda asked in a worried tone.

"Yes. The use of some talents carries a heavier price than others. I just need to sit for a while."

Lady Miranda led her to a bench and helped her to sit.

"Ask your questions," Sonje said after a while.

"Your additions to the map have already answered some of my questions. Some of the others are much more personal."

Sonje nodded.

"Do you love my son or are you marrying him just to save Glynis?"

"When I first met Bryant, I was both afraid of and attracted to him. I heard of the villagers fears of him before I really got to know him. After arriving at the castle, I discovered him to be kind and thoughtful. Through the books in the library I discovered the origins of the people of Dracona. But, by then I already was prepared to give up the Quest and everything else to marry Bryant. I had always been afraid of actually finding the man of the Riddle and not loving him. Then I was afraid that Bryant didn't love me."

"Why has Bryant gone to Burton alone?"

"When my parents and I were in Burton, Gustave killed my mother and I cut off his hand. Bryant thinks Gustave may descend from the thirteenth member of Fanchon's group," Sonje explained. "He felt that he must go alone to protect Dracona, Glynis and me."

Sonje drew her half of Malvin's Heart from under her bodice.

"He wears the other half of Malvin's Heart. It allows us to speak through thought. Also, he carries Fanchon's sword."

"I have seen that sword kill those who tried to claim it," Lady Miranda said with alarm.

As she began describing what the inscription on the sword meant and what had happened when Bryant first picked it up Lady Miranda's expression betrayed her amazement. She told about Gale preserving her mother's body and that Bryant had promised to take her body for a proper burial when he returned to Dracona. She felt the tears began to form.

"You miss him," Lady Miranda said.

"Yes I do," Sonje said softly. "I don't know how I could go on if he did not return. Through Malvin's heart I can sense his emotions if I concentrate. It is a great comfort to me right now."

* * * * *

Miranda's heart ached as she saw the tears streaming down Sonje's face. She knew how it felt to lose someone she loved. She put her arms around Sonje and held her.

"Eamon and I had both hoped for and dreaded the day that Bryant discovered love," Miranda said softly. "After Rolf's tragic end, we were afraid that Bryant might suffer the same fate. I am happy that he found you. In reading his journal, I discovered how very lonely he was. He was actually afraid of falling in love with you. When he finally understood that you would live as long as he would, it was like the sun had pierced through the dark clouds overhead. He loves you very much, and so do I."

"I had a gift for you in my saddle bags," Sonje said as she began to dry her tears. "Everything has happened so fast that I haven't even had time to ask where they are or how Guen is doing."

"She has several scratches on her rump, but she will heal nicely. Your saddlebags are in the stable behind Brenndah's house," Miranda answered. "Let's get back so that you can rest before this afternoon's meeting."

The two women rose and walked slowly back to Brenndah's house. Guen whinnied in greeting to Sonje. The scratches were deep and just starting to heal.

"Bring Brenndah out here. I think she can help," Sonje said.

Miranda was puzzled, but went to get Brenndah. The girl put her hand over her mouth in horror as she saw Guen's injuries.

"Do you think you can help her?" Sonje asked.

Brenndah glanced at Miranda and back to Sonje.

"I have shown her what I can do and explained about our people's talents," Sonje said.

Brenndah opened the door and entered the stall. She began to have a red glow around her as she placed her hands on the mare. Miranda watched in amazement as Brenndah moved her hands over the wounds, they closed. Soon all the wounds were closed and only faint scars showed in her hair. Guen turned and nuzzled Brenndah's cheek softly.

"She is grateful," Sonje said. "Thank you."

"I had always suspected that Brenndah's healing abilities were extraordinary, but I had no idea that she could do that," Miranda said stunned that Brenndah had such a talent. "I think I need to sit down."

Sonje shut the door and picked up the saddle bags. The three went into the house and sat at the table. Sonje drew a small jeweled dragon from the saddlebags and gave it to Miranda.

"You made this for me?" she asked in amazement. "It is beautiful."

"I wanted so much for you to like me. I thought a gift might help."

"The happiness you brought my son is enough to make me love you," Miranda said. "Can you teach me how to glow and help me find my talents?"

"Close your eyes and desire to glow. Think about the light surrounding you."

Miranda closed her eyes and followed Sonje's instructions

"Now open your eyes."

Miranda saw a bright blue glow surrounding her.

"It's amazing!"

"With time you will learn to use it and your talents as Brenndah learned to use hers," Sonje said.

"I've noticed Bryant talking to Llewellyn and Evelina once told me that the horse understands him perfectly," Miranda said, then paused as Evelina spoke to her. "She says she doesn't think Bryant realizes that he is doing something others can't."

They all jumped in surprise at the knock on the door. Miranda extinguished her light as Brenndah opened the door. A young boy stood at the door. He bowed low before speaking.

"The ships are in," he said. "The feast begins in two hours."

"Thank you," Miranda responded.

The boy bowed and left.

"Come, my dear," she told Sonje. "Let's get you fancied up for the feast."

* * * * *

Sonje followed Lady Miranda to a large stone house on a point that jutted out into the ocean north of most of the other homes. Brenndah followed carrying Sonje's things. Soon they had a tub of water for her to wash in. It felt good to wash away the dirt of her journey. She loosened her hair and washed it. Lady Miranda brought her a beautiful maroon dress with white trim. After putting on the dress, she began to brush her hair.

"I had no idea your hair was so long!" Lady Miranda said in surprise. "It is beautiful."

Brenndah nodded in agreement. Sonje smiled.

"In Glynis, the women do not cut their hair," she explained. "I have kept it braided to hide its length while traveling. We wanted to blend in and noticed most women's hair was shorter."

Sonje braided her hair to encircle her head like a crown.

"It is time for the feast," Lady Miranda said.

The women walked to a large building near the doors in the cliff. Many people were already in the building. A few were still arriving. Sonje was amazed at the amount of food as she sat where Lady Miranda indicated.

"We celebrate the return of our ships and the safe return of their crews," Lady Miranda said. "We welcome Gwladys Sonje to our home. We pray for the safe return of our beloved Lord Bryant. Let us eat."

Soon everyone was eating. The flavors were strange and new to Sonje. She guessed that most of the foods must have been harvested from the sea. Sonje watched the people eat and talk among themselves. Many cast curious glances towards her as she ate. When the meal was over, Lady Miranda stood. Soon the room fell silent.

"The time has come to vote on the proposal to move Glynis by ship," she said. "All in favor, say 'yes'."

The room resounded with the response.

"Any opposed?"

Sonje felt greatly relieved by the silence that followed. She glanced to Lady Miranda and was rewarded by a smile.

"I thank you for your support," Sonje began. "The people of Glynis are looking forward to coming to their new home and meeting all of you. There are a few things about our people that have been forgotten here in Merton and Dracona."

A murmur went through the room. Sonje waited before resuming.

"Many of the women do not cut their hair. They understand that shorter hair is customary here."

Sonje loosened her hair and shook loose the braids.

"I did not want this difference to alarm anyone. Also our people have the ability to produce a colored light."

Sonje slowly let her light grow. She was pleased to see that Lady Miranda and Brenndah also let their lights glow. She saw the surprise on the faces of the people. Sonje smiled as a few others begin to glow also.

"Along with this there are talents that our people possess. Some are able to shape metal and stone with a touch of their hand. Others can heal injuries. There are many things that our people can do, yet we do not

156

completely understand how. I wanted to tell you now so that these things would be easier to accept when the people of Glynis arrive."

"We have much to prepare," Lady Miranda announced. "All ship's captains and navigators should report to the map chamber in a quarter of an hour."

Sonje and Lady Miranda left the feast and went to the map chamber. Soon they were joined by a man and a woman. Their weathered faces told of many hours in the sun and wind. They bowed low before Lady Miranda and Sonje.

"My Lady," the man spoke first. "The island was glowing again."

"Like after the death of Lord Eamon," the woman finished.

"Thank you," Lady Miranda replied. "I wish I knew what it meant."

Sonje felt for Bryant's thoughts and could feel that he was still alive. She didn't feel any panic or distress from him.

"Malvin's Heart would let me feel if Bryant had died," Sonje offered. "So it must mean something else."

Sonje wondered what it all meant. There were too many people coming in to discuss it further. She noticed that the additions to the map seemed to interest the people. Lady Miranda stood before the map and raised her hands. Soon the cavern was quiet.

"Gwladys Sonje will explain the changes to the map and propose a course."

Sonje took the long stick that was offered to her and pointed to the map.

"This is Glynis. Our people should be able to travel in safety to this point. There is a passage between these villages and the ocean. If they could be loaded onto ships, they would be safe from Burton's army. Even if the rightful king gains the throne and Lord Bryant strikes a peace agreement with him it will take time for all the soldiers to be notified and withdrawn."

One man stood and said, "The river provides a natural harbor. It should be a simple matter to load the people and their belongings there. It will take a three days sail to get there providing the wind is good. When will they be there?"

"I will give you an answer in the morning."

"How many people are there?" another man asked.

"About one thousand in all."

"How will they be transporting their belongings to the villages?" a woman asked.

"By wagons or carts pulled by one or two horses each," Sonje answered. "Glynis has been preparing for this move for a long time. They are ready to load and move at any time. It would be best to move them before the winter storms set in.

"Then it is settled. It might take several trips to get everyone transported." Lady Miranda said. "We will pass the word of when the move will begin in the morning."

As the others began to leave, Sonje turned to Lady Miranda.

"What island was glowing?" Sonje asked.

"It is not on the map because it has been moving slowly from the north to the south. No one has dared get very close to it. We think perhaps it might be the island that Malvin visited before his death."

"It could be," Sonje agreed. "I will need a large polished shield or reflective surface to make contact with my aunt. Also, I will faint after I have finished. The effort is very draining."

"I read Bryant's account of your previous communications," Lady Miranda acknowledged. "Brenndah and I will care for you. You will have the room Bryant uses when he visits. Let's go back to my house and prepare for this evening."

Sonje walked in silence to the house. She wondered just what Bryant had written in his journal. Even what they shared through Malvin's Heart had not given her that specific of information.

* * * * *

Miranda saw the look on Sonje's face as she showed her to Bryant's room. She knew that so many things were happening that it must be difficult for Sonje. What she was doing would change the lives of everyone in Glynis, Merton, and Dracona.

"Come and sit," Miranda said after Brenndah had gone. "You seem preoccupied. Would you like to talk about it?"

"Even though we shared our memories when Malvin's Heart joined our minds, I realized that I still do not know what Bryant wrote in his journal about me and about before he met me," Sonje admitted, knowing that she could not hide the truth from Bryant's mother. "My presence has thrust a whole new responsibility on Bryant."

"After Eamon died, Bryant seemed to be only a hollow shell of his former self. He seemed to do things automatically, without thought. He was changed. In his journal, he seldom mentioned any feelings. Those he did write about were loneliness, sorrow, and even anger."

"When I first met him in the forest, he seemed cold and forbidding. After he brought me to the castle, he seemed less cold, but still somewhat aloof until his birthday."

* * * * *

"When he met you, his world changed," Lady Miranda said. "He was unsure of what he was feeling. He was afraid of loving you and wrote

158

about it in detail. The first time you fainted, it began to hit him. The second time, he realized that he had been denying his true feelings. He wanted to hold you and kiss you, but was afraid of what would happen if he let himself."

"That night he had a nightmare about his Uncle Rolf," Sonje said slowly. "It was that morning that I began to understand my feelings for him. He was so different from the other men I had met. I think I saw in him some of what I felt. I was bound by responsibility, yet uncomfortable with the position and power that I have over the lives of others."

"He never seemed to be comfortable with being served by others. He was always trying to be just like everyone else."

"I took him on a picnic in the meadow, hoping that I could get him to talk about his age and the dragons that he was keeping a secret. I knew he was hiding something, but the books were not very clear on the fact that Malvin was a dragon."

"That night he wrote in great detail about the day and his feelings for you. You were still very mysterious to him, but he knew that he wanted to marry you."

"That was the day that I knew too," Sonje said. "I feel better about things now."

"Good. It is almost time to eat."

The meal was eaten in silence. Sonje looked from Lady Miranda to Brenndah. In such a short time, they had become her friends. She hoped that things were going as well for Bryant.

After the dishes were cleared and washed, the three women went to Bryant's room. Sonje prepared for bed before standing before the large shield. Her light was nearly white as it filled the room. Soon her aunt's image replaced her own in the reflection.

'Greetings Sonje,' she said and Evelina repeated it for Miranda.

'The time has come for Glynis to move,' Sonje said. "Out of division will come union."

'We will be ready to leave the day after tomorrow. What will be our route?'

'South to the villages at the break in the mountains. Then east to the ocean.'

'We will begin to arrive in two weeks from our departure.'

'The ships of Merton will be there to meet you.'

'It will be good to see you in person,' Sonje's aunt said. 'Farewell until then.'

'Farewell.'

As the reflection returned to normal, Sonje began to crumple towards the floor. Miranda and Brenndah caught her and carried her to the bed.

"Let's get some sleep ourselves," Miranda said.

Brenndah nodded in agreement.

Chapter 15 – The Rightful Heir

Bryant and Riva went to wait at the castle gate for the boy.

"Last night I remembered something I hadn't thought about in years," Riva said. "I know it is important for you to know about it."

Bryant was curious.

"There was once a prince with no name in a kingdom south of here," Riva continued. "I told him that his true heir would be hidden, but would return to claim the throne. You will be the one that will enable his true heir to find their way back to rule the kingdom. Without your intervention the entire kingdom would be lost."

"Me?" Bryant asked. "Why would the prince have no name?"

"Only by true love could he be named," Riva said. "I saw the shadow of a dragon when I had visions of his true heir. I now know that you have met the son of this prince and will provide everything his child needs to assume their birthright."

Bryant realized it had to be someone in the village, but whom?

"Do not worry about finding this child," Riva said. "You will be there when they are ready and need you the most. Also it is very important that they discover their past for themselves."

Bryant was confused as he saw the boy come through the gate without looking at them. They followed at a distance as the boy walked through the streets, then to where the east castle wall met the cliff edge. He led them to a narrow trail just wide enough for a horse that edged down the cliff. After rounding a bend, the trail ended on a ledge with trees along the side of the cliff. The boy doubled back through the trees into a cave. The boy paused and looked from them and back into the black maw that opened before him.

"Do you have a light?" Bryant asked.

The boy shook his head.

"I will provide a light," Bryant said. "Please do not let it frighten you."

They both gave him a puzzled look, but as Bryant's glow lit up the entrance the boy grinned while Riva looked stunned. The boy led the way through the cave. Soon they saw a light around the bend. Bryant extinguished his light before turning the corner.

The cavern was well lit and simply furnished. A woman turned to greet them.

"Come, Archelaus," she said.

A green glow centered around her as she laid her hands on the boy's shoulders. Soon he stood straight and tall. The boy had become a handsome young man when he turned to face Bryant and Riva.

"This is my Aunt Althea," Archelaus said. "And this is my true form. When Uncle Gustave killed my father and mother, we hid here in this cave. We decided that if I were to ever have a chance at the throne, I would have to stay near the castle."

"To avoid discovery by my twin I changed his appearance," Althea said, "Gustave must be stopped. The people of Burton suffer greatly under his rule."

"I come from the land to the southeast of Burton," Bryant said. "I am Bryant Donley, Lord Dracona. My ancestors came from Glynis which is far to the north of Burton. The people of Glynis are going to move to Dracona soon. Gustave has threatened them with slavery. My mission in Burton is to place the rightful king on the throne and strike a peace treaty with him."

"The opportunity may come very soon," Archelaus revealed with a smile. "The word in the castle is that Gustave has heard of the fortune teller. He may soon command a private meeting with Madam Riva."

"We will be ready when the time comes," Riva said.

"It would be best if I could be nearby without being recognized," Althea said.

"If we could disguise you as an old woman, you could be part of the show," Bryant suggested.

"I will stay near Gustave until that time," Archelaus said. "We should hurry back before anyone gets suspicious."

Althea returned Archelaus to his scullery boy disguise and then transformed herself into an old woman. Soon they were back in the city.

Bryant and Riva prepared a simple noon meal while Althea sat on a small stool nearby. He was pleased with her appearance. As they ate, a group of soldiers approached them.

"King Gustave commands a private meeting with Madam Riva tonight," the leader announced. "He invites you to share his evening meal. You will set up your tent in the castle garden this afternoon."

Bryant's heart jumped into his throat as Riva stood up.

"Tell King Gustave that we accept his invitation," Riva replied.

Bryant met Riva's gaze as the soldiers left.

"This evening I will wear my cape," Bryant said. "Can your nephew handle a sword?"

"Yes," Althea responded. "I have been trying to school him in the skills he will need."

No more was said as they finished their meal. Soon everything was packed in the wagon. Bryant was nervous as they entered the castle gates. There could be trouble if Gustave recognized him. Bryant parked the wagon where the soldiers indicated and unhitched the horses. The soldiers took the horses to the stables and left the garden. Bryant and Riva set up the tent and lamps between the castle and the well. When all was ready, they sat in the wagon to make further plans.

"I think it would be best if Gustave did not recognize me until after dinner." Bryant began. "The change in hair color might not be enough to fool him."

"I agree," Althea said. "What did you have in mind?"

"A scar under my chin might do the trick," Bryant said. "He would know that Lord Dracona did not have such a scar."

Riva nodded as Althea traced under his chin and along his jaw with her finger. Bryant smiled as he felt the unfamiliar scar.

"We will call you 'Mother' tonight," Riva said as she pulled some clothes from a trunk. "You can wear these."

"I suggest that we rest for a while," Bryant said. "It will be a long night."

The women nodded and Bryant left the wagon. He drew a drink from the well before settling down against one of the wagon wheels. He closed his eyes and wondered how Sonje's mission was progressing. He thought about Althea's amazing talent for changing appearances, and wondered if he might have any such talent within him. He missed Sonje and wondered if she had arrived in Merton safely. He concentrated and could feel that she was not in distress. As the sound of footsteps approached, Bryant realized that he had been asleep. He looked up to see the soldier pass the well.

"Dinner will be in an hour," he announced. "I will return to escort you to the dining hall."

"Thank you," Bryant responded as he stood up. "I will inform Madam Riva."

Bryant woke the two women and began to prepare. First he tied the scarlet sash about his waist. Then he unwrapped the swords and strapped them to his back. He settled his cape over the swords. Riva tied a scarlet cloth about his neck with the ends lying over his shoulder. Bryant left the wagon as the women prepared. He helped Althea out of the wagon. Her dress was dark blue silk with small shiny disks dangling from the hem of her overskirt and from the scarlet shawl covering her hair and shoulders.

Riva wore her scarlet dress accented by a dark blue overskirt and shawl about her shoulders that had shiny disks dangling from their hems.

The three stood between the wagon and the well when the soldier returned to escort them to dinner. They walked in silence to the dining hall. The opulent decorations and furniture made Bryant uncomfortable. Dracona was beautiful, but plain in comparison. He wondered about the sacrifices the people of Burton must make to enable such ornamentation of the castle. The dining hall was enormous. A vaulted ceiling and ornate stained glass reminded Bryant of the church in Dracona's town. King Gustave greeted them in an elaborate outfit accented with fur and jewels.

"Welcome, Madam Riva," Gustave said. "I have heard good things about the accuracy of your fortune telling."

"It is a skill passed from mother to daughter," Riva said as she put an arm around Althea's shoulders.

"And what of this man? His face seems familiar," Gustave said.

Bryant's heart pounded in his chest as he waited for Riva's response.

"My brother cannot foresee the future, but he is an excellent provider of food, shelter and safe roads in our travels," Riva replied. "He has an interest in architecture and finds the most wonderful buildings for us to visit."

"What do you think of my humble abode?" Gustave asked as he looked Bryant in the eye.

"This workmanship is unsurpassed," Bryant said as he looked up at the ceiling. "The size and spacing of the support beams are perfect in proportion."

"You have a good eye," said Gustave. "Come, let's eat. I have chosen a mute servant to wait on us tonight. He is not much to look at, but he will not repeat our conversation."

Bryant shot a glance a Riva behind Gustave's back. She smiled in return. Bryant helped Althea to her seat and helped her to sit. Gustave rang a gold bell and the doors opened. Bryant tried to look as if Archelaus' appearance disgusted him.

"Do not mind his looks," Gustave said, noticing Bryant's reaction. "He has been working here since he was a young lad. I trust him with my most important errands because he is mute. Eat and enjoy."

Bryant had seldom seen such an extravagant feast. He was glad to see that Gustave took his eating quite seriously. He was not looking forward to a lot of talking. Bryant ate slowly and tried to appear relaxed.

"I am excited to learn what my future holds," Gustave said as he wiped his mouth. "I simply cannot wait any longer."

"We have set up my crystal sphere in the castle garden," Riva replied. "We may retire there at your leisure."

"Then let us go there now."

Gustave stood and the others arose as well.

"Come walk with me, Madam Riva," Gustave commanded.

She took the arm he offered and Bryant offered his arm to Althea. Archelaus followed behind. Soon they reached the garden. Riva and Gustave entered the tent. Bryant lit the lamps while Archelaus checked for guards and soldiers. Bryant was relieved to see the boy return with a smile on his face. As Archelaus and Althea ducked into the wagon to change Archelaus back to his true appearance, Bryant stepped closer to the tent to listen. It was a few minutes before Riva spoke.

"As the season is changing, so is the city. What seemed a dark cloud will usher forth a bright new era. Blood will run true and wrongs will be righted. The hilltop and the dragon will be at peace."

Archelaus and Althea had joined Bryant in time to hear Riva's prediction. Bryant entered the tent to see Gustave draw a dagger from his belt. Bryant shed his cape and drew Fanchon's sword. Gustave turned to Bryant.

"So this wanderer is the dragon lord after all," Gustave growled with disgust. "I thought there was something familiar about you."

Gustave paused and his face grew pale. He snarled as he lunged to Bryant's left. As Bryant swung the sword, the blade appeared to be a flame as it cut Gustave in two. In stunned silence, the four stood in Bryant's light watching the blood stream towards the gates. The shouts of approaching soldiers startled them back to awareness of the danger they were still in. Archelaus and Bryant stood with swords drawn while the women sought shelter in the wagon.

"The king has been killed!" the first soldier shouted.

"They have killed the king!"

"Kill them!"

The soldiers stopped short as the blade of the dragon grip sword turned to flame.

"I will defend the rightful king of Burton as he assumes his birthright," Bryant announced calmly as he stepped forward.

"Prince Archelaus disappeared long ago," the captain replied in challenge. "He died when his parents did."

Archelaus stepped forward and ripped his shirt open in front. The soldiers fell to their knees and bowed. As Archelaus turned, Bryant could see the birthmark in the shape of a crown and scepter on his chest. Bryant sheathed his sword.

* * * * *

Sonje awoke feeling very hungry. As she sat up, Brenndah entered the room. Brenndah brought her a dress and then left the room. She quickly dressed and joined Lady Miranda and Brenndah at breakfast.

When they arrived at the map cavern, many of the people were already waiting. As soon as everyone had assembled, Lady Miranda stood. Silence fell over the cavern.

"Gwladys Sonje has been in contact with Glynis," she said. "We will coordinate the move and prepare the ships to meet in two weeks. This will allow the move to be completed before the rainy season."

As the people began to drift out in groups discussing the preparations, Sonje touched Lady Miranda's arm.

"I feel strongly that I should visit the glowing island," Sonje said as Lady Miranda turned to face her.

"I have a small boat we can go in," Lady Miranda replied without argument. "Brenndah can come with us."

In an hour, they had packed a lunch and cast off for the island. Sonje was amazed at how swiftly the wind pushed the boat. Before noon, they sighted the low lying island.

"Can we get in closer?" Sonje asked.

"Yes, but this is as close as anyone has ever been."

Brenndah nodded. As they neared the island, Sonje noticed that it seemed to be a very symmetrical shape. Soon she noticed the bottom sloping beneath their boat. When the boat touched the bottom there was an oddly metallic thud.

There was silence other than the lapping of the waves on the boat and shore. Sonje stepped carefully out into the edge of the water. A short distance inland, she could see a ridge. She motioned for the two to stay in the boat and proceeded alone.

Sonje noticed that the island seemed to be devoid of life other than the plants that clung to its surface. As she neared the ridge, she could see that there was writing on the face of the ridge. As she touched it she knew that it was made of metal, not stone. As she followed the ridge around, she made out a word or two, but most of it was not familiar. Soon she found what appeared to be a doorway that was tightly sealed. She gasped as she realized that the symbol that covered the door was the same as on her mother's signet ring. She could see the details that were mere specks on the ring. Two pairs of hand prints were on the door with a small slit opening between them and writing above.

"Temple of Origin," she read aloud softly. "The path leads to the future."

Sonje studied the door for another moment before returning to the boat. She pushed the boat loose and climbed in. Soon the sail had caught the wind and they sped back towards land.

"It is not an island," Sonje said in answer to their questioning stares. "It is out of our past."

Brenndah passed her a slice of bread with some dried fish and cheese while Lady Miranda turned her attention to sailing back to Merton.

* * * * *

Bryant awoke with a start. He felt disoriented as he sat up and looked around. His eyes fell upon the two swords and the rough cape hanging incongruently on an elegant chair at his bedside. Memories of the night before came flooding back. After Gustave's body had been taken by the soldiers, Archelaus ordered rooms be given to Bryant, Riva, and Althea. A quiet tap at the door broke into his thoughts.

"Come," he responded.

A servant entered and bowed.

"His Highness sent some clothes for you and a bath is being made ready, My Lord."

The man opened a door to an adjoining room and bowed.

"Thank you," Bryant said as he entered the room.

There were two more servants standing near a tub of water. The first servant bowed and motioned towards the tub.

"I require no further assistance, thank you," Bryant said.

"But, My Lord," the man protested.

"I keep no personal servants at Dracona," Bryant replied with an upheld hand. "I am not comfortable with such treatment."

"We will be right outside if you need us."

The servants bowed and left. Bryant undressed and stepped into the tub. As he settled into the water, he wished he were back home in his own spacious bath. Soon he had washed away the dirt of his travels. It felt good to wash his hair again.

He dried himself and put on the pants. The clothes were more elegant than he was accustomed to. As he shaved, he noticed that his hair was much lighter. A tap on the door caught his attention.

"Come," Bryant said as he finished buttoning the jacket.

"His Majesty awaits you, My Lord," the servant said with a bow.

"Thank you," Bryant answered.

"Your hair, My Lord," the man said as he stood and faced Bryant. "How did you change its color so swiftly?"

"It had been dyed," Bryant responded.

Bryant returned to the bed chamber and retrieved Fanchon's Sword.

"You will not need a weapon, My Lord."

"This is no ordinary sword," Bryant responded. "It is safer for all if I do not leave it unattended."

The man bowed and opened the door to the hall. Bryant followed the man down to the throne room. Riva and Althea were already waiting with Archelaus. Bryant bowed with a smile.

"I trust you slept well, my friend," Archelaus said in greeting. "Bring some food at once."

The servant bowed and left.

"I did," Bryant said. "Thank you for your hospitality,"

"It would not be possible if not for your aid. I am eternally grateful."

"Rule your kingdom wisely and with kindness, my friend," Bryant replied.

"There are a few things to attend to before you leave for Dracona," Archelaus said. "I wish for you to stay for my coronation tomorrow afternoon. And then there is the matter of the body."

"I wouldn't think of leaving before your coronation," Bryant responded. "And I know exactly what to do with the body. We can bury it near the northern border of Dracona beside the grave of the man who is Gustave and Althea's great grandfather."

Archelaus smiled as the servants brought in Bryant's breakfast. Bryant ate as plans were made for the coronation. As soon as he finished eating, Bryant realized that he should try to retrieve the box before contacting Sonje and Haskell.

"If you will excuse me," Bryant said. "There are a few things that I need to attend to."

"Charles will assist you with anything you need," Archelaus said.

"Thank you," Bryant said with a bow.

The servant who had brought Bryant to the throne room followed him as he left.

"First I need to go to the well in the castle garden," Bryant told him. "I need some rope and a hook."

"Yes, My Lord," Charles replied.

He led Bryant to the garden and went to get the rope. As Bryant stood at the well, he thought of the conflicts the garden had seen. He saw where Gale must have hid with the body of Auberon's wife after Sonje and Auberon's hasty departure. Last night seemed to be a disjointed dream except for the stain of blood trailing from Riva's fortune telling tent. Bryant turned away from the tent to see Charles coming with a rope and a hook. Bryant soon had the hook lowered into the well. He thought he could feel the hook bumping against something, but only came up with an empty hook. After several unsuccessful tries, Bryant sighed.

"What are you trying to hook, My Lord?" Charles asked.

"A box left for safe keeping in this well by My Lady," Bryant answered. "I am going to try something different. Do not be alarmed at what happens."

"The stories going around the castle about last night credit you with some very unusual abilities, My Lord."

Bryant grinned as he closed his eyes to concentrate. He relaxed and focused his mind on the box in the well. He could feel it sitting at the bottom of the well. He placed both hands on the rim of the well and willed the box to rise. His concentration was broken with Charles' gasp. He opened his eyes to see Charles snatch the box before it plunged back into the well.

"Well done, My Lord," Charles said. "I didn't know that anyone could do such a thing."

"Neither did I until I tried," Bryant admitted. "Now I think I had better sit down for a while."

Charles set down the box and brought a chair from Riva's tent. Bryant sat down gratefully. Now he understood why Sonje had passed out when contacting her aunt. He hoped it would be less draining if he practiced on smaller things.

"Will you be alright, My Lord?" Charles asked in a worried tone. "You look pale."

"That took more effort than I expected, but I will be fine." Bryant replied. "Let's take the box to my room and I will take a nap before lunch."

Charles bowed before helping Bryant to his feet. He picked up the box by the ring and they walked slowly back to Bryant's room.

"I will wake you for lunch," Charles said as he put the box down. "Call out if you need anything."

"Thank you," Bryant said as he pulled off his boots and removed his sword.

Charles bowed and closed the door quietly behind him. Bryant lay down and closed his eyes. It seemed only moments before Charles awakened him.

"It is time for lunch, My Lord."

Bryant sat up and stretched. He pulled on his boots and picked up Fanchon's Sword. He examined the dragon grip for a moment.

Bryant drew the blade from the sheath.

"I swore an oath on this blade to protect those in need," Bryant said.

"And the people of Burton are grateful. Even the soldiers are rejoicing at the true king's return."

"And after tomorrow, I will return to Dracona to prepare for my own coronation and wedding."

"Congratulations, My Lord," Charles responded. "Come now. His Highness is waiting for you."

Bryant sheathed the sword and followed Charles to the dining hall. The conversation was light and the food was delicious. After the meal, Archelaus motioned for Bryant to follow him. They entered a small sitting room just off the dining hall.

"I am glad that you will stay for my coronation," Archelaus began. "Without you, it would not be possible. There are many wrongs done by Gustave that I must strive to undo. I have started by recalling all of the soldiers that were sent to the neighboring lands including Dracona."

"Thank you," Bryant said with a smile. "I am certain that you will make a kind and wise ruler. You and the people of Burton are welcome to visit Dracona. We wish to be at peace with our neighbors."

"I will make Burton a better neighbor," Archelaus promised. "I know that it was Gustave's greed, not the people's needs that was behind Burton's plans to conquer. I understand that you retrieved your lady's box from the well."

"Yes. I still need to send for the minstrel who concealed her mother's body so it might receive a proper burial."

"I can dispatch a messenger for you."

"That will not be necessary," Bryant said as he sat down. "I can contact my dragon, Haskell, with my mind. He will pass the message along to the minstrel."

"Could he also pass a message to your lady?" Archelaus asked. "I would love to have her attend my coronation also."

"I can give her your message myself," Bryant said with a smile. "I will contact her first."'

Archelaus nodded and sat down. Bryant closed his eyes.

'Sonje!' he called out with his mind.

'Bryant! You are safe!' Sonje replied with a mix of excitement and relief.

'Yes, My Love. I am safe. The scullery boy is now the king of Burton. He invites you to his coronation tomorrow afternoon.'

'I would love to attend. I have so much to tell you, but I would have to fly to get there in time.'

'I will ask Haskell to take you to the village. From there you and the minstrel can come with a team of horses and a wagon.'

'I will see you tomorrow morning then. I love you.'

'Tomorrow then.'

"She is coming?" Archelaus asked as he saw Bryant's smile.

"Yes," Bryant answered. "I will now arrange things with Haskell."

Bryant closed his eyes again and concentrated.

'Haskell!' Bryant called.

'I am glad to hear from you. Is everything going well?' Haskell replied with a pleased tone.

'Yes, things are going quite well, my friend. I need you to pick up Sonje in Merton and take her to the village.'

'Will she know I am coming for her?'

'Yes. Tell Hoyt and Auberon that Sonje and the minstrel are to attend the coronation of Burton's new king tomorrow. Ask Auberon to have a team of horses and a work wagon ready for them at the village. After the coronation, we shall return to Dracona.'

'I will. We will all be glad to have you back. You must tell me everything later.'

'I will Haskell. Thank you.'

Bryant smiled and opened his eyes.

"Everything is arranged," Bryant said. "Sonje and the minstrel should arrive just before noon."

"Wonderful," Archelaus exclaimed. "Come, I need your advice on the preparations."

"I've never even seen a coronation, but I'll give you my honest opinions," Bryant said with a smile.

Chapter 16 – Return to Dracona

"Are you alright, Sonje?" Lady Miranda asked in a worried tone.

"Yes," Sonje replied. "I just spoke to Bryant. The conflict with Burton is over and the new king has invited Bryant and me to the coronation."

"When is it?"

"Tomorrow. Haskell will be coming to take me to Dracona's village."

"We will be ashore soon," Lady Miranda said. "We will have to hurry to get your things together."

As soon as the boat was docked, the women hurried to pack Sonje's saddle bags. Just as they had finished packing, they heard the sound of Haskell's wings.

"Return this to Bryant and give him my love," Lady Miranda said as she handed Bryant's journal to Sonje.

"I will," Sonje said as she tucked the book in the bags. "I am going to miss both of you."

Brenndah nodded as she handed Sonje her cape. She flung her arms around Sonje and held on tight.

"I know Brenndah," Sonje said as she hugged back. "I will see you again soon. Take good care of Guen until I can take her back to Dracona."

When Brenndah released her, Sonje found herself being hugged by Lady Miranda.

"I know that you and Bryant will be very happy. That is all I have ever wanted for him."

Sonje nodded, afraid that the lump in her throat would betray her emotions. Lady Miranda opened the door and Sonje hurried to mount Haskell. She held her breath as Haskell leapt off the cliff edge over the sea. Soon his outstretched wings lifted them and he circled towards Dracona.

'He misses you too,' Haskell told her.

'I have always dreamed of being in love, but was doubtful that it would actually happen.'

'Bryant always feared love after Rolfe. You have made him happier than he has ever been. You showed him that he could let himself love again.'

172

Sonje smiled as they landed just outside the village. Her father and Gale were waiting with the wagon.

'Thank you, Haskell,' Sonje said as she dismounted.

Her father was waiting with the rest of the family.

"We'll meet you in Dracona," Father said. "It is good to know that your mother will at last have a proper burial."

"We should be back in Dracona in four days," Sonje said before she kissed her father and climbed into the waiting wagon.

Gale urged the horses forward and they traveled in silence until it was dark. They ate a quick supper without lighting a fire and laid down to sleep for a few hours before continuing the journey to Burton. It seemed to Sonje that she had just gone to sleep when Gale awakened her. The moon was full and sinking into the trees He handed her a hot cup of tea when she sat up.

"Thank you, Gale," Sonje said.

"I was up early, My Lady," Gale replied. "I didn't sleep well remembering the last time I was in Burton."

"We appreciate what you did for us in Burton. It is very important to us to know her body was so well cared for."

Gale nodded and went to hitch the horses. Sonje helped clear their campsite and soon they were on their way. Within an hour of noon, Burton came into view. As they approached the southern gate, a man on horseback rode forward to meet them.

"Bryant!" Sonje exclaimed as she recognized him.

"Welcome to Burton, My Lady," Bryant answered with a smile. "Thank you for coming, Gale."

Bryant turned his horse and led the way to the castle. As soon as they arrived in the castle courtyard, Sonje was whisked into the castle before Bryant could dismount. She found herself surrounded by servants who bathed and dressed her. Then she was escorted to the dining hall. Bryant was waiting for her at the door. He bowed and kissed her hand before escorting her to her seat. Gale was seated along with three people she did not recognize.

"Welcome, Gwladys Sonje," the young man said in greeting. "I am so grateful that you could attend my coronation. Without you and Bryant, I would still be a scullery boy."

"Gustave's sister, Althea, and Archelaus had been trying to find a way to dethrone Gustave ever since he tried to have them killed," Bryant explained. "Riva and her sister saved me from Gustave's soldiers and made it possible for me to find Archelaus and help him claim his birthright."

"I am glad that Dracona and Burton can now live in peace," Sonje said.

Servants brought in food and while they ate they talked about the past and the future of their kingdoms. By the end of the meal Sonje felt at ease. As the servants came to clear the table, Archelaus stood.

"The coronation will take place in half an hour. Servants will bring you to the balcony when it is time," he said. "Minstrel, I could use a song to steady my nerves."

"My pleasure, My King," Gale said with a bow.

Bryant took Sonje's hand and led her to the room he had stayed in. As soon as the door closed behind them, he turned towards her. Her heart leapt as she looked into his eyes.

"You are even more beautiful than I remember," he said. "I have missed you so much."

"Every moment of every day I wished for you to be with me."

Sonje felt herself tremble as she felt Bryant's hand lift her chin and his lips met hers. As he drew her even closer, she put her arms around his neck. When their lips parted, Sonje laid her head on his shoulder. She felt his heart beating against her cheek.

'I feel whole at last,' Bryant's words came softly to her mind.

'Your mother told me that she was grateful that I had opened your heart to love,' Sonje thought back. 'She has been very worried about you and was praying for your happiness.'

'It sounds as though you had no trouble in Merton then.'

'Except getting attacked by a mountain cat, I had no trouble in Merton. In two weeks the people of Glynis will be safely on board Merton's ships.'

Bryant pulled back.

"You were attacked?" Bryant said aloud. "Are you alright?"

"Yes, Brenndah is a very talented healer and was even able to heal Guen."

"Speaking of talent," Bryant said with a mischievous grin. "Here is the box from the well."

To her amazement, the box lifted up off the floor and floated onto the table.

"Bryant! How did you do that?" she exclaimed.

"The hook and rope idea wasn't working," Bryant explained. "So I tried something different."

"Give me the circlet and the ring." Sonje said with a smile. "It is my turn to use a talent."

Bryant handed over the circlet and ring. Sonje concentrated and soon restored them to their original forms. After settling the circlet back on his head, she smiled. Bryant leaned forward and kissed her again.

"I don't ever want to take that ring off my finger again," Bryant said as she slid the ring onto his finger.

Just then there was a quiet knock at the door.

"Come," Bryant ordered.

Charles opened the door and bowed.

"It is time." he announced.

Bryant nodded and placed Sonje's hand on his arm. They followed Charles up stairs and to a wide balcony above the city plaza. The others were gathered there as well. Archelaus looked nervous but happy. Bryant could hear the noise of the people crowded into the plaza below. Archelaus stepped to the railing and raised both hands. As soon as the crowd quieted, he began to speak.

"Good citizens of Burton, today is a day I know that you have waited for too long. While Gustave was in power, I prepared for this day and the years to come. I lived among you in disguise. I knew first hand your discontent under Gustave's rule."

Archelaus waited for the crowd to quiet again.

"With Gustave's death, we will begin a new era of peace. We will live in peace with our neighboring kingdoms. We will lower our taxes so that everyone can prosper."

The roar of the crowd was deafening. It was several minutes before Archelaus could continue. He gestured to Bryant and Sonje.

"This is the Lord and Lady of Dracona, our neighbor to the southeast. They have agreed to peace with Burton and have made it possible for me to claim the throne of Burton."

Archelaus paused as Charles and another servant brought a small chest forward. He opened the clasp on the top and it opened on hinges at the bottom corner of each side. The sides swung all the way around to form a stand under the chest bottom. A plain gold crown with a purple gem at the top of each of the six points was revealed.

"I will wear this, the original crown of Burton, instead of the crown that Gustave wore. That crown will be taken apart and used for the people of Burton."

A cheer went up among the crowd. Bryant smiled at Sonje; Archelaus would make a good ruler over Burton. When the people were quiet again, Archelaus lifted the crown above him with both hands.

"Upon this crown I swear to the people of Burton that I will serve as your ruler, caring for the needs of the people before my own."

As Archelaus settled the crown upon his head the crowd cheered again.

"When I choose my queen, I will take care to select one who is kind and noble of spirit and pure of heart. We will be your representatives and your servants."

The plaza echoed with shouts of "Long live the king!" and "Hail Archelaus!" Archelaus bowed and left the balcony.

'He will make a good king,' Sonje's voice said in Bryant's mind as they entered the castle.

Bryant smiled and nodded in agreement.

'I hope that our coronation goes as smoothly,' Bryant thought back.

'It will,' Sonje replied. 'Hoyt and Agatha are experienced in planning such events. My father will pass his crown to you and my aunt will stand in for my mother.'

They followed Archelaus into the throne room.

"I have always looked forward to the day that I could sit here," Archelaus said softly. "But I thought that it would be the same throne that my father used."

"I had some of the servants that were loyal to your father volunteer to dispose of it," Althea said. "They put it in safe keeping until it was needed. Charles can have it brought back for you."

"Thank you, Aunt Althea," Archelaus said. "It does mean a lot to me. Please do so at once, Charles."

Charles bowed and left the room.

"I have always felt that Gustave abused his power and the people of Burton to satisfy his extravagant tastes," Archelaus continued. "There will be a lot of changes to be made. One of the first will be to remove the excess ornamentation from the castle and return the materials to the people."

"That would be most noble of you," Bryant said. "When I first entered this castle, I thought of the sacrifices forced upon the people of Burton. Our castle at Dracona is beautiful, but much simpler. The castle was always open to every citizen to enjoy, not just the select few. That is the way it will always be."

"That is a wonderful idea," Archelaus responded with interest. "I must come to see Dracona's castle. It may give me some ideas on how this castle can be better used by and for the people of Burton."

"You must attend our wedding and coronation in about four weeks," Sonje said with Bryant's approving nod.

"I would be delighted and honored," Archelaus responded. "Send a messenger with the exact date as soon as possible."

"I wouldn't miss it," Althea said.

"We must now finish our business here and return home," Bryant said. "There is much to be done."

"You may go, my friends. We will look forward to seeing you again soon," Archelaus responded.

"Take care friends," Althea said.

"Tell Xylia that I will remain in Burton until we come for your wedding." Riva said. "Your future shows that you will take your people farther than you can imagine. You will find the way to open the door."

Bryant felt the shock that passed through Sonje's mind.

"May fortune smile upon you, friends," Bryant said.

Bryant led Sonje and the minstrel back to the room he had stayed in to collect the rest of his things. Gale remained in the hall while Bryant and Sonje went in the room.

'Something Riva said startled you,' Bryant thought to Sonje.

'It will take time to explain it,' Sonje replied. 'I will tell you when we return to Dracona. She referred to a door that I discovered while in Merton.'

When they opened the door they found Charles waiting with Gale in the hall. When they reached the wagon, Sonje's things had been loaded and there was a carved coffin in the wagon. A second wagon containing a plain wood coffin with two soldiers was also there. Bryant turned to Charles.

"King Archelaus wanted her to have a coffin more befitting a queen," Charles said in answer to Bryant's questioning look. "The soldiers and I will accompany you to bury Gustave."

"Thank you," Bryant said.

"It means a lot to my father and me to know that Mother will receive a proper burial," Sonje added.

Bryant helped Sonje up to the wagon seat.

"When you have shown us the cave, you may remain in Burton or return with us to Dracona," Bryant told Gale.

"King Archelaus is grateful for your part in bringing Lord Dracona to Burton," Charles added. "You will be always welcome to stay in the castle when you are in Burton."

Gale smiled at them and said, "I will have to think about it. I would like to be in Dracona for the wedding and coronation."

"We wouldn't have it otherwise," Sonje said with a smile.

Bryant took his place beside Sonje and took up the reins. Charles and Gale sat on either side of the coffin. Bryant was glad to see the change in the citizens of Burton. As they rode through the streets, many of the people waved or bowed and all seemed more cheerful. Soon they arrived at the city gate. Gale got out and led them to the cave. Bryant and the other men removed the rocks from the simple coffin as Sonje watched. With great care, the coffin was carried out to the wagon. The two coffins looked so incongruent lying beside one another. Bryant and Gale carefully lifted the body from the old coffin and placed it in the new one.

Sonje felt her mother's presence as she watched. It comforted her to see the care that Gale had taken to wrap her body and prepare her for burial. She watched as the old coffin was returned to the cave and Bryant knelt beside the new one. He placed one hand on the side of her mother's head for a moment before closing the lid.

"I would have liked to have known her," Bryant said softly before standing up.

Sonje could see the tears in his eyes and feel them in his thoughts. In silence they continued their journey towards Dracona. They traveled quickly until the sun was beginning to set. They found a small clearing to make camp for the night. Everyone was just finishing the cold supper that had been packed for them when a wolf howled nearby. Bryant raised his hands as the soldiers reached for their swords. A large black wolf stepped into the clearing.

"I am glad to see you, my friend," Bryant said. "Will your pack keep watch for us tonight?"

Sonje was amazed to see the wolf bow its head before turning and disappearing into the trees.

"We will have no need to keep watch tonight," Bryant said as he turned to face the others.

"My Lord," Charles said in a nervous tone. "Are you certain?"

"Those wolves traveled with Riva and me before we arrived in Burton," Bryant replied. "They will make certain that no harm comes to us while we sleep."

* * * * *

Bryant could see the uncertainty in the others. Sonje seemed especially nervous.

'These wolves saved my life,' Bryant thought to her. 'I trust them to keep us safe.'

'I trust you,' Sonje's words came into his mind. 'It seems we will have a lot to talk about when we reach home.'

'Yes, My Love,' Bryant thought back as he kissed her.

Bryant settled down against a tree. He fingered the dark brown cape as he watched the others lie down and go to sleep. It would be good to get back home to Dracona. So much had changed since he had met Sonje. He smiled at the thought that nothing would ever be the same.

As the grey dawn was still upon the clearing, Bryant woke up. The horses were grazing nearby, but no one else had awakened yet. He

178

shook off the cape before placing it about his shoulders. The black wolf silently entered the clearing and faced him.

"Thank you," he told the wolf. "You are welcome in Dracona's forest at any time."

The wolf bowed and disappeared back into the forest. As Bryant turned he saw that the others were beginning to awaken.

"We will be able to reach Gustave's burial site just after noon tomorrow," he announced. "And we will reach Dracona by that nightfall."

After a quick breakfast of bread and cheese, the horses were hitched up. They started out in silence. As he drove the wagon he caught an occasional glimpse of one of the wolves moving through the trees. They camped another night and continued their journey the next day. Suddenly the trail left the forest and they were surrounded by a sea of grass and flowers. Bryant paused to get his bearings, and then turned the wagon east. Soon they arrived at the place chosen for Gustave's grave.

"Why is there bare dirt here and nowhere else?" Charles asked.

"Is this a new grave?" Gale added.

"It is the grave of Gustave's great grandfather," Bryant said. "Nothing has grown here since he was buried here. Perhaps it is because of his misdeeds in Burton."

The soldiers brought shovels out of their wagon and began to dig beside the existing grave. As the soldiers began to tire, Bryant and Charles took the shovels and continued the digging. After three hours the grave was finally finished. The men removed the plain coffin from the wagon and lowered it on ropes into the grave.

Sonje breathed a sigh of relief when the last of the dirt was placed on the fresh grave.

"It is good to know that he is no longer a threat to Glynis' safety," she commented.

"It is a relief to no longer have to serve him," Charles said. "It will be a pleasure to serve King Archelaus instead."

"I am looking forward to having time to spend with my family instead of being sent to conquer other lands to pay more taxes to Gustave," one of the soldiers said in agreement.

"It is good to lay to rest this shameful piece of Dracona's history," Bryant added. "I can return home knowing that Dracona's honor has been completely restored."

Charles stepped forward and bowed to Sonje and Bryant.

"We must return to Burton, but we will look forward to seeing you again soon," Charles said.

"May your travels be safe and your road smooth," Bryant replied.

"I will stay in Dracona until the wedding date has been set. Then I will return to Burton with the news," Gale said.

"King Archelaus will anxiously await your return," Charles replied.

Charles climbed into the wagon with the soldiers and they turned back into the forest. Bryant, Sonje and Gale climbed into their wagon and turned towards Dracona.

'Haskell!' Bryant called out in his mind.

'Bryant! It is so good to hear you again,' came the response.

'It will be even better to see you again. Please tell Agatha that Sonje, Gale and I will be arriving in an hour. We would love to have a good hot meal.'

'I will tell her,' Haskell said. 'I will see you after your dinner.'

Bryant turned to the others and told them, "We will have a hot meal and soft beds waiting for us when we arrive in Dracona."

"It will be good to be home again," Sonje said.

'Bryant,' Haskell called.

'Yes, my friend?' Bryant responded.

'Hoyt has set up a table in the great hall for the coffin you are bringing. The burial will be tomorrow afternoon. I will be bringing Lady Miranda and Brenndah from Merton in the morning. Regis Auberon and others from the village should arrive by noon. Young Wyman arrived earlier today with the news.'

'That will be great. It will be wonderful to see my mother again.'

Sonje gave him a questioning look as she saw his smile.

"Haskell said that Hoyt has made the arrangements for your mother's burial tomorrow. My mother and Brenndah will be there for the burial in the afternoon," Bryant explained. "Your family will arrive around noon."

"I will contact my aunt tonight after we eat," Sonje said. "Now that Burton is no longer a threat anyone not able to come by ship can travel by land."

The rest of the trip went quickly. Bryant smiled to see Edgard and Philip waiting for them at the edge of Dracona's town. Soon they were entering the castle gate. Bryant noticed that the large doors were open and there was a large group of people waiting. Bryant helped Sonje down from the wagon seat. Bryant and Gale pulled the coffin to the back edge of the wagon as Hoyt, Edgard, Philip and Wyman Jr. stepped forward to help carry it. The people opened a path into the great hall as a light rain began to fall.

Sonje followed the coffin into the castle. She watched the men gently place the coffin on a table in the center of the great hall. She could see that Hoyt had placed candles and flowers for a backdrop for the coffin. She placed her hand on the coffin. Bryant took her free hand in his and placed his other hand on the coffin. A feeling of peace fell over her as she stood there.

"Thank you," Sonje told Hoyt. "This means a lot."

Hoyt bowed his head slightly as she met his gaze.

"It has been a long day," Bryant said. "We should eat and prepare for tomorrow."

"Come," Agatha said as she stepped forward. "Your meal awaits you."

Sonje, Bryant and Gale followed her to the dining hall. Sonje could smell the food as soon as they entered. Soon they were seated at the head table and eating. The food tasted as good as it smelled. As soon as she finished eating, Sonje put her hand on Bryant's arm.

"I am going upstairs to contact my father," she said. "I will see you in the morning, My Lord."

"Haskell asked me to see him after eating," Bryant responded. "I will come check on you in a few minutes. Haskell can wait a little longer."

"Thank you," Sonje said and kissed his cheek.

Bryant turned to Gale and said, "Agatha will show you to your room."

* * * * *

As Sonje entered the great hall, she found it to be deserted except for her mother's coffin. She placed her hand on it and gently stroked the carvings on the coffin. A soft red glow began to surround Sonje and the coffin.

'My Gwladys,' her mother's voice said softly in her mind. 'You are the one chosen to lead our people back to where they belong. I am proud of what you have done.'

"I miss you, Mother," Sonje whispered.

'I will always watch over you,' the response came. 'You and Bryant will see many changes in your lifetime. The destinies of the dragons and our people are intertwined. Remember that always.'

'I have felt so since I discovered that the dragons truly existed.'

'Remember that I love you and will watch over you. Farewell Daughter.'

The red glow faded as Sonje lifted her hand from the coffin to her cheek. She used her own light to get upstairs to her apartment. The fragrance of fresh flowers greeted her as she opened her door. She stood before the polished shield. She sighed as she saw how tired she looked. Gathering her strength, she concentrated on the task at hand. Soon her image dissolved and was replaced by her aunt's image.

181

"You look tired, Gwladys," she said.

"It has been a long day," Sonje responded. "Mother's body is safely at Dracona. Hoyt has arranged the burial for tomorrow afternoon."

"I wish I could be there with you."

"I have good news. Gustave is dead and King Archelaus of Burton is withdrawing all soldiers from other kingdoms. Those unable to travel by ship can continue the journey safely by land."

"That is good news. I will select those who would struggle to keep up to travel by ship. I'll come by ship leaving your Aunt Lillian to lead the rest to Dracona."

"I look forward to seeing you. Goodnight."

"Goodnight."

* * * * *

As her image faded, Sonje slowly collapsed. Bryant opened the door just in time to see her go down. Quickly he crossed to her side. He gently took her in his arms and carried her to the bed. He gently loosened her dress before covering her with a quilt. He sighed as he headed towards the door.

'She sleeps,' Haskell thought to him. 'Come and talk.'

'Yes,' Bryant responded. 'I have much to tell you.'

Soon Bryant was in the cavern and climbing the stairs to Haskell's cave. He placed a hand on Haskell's enormous cheek before sitting down.

'You look older, Bryant,' Haskell commented.

'I feel older,' Bryant responded.

'Something troubles you,' the dragon prompted.

'I have seen evil,' Bryant began. 'Gustave was bent on the destruction of all for his own gain. He even tried to kill his twin sister.'

'It is important that you recognized his evil and wanted no part of it.'

'I will always remember the snarl on his face as he recognized Archelaus and lunged forward to kill him. The next thing I knew, I stood over his body with Fanchon's Sword in my hand.'

'At that moment, you had acted to protect more than just Archelaus. You were protecting Burton, Glynis, Dracona, and many others,' Haskell told him. 'You will make a great leader because you are willing to put others before yourself.'

'I still sometimes wonder how Dracona and Glynis will be under my leadership.' Bryant said with a sigh. 'I have lived alone for so long that I am not sure if others will accept me.'

'Even the villagers were concerned for the safety of both you and Sonje.' Haskell reassured him. 'You have already improved their lives. You do not need to worry about them accepting your leadership.'

'That does make me feel a bit better,' Bryant admitted.

'Good,' Haskell said as he lowered his head. 'Now go to bed and get some sleep.'

'Good night, my friend,' Bryant said as he patted Haskell's cheek.

Bryant closed the doors behind him. The great hall was dark except for the soft glow of the candles about Regina Elva's coffin. Bryant walked around to the coffin. He realized the appreciation that Archelaus was expressing with the gift of Regina Elva's coffin. As he softly traced the carvings with his hand, a red glow surrounded him and the coffin.

'Lord of Dragons,' a woman's voice said softly in his mind. 'You have risked much for so many. I am proud that Sonje has chosen you as Glynis' regis, and proud to call you my son. You will lead our people back home. Please thank the minstrel for his efforts in my behalf.'

"I was taught as a child that my duty was to serve and protect our people. Sonje has made me complete," Bryant responded in a whisper. "I love her with all of my being."

'Let that love guide you as you guide our people into the future. The things you were given on your journey are vital keys to our people's future.'

The red glow faded leaving Bryant in the candlelight that created a pool of light in the center of the darkness of the great hall. Bryant let his glow light his way to the stairs. He was surprised to see that his glow was almost entirely white. The stairs seemed longer than he remembered as he climbed to reach his room. He shut his door and got undressed for bed. As he thought about the day's events, he drifted off to sleep.

Chapter 17 – Family Gathering and Funeral

Bryant awoke to a knock at his door.

"Come in," he said as he sat up in bed.

Hoyt entered with a bundle of clothing in his hands. He bowed before placing the bundle on the foot of the bed.

"Here is the clothing that you sent with Gwladys Sonje," Hoyt told him. "Stanislaus has completed a grave marker for Regina Elva. He noticed that your father's grave was marked with just a faded wooden plaque. He has prepared a marker for Lord Eamon to replace it. He wishes for you to see it before it is placed on the grave."

"That is most kind of him," Bryant replied. "I will look at it right after breakfast."

"I will tell him, My Lord."

"Thank you, Hoyt."

Hoyt bowed and left. Bryant quickly bathed and dressed. He put the black cape over his arm before heading to Sonje's apartment. Sonje opened the door when Bryant tapped on it. Even dressed in a somber black dress, she was beautiful.

"Bryant," she said as she fell into his arms.

'Are you alright?' he asked silently.

'My mother spoke to me last night,' came the response in his mind.

'She spoke to me also,' Bryant replied. 'She gave her blessings on our marriage and expressed gratitude for the care taken with her body.'

Sonje lifted her head to meet his gaze. He wiped the tears from her face and kissed her.

'Stanislaus has prepared a marker for her grave. We can see it after breakfast.'

Sonje nodded and retrieved her cape from the chair next to the door. Breakfast was eaten in silence. Bryant placed Sonje's cape about her shoulders before putting his own cape on. Hand in hand, they left the dining hall. Hoyt met them in the great hall near Regina Elva's coffin.

"King Archelaus was most generous to provide such a beautiful coffin for Regina Elva," Hoyt commented.

"He will be a kind and generous leader for Burton," Bryant replied. "He wanted her to have a coffin more befitting a queen than the plain wooden box that the minstrel had put her in.

"The markers are in the armory," Hoyt said. "Follow me."

Hoyt led them into the armory. Stanislaus and Edgard were busy sweeping the floor around the two stones. The two men bowed as Bryant and Sonje approached. Regina Elva's grave marker was a large white stone that had been smoothed and polished on one side. A crown was carved across the top of the stone with the words, 'Regina Elva' carved into it. Below the crown were the dates of her birth, coronation, and her death. Below the dates were carved the words, 'Beloved Queen.'

"It is perfect," Sonje said. "Thank you."

The other stone was white flecked with black. The face of the stone was a dragon carved in relief. On its outstretched wings was carved, 'Eamon Donley' and 'Lord Dracona.' Under the dragon was carved his birth and death dates.

"Thank you, Stanislaus," Bryant said. "This is a fitting marker for my father. My mother will be as pleased as I am."

Stanislaus bowed and smiled.

"It is a pleasure to know that," he said. "You have done so much for us. I present these to you in appreciation for your leadership."

"Thank you," Sonje said.

"A carriage awaits to take you to the church to inspect the preparations there," Hoyt said.

Bryant and Sonje left the armory to find Philip waiting with Llewellyn hitched to a carriage. Bryant helped Sonje to her seat before sitting beside her. As they rode through the streets to the church, Bryant noticed that many buildings were showing signs of activity.

"It was very thoughtful of him to prepare a marker for my father's grave," Bryant commented.

"You are respected and loved by all of the people," Sonje replied.

"Last night, I noticed that my glow is almost completely white," Bryant said.

"I noticed the same has happened to my glow," Sonje said. "Soon the process of becoming the king and queen of our people will be complete."

As they arrived at the church, they could hear someone playing the organ. Bryant patted Llewellyn's neck as they walked towards the door. As Bryant opened the door, he noticed the smell of flowers. Gale was playing the organ while Florene and Aloysia were arranging flowers. Sonje smiled as she saw the preparations that were being made. Bryant kissed her cheek before going to the organ consol. Gale stopped playing as Bryant approached.

"I have a message for you," Bryant told him.

"A message?" Gale asked in a puzzled tone.

"Last night, Regina Elva spoke to me," Bryant paused as Gale's expression changed to shock. "She asked me to thank you for your efforts on her behalf."

"She really said that?"

"Yes. Sonje and I want you to know that we are all very grateful to you for how you cared for her after her death."

"Yes," Sonje said as she joined them. "What you did was very brave and means a lot to us."

"I just couldn't bear to see her body left to Gustave," Gale said. "I could not have lived with myself if I hadn't done something."

Sonje smiled and put her hand on Gale's shoulder.

"You are a good man," she said. "I would like to play something for you."

Gale stood up and Sonje took his place at the keyboard. Bryant led Gale to the front bench as she began to play. Bryant watched the minstrel relax. Soon his eyes were closed and there was a smile on his face. As Bryant listened to the music of Glynis, he began to feel more relaxed and confident. When Sonje had finished playing, Gale opened his eyes.

"That was so beautiful," he said. "I have never heard anything like it."

"It is the music of Glynis," Bryant explained.

"I thought that you might want to hear it before this afternoon," Sonje said.

"I can still hear it in my head," Gale said. "It should be played at the services."

"I want you to keep your place carrying Mother's coffin. Darryl plays the organ. You can find her at the tailor's shop." Sonje told him. "She can play the music for the services.

Gale returned to the organ and began playing the melody. Bryant led Sonje from the church and to the carriage. They returned the carriage to Philip and entered the castle. Xylia and Hoyt stood by the coffin.

"I'm glad you are here," Bryant said. "We would like to discuss a few things with both of you. Please bring the box that Xylia brought to my office.

"The box was put there as soon as she arrived," Hoyt responded.

Bryant nodded and led them to his office.

"Sonje, this is Xylia. Riva is her older sister. Riva's father was from Glynis. He brought some things from Glynis that have suddenly become important to our people's future," Bryant said.

Xylia felt around in the box for a moment then took the thinnest book from the box and held it up.

"Bryant read the first bit of this journal. Riva's father was looking for the man in the riddle to give him the other journals and these mysterious objects," Xylia said as Sonje looked into the box.

Bryant took everything out of the box and laid them out on the table. Hoyt picked up one of the books and opened it. Sonje picked up one of the metal objects.

"This may be a key of some sort," Sonje said, handing the flat piece of metal to Bryant.

Bryant noticed that there was a shiny black stripe along the length of one side of the metal piece. There were markings on the other side.

"The markings seem to match part of the markings on Mother's signet ring and the door," Sonje explained.

"The lettering is different than what we use in Glynis," Hoyt said as he closed the book he was looking at. "But it seems to be in our language. I do not recognize all of the words however."

"Where was the door that you saw in Merton?" Bryant asked Sonje.

"The floating island had been seen glowing as it did when your father died," Sonje began. "I felt strongly that it was important for me to visit the island."

"No one has ever set foot on that island," Bryant said shaking his head.

"Your mother and Brenndah took me in a boat to see it up close," Sonje replied. "As we neared the shore line, the bottom rose up in a smooth slope. As the boat touched bottom, there was a metallic thud instead of what I expected."

"Metal?" Hoyt asked in a surprised tone.

"The whole island appears to be made of metal. There are plants growing in patches of soil, but no other life. It is shaped like a wide, shallow bowl that is upside down with a raised center. Along the edge of the raised part there is strange writing."

"Is the writing similar to this?" Hoyt asked, handing the book over to Sonje.

"Yes," she answered. "I followed the raised part around until I found the door. It looked like the stone on this signet ring."

Bryant and Hoyt examined the ring that Sonje wore on her right hand.

"There is a slot between two pairs of hand-prints. Above this was an inscription that read, 'Temple of Origin, The Path Leads to the Future.'"

"That is why Riva's words shocked you," Bryant said. "Your mother's words make more sense now too."

"Yes," Sonje agreed.

"If this island is metal," Hoyt said. "It may have been constructed by our people before they reached Glynis."

"If it floats, perhaps it is a ship of some sort," Xylia commented.

"Hoyt, we need to try to decipher this writing as soon as possible," Bryant said. "Because this seems to be written before our people arrived in Glynis, some of the words may refer to things forgotten by those in Glynis."

"Just as Dracona had forgotten the language of Glynis," Sonje said.

"Exactly," Bryant said.

Hoyt nodded in agreement. Bryant put everything back into the box.

"Let's see if lunch is ready," Bryant suggested.

He locked the door behind them and led the way to the great hall.

'Bryant,' Haskell's voice said in his mind.

'Yes, my friend?' Bryant responded.

'We will arrive in the courtyard in a few minutes,' Haskell answered.

'We will meet you there,' Bryant thought back before relaying the message to the others.

"I would like to meet your dragon," Xylia said.

The group went out to the courtyard to greet Haskell and his passengers. Hoyt put his arm around Xylia's shoulders to steady her in the wind created by Haskell's wings. Bryant ran to Haskell's side as soon as he had landed. He helped his mother down and embraced her before helping Brenndah down.

"It is so good to see you again," Mother said. "You have changed since I last saw you."

"Everything has changed since I last visited Merton," Bryant said. "Please come and meet Hoyt and Xylia."

"It is good to see you again, my daughter," Mother said as she embraced Sonje.

"It means a lot to me for you to come," Sonje said. "Your presence is a comfort. I am glad that you have come as well, Brenndah."

Brenndah smiled and nodded.

"This is Hoyt," Bryant said. "He has been a great help in arranging everything. This is my mother, Lady Miranda and Brenndah, her assistant and Merton's healer."

Hoyt bowed low to the women. Bryant took Xylia's hand and led her forward.

"This is Xylia," Bryant said. "She and her sister Riva saved me from Gustave's soldiers and helped me complete my mission in Burton. She has traveled alone to Dracona to deliver some things that are important to our people's future."

Brenndah gestured towards Xylia and then touched her own eyes.

"Yes," Bryant said. "She is blind."

"Could you help her?" Sonje asked.

Brenndah nodded. Bryant shot Sonje a puzzled look. Sonje nodded in response as Brenndah began to glow. She reached out and gently touched Xylia's eyes. When she removed her hands, Xylia blinked several times and put one hand above her eyes to shade them.

"How did you fix my eyes?" Xylia asked in amazement.

"The same way that Riva is able to foretell the future," Sonje answered.

Xylia turned to Haskell.

"I never thought that I would actually be able to see you with my eyes," Xylia said. "But I have wanted to meet you ever since Bryant told us of you. You are beautiful."

'Thank you,' Haskell thought to her. 'I am honored to meet you at last. Thank you for saving Bryant. He is like a son to me.'

Xylia turned back to the others and looked at each of them in turn.

"Thank you for giving me my sight," she said. "I have missed being able to see."

Brenndah smiled. Agatha appeared at the door.

"Lunch is ready, My Lord," she announced.

"Agatha, I would like you to meet my mother, Lady Miranda, and Brenndah," Bryant said.

"It is a pleasure to meet you, My Lady," Agatha said as she curtsied. "You son is a fine young man and we are grateful to have him as our leader."

"I am glad to hear that," Mother responded.

They entered the castle as others began to arrive for lunch. Haskell returned to his cave. Soon they were enjoying the delicious meal that Agatha had prepared. When everyone had finished eating, Hoyt stood in front of the head table.

"Please meet in one hour at the church for a farewell service for Regina Elva," he announced.

189

Bryant turned to Sonje and took her hand in his. Sonje smiled at him. He then turned to his mother.

"I have a surprise for you, Mother," he said. "It is in the armory."

"Let's see it then," she answered.

Bryant led her out to the armory while Sonje stayed in the dining hall. The armory was empty when they entered. Bryant led her to where the grave markers were.

"Oh, Bryant!" she gasped. "Your father would have loved it."

"One of the men from Glynis surprised me with it."

"I must thank him in person."

"It seems that Dracona has finally moved out of the past," Bryant said. "The town has been repaired. The people of the village have forgiven Uncle Rolf's actions and pledged their loyalty to Dracona. The evil wrought by the thirteenth member of Fanchon's group has been laid to rest."

"Yes," she agreed. "Dracona is ready for the future, and you are doing a fine job as Lord Dracona. I am so glad that you have at last found love. I have been so very worried about you. It was like I could see the life slowly draining out of you, but today you are alive again."

"I am more alive than I've been for a very long time."

Bryant led his mother out of the armory and met Philip and Stanislaus outside the stables.

"Mother, this is Philip and Stanislaus," Bryant said. "This is my mother, Lady Miranda."

Both men bowed.

"Stanislaus is our talented and thoughtful stone cutter," Bryant explained with a smile.

"I want to thank you for the grave marker for my beloved husband," she said. "Eamon would have loved your design."

Stanislaus bowed again. Bryant noticed his cheeks were turning red as he rose.

"You are too kind, My Lady," Stanislaus replied. "It was done as a small token of appreciation for what Lord Bryant has done for all of us."

"We will move the stones to the graveyard before taking Regina Elva's coffin to the church," Philip said.

"Thank you," Bryant replied.

The clattering of hooves on the cobblestone streets drew their attention to the courtyard entrance. Bryant was glad to see Regis Auberon and the rest of Sonje's family enter in a wagon followed by several other wagons with some of the villagers including the village council. Bryant bowed as Regis Auberon left the wagon and approached him. Regis Auberon bowed to Bryant.

"This is Sonje's father, Regis Auberon," Bryant said. "This is my mother, Lady Miranda."

"It is a pleasure to meet you, My Lady," Regis Auberon said with a bow.

"It is a pleasure to meet you as well," she replied with a curtsey.

"Philip can take care of your team and wagon. Please come and see the beautiful coffin provided by the new king of Burton," Bryant said as he indicated the castle door.

Cherie and Olvan followed with their children after Bryant had introduced them to his mother. Sonje, Brenndah and Xylia were just coming out of the dining hall as Bryant held the door open for the rest to enter the castle.

"Father!" Sonje exclaimed when Regis Auberon entered.

"Gwladys, it is so good to see you," Regis Auberon answered.

"Mother will finally have a proper burial," she said as she embraced him. "Stanislaus has carved a beautiful marker for her grave."

"This is a beautiful coffin. It pleases me," Regis Auberon commented.

"King Archelaus gave it to us in gratitude for our help," Sonje replied.

"Remember the mute kitchen boy?" Bryant asked.

"Yes," Regis Auberon acknowledged.

"That was Archelaus in disguise," Bryant explained. "Gustave's twin sister has the ability to change physical appearances. Archelaus will be attending the wedding and coronation."

"Were you able to retrieve the box from the well?"

"Yes, but the hook and rope didn't work," Bryant said with a grin. "I found that I can lift things with my mind."

Regis Auberon's face showed surprise.

"I can show you later if you would like," Bryant said. "But we had best let you get something to eat before the service begins."

Sonje led her family and the villagers into the dining hall. Bryant excused himself to see if Philip and Stanislaus needed his help. He soon found that they had left with the stones already. He went to the pasture fence to check on the horses. Llewellyn whinnied and trotted over to the fence.

"I've missed you," Bryant told him as the horse nuzzled his cheek. "Has Philip been taking good care of you while I was gone?"

Llewellyn nodded his head up and down. Bryant rubbed the horse's nose before turning to leave. He heard the wagon return to the courtyard and stop. Bryant quickly returned to the castle doors as they were opened. Hoyt was waiting with the others who had carried the coffin the night before.

No words were spoken as the men lifted the coffin and moved it to the wagon. The men took their places beside the wagon as Sonje and her family took their place behind. Gale and Bryant were on each side of the horses pulling the wagon. Bryant put his hand under the horse's chin and clicked his tongue. As the horses began to move, Bryant dropped his hand knowing that the horses would stay between him and Gale.

They proceeded slowly to the church. At the church, the men carried the coffin in and placed it on a table in front of the benches. Bryant took his place beside Sonje as Darryl began to play the organ. Bryant took Sonje's hand in his as Hoyt stood on the stand waiting for the last of the people to take their seats. Hoyt nodded to Darryl and stepped up to the podium.

"We are here today to bid farewell to Regina Elva," Hoyt began. "We are sorrowed at her death and she is missed by all who knew her. Many of you know her only as wife of Regis Auberon, mother of Gwladys Cherie and Gwladys Sonje. To those from Glynis, she was much more."

"As queen of Glynis, she ruled in kindness and fairness. As a true servant of the people, she risked her life for the protection and safety of Glynis. In Burton, she paid for that safety with her life. We will always remember the minstrel, Gale, with gratitude for his brave actions in preserving her body so that Gustave would not have it. Today we bid Regina Elva farewell and pray that she will now be in peace. Let us all take a few moments of silence to honor her memory," Hoyt said.

The church fell silent for a time. Bryant put his arm around Sonje's shoulders as he saw the tears begin to roll down her cheeks.

Hoyt at last broke the silence and said, "At this time, we will also be placing a grave marker for Lord Eamon Donley, Lord Bryant's father. We will now adjourn to the grave yard."

Bryant squeezed Sonje's shoulders before taking his place with the others carrying the coffin. Slowly the procession made its way out of town and onto the foothill. Near Father's grave was a freshly dug grave. Hoyt nodded to Regis Auberon who stood at the head of the grave.

"We dedicate this grave for the body of Regina Elva. May she rest peacefully in this beautiful place," Regis Auberon said.

The men took the coffin from the wagon and carried it to over the grave. Bryant concentrated and felt the weight of the coffin lift from his hand. Slowly, Bryant lowered the coffin into the grave. Regis Auberon smiled at him and nodded. Stanislaus, Keith and Absalon began shoveling dirt into the grave. Bryant turned his attention to the grave markers.

"When my father, Lord Eamon, died, I was unable to provide more than a simple wooden marker for his grave," Bryant said. "Today through the generosity and talents of Stanislaus, his grave will have a proper stone marker."

Bryant concentrated on the marker stone for his father's grave. Slowly it lifted off the ground. Bryant set it down where the wooden marker had been. Sonje joined him as he looked at the newly placed stone.

'It is good to see a proper stone on his grave,' Bryant thought to her. 'I feel that I can begin to move on now.'

'I feel the same about my mother,' she responded. 'I never was able to mourn her death.'

Bryant put his arm around her shoulders.

'I have been in mourning ever since my father's death.'

Mother and Regis Auberon joined them.

"That is quite a talent you have," Regis Auberon told him. "I have never met anyone who was able to lift things with their mind."

"I discovered it when I couldn't get the box in the well hooked."

"It is amazing," Mother remarked. "I am so proud of you, Bryant. I have been watching you today. I can see how much you have grown and changed. You are finally ready to be the leader of our people."

"Sonje has been a ray of light leading me out of darkness. With her I am complete and ready to face the future," Bryant said with emotion.

"You have changed a lot since I first met you," Regis Auberon admitted as he placed his hand on Bryant's shoulder. "I will be proud to call you Regis Bryant."

"Now that the past has been laid to rest, we can concentrate on the move of Glynis and on your wedding," his mother said.

"Hoyt has started making the preparations for the wedding and coronation already," Sonje said.

"We can go over those plans tomorrow," Hoyt said as he approached the group. "We are ready for you to set the stone, Lord Bryant."

"Thank you, Hoyt," he replied.

Bryant stood near the foot of the new grave as he concentrated on the grave marker. As he set the stone in place, he began to feel very weak. He turned to find Hoyt at his side.

"Come, My Lord," Hoyt said as he took Bryant's elbow. "You need to rest after using your talent so much."

Hoyt helped Bryant into the wagon and Sonje sat next to him. Bryant was grateful for her arm around him to keep him upright. Soon they arrived at the castle. Hoyt and Sonje helped him to his room. Bryant sat down on the bed.

"Rest, My Love," Sonje said softly. "I will bring some food up to you in about an hour."

She kissed his forehead as she turned to leave. Bryant settled gratefully onto the bed and slept.

* * * * *

"He is very strong," Hoyt told Sonje as they walked down the hall.

"Yet at the same time, he is fragile," Sonje replied. "He needs our support as much as we need him."

Hoyt nodded in agreement. At the great hall, Sonje paused to contemplate the day's events.

'I wish to speak with you, Sister Queen,' Evelina's voice said in her mind with a sense of urgency. 'Come to me.'

'I will be right there,' Sonje replied.

She quickly turned the mechanism and opened the doors just enough for her to enter. She paused for a moment to remember which tunnel would be the shortest route before continuing. Her light reflected off flecks of metal in the tunnel walls as she hurried to where Evelina waited for her.

'Thank you for coming,' Evelina greeted her.

'You are welcome to call me at any time,' Sonje replied with a curtsey.

'My sleep has been filled with strange dreams,' Evelina began. 'I see a place of tall red cliffs against a light violet sky. In this place, I see dragons and people living together.'

'I have traveled to many lands, but have never seen such a place,' Sonje commented puzzled by the description.

'It did not mean much until I heard you talking about a metal island. In my dreams there are houses and wagons of some sort that are made of metal,' Evelina explained. 'I don't know if it means anything, but I thought I saw you and Bryant in this place. I thought you should know.'

'Thank you,' Sonje said. 'Bryant was given some metal objects and some books. We do not understand some of the words yet, but we are going to try to learn as much as we can from these things.'

'I must sleep now,' Evelina thought as she yawned.

'Sleep well,' Sonje replied.

Sonje was deep in thought when she reached the kitchen. Since Agatha was not in the kitchen, Sonje gathered a tray of food herself. She went to Bryant's room and set the tray quietly on the table. Bryant was sleeping soundly, so Sonje sat in a chair to wait.

She went over Evelina's dream in her mind. The dragon's thoughts had provided her with some images from the dream.

'Where is that?' Bryant's question broke through her thoughts.

'I don't know,' she thought back. 'It was part of Evelina's dream.'

Bryant sat up on the edge of the bed.

"You look tired," he said aloud.

"I'm beginning to be hungry too," she admitted. "It has been a long time since lunch."

They shared the tray of food that she had brought. After she finished eating, Sonje went to the window. After a few minutes, Bryant joined her at the window and put his arm about her shoulders. They stood in silence for a while.

* * * * *

'What's wrong?' Bryant thought to her when he felt the tremor go through her.

She turned and buried her face in his chest. He felt the overwhelming sadness in her thoughts as she opened her mind to him. He gently stroked her hair as she wept. He remembered the time just after his father's death. He knew that she was finally mourning for her mother. He felt her begin to collapse. He turned her and lifted her into his arms. He carried her to the chair near the bed and sat down with her in his lap.

'I understand what you are feeling,' he thought to her gently. 'I felt the same way when Father died. You have hidden it deep inside for too long. Let it out. I will hold you and keep you safe.'

Bryant drew her closer as she cried. He watched the sun sink lower in the sky as he held Sonje in his arms. He felt Haskell's presence knowing the dragon was keeping his own watch.

'They are looking for you two,' Haskell's voice broke through Bryant's thoughts. 'Dinner is almost ready and they are very worried.'

'Explain to Mother and Auberon,' Bryant replied. 'I think Sonje needs more time before she is ready to face anyone.'

'I agree. I will tell them.'

Bryant kissed her hair and held her tighter. He knew that she was nearly exhausted, but still too distraught to sleep. Bryant caught a movement out of the corner of his eye. He turned his head to see Brenndah enter the room and close the door. She placed a hand on Sonje's head and closed her eyes. A red glow centered around Brenndah and Bryant felt Sonje relax in his arms.

'She sleeps,' Haskell told Bryant.

"Thank you, Brenndah," Bryant whispered. "Help me put her in the bed."

Brenndah nodded and pulled the quilt back as Bryant laid Sonje gently on the bed. She took off Sonje's boots. Brenndah gestured to Bryant, then to her mouth as if eating.

"No, thank you," he responded as he gestured towards the tray on the table. "We have eaten. I will have Haskell tell Agatha if I am hungry."

Brenndah nodded and smiled.

"I will keep watch over her. She needs me just to be here."

Brenndah nodded and placed her hand on his forehead. Bryant felt her energy flow into him through her hand.

"Thank you, Brenndah," Bryant said as she removed her hand. "Go get some sleep. Tell Mother that I will see her in the morning."

Brenndah smiled. She turned and took the empty tray with her. Bryant closed the door behind her. He pulled the chair and footstool up to the bed and took off his boots. He settled into the chair and took her hand in his. As the room darkened with the setting of the sun, Bryant let his light glow softly.

He thought back on the events that had happened since he met Sonje. He knew that it had been just as difficult on her as it had been on him. His father's death had been hard for him to endure watching. He knew that it must have been even harder for Sonje to have to flee for her life and leave her mother behind knowing there was no way they could take the body with.

He shifted so that he could see her face. Her face seemed so beautiful and delicate, yet he well knew the strength and determination that she had in her. He watched her face as the hours passed. Suddenly, she winced as if in pain. Quickly he shifted from the chair to the bed and stroked her hair. Her hand grasped his tightly before she relaxed again.

'You are correct,' Haskell said to him. 'The circumstances of her mother's death have left her feeling that she should have done more to save her mother. She has kept this buried deep inside. She needs you more than ever to help her get through her sorrow.'

'I will not leave her side until she is ready.'

'Try to get some sleep. It will be dawn in a few hours and she will need you awake then. I will keep watch over her dreams.'

'Thank you, Haskell. It is good to have one such as you to turn to in times of need.'

Bryant shifted back into the chair. With her hand still in his, he closed his eyes and drifted off to sleep.

Chapter 18 – Mourning the Past and Saying Goodbye

The room was still dark except for the silver light of the dawn shining softly through the window when Sonje awoke. She felt disoriented at the unfamiliar surroundings and her head hurt a little. As she let her light increase, she saw Bryant asleep in a chair with her hand in his.

'How are you feeling this morning?' Haskell asked in a concerned tone. 'We have been very worried about you.'

'A little better I think,' Sonje replied as she recalled the previous night. 'Everything that I had tried to not think about suddenly hit me yesterday.'

'Bryant understood what you were going through. He has not left your side since you began to cry. Brenndah came and helped you to finally fall asleep. She also gave energy to Bryant so he could stay up watching over you.'

'I should let him sleep.'

'No. He has had enough sleep. He will wake when you move your hand.'

'Thank you, Haskell.'

Sonje carefully moved her hand and sat up. She was surprised to see that she was in Bryant's bed. Bryant began to stir. Tenderly she put her hand on his cheek. He opened his eyes.

"Are you alright, Sonje?" he asked with concern. "I'm sorry that I fell asleep."

"I felt your presence in my dreams. It helped me get through my grief knowing that I was not alone."

"Right after my father died, I felt so alone and all empty inside. I knew that you needed me here with you."

A quiet knock drew their attention to the door.

"Come," Bryant responded.

Father and Lady Miranda entered followed by Brenndah.

"We have been so worried," Lady Miranda spoke first.

"Haskell said you were doing better this morning," Father finished for her.

"I don't know if I would have made it if not for Bryant," Sonje answered. "My only awareness beyond the grief was Bryant's presence. I think I will be alright now."

Sonje stood and hugged first her father, then Lady Miranda, and finally Brenndah.

"Breakfast will be ready soon, Gwladys," Father said. "Do you feel up to coming to the dining hall?"

"I want to take a quick bath and put on a less somber dress first," Sonje replied.

"I think I will do the same," Bryant said as he stood and stretched out his stiff muscles.

"May I have a word with you, Lord Bryant?" Father asked.

"Certainly. We can talk while I get cleaned up," Bryant replied.

"Brenndah and I will stay with you while you get cleaned up, Sonje," Lady Miranda said as she put an arm across Sonje's shoulders.

"Thank you," Sonje said.

* * * * *

After the women left, Bryant and Regis Auberon went into the bathing chamber. Bryant began to run the water for his bath then sat down to shave.

"I wanted to thank you for all that you have done for my family," Regis Auberon began. "I knew that Sonje had not yet let herself grieve for her mother's death and I have been very worried about how she would finally deal with it."

"I grieved for my father for five years after he died in my arms," Bryant admitted. "I was still grieving when I came across you and Sonje in the forest. When I saw her trying to protect you, I also saw myself trying to keep my own father from dying."

Bryant paused to undress and step into the basin of water.

"Is that why you decided to save my life?"

"Partly," Bryant replied after a moment. "To this day, I still cannot answer that completely. At times I feel compelled to do something without any clear reason. When I was prompted to open the box containing Malvin's Heart, I did not have any clear reason to do so."

"Yet that has been very important to our people's safety and to Sonje just last night."

Bryant nodded before washing his hair.

"After I had spoken the words to open the box, a woman appeared over the volcano's pit. She said she had been calling me to open the box."

"Perhaps she was prompting you that morning in the forest."

"If so, I am glad that she did. I hope she continues to guide me," Bryant said as he exited the basin. "I am beginning to believe that Dracona is only a temporary home for our people."

Regis Auberon seemed stunned as Bryant dried himself. He followed Bryant to the bedroom.

"On my way to Burton, I met the two sisters, Riva and Xylia. Riva's father was from Glynis. She gave me a box of journals and some strange metal objects," Bryant continued as he began to dress. "Then Sonje discovered a door on a metal island that Merton's ships have seen glowing. On the door are marks matching the ring Gale brought from Burton. Above those marks are the words 'Temple of Origin, The Path Leads to the Future.' The island has been slowly drifting south."

Regis Auberon looked even more puzzled.

"Sonje told me that Evelina's dream showed people and dragons living together in a place with tall red cliffs and a light violet sky."

"I hope that you can find out what all this means," Regis Auberon said. "I have no idea what to think of any of it."

"That is why I have decided that learning what those things mean is second only to the move of Glynis," Bryant replied as he combed his hair.

"What about your wedding and coronation?" Regis Auberon asked.

Bryant turned to face him.

"My wedding to Sonje is the most important event in my entire life. Not even the coronation will come close to it in the life of Bryant Donley. The coronation, the move of Glynis, and the future of our people are the most important things for Lord Dracona and Regis Bryant. For over a hundred years I put aside Bryant Donley for Lord Dracona. I now know that never again can I put aside the needs of Bryant Donley for Lord Dracona. Both are equally important. Yet I know with all my heart that if I had to choose, I would give up everything for Sonje in a single heartbeat."

Bryant was surprised as Regis Auberon hugged him tight and patted his back.

"I am proud to call you my son," Regis Auberon told him. "And proud to have you as my regis."

Bryant stood in stunned silence for a moment after Regis Auberon released him. He numbly followed Regis Auberon to Sonje's room. Sonje was brushing her hair as they entered. Bryant took the brush from her, kissed her hand and began to brush her hair. The others quietly left.

* * * * *

"Bryant has changed so much since the last time he visited Merton," Lady Miranda told Auberon. "He seems to be whole again, and more mature."

"He has changed a lot since I first met him," Auberon said in agreement. "He is a remarkable man to have dealt so well with everything that he has been through. I think he is ready to be regis."

"He has done so much in such a short time. He has forever changed the lives of our people for the better."

"Yet he now understands that to be a true leader, he cannot put aside his own needs. He will make as good of a husband as he does a king."

"And Sonje will make the perfect wife and queen for him," Lady Miranda added with a smile.

* * * * *

Sonje watched Bryant's face in the polished shield as he brushed her hair. He seemed to be deep in thought. When he set down the brush, he knelt beside her. She turned to face him. He tenderly took her hands in his before he spoke.

"Your father has given his blessings on our marriage," Bryant said as a tear ran down his cheek. "The first thing that he ever said to me was that it was a cruel thing to take a man's daughter away from him. This morning, he said he was proud to call me his son and his regis. I didn't expect to ever hear him say that."

"I know that you and Father will be friends just as your mother and I have become," Sonje said as she stood up.

She pulled him to his feet. Her heart leapt as he leaned down and kissed her lips. He released her hands and pulled her closer. Her head began to spin as he kissed her again. She laid her head on his shoulder to catch her breath. She could hear his heart beating as quickly as her own.

'We had better get down to breakfast,' she thought to him.

He kissed her hair before releasing her. They went down to the dining room and sat between Lady Miranda and Father at the head table. After they were finished eating, Bryant turned to Sonje.

"I want to see that door," he told her. "Haskell can take us."

"We should take paper, pen and ink with us so we can copy the writings on the island," she replied.

'Come to my cave when you are ready,' Haskell told them.

Soon they had a pair of saddlebags packed with the writing materials and a lunch. Bryant found a fur lined jacket and gloves for Sonje to wear. Haskell was waiting for them when they reached his cave. They mounted and Haskell carried them to the opening of the cave. Bryant felt Sonje's arms tighten around him as Haskell launched himself into the sky.

'I have always been curious about this island,' Haskell told them as it came into sight.

* * * * *

Bryant looked down as Haskell circled to look for a place to land. He could see that the island did make a complete circle that stood out against the darkness of the deep water. He thought he could see a long rectangular shape trailing to the north under the island.

'This is very big,' he thought to Haskell and Sonje. 'Only a small portion is above water.'

Haskell landed on top of the raised center. Bryant helped Sonje to dismount. Sonje got out the paper, ink and pen as Bryant looked over the edge.

"I think I had better lift us down," Bryant said as he took her hand.

She gasped in surprise as their feet lifted off the ground. Bryant set them down carefully on the lower surface. They followed the ridge around to their left until they found the door. Sonje drew a diagram of the door before beginning to copy the writing along the ridge. Bryant knelt on one knee and wiped some of the dirt and plants from the surface. It was indeed too smooth and metallic to be a natural island. After brushing more, he found a straight line with round marks on either side in regular intervals. He returned to the door as Sonje was coming around from behind the ridge. He pulled off his glove and put his hand on one of the hand prints. He pulled back with shock when he felt a tingling and energy flowing from the metal into his hand just as Brenndah had done the night before.

"What is it?" Sonje asked with concern.

"This is no island," he said. "We must learn as much as possible from these writings and the journals before returning. There is more power here than I know what to do with."

"I have seen what seems to be the word 'vessel' several times," she said as she wrote down the last few words. "I also saw 'lift', 'energy', and 'lead'."

* * * * *

Bryant put his glove back on and lifted them both back up to where Haskell was waiting. Sonje took the lunch out of the saddle bags. She watched Bryant closely while she ate. He did not eat much and seemed lost in thought as he read over what she had written down.

"When will Glynis arrive?" he asked suddenly.

"In about two weeks," she answered, wondering why he asked.

"And about two weeks after that to get them settled before our wedding and coronation."

"Yes."

"Agatha and Hoyt have things under control and on schedule, leaving this to you and me."

"I suppose so."

"I think Xylia was right about this being some sort of ship," Bryant said as he began to pack the saddle bags. "I want to get back home now. Our wedding and coronation will prepare us to open that door. Only you and I can open it."

Sonje mounted Haskell and held on tight to Bryant as she tried to sort out what he meant. When they arrived at Dracona, Bryant led her straight to his office. "I think I understand what this is saying," he told her as he pulled the papers from the saddle bags. "When I touched one of the hand-prints with my bare hand, I felt energy flowing into me. I believe it would provide me enough energy to raise the whole thing up out of the water."

"And what about opening the door?" Sonje asked.

"Here in front of the word 'lead'there are two marks," Bryant said as he pointed to it on the paper. "This mark appears in front of 'lift', and the other in front of this word."

"What does that word mean?"

"The last part seems to say 'opening', but I don't recognize the first part. I think it refers to the door, because the next section refers to 'lead' with the two marks again."

'Aurora and Darryl need you two at the tailor's shop,' Haskell interrupted.

"We can work more on this later," Bryant said.

* * * * *

When they arrived at the tailor's shop, Aurora and Darryl took some more measurements and showed them some of the things that they had finished. Bryant gently touched the finished embroidered dragon on his cape. They had trimmed the cape with black fur. The women had finished a suit of clothes for him that was all white.

"You will need a pair of white boots," Aurora told him as he examined the white jacket. "Please sit down and remove your boots, My Lord, and I will take the necessary measurements."

Bryant complied as she set a stiff piece of leather on the floor. She asked him to stand on it while she traced around his feet with a pen and ink. Soon Sonje was the one getting her feet traced. Bryant marveled at the detail put into each item of clothing.

"Is everything to your liking, My Lord?" Darryl asked, noticing his interest in the clothing.

"I have never worn anything this elegant, nor this," he paused for a moment, "white."

"The coronation clothes will be more colorful," she assured him. "White clothing is customary for a bride and groom in Glynis."

"It has been too long since I have attended a wedding. I do not remember much about the last one that I attended," he explained. "I suppose I should ask Hoyt to tell me what to expect."

"Hoyt will also be able to tell you what to expect at the coronation ceremony the day after the wedding," Aurora added as she came out of the back room.

Sonje came out of the back room soon after and they returned to the castle. Bryant's stomach rumbled as soon as they entered the castle. Agatha stood in the doorway to the dining hall.

"I've saved some supper for you," she said. "Everyone else has finished already."

Bryant and Sonje ate while Agatha worked in the kitchen. Bryant looked around the room as if seeing it for the first time.

* * * * *

"Are you alright?" Sonje asked as she saw the faraway look in his eyes.

"Just thinking about how much things have changed," he replied.

"The last several days have been tough on you," Sonje said, sensing what he was thinking. "Perhaps you need to spend some time alone tomorrow. Haskell and I can be there if you need us."

"Maybe you're right," Bryant admitted. "I will take a long ride on Llewellyn right after I give Mayetta and Alleyn a ride on Haskell. I did promise them that when they visited the castle."

"Good. Let's get some sleep then," Sonje said as she stood.

They walked arm in arm up to Sonje's apartment.

"Will you be alright tonight?" Bryant asked her.

"I will be fine," Sonje reassured him.

Her heart skipped a beat as he kissed her goodnight. She watched him as he went to his room and shut the door behind him. There was a sadness about him, but she could not read his thoughts.

'He is trying to keep it all hidden even from me,' Haskell said to her in a worried tone. 'I will keep watch over him tonight.'

'Wake me if I am needed,' Sonje said as she closed her door behind her.

* * * * *

Bryant awoke at dawn after a restless night. He bathed and got dressed. The familiar black clothing somehow felt comforting although he had not worn them since before the village fair. His sword hung in its scabbard underneath his black cape. After a moment of hesitation, he buckled its belt around his waist. He tied the sheath with his hunting knife

203

to the belt before settling his cape about his shoulders. He took a rolled quilt from the closet and his journal from the night stand. He put the pen and ink in his jacket pocket and left the room.

The hall was silent and empty. Quietly, he descended to the great hall. There was no light yet in the great hall, but Bryant made no effort to light his way. He knew by heart the entire castle. Out in the courtyard, he crossed to the stables, the echo of his footsteps the only sound. He found a saddlebag and Llewellyn's saddle and bridle. The horses were still sleeping as he placed the things by the pasture gate. He packed the saddle bags with the journal, pen, ink and two skins of water.

He knew that soon enough others would be awakening. He still was not ready to have intrusion into his solitude, not yet. He went behind the armory and climbed the stairs to the top of the wall. He went to the corner of the wall and looked towards the village. He watched the shadow of the mountain slowly retreat towards the castle, just as the darkness and shame of Dracona's past had slowly retreated. It felt good to know that the darkness was finally gone, yet something inside wanted things the way they were before.

* * * * *

Sonje knocked quietly on Bryant's door, knowing full well that he was not there. She glanced down the empty hall before entering. She felt drawn to the window. As she looked out, at first nothing was out of the ordinary. As a breeze played across her face, a movement caught her eye. To the right she could see Bryant standing as still as a statue with his black cape gently billowing in the breeze.

'What is he thinking, Haskell? I still am inexperienced in listening in on his thoughts,' Sonje said with her mind.

'I see images of his past,' Haskell said. 'I think he needs a chance to reconcile with the past, so he can leave it behind him and face the future.'

'Then we must let him do so,' Sonje replied. 'He said that he had been mourning his father's death still.'

'Eamon died in Bryant's arms after being ill for several months.'

'That was probably harder than my mother's death to accept.'

'Let him stay where he is. I think breakfast is the last thing on his mind.'

Sonje went down to breakfast alone. Her father and the others were there already. She could read the question in their eyes.

"Bryant has been up for a few hours already," she said in answer. "I don't think he'll be joining us for breakfast."

Everyone seemed satisfied with her explanation. Sonje ate as she listened to the conversation of the others. She was still eating when Cherie sat down next to her.

"I don't have to hear your thoughts to know you are worried about Lord Dracona," Cherie said softly to her.

"The funeral and burial have been very hard on both of us," Sonje admitted. "He has been mourning his father's death for a long time. It is now time for him to put that past behind him, but that is something that he must do alone."

"Father told me that Mother's death hit you pretty hard the other night."

"Yes, but I think I am through the worst of it."

Cherie gave Sonje a quick hug as Bryant walked through the door. Mayetta and Alleyn leapt from their seats and ran towards him.

"Uncle Bryant!" they exclaimed.

Bryant knelt as the children reached him. They flung their arms around his neck. Sonje smiled to see him return their hug.

'I can hardly wait for us to have children of our own,' Bryant's words sounded wistful in her mind.

'I am looking forward to that time as well,' she replied to him.

* * * * *

Bryant had a child holding on to each hand when he reached the head table.

"I promised these two a ride on Haskell," Bryant said. "If you would like to come with, Olvan, they could both ride at the same time."

"Certainly," Olvan replied.

Haskell was waiting in the courtyard when they got there. Haskell put his chin on the ground so the children could get a closer look. Soon they were mounted. Haskell leapt into the air as the children squealed with delight. After circling a few times, Haskell set down gently in the courtyard.

"That was great!" Mayetta said with enthusiasm.

"Thank you, Haskell! Thank you, Uncle Bryant!" Alleyn added.

Bryant smiled, but Sonje glimpsed a tear in the corner of his eye. She took his hand and walked with him into the stables.

"Things are alright here," she told him. "I understand that you need time to sort things out."

"I am going to a place my father used to take me," Bryant replied.

"Do you have everything you need?"

"Yes."

"If I don't hear from you tonight, I will come after you," she said as she put her hand on his cheek. "I just need to know that you are safe."

"I will be back in a day or so. It is not very far from here," he said as the tear finally rolled down his cheek. "There is too much here for me now to not return."

He leaned down and kissed her lips.

"Tell them not to worry," he said as he picked up the saddle.

"They understand, but they will still worry because they love you," Sonje replied.

Soon Llewellyn was ready to go. Bryant led him out of the stables. He was grateful to find the courtyard deserted except for Sonje and him.

"Safe journey, Bryant," Sonje said. "I love you."

He kissed her hand.

"I love you," he replied before mounting.

He held Llewellyn to a trot until they were off the cobblestone streets. He turned Llewellyn onto the mountain trail and gave him his head. It felt good to ride again. Before noon, they had reached the summit. Bryant turned his mount off the trail and around an outcrop of rock. On the other side was a grassy area tucked in the curve of the ridge.

Bryant dismounted and unsaddled Llewellyn. He placed the saddle and bridle on a small ledge of rock. He took out his journal and began to thumb through it. He sat down on a rock and began to read. As the sun crept down to the west, Bryant read what he had written before Rolf destroyed the town and after. He read what he had written during his father's illness. As he was reading the day of his father's death, he had trouble making out the words in the dark.

He set the journal beside the saddle and picked up some of the wood he and his father had sheltered amongst the rocks years ago. He placed the wood in the rock lined fire pit and lit the fire. He sat down by the fire and watched it lick at the wood.

As he watched the dancing flames, he remembered the many times that he and his father had camped there. Slowly he began to relax. Beyond the rocky ridge, the stars dotted the sky like bright diamonds. Softly he heard a voice, at first too quiet to understand, then louder.

'It is time to let me go, My Son,' said the voice in his mind. 'I am proud of how you have cared for Dracona, but you have much more important responsibilities now.'

"I feel I still need you," Bryant answered in a whisper.

'I still watch over you, but you have others now who love you as much as I do. You have Sonje at your side. Together you will lead our people. She is the one you need now.'

"I love her with all of my being."

'As I still do your mother. Put the past behind you and mourn no more. I love you, Bryant.'

"Farewell, Father. I will always love you."

Bryant sat for a moment before getting up. He got the quilt rolled out and laid down.

'Sonje,' he called to her with his mind.

'Bryant!' she answered. 'How are you doing?'

'A little better.'

'Good. Everyone has been worried about you and they want to know when you will return.'

'I miss you. I will come home sometime tomorrow.'

'I miss you too. Take your time coming home. The body heals faster than the mind and heart.'

'That is so true,' he answered with a sigh. 'I'll call you when I am on my way. Meet me in the meadow where we first kissed.'

'I will and I will bring some food. I noticed you didn't have any when you left.'

'It just wasn't a priority this morning.'

'Get some sleep and I will see you tomorrow. I love you.'

'I love you.'

Chapter 19 – Planning a Surprise

Bryant woke with a start and discovered Llewellyn nuzzling his cheek. The horse moved away after Bryant rubbed his nose. The sun was well on its way towards noon. Bryant got up and stretched. He opened his journal and began writing about the last few days. As soon as he finished, he broke camp and saddled up Llewellyn. The horse pranced with eagerness as he mounted.

"Let's go," Bryant told the horse.

Soon they were on the gentle rolling slopes where the cattle were kept. Llewellyn stretched his long legs as he galloped full speed across the grassy slopes. Bryant slowed him as they neared the trail down to Dracona.

'Sonje,' Bryant called.

'I've been waiting to hear from you. I will leave at once,' Sonje answered.

'I will see you soon.'

Bryant reached the meadow first. He found a spot on the stream that gave a good reflection and used his hunting knife to shave. As soon as he finished, he heard hoof beats approaching. He turned to see Sonje enter the meadow on one of the tan horses. Bryant hurried to help her down as she drew her mount to a halt.

* * * * *

A shiver went up her spine as he put his strong hands on her waist and lifted her down. Bryant pulled her close with his arms around her and held her. Sonje could feel him tremble as he held her tight.

'My father spoke to me last night,' Bryant's words came to her mind. 'My place is here with you, not in the past. I know that I can let go of him now.'

Sonje looked up at him. She could see the determination on his face as he leaned down and kissed her. Her head was spinning when he finally released her. When her head cleared, she found that he had taken her saddlebags and sat down near the stream. She joined him and began unpacking the food. Sonje watched him while they ate. He seemed less anxious and moody than he had since she met him in Burton.

"I'm glad that you are feeling better about things," she said aloud.

"Last night, I read back through my journal. After my father spoke to me, I began to understand that my life has been preparing me for now," Bryant replied. "I just needed to accept that. Part of me was afraid of marriage and leadership, but that part is gone now. The time I have spent with Olvan's children helped me understand how alone I have been and how very much I need you. It will be wonderful to have children of our own."

"I am so happy to hear that," Sonje said. "The only other thing that might make me happier is to hear that our wedding was tomorrow."

* * * * *

Bryant's heart leapt at her admission. He stood and drew her to her feet.

"That would be welcome news for me as well," he said as he drew her closer. "It seems forever away."

He lifted her chin and kissed her tenderly.

"I think it would be best for us to return to the castle now," he reluctantly admitted.

Sonje nodded. Together they packed the saddle bags and were soon headed back towards the castle. He was grateful to see that some of the villagers had remained in Dracona and were helping with the rebuilding of the town. As they made their way to the castle, he began to see how much concern the people did have for him. As they passed, everyone smiled and waved to them. As they entered the castle courtyard, they were greeted by a large group.

"Bryant!" Mother said as he dismounted. "You have worried all of us."

"I just needed some time alone to sort things out," Bryant replied as he hugged her.

"I'm glad you were able to do it before Glynis arrived," Regis Auberon said as he hugged Bryant.

Bryant turned to take his saddlebags from the horses and hide the fact that his face was turning red. Haskell's chuckle rumbled in his mind.

'You knew it all along,' Bryant told Haskell. 'Auberon has forgiven me completely.'

'I couldn't tell you,' the dragon admitted. 'You had to learn it for yourself.'

Philip took the horses as soon as Bryant had removed the saddle bags.

"We can take those, My Lord," Hoyt said as he and Agatha stepped forward.

"Please put this on the table in my room," he responded, handing Hoyt the one with the quilt attached.

Bryant handed the other to Agatha. As the crowd began to disperse, Bryant noticed Sonje was talking with her sister. He placed a hand on Regis Auberon's arm.

"I need to ask you something about your daughter," Bryant said quietly. "Could you come to my office? It is more private."

"Certainly," Regis Auberon responded.

Bryant led Regis Auberon to his office without attracting Sonje's attention.

"This was my father's office. I have had little use for it before now," Bryant told him as he shut the door.

"It is a beautiful castle you have," Regis Auberon commented. "Yet not excessively ornate."

"Like Burton's castle," Bryant finished for him. "It was built for the use of the people. There is a library, a theater, and a music room, in addition to the dining hall and great hall. I remember during my childhood attending many events in those rooms. I remember attending classes in the theater with the other children."

"You wished to ask something about Sonje," Regis Auberon said, bringing him back to the present.

"Yes," he said as he sat down. "Last night I read back through my journal. This morning I remembered something important when you mentioned Glynis."

"That being?"

"When Sonje first told me she was from Glynis, she said she would be two hundred sixty-six on her birthday that was in a month. I realized that it must be sometime soon."

"You're right," Regis Auberon said. "It will be the day after tomorrow."

"I think that what we need then is a big party," Bryant said with a grin as he began to form a plan. "The hardest part will be keeping it a secret from her."

"I like that idea," Regis Auberon said. "I think it is a perfect idea. It would help all of us get over the funeral."

"Hoyt and Agatha are pretty busy already, but my mother might be able to help."

"Cherie can help distract Sonje."

"I think I know where to find a dress for her that would fit the occasion."

"Music should be no problem."

"With some help, Mother and Agatha could have enough food prepared for everyone."

Bryant could see that Regis Auberon was going to enjoy their first cooperative effort.

"I remember there is a tiara that my mother would wear to such a party," Bryant said. "And another my father said belonged to my grandmother."

Bryant stood and released the hidden door behind the bookcase. He was pleased by the look of surprise on Regis Auberon's face as he saw what was behind the bookcase. After a few moments, Bryant found what he was looking for. Next to the tiaras was a pin that he had forgotten about. As he picked it up, he remembered his father had worn it on special occasions. The pin was a dragon in a circle. On the back of the pin was some writing. He could now read the words that had fascinated him as a child, 'Service, Loyalty, and Honor.' Bryant held the pin for a moment before turning to Regis Auberon.

"This is something my father sometimes wore. He said his father had worn it," Bryant told Regis Auberon. "It would mean a lot to me if you would accept it as a token of our new friendship. As I have gotten to know you better, I have found you to be an example of these very traits."

Regis Auberon took the pin as Bryant handed it to him and read the back.

"I don't know what to say," Regis Auberon told him.

"I want you to have this, because you are now a father to me," Bryant explained both to Auberon and himself.

Auberon smiled and said, "Let's get this party plan in action. Will you be able to keep it hidden from Sonje if you two can speak through thought?"

"I think so. I have learned much about keeping my thoughts hidden."

'Bryant has even kept me from reading his thoughts lately,' Haskell spoke to both men. 'I have told Lady Miranda of your plans. She is on her way to join you.'

"Thank you, Haskell," Auberon said aloud.

Bryant brought the two tiaras into the office as his mother walked in the door. Soon the three had everything worked out. The next day, Auberon had Cherie and Sonje go on a horseback ride. The castle bustled with activity as everyone helped get things ready.

* * * * *

The morning began as any other morning for Sonje. After getting dressed, she brushed and braided her hair. As she finished, there was a knock at her door.

"Come in," she answered.

She was pleased to see Bryant enter. He was carrying a bundle of clothing.

"Mother and I were going through some things and we came across a few things we thought you might like," he said as he put the bundle on the table. "I missed you yesterday."

"I missed you too."

Bryant lifted her chin and kissed her gently before drawing her closer. She looked into his eyes before he kissed her again, this time harder and more demanding. He held her close for a moment before releasing her. She felt a little dazed as she watched him undo the bundle.

"This was my grandmother's," Bryant said as he drew a delicate tiara from the bundle. "She wore it on special occasions."

"It is beautiful," she exclaimed as she watched the gems sparkle.

"I want you to have it."

Sonje sat down in front of the polished shield after he had placed it on her head.

"There are some dresses that you can try on after lunch," he said.

Reluctantly, she placed the tiara on the table and went down to breakfast with him. Everyone seemed unusually cheerful. She was beginning to wonder if there was something she was missing. She jumped when Bryant touched her arm.

"Why don't we go for a ride this morning?" he asked her.

"That would be nice," she replied, glad that he didn't seem to notice he had startled her.

Soon they were headed up the trail behind the castle. They galloped across the foothills and up to the summit. Bryant led her around an outcropping of rock into a tiny meadow.

"This is one of the places my father used to take me," Bryant explained. "It is where I stayed the other night."

"Someday you can bring your own son to camp here," she replied.

"It will soon be lunch time," Bryant said. "We had best get back before everyone starts looking for us."

Sonje followed as they returned to the castle. Philip came out of the stables as they entered the courtyard. Bryant lifted her down from the saddle and kissed her forehead.

"Let's go clean up a bit before lunch," Bryant suggested.

"Yes," she agreed.

As she washed her face, she realized how tired she felt. The last week had left her feeling drained.

'Bryant,' she called in her mind.

'Yes?'

212

'I am feeling tired. Could you have a tray of food brought up? I just want a light lunch and a nap.'

'I'm sorry to have worn you out.'

'It's alright. I just need some rest.'

'I will bring some food up for you.'

'Thank you, My Love.'

* * * * *

Bryant smiled with delight. This would make hiding the unusual activity from her much easier. He had Haskell relay Sonje's request to Agatha as he started down the stairs. The tray was waiting when he entered the kitchen. He took the tray up to Sonje's apartment. She was waiting at the door for him.

"Here you go," Bryant said as he placed the tray on the table beside the bundle of clothes. "A nice warm bath after you eat would help you sleep better."

"Yes, that would feel good," she replied.

Bryant kissed her lips and turned to leave.

"Sleep well, My Love," he told her before closing the door behind him.

He hurried down to the dining hall as everyone was just sitting down. He stood at the head table until everyone was quiet.

"I have good news," he announced. "Gwladys Sonje is a bit tired after this morning's ride, so she will probably stay in her apartment for most of the afternoon."

As Bryant sat down to eat, he could see that everyone seemed pleased by the news. He ate quickly, excited about the evening's plans.

"Let me know when she wakes up," his mother told him. "I think I can keep her up there the rest of the afternoon trying on dresses."

"Good," Bryant said with a mischievous grin. "Let's get to work."

Soon everyone was busy preparing for the party. Gale had found people to play music and had them rehearsing in the music room. Garlands of flowers and vines were brought in from the armory to be hung from the balconies in the great hall and laid down the centers of the tables in the dining hall. Agatha and several others were busy in the kitchen. Bryant slipped off into his office to get his gift for Sonje out of the jewel chamber. Soon he found a matched set of earrings and a necklace. He found a box to put them in before leaving the jewel chamber.

'She is beginning to awaken,' Haskell informed him as he left his office.

'Good. Tell Mother it is time for her to go up to Sonje's apartment,' Bryant replied.

Mother waved to Bryant from the balcony before continuing upstairs. He was pleased to see that everything was right on schedule. After helping Hoyt set up the lamp poles that were for such occasions, he went to the kitchen.

"You're just in time, My Lord," Agatha told him. "Taste this."

Bryant put the bit of food she handed him in his mouth.

"This is so good," he said after swallowing.

She smiled.

"Look in there," she said, pointing to the cold storage doors.

He opened one door and entered. He used his light to help him see in the unlit room. On the storage racks he could see many delicious looking things and on a table in the center was the biggest cake he had ever seen.

"I finished it last night," she said from the doorway.

"This is more than I expected," Bryant told her.

"I needed the practice," Agatha said casually. "The one for your wedding will be bigger."

Bryant stood stunned for a moment.

"Bigger," he said to himself.

'You have no idea,' Haskell told him. 'This little party is nothing in comparison to their plans for your wedding and coronation.'

Bryant left the kitchen and sat down in the dining hall for a moment. He was lost in thought with Sonje's gift in his hands when Auberon found him.

"Something wrong, Son?" Auberon asked.

"Was your wedding bigger than this party?"

"Much!"

"I just saw Sonje's birthday cake and Agatha said the wedding cake would be even bigger."

"Come," Auberon said as he put his hand on Bryant's shoulder. "Let's go up to your room and talk while you get dressed. You have the two most capable people in all of Glynis taking care of your wedding and coronation. All you need to do is decide on who will be your best man."

"Best man?" Bryant asked as he heard Haskell laughing.

Bryant learned a lot from Auberon as he bathed and dressed. Soon it was time to return for the party. Everyone was assembled in the dining hall, waiting for Lady Miranda to bring Sonje down.

* * * * *

Sonje stood in front of the polished shield in awe of what she saw. Lady Miranda had given her a dress to try on that was one of the most beautiful she had ever seen. The bodice was white and covered in tiny gems that sparkled in the light. The skirt was deep rose. Lady Miranda had put her hair up so the tiara set just in front of a mound of curls. Sonje could barely recognize herself.

"I think we should show Bryant and your father," Lady Miranda said with a smile.

She had also done her own hair up with her tiara. Sonje followed Lady Miranda down the hall. They went all the way across to the library mezzanine before going down.

"I thought Bryant said he would be here," Lady Miranda said as she looked around the empty library. "Maybe he is in the dining hall. It is almost time to eat."

"I'm feeling a bit hungry," Sonje admitted.

She followed Lady Miranda through a door she had not noticed before. She let her light glow in the darkened stairway.

"This goes directly to the dining hall," Lady Miranda explained as they reached the bottom. Sonje followed her out into the dining hall.

"Happy Birthday!" everyone exclaimed, leaving Sonje stunned and speechless.

Bryant bowed to her and kissed her hand. He was dressed more elegantly than she had ever seen him dressed before. The royal blue jacket and pants made him look regal.

"Come, sit and eat," Bryant said as he placed her hand on his arm. "A few days ago, I remembered that your birthday would be coming up. Your father gave me the exact date."

"You planned all of this just for me?"

"It was the least I could do after what you did for me on my birthday."

"The picnic?"

"You gave me a whole new life on that day. A life I had never dared dream of."

Sonje turned to him and saw the sincere look on his face.

"It was a greater gift than any other," he said. "You gave me hope."

Sonje looked around the room as she ate. Bryant was right about how much things had changed. She caught herself wondering how this would compare to their wedding and coronation. As soon as the meal was finished, Bryant led her out to the great hall. The decorations in the dining hall paled in comparison. Music was playing. Bryant led her to a table laden with a wide variety of things.

"These are all gifts for you," he explained as he picked up a flat wooden box. "This is my gift to you."

She gasped as he revealed the contents of the box. He put the necklace around her neck. With trembling hands, she put on the earrings. He bowed low before her.

"May I have the pleasure of this dance?" Bryant asked as he took her hand in his.

She curtsied and replied, "The pleasure is mine, My Lord."

Time lost all meaning as she danced with him. She only wished the night could last forever. She felt happy and content. He was watching her with a smile on his face. She laid her head on his shoulder with a sigh.

'Having a good time?' he asked her silently.

'I'm having a wonderful time,' she replied. 'But the best part is just being with you.'

'There's nothing else I'd rather do. I'm hoping our wedding goes as smoothly.'

'It will,' she reassured him.

'Your father told me some things about weddings. He said I needed to choose a best man.'

'Yes. I have asked Brenndah to be my maid of honor.'

'I have been thinking of asking Olvan to be my best man,' Bryant said. 'He was the first person who accepted me as I am dragons and all.'

'I think he would be honored.'

Their conversation was interrupted when the music stopped. Hoyt opened the doors to the dining hall and four men entered carrying the cake. Bryant and Sonje made their way to the table that the cake was placed on. Hoyt handed Sonje a knife. Bryant watched as she carefully cut two pieces of cake before handing Hoyt the knife back.

"I would like to thank all of you for this wonderful surprise," Sonje said. "I really had not expected a party. Thank you."

'It was hard to keep this a secret from you,' he told her silently. 'I had to be very careful not to think too loudly.'

'Haskell told me you are able to keep even him from reading your thoughts,' she replied as they ate the cake. 'Thank you again for this surprise. I'll never forget tonight.'

'I'll never forget how beautiful you look in that dress.'

Sonje blushed then said, "You are the one who picked it out, not your mother.'

'Yes.'

'When I saw myself in it, I almost didn't recognize myself.'

'I saw how beautiful you are the first time we met,' Bryant thought back to her. 'And to know that I can look upon your beauty every day for the rest of my life makes me happier than I knew was possible.'

He took her hand in his and kissed it.

216

"It is getting late and you are looking tired, My Love," Bryant told her. "May I escort you to your room?"

"Yes," Sonje replied.

* * * * *

Lady Miranda and Auberon watched as Bryant and Sonje made their way upstairs.

"They look very happy together," Auberon commented.

"Yes they do," Lady Miranda replied.

"Lord Bryant is still getting used to his new role as leader," Auberon said. "He will be a good king."

"I'm glad to hear that from you. Whether you know it or not, your opinion is very important to Bryant."

"I guess our first meeting couldn't have gone worse. I think that Hoyt and I will have to spend a lot of time in the next weeks to prepare him for what is ahead of him."

"Yes, I think so too."

Chapter 20 – Bringing Glynis Home

As the days passed, Bryant spent his mornings in the library with Auberon and Hoyt instructing him about Glynis. After lunch he usually went to the armory for a practice duel with Edgard before taking a long ride on Llewellyn. Some afternoons he spent his time pouring over the journals that Riva had given him. Sometimes Sonje joined him, but her days were busy with wedding plans. Each evening was spent on the move of Glynis. Housing assignments were made and changed. Food supplies were discussed.

Two days before Merton's ships were due in the harbor, Gale and Xylia set off for Burton. Sonje and Auberon set out for Merton that same day. Bryant sent Llewellyn with them, but stayed behind.

"I will miss you," Sonje told him. "I wish you were coming with us."

"I want to take care of a few things here," he replied. "Haskell and I will arrive just after dawn on the day the ships are due."

"I want to hear from you tonight and tomorrow night."

"I promise," he assured her as he lifted her chin.

He kissed her tenderly before helping her mount Llewellyn. He patted the horse and rubbed his nose. He would need the stallion in Merton for the trip back to Dracona. He stood and watched them until they were out of sight. He turned to find Hoyt standing at his side.

"My Lord," Hoyt said with a bow. "I did not realize you were not going with them."

"I think I need a day or two alone to prepare myself. Haskell and I will join them in time for the ships to arrive," Bryant explained.

"Auberon told me about when Gwladys Sonje presented you at the Grand Council," Hoyt said as they walked back to the castle. "The people of Glynis already see you as their regis. The coronation is a mere formality. For Glynis, your word is law."

"I know that should make me less nervous about meeting the people of Glynis," Bryant said. "But, this is still feeling quite new to me."

Hoyt smiled and patted his shoulder.

"I will be in the library if you should need me," Hoyt told him.

"I think I will spend some time in my office. I will be using it a lot more than I used to."

Bryant spent much of the next two days going through the things in his office. There were many things that brought back memories of the past. The box on the desk was a reminder of the future. The night before Glynis was to arrive Bryant went to bed right after supper. He woke an hour before dawn, and dressed in the clothes that Hoyt had helped him choose the day before. He settled his cape about his shoulders and picked up the saddle bags and gloves for the journey.

The air was crisp and cold as he mounted Haskell in the courtyard. The ride to Merton was colder than Bryant had expected. He was glad when Haskell landed on the cliff above the harbor. He walked the short distance to his mother's house just as the sun began to rise above the distant horizon. When he opened the door, he could smell something cooking.

"You must come and have some breakfast," Mother said in greeting. "We are just ready to eat."

"Thank you, Mother," Bryant said in greeting. "I need something to warm myself up with."

"Bryant!" Sonje said as he entered the kitchen. "You look cold. Come eat this. It will help you warm up."

Bryant noticed the smile on Auberon's face as he sat down at the table. Bryant felt much warmer after he finished eating.

'The ships are approaching the harbor,' Haskell told Bryant.

"The ships are in sight," Bryant told the others.

Sonje kissed him on the cheek after he helped her put her cape on.

"It is a wonderful idea to greet the ships," Auberon said as he put his hand on Bryant's shoulder.

"I wanted them to feel welcome," Bryant said. "New beginnings can be difficult enough. It must have been very hard for them to leave the only home they had ever known. We'll have them camp just on the other side of the tunnel for the night and we'll meet them in the morning to lead them to Dracona."

Auberon smiled and nodded. Soon they were waiting at the dock for the first ship to arrive. As the ship drew nearer, others joined them. As soon as the ship was docked, a bridge was lowered from the deck of the ship. The first wagon to leave the ship was soon followed by another. Soon a ship docked at the second dock. Bryant went over to the second dock to greet the families from that ship leaving Sonje to greet the families on the first dock. Bryant was encouraged by the warm response of the people of Glynis.

The day wore on as each ship docked and unloaded in turn. At last the final ship was docked. As the people and wagons left the ship, a woman walking beside a wagon lost her balance and fell from the bridge.

Bryant saw her begin to fall and quickly used his talent to lift her safely to the dock.

"Are you alright?" Bryant asked her in the language of Glynis.

"I think so," she replied in a shaky voice. "How did I land safely here instead of in the water?"

"I am able to lift things without touching them," Bryant explained as Sonje joined him.

"You have saved my life, Regis," she said as she curtsied low before him. "I am in your debt."

"Rise," Bryant told her. "It is my duty to serve the people of Glynis, and I am glad to be of service."

"We are happy to welcome the people of Glynis to Merton," Sonje added as she joined them.

The woman curtsied again as her husband joined them. Soon the last wagon was on its way up the road to the top of the cliff overlooking the harbor. Bryant and the others followed. Bryant was glad to get back to his mother's house and sit down. Brenndah had prepared a meal which they gratefully ate.

* * * * *

It was early when Bryant, Sonje and Auberon joined the people of Glynis to lead them to Dracona. Bryant's mother stayed in Merton. At dusk, they had reached a mountain valley large enough to camp in for the night. Bryant walked the perimeter of the camp after supper. He climbed an outcropping of rock to get a better view of the camp. He extinguished his light completely while he stood looking over the camp. He was struck by the many different colors of light as the camp settled in for the night. He turned as he heard a movement behind him. The black wolf stepped onto the rock and sat down beside him.

"I see you like Dracona," Bryant said. "Are you keeping watch on camp tonight?"

The wolf nodded.

"Thank you. I will sleep better knowing you are on guard."

He placed his hand on the wolf's head as he looked over the camp. He could see Sonje's white light plainly among the many colored lights. He sighed and scratched the wolf behind the ears before climbing down the rock. As he used his light to make his way toward Sonje, he could see that, like hers, his light had lost all sign of color. Many of the people bowed as he passed by. He still wasn't used to that.

"There you are," Sonje said as he came into view.

"I just wanted to make certain that the camp was secure," Bryant said.

"You need your sleep as much as anyone else," Sonje replied. "The watch is posted already."

"There is a second watch on duty tonight," Bryant said.

Sonje looked puzzled for a moment before nodding.

"Good night then," Sonje said.

"Good night, My Lady," Bryant replied and kissed her hand.

Bryant woke up at the first light of dawn. Again he walked the perimeter of the camp. When he returned, Sonje was stirring their small fire. Soon they had eaten breakfast and were ready to go. The rest of the camp took a little longer to be ready. At this pace, Bryant knew it would take several days to reach Dracona.

"Anxious to get home, Bryant?" Auberon asked.

"Anxious to get these people safely to Dracona," Bryant answered. "There are unseen dangers in these mountains. Snakes and wildcats to name two. These people are my responsibility now."

"They have traveled hundreds of miles already. They knew the risks of the journey before they left Glynis," Auberon reassured him. "Let's get back on the road."

The day was long and uneventful as was the next day. On the fifth day, they finally reached the valley as a light rain began to fall. By noon the sky began to clear as they reached the outskirts of Dracona. Bryant was relieved to see the familiar walls and streets once again. Haskell was perched on the courtyard wall with Agatha and Hoyt waiting at the gate. Auberon, Bryant and Sonje entered the courtyard and dismounted. Philip took the horses into the stable.

"Agatha has prepared lunch for you, My Lord," Hoyt told Bryant. "Go eat and get cleaned up."

"Thank you," Bryant answered. "Thank you both."

The three weary travelers found a generous meal waiting on the head table in the dining room. They ate in silence before going up to their rooms to get cleaned up. Bryant was grateful to get into a basin of warm water and soak. His muscles began to relax in the warm water. Slowly he washed the dirt from the trip off and began to feel more like himself.

He dried himself and shaved before getting dressed. After pulling on his boots, he went to the window. He looked out on the courtyard and saw that there was still a line of wagons waiting to be told where to go. He noticed a few wagons that were standing empty in the courtyard.

'Sonje?' he called in his mind.

"Yes, Bryant?' she responded.

'Those people are as weary and hungry as we were.'

'Yes.'

'Maybe there is more of the soup that we had for lunch. The people staying in the castle will have no way to prepare their own food.'

'Good idea. Let's go down to the kitchen and see.'

Bryant met her in the hall and they went down together. Once in the kitchen, they discovered a large pot of soup on to simmer. They got out some bowls and put them on the counter.

"I'll go tell someone that there is food ready," Bryant said. "They can spread the news to the rest."

Sonje nodded as she got out the spoons. Bryant went to the great hall and then to the courtyard. He crossed to where Agatha and Hoyt were standing.

"Sonje and I are ready to serve the soup to those who are staying in the castle," he told them.

"I have been waiting for Darryl and Aurora to take care of that, My Lord," Agatha said. "But they haven't come yet."

"They can help when they get here. Until then, tell the people about the soup. I will tell those who are already here about it."

"They are all on the second floor so far, My Lord," Hoyt said.

"Thank you."

Bryant returned to the castle and climbed the stairs to the second floor. Soon he located an occupied room. He knocked on the door which was quickly opened by a man who dropped to one knee and bowed to Bryant.

"Regis," the man said. "We are honored by your presence."

"Rise," Bryant said. "We are serving soup in the dining hall. It is on the other side of the great hall on the ground floor."

"Thank you, Regis," the woman said as she curtsied.

"Please tell others on this floor about the soup," Bryant told them. "We don't want anyone to go hungry."

"Yes, Regis," the man said as he bowed again.

As he returned to the kitchen, he heard Haskell say, 'They were very surprised to see you at their door.'

'I am certain of that,' Bryant said with a mischievous grin. 'They will just have to get used to the fact that things are a little different around here.'

Sonje was stirring the soup as he entered the kitchen.

"What was the castle in Glynis like?" he asked her.

"Well," she said as she turned to face him. "There was a section of living quarters for the immediate family, and a very large throne room where meetings were held. There was an amphitheater within the castle wall where all of Glynis could assemble and then the servants' quarters."

"Very different from Dracona."

"Definitely."

"I am glad there is no throne room here," Bryant said as the first people entered the dining hall. "That would be too uncomfortable for me."

"I think many things about this castle will be much better than the castle at Glynis," Sonje answered as she dished out the first bowl of soup.

Bryant smiled as he began to hand out bowls of soup. He was glad that she felt that way.

'Something's wrong,' Haskell's voice had a sense of urgency. 'Darryl is telling Agatha that Aurora broke her ankle.'

Bryant nearly dropped the bowls of soup he was holding.

'Agatha hasn't seen the healer from Glynis yet.'

'Tell Agatha to send Darryl in to help Sonje,' Bryant replied. 'Tell Philip to saddle Llewellyn quickly. Then go get Brenndah from Merton. Explain it to Mother as soon as you can.'

"What's wrong?" Sonje asked.

"Aurora broke her ankle. Darryl will come help here," Bryant said as he opened the door and went out to the garden.

Soon he had several of the leaves he needed and was on his way to the stables. Philip was leading Llewellyn out of the stable as Bryant came around the corner. He vaulted to the horse's back and urged him forward. As soon as they were past the wagons at the gate, Bryant urged Llewellyn into a gallop. Bryant dismounted before the horse could fully stop and ran into the tailor's shop. He found Aurora in the back near some shelves and a broken stool. She was propped up against the wall and her ankle was swollen.

"Here," Bryant said. "Chew this and swallow it. It will ease the pain. Haskell has gone to get Brenndah. She can help you."

Aurora nodded and put the leaves he offered her in her mouth. Bryant went through a door to the living quarters behind the shop. He found a rag and wet it with cold water. He wrung most of the water out and put it on Aurora's ankle.

"This should help too," he told her.

He went back outside and found Llewellyn waiting.

"Go to the castle and wait for Haskell," he told the horse. "Bring the girl back here. Understand?"

Llewellyn nodded and turned towards the castle. Bryant heard the hoof beats fade as he returned to the shop.

"Help is on the way. Now all we can do is wait and keep that ankle cold," Bryant said as he sat down beside her. "How is the pain?"

"A little better, My Lord," Aurora whispered. "I'm mostly embarrassed and sorry to put you to this trouble."

"You could not have known that the stool would break. I will make sure a new one is made immediately."

"Poor Darryl. There is still much work left on the clothes."

"Don't worry about it," Bryant reassured her. "Your ankle is more important right now than any clothing could be."

"We want everything to be perfect for you and Gwladys Sonje."

"I know so little about weddings and coronations that the clothes don't matter as much as the welfare of everyone in Dracona."

She smiled weakly. As the minutes crept by, Bryant kept the cloth on Aurora's ankle wet and cold. It seemed as though half the day had gone by before he heard hooves clatter to a stop outside the tailor's shop. Bryant stood as Brenndah burst through the door.

"Can you heal it?" Bryant asked as she put her hands on Aurora's ankle.

Brenndah nodded after a moment. She sat back and looked at Bryant. She put her hand to her forehead then pointed to him then to herself. Bryant was puzzled. Brenndah reached out with her hand and placed it on his forehead. He began to understand.

"This will require help from me?" Bryant asked. "My energy?"

Brenndah nodded.

"Of course," he answered her silent request.

He knelt behind her and put a hand on each side of her head. Brenndah placed her hands on Aurora's ankle and began to glow. Bryant let his light glow as he felt his energy begin to flow from his hands. Bryant saw Aurora wince once and then relax. He began to feel a little dizzy.

* * * * *

"Oh, Bryant," Sonje said softly as she knelt beside him.

Aurora had explained how when Brenndah had healed her ankle, she and Bryant had both passed out. Edgard shook his head.

"They will have to sleep it off," he said.

'Maybe not,' Haskell told Sonje. 'Bryant was giving some of his energy to Brenndah. If you and Edgard could give them some of your energy, perhaps they would wake up.'

"It's worth trying," Sonje said aloud.

"What is, Gwladys?" Edgard asked.

"Brenndah used both her energy and Bryant's to heal Aurora," Sonje explained. "We could give them some of our energy."

"If they wake up long enough to eat something and get to bed, it would make things a lot easier," Edgard agreed.

"You should give Bryant your energy," Sonje said after a moment of thought. "I will give mine to Brenndah."

Sonje put her hands on either side of Brenndah's face. She concentrated on feeling energy flow from her hands to Brenndah. After a moment, the girl began to stir and her eyes opened. Sonje turned to see that Edgard was getting similar results with Bryant.

"You should have called for some more help," Sonje said as she stood up slowly. "Aurora's ankle is sore, but can hold her weight."

"There is a carriage outside waiting to take you to the castle," Edgard added.

"Thank you," Bryant responded.

Brenndah nodded. Aurora insisted on staying at the tailor's shop, while the rest returned to the castle. Llewellyn trotted along behind the carriage. When they reached the castle gate, Bryant could see that there were only a few wagons left. The wagon at the front of the line held an elderly man, a young man and a young woman.

"My Lord, this is Eban, Glynis' healer," Agatha said.

"These are my two apprentices, Bethesda and Raphello," Eban said.

"This is Merton's healer, Brenndah," Bryant said. "She will be staying in the castle tonight. You should come to the castle tomorrow morning and get acquainted."

"We will be there," Eban said.

Eban turned his wagon towards the healer's cottage. Agatha looked through her lists.

"There has got to be a spare room somewhere she can stay," Agatha muttered.

"Brenndah can stay in my room," Sonje said.

"Thank you, Gwladys. That will help so much."

"It will be no trouble at all."

Edgard pulled the carriage up to the castle door. Philip took the carriage after they had gone inside. Sonje was glad that the great hall was empty. She knew Bryant would not want anyone else to know how weak he was. After Bryant and Brenndah were seated, Sonje prepared two bowls of soup.

"Eat," she told them. "It will help you regain your strength."

"I'm going to need it just to get up those stairs," Bryant said.

Brenndah nodded in agreement. Sonje watched as they ate. She was glad to see that they were beginning to look less pale. When they finished eating, Sonje and Edgard walked upstairs with them. Sonje paused as Edgard took Bryant into his room.

'Sleep well, My Love,' she thought to him.

'Good night,' he responded.

Sonje took Brenndah to her apartment and helped her get into bed. Soon Brenndah was sound asleep. Sonje slipped quietly out into the hall and found Edgard talking with Agatha and Hoyt.

"Lord Bryant is sleeping soundly," Edgard told her.

"Edgard explained what happened in the tailor's shop," Hoyt said. "I did not think it possible to give one's energy to another."

"We don't know something is impossible until we try it," Sonje responded. "I'm just glad that Aurora is able to walk."

"Brenndah is a good healer," Agatha agreed. "But why doesn't she speak?"

"You saw her scars," Sonje said. "She was very young when Rolfe burned the town. She watched her parents die in that fire. She has not spoken since."

The others stood in stunned silence.

"She has the power to remove the physical scars," Sonje said. "But she is not ready yet. I am beginning to feel tired. I will see you tomorrow."

The others bowed as she returned to her room.

* * * * *

The next morning both Bryant and Brenndah were feeling stronger. Eban and his two assistants came to the castle after breakfast. They met with Brenndah, Bryant and Sonje in the sitting room of Bryant's office.

"Agatha told us about what you did yesterday," Eban began. "I have been able to set a broken bone, but never to heal it instantly. How were you able to do that?"

Brenndah motioned to Bryant.

"It required more than just her own energy," Bryant explained. "So I gave her my energy. Then she had enough to heal the bone. Aurora is sore, but able to walk now."

"Transferring energy?" Eban responded in a puzzled tone. "How?"

Brenndah stood up and went to stand in front of Eban. She put her hand on Eban's forehead and began to glow. After a few seconds, she removed her hand.

"Incredible," Eban said.

Raphello reached out and touched Brenndah's arm.

"What happened to you?" he asked her.

She turned to Sonje and nodded. Sonje explained Dracona's past and how Brenndah had been injured.

"Certainly if you can heal bone, these scars could easily be removed," Bethesda said.

Brenndah smoothed the scarring on her arm and then returned it to the way it had been.

"She chooses to keep the scarring for now," Sonje said. "It is a reminder of the past just as her silence mourns the deaths of her parents."

"Perhaps I should send one of my assistants to Merton with her to learn what she knows," Eban suggested.

Brenndah nodded.

"Bethesda, go to Merton with Brenndah," Eban said.

Brenndah nodded then she pointed to Sonje and Bryant before putting her hands on her head like a crown. Next she pointed to Raphello and Bethesda and then crossed her arms and pointed to them again.

"Have them trade places when the coronation takes place?" Eban asked and Brenndah nodded. "Yes, that's a good idea."

"Then it's settled," Sonje said. "Bethesda and Brenndah can fly to Merton after lunch."

"F-fly?" Bethesda stuttered in alarm. "On the dragon?"

Brenndah nodded and patted her shoulder with a smile.

"Don't worry," Bryant said. "Haskell will take good care of you."

Bethesda nodded, still looking unsure of the idea. Brenndah went with Bethesda to help her pack. Bryant went to the tailor's shop to see how Aurora's ankle was doing. Sonje gave Eban and Raphello a tour of the castle and of the town. Bryant was still at the tailor's shop when they arrived there. Brenndah and Bethesda were there as well.

"How is your ankle today?" Sonje asked when Aurora came out of the back room.

"Much better. It is still a bit sore though," Aurora answered. "Lord Bryant brought a new stool to replace the one that broke."

Brenndah motioned to Aurora and to a chair. Aurora sat in the chair while Brenndah examined her ankle. Brenndah smiled and patted her ankle.

"Thank you, Brenndah," Aurora said. "I'm glad to see that you have recovered your strength. I also want to thank you, My Lord."

"The work you and Darryl are doing is thanks enough," Bryant said with a smile. "We should be getting back to the castle for lunch."

They left Aurora and Darryl to do their work and walked back to the castle. Hoyt was waiting for them at the door with a woman beside him.

"Aunt Ruth!" Sonje exclaimed as she ran to the woman and hugged her.

"Sonje," the woman responded. "It is good to see you in person again."

"Bryant, this is Ruth, my father's sister and Hoyt's wife," Sonje said in introduction. "Aunt Ruth, this is Bryant Donley, Lord Dracona."

Bryant bowed to her as she curtsied to him.

"You didn't tell me you had such a beautiful wife, Hoyt," Bryant said with a grin. "Nor that we would be related when I married Sonje."

"I came to Dracona as your teacher," Hoyt said. "My personal life did not seem as important as preparing you to be Regis."

"I suppose I will have to call you 'Uncle Hoyt' now," Bryant responded.

"Absolutely not. If I won't let Gwladys Sonje call me that, I certainly am not going to let you do it either," Hoyt replied. "Lunch is ready."

'He was worried about what you would think about becoming his nephew,' Haskell told Bryant as they entered the castle. 'That is the real reason that he didn't tell you before. Even though he and the others had been sent knowing that Sonje would marry you, he didn't want you to feel uncomfortable and forced into it.'

'I will have to find a way to thank him for that,' Bryant replied as they sat down to eat.

As lunch was being eaten, Bryant looked around. It seemed good to see so many people in the castle again.

"This is the way I remember the castle," Bryant told Sonje as they walked with Brenndah and Bethesda out to the courtyard. "Busy and full of life."

"I'm glad that you like it this way," Sonje replied. "I like it better this way too."

Sonje hugged Brenndah goodbye before she mounted Haskell. Bethesda hesitantly mounted behind her.

'I think having an apprentice will be good for her,' Sonje told Bryant silently as they watched Haskell disappear over the castle.

'I noticed the way she was watching Raphello,' Bryant responded. 'We may not be the only ones anxious for our wedding day to arrive. I'm really glad she is ready to open her heart to love again. She was the one person who seemed to understand what I was feeling better than anyone else.'

Chapter 21 – Preparations and Revelations

For Bryant, the days seemed to crawl by. Some afternoons he helped the men build new houses since there would not be enough once Sonje's Aunt Lillian arrived with the rest of the people of Glynis. Hoyt protested, but could not stop him. Bryant felt the need to do something physical to help pass the time. The new homes were completed quickly with the many hands to help. The men from Glynis were nervous around Bryant at first, but soon began to look forward to his arrival. This pleased Bryant very much. The new homes allowed some of the people in the castle to vacate rooms that were needed for the wedding guests that would be coming from Merton and Burton. Agatha promptly had Aloysia and Fluorine clean the rooms for the guests.

The day before the guests were to arrive Bryant went to the library after breakfast as he had been doing every morning. This morning he just couldn't seem to concentrate on what Hoyt was saying. Sitting still was not easy either.

"I don't think you have heard a word I've said," Hoyt said as he laid a hand on Bryant's shoulder. "Is everything alright, Lord Bryant?"

"I just can't focus today. I need to be up doing something instead of just sitting here," Bryant admitted. "I just need to do something, but I don't know what."

"Are you nervous about the wedding?"

"Yes, yet there is nothing in the world more important to me."

"Maybe that is why you are nervous."

"I don't seem to be doing anything productive. I feel as though there is something I should be doing or building. Everyone else seems to be doing something for the wedding and I am doing nothing."

"I think these lessons can wait for another time," Hoyt said with an understanding smile. "Go find something to build. Perhaps something for your bride."

Bryant passed Ruth on the way out of the library.

* * * * *

"Where is he going in such a hurry?" Ruth asked Hoyt.

"I can't keep him busy with study any longer," Hoyt replied. "He is too used to physical activity to bury himself in books as I did before our wedding."

"I saw him out building houses with the other men last week," Ruth commented. "He seemed to know what he was doing."

"Before we arrived, he was repairing Rolf's damage to the town."

"He is very different from any regis Glynis has ever had."

"Yes, but I think that is exactly what we are in need of," Hoyt said with a smile. "He is a very remarkable man."

* * * * *

Bryant went to his room and got his cape. He was back in the hall before it was settled around his shoulders. When he reached the stables, Philip was not around. Bryant saddled and bridled Llewellyn himself. He rode out of the courtyard not really knowing where he was going. As he reached the edge of town, he found himself on the trail to the meadow. When he reached the tiny meadow, he dismounted and left his horse loose to graze. He noticed a fallen tree on the other side of the brook. He crossed the stream to examine it more closely. The branches were not straight, but were intertwined with each other. It reminded him of the carved back of the chair at his desk.

"Now I wish I had brought an axe," he said aloud. "I could cut this trunk off below the branches and make a chair for Sonje."

Llewellyn lifted his head and snorted in response. Bryant put his hand on a branch that was sticking out at an odd angle. The branch bent as easily as a green vine under his hand and wove itself into the rest of the branches. Bryant stood in shock for several minutes.

He closed his eyes and shook his head. He could see the finished chair clearly in his mind. He opened his eyes and looked again at the branches. He knelt on one knee and put his hand on the trunk below the branches. The trunk felt soft at his touch like the branch had. He concentrated on the tree, thinking about cutting the trunk. A split began to form under his hand. He concentrated harder and the split grew until the trunk was cut in two.

Bryant smiled and rubbed his hands together. The wood responded to his touch as he shaped it into a beautiful chair. When the chair was finished, he felt tired but satisfied. He laid out on the grass and fell asleep.

* * * * *

"Have you seen Lord Bryant?" Hoyt asked Sonje as they entered the dining hall for lunch.

"I thought he was with you this morning," Sonje said as she shook her head.

230

"He just couldn't concentrate and he left to find something more physically productive," Hoyt answered. "He's been gone for hours and I'm getting worried."

'He has been busy this morning,' Haskell told them. 'He is taking a nap.'

"Where is he?" Sonje asked aloud. "Is he in his room?"

'No, but he is safe.'

Sonje sighed as she sat down next to Bryant's empty chair. Hoyt could see that she was also impatient for the wedding day to arrive.

'Bryant has found a new talent,' Haskell told Hoyt. 'I did not want to spoil his surprise.'

'What surprise?' Hoyt asked.

'He has made her a chair similar to the one at the desk in his office,' Haskell explained. 'He made it with his bare hands.'

'That talent is a rare one,' Hoyt replied. 'When he wakes up, tell him to contact Gwladys Sonje. She seems very worried.'

* * * * *

When Bryant woke up it was mid-afternoon and he felt hungry. He stood up and took another look at the chair he had made. All it needed now was some oil to protect the wood.

'It's about time you woke up,' Haskell told him in a stern tone. 'Sonje is worried sick about you.'

'Everyone has been so busy, I thought no one would notice my absence,' Bryant replied.

'You had better talk to her so she can stop worrying.'

'Sonje!' Bryant called out to her in his mind.

'Bryant!' Sonje's voice was anxious. 'Where are you? I've been looking for you.'

'I'm sorry,' Bryant replied. 'I thought you would be too busy to notice.'

'I know when you are here even if I can't see you. What if you had gotten hurt going off all alone?'

'I'm sorry. I just needed to get out of there for a while,' Bryant replied apologetically. 'I have something to bring back to the castle. I'll explain later.'

'Alright. Meet me at the tailor's shop as soon as possible.'

'I will, My Love.'

Bryant put his cape around the chair and set it upside down across the saddle. He led Llewellyn back to the castle. It seemed to be farther than he remembered. When he reached the castle, Bryant was surprised to find that a platform had been built on the wall near the courtyard gate with a staircase built along the outside of the courtyard wall. Philip met him at the stable door with a puzzled look.

"It's a gift for Gwladys Sonje," Bryant said. "Leave Llewellyn saddled. Take the gift to Haskell's cave and bring the cape to me in the dining hall. I am starving."

Philip bowed and tied the horse to a post. Bryant found Agatha in the kitchen.

"You look a little pale, My Lord. Are you ill?" Agatha asked with concern.

"No, just hungry. I suppose that's what I deserve for missing lunch."

"Go sit down. I'll put together some bread with meat and cheese on it for you."

Bryant gratefully ate the food she brought. Philip brought his cape to him before he was finished.

"That chair is beautiful!" Philip exclaimed. "Is that why you weren't here for lunch?"

Bryant nodded.

"I've got some dark oil out in the stable. I'll put some aside for you to use on the chair."

"Thank you," Bryant said after he swallowed the last of the meal. "I want it to be finished before the wedding."

Philip bowed and followed him out to the stable. Soon Bryant arrived at the tailor's shop. He hesitated and took a deep breath before entering.

"What were you doing that was more important than lunch?" Sonje asked before he could shut the door behind him.

"I'm sorry to worry you," Bryant said. "I was making you a gift and completely lost track of time."

"A gift?"

"A wedding gift."

"Oh, Bryant!" she said. "Next time at least tell someone where you are going."

"I will," he promised as he took her hand. "I have felt so restless for the last couple of weeks. I just hope I can survive another couple of days."

"I know what you mean," Sonje admitted. "I've been here a lot helping with the sewing."

Bryant laughed and kissed her hand. Sonje took his other hand and looked into his eyes. He did not have to read her thoughts to know what she was thinking. He leaned down and kissed her lips.

"It won't be much longer," she said with a sigh.

"Yet it will still seem too long," he answered.

"Darryl wants you to try on your clothes for a final fitting," Sonje told him. "I'll see you at supper."

Bryant bowed to her as she left. He went into the back room where Aurora and Darryl were busily working. Darryl stood up and brought him two hangers of clothes.

"Try on the white ones first," she told him. "Come out when you are changed so we can check the fit."

She opened a door to a tiny room with a hook on the wall and a stool in the corner. He felt self conscious about the whole idea as the door closed behind him.

'You're not going to get out of it,' Haskell told him with a chuckle. 'They are not going to let you leave without making certain those clothes fit perfectly.'

'It seems that I should have more say in this since I am the king,' Bryant said as he reluctantly began to change his clothes.

'Not when you are the groom,' Haskell said with a full laugh. 'Don't worry. I think you'll find that it will be well worth it.'

'You know how much I dislike all this formal stuff,' Bryant replied. 'Why can't the coronation be right after the wedding ceremony?'

Haskell's only response was to laugh again.

'What?' Bryant asked as he put on the white jacket.

'From what I have learned, there is one formality that must take place after the wedding and before the coronation that might change your mind.'

Bryant opened the door and stepped out. Darryl had him stand with his arms held straight forward before checking the length of his pants. Then she gave him a pair of white boots to walk around the room in.

'What formality?' Bryant asked.

'I'll tell you when you come to oil the chair.'

Bryant sighed as he entered the room to change again. As promised, the coronation clothes were more colorful. The pants and jacket were royal blue. The shirt was white. The jacket was trimmed with scarlet. The short dragon cape and a pair of black boots finished the outfit.

"Good," Darryl said as she stood back to look at him.

"The sword will be the finishing touch," Aurora commented.

"Sword?" Bryant asked.

"Fanchon's Sword," Hoyt answered as he and Auberon entered the room.

"You look like a king," Auberon added with a smile. "Now get changed. We want to look at what you've been up to this morning."

Darryl nodded and Bryant went back in to change again. He was glad to get out of the tailor's shop and away from the women's critical gaze. The three walked to the castle with Bryant's mount following behind. Philip met them at the stable door and handed Bryant the bucket of oil and some rags. Bryant led them to the doors of the caverns. As he entered, Auberon drew a quick breath.

"You hadn't shown me this," he said. "What is in the sand?"

"Dragon eggs," Bryant responded, pleased with the look of awe on Auberon's face. "They should hatch before the warm season returns."

Bryant led them up the stairs to Haskell's den.

"Beautiful!" Hoyt said as Bryant's light exposed the chair.

"Where did you get this?" Auberon asked.

"I discovered another talent," Bryant answered.

Haskell joined them as Bryant began to put the oil on the chair.

'Bryant asked me why the coronation is on the day following the wedding instead of the same day,' Haskell said in the minds of all three men. 'Perhaps one of you would like to explain why.'

When there was no response, Bryant glanced up to find both men looking very uncomfortable. He knew that Haskell was enjoying this immensely.

"There is a reason for that," Hoyt said after clearing his throat.

"Yes," Auberon added. "It's a long held tradition really."

Bryant was even more puzzled by the way they seemed unwilling to get to the point.

"Technically speaking, Glynis has been without a Regis and Regina ever since Regina Elva died," Hoyt explained.

Bryant shot a questioning look at Auberon.

"The leadership of Glynis is given to a couple," Auberon explained. "Not to an individual."

"The princess must marry in order to become queen," Bryant repeated the words he was told what seemed like so long ago.

"Exactly," Hoyt responded. "But there is more to getting married than saying some words and exchanging rings."

"Why do you think the coronation is held the next evening? No one expects you two to get much sleep on your wedding night." Auberon said with a grin on his face that surprised Bryant.

Bryant dropped the rag he was holding. He could hear Haskell laughing. Even Hoyt was beginning to grin. A slow smile began to form as he realized what they meant.

"We thought you would have guessed that by now," Hoyt said.

"Considering she is able to read my thoughts, I have been trying to avoid that particular subject," Bryant explained.

"No wonder you haven't wanted to sit around studying," Hoyt said with a laugh. "I could think of little else the week before my wedding. It would have been extremely difficult to bury that."

"Impossible!" Auberon exclaimed in agreement. "If it is any consolation, I think she is having the same problem."

Bryant sat down in surprise, sending the others into a fit of laughter.

"I've seen the way she looks at you when she thinks no one is noticing," Hoyt said as soon as he caught his breath.

"I have too," Auberon said. "If she takes after her mother, Son, you are definitely not getting much sleep that night."

Bryant picked up the rag and began rubbing oil into the chair again. He jumped as Auberon put his hand on his shoulder.

"Don't be embarrassed," Auberon said. "We all go through this."

"I just didn't expect to hear it from you," Bryant admitted. "She is your daughter."

"She's not a little girl anymore," Auberon replied. "She is a grown woman. She has chosen you among hundreds to be her husband. I know that you two will be very happy together."

"How will I know what . . .," Bryant began to say and then trailed off, searching for the right words.

"Don't worry," Auberon said, interrupting him. "You two will figure it out."

Auberon and Hoyt left him alone to think about what they had said. As he finished with the chair he turned to Haskell.

'No wonder you were laughing,' Bryant said as he stood with his hands on his hips. 'You knew how I would react.'

'Of course. I have known you too long not to,' Haskell said. 'But I still thought it might be best if that was explained to you by one of your own kind.'

'I guess so,' Bryant replied.

'Go eat,' Haskell said. 'Sonje is looking for you.'

Bryant wiped his hands on a clean rag before going to the dining hall. Sonje came out of the kitchen.

"There you are," she said. "Where have you been hiding this afternoon?"

"Oh, nowhere," Bryant replied. "Just having an important talk with your father and Hoyt."

"Oh," she said as if expecting more.

He kissed her cheek before sitting down. He ate slowly, enjoying both the food and the company. When the meal was finished, Bryant leaned back in his chair. Sonje looked at him and then at her father. When she turned back to face him she shook her head.

"I don't know what you talked about," Sonje said. "But I'm glad you did."

"Let's take a little walk," Bryant said.

He took her hand and led her outside. He took her up the stairs behind the armory.

"The view here is great," Sonje said. "You can see the whole town from here."

"It was one of my favorite spots when I was younger. Now that the people are here, I wanted to show you."

"I'm glad you did."

"I realize that we haven't spent much time together lately."

"Everything has been so busy," she said turning away from him.

"No," he said as he stepped behind her, took her hands in his and wrapped their arms around her. "It's more than that."

"Yes," she whispered.

"It's alright, Sonje," he whispered in her ear. "Everyone goes through this. It's just harder for us because we can speak through thought."

He felt her slowly let out her breath and relax against his chest. She leaned her head back against his shoulder.

"You are right," she finally said. "Is that what you talked to Hoyt and Father about?"

"Yes," Bryant said after a moment. "I know that tomorrow will be a long, hard day for us and the next even harder, but we can make it."

"You know, it does make me feel better to know that what we are going through is what everyone goes through."

"Still it would make me less nervous if our wedding was a small quiet ceremony."

"Instead of in front of all of Glynis," she said with a laugh.

He turned her around to face him. He looked into her eyes.

"But then again, this way I can tell the whole world that I love you," Bryant said as he leaned down to kiss her lips.

"I love you, Bryant Donley," she said before he kissed her again.

She sighed as she laid her head on his shoulder. He stroked her hair before releasing her.

"I'm getting tired," he said.

"I'll walk you to your room," she replied.

* * * * *

When they reached the bottom of the stairs, he put his arm around her shoulders as they walked into the castle. It felt good to her to have it there. It seemed to her that they reached his room all too soon.

"Sleep well, Bryant," she told him.

"You too," he replied before kissing her. "Good night, Love."

She quickly went to the library where she found Father, Hoyt, and Aunt Ruth.

"I thought I might find you here," Sonje said. "Thank you for talking to Bryant."

"It was Haskell's idea actually," Hoyt replied.

"It was just what he needed," Sonje said. "I was beginning to get very worried about him."

"He did seem more relaxed at supper," Father commented. "You seem a bit more relaxed now too."

"Yes," Sonje said and kissed him on the cheek.

"You need your rest, Sonje," Aunt Ruth said. "Tomorrow will be a busy day."

"Good night," she replied and kissed Hoyt and Aunt Ruth each on the cheek before leaving.

She paused in front of Bryant's door before going to her apartment. She got ready for bed before standing at the window. The stars were just beginning to come out.

"Thank you, Haskell," Sonje whispered aloud.

'You are not the only one who was worried about Bryant,' Haskell replied. 'Sleep now.'

'Good night, my friend,' Sonje said as she turned from the window.

Sonje woke just after dawn. She bathed and was trying to decide on what dress to wear when there was a soft tap at the door.

"Who is it?" she asked.

"It's me, Sonje, Aunt Ruth."

"Come in," she said with relief. "I could use some help."

"I thought you might," Aunt Ruth said as she entered.

She looked at the several dresses Sonje had laid on the bed.

"You would look stunning in this one," Aunt Ruth said as she picked up one of the dresses.

"I wore it the evening Bryant and I first spoke through thought," Sonje said. "I like it a lot, but isn't it a bit too fancy for the daytime?"

"I don't think so," Aunt Ruth said. "You are to be our Regina. People expect you to dress fancy for this sort of occasion."

Sonje put the dress on and sat down at the dressing table. She opened a drawer and drew out the ribbons she had worn with the dress before. Aunt Ruth helped her do her hair and set the tiara on Sonje's head.

"There," Aunt Ruth said. "Now you look like Gwladys Sonje. A necklace besides that chain would complete the look."

Sonje drew her half of Malvin's Heart from the bodice of her dress.

"This is half of Malvin's Heart," she said as she faced Aunt Ruth. "Bryant wears the other half. It was this that gave us the ability to speak through thought with each other."

"Hoyt told me about that night," Aunt Ruth replied.

"I will keep this on, but I think this is more what you had in mind," Sonje said as she opened the box with Bryant's gift in it.

"Yes," Aunt Ruth answered. "Where did you get them? Did you make them?"

"No," Sonje replied. "Bryant gave them to me for my birthday."

Aunt Ruth helped her with her necklace. As Sonje put on the second earring, there was a knock at the door.

"It's Bryant," Sonje said as Aunt Ruth went to the door.

"Come in, Regis," Aunt Ruth said with a curtsey.

"I was hoping you would wear that," Sonje said when Bryant entered wearing the same clothes he had worn for her birthday party.

Sonje smiled at the awestruck look on his face. He bowed low to her.

"You grow more beautiful with each passing day," Bryant said before kissing her hand.

"And you more handsome," she replied. "I like your hair cut."

"Hoyt insisted," Bryant said with a laugh. "I suppose it was getting a bit long."

"It suits you," Aunt Ruth said. "Let's get some breakfast before the guests start arriving."

Hoyt met them in the hall outside of Bryant's room. They met Auberon and Agatha in the dining hall.

"Here is a copy of the room assignments for you to look over," Agatha said as she placed a piece of paper on the head table. "Lord Bryant, your mother and Brenndah will stay in the children's rooms in Gwladys Sonje's apartment tonight and move to your room for tomorrow night."

"Thank you, Agatha," Bryant said. "This looks good."

After breakfast, Hoyt went out to the courtyard with Bryant and Sonje.

"Everyone will get to the platform by the staircase except you, Lord Bryant," Hoyt explained. "Haskell will bring you to the wall near the castle. Gwladys Sonje and Regis Auberon will arrive in a carriage from just outside of town along the road to the village."

The sound of horses and wagons approaching interrupted Hoyt's explanation. A large enclosed carriage pulled by four matched horses stopped in front of them. The carriage was followed by some wagons. A guard dismounted and opened the carriage door for the passengers.

"Welcome to Dracona," Bryant said with a bow as Archelaus stepped out of the carriage.

"We're so glad you could attend," Sonje said with a curtsy.

"I wouldn't dream of missing it," Archelaus replied as he bowed.

"Neither would we," Althea said as she stepped from the carriage and turned to help Xylia out of the carriage.

Gale, Riva and Charles followed.

"We come with a gift that was contributed by all of Burton," Archelaus said with a smile. "This year's harvest was quite generous and it was decided that in appreciation for your help, Burton presents you the gift of ten wagons of grain, potatoes, and squash."

"Burton is too generous," Bryant said.

"I knew that with the people of Glynis arriving, that food would be the one thing that you would need the most," Archelaus said with a smile. "Just as you gave me the help I needed the most, I asked the people of Burton to give what they felt they could spare, and this is what they gave."

"Thank you," Bryant replied. "And relay our gratitude to the people of Burton."

Soon introductions were made and Bryant gave the guests from Burton a tour of the castle. When they arrived back in the great hall, Sonje and Auberon were there.

"Father, do you remember the scullery boy with the bent back?" Sonje asked.

"Yes," Auberon answered. "It is amazing! I can hardly believe it is the same person."

"It would not be possible without Aunt Althea," Archelaus said with a grin. "You've met Xylia, this is her older sister, Riva and this is Charles."

"Bryant speaks highly of you," Auberon said.

"Charles is now my advisor," Archelaus said. "I wanted him to see this marvelous castle that I have been hearing about."

"There is someone else that I would like you to meet," Bryant said. "He is waiting for us."

* * * * *

Sonje and Auberon went back out to the courtyard. Bryant led the others to the back of the great hall and opened the doors.

"Why are the doors so tall?" Charles asked.

"The same reason that the front doors are so tall," Bryant said with a mischievous grin. "Follow me and you will understand."

Bryant led the group into the cavern where Haskell was waiting for them on the ledge in front of his cave.

"It's a d...d...d," Charles stuttered.

"Dragon," Bryant finished for him. "Lord Dracona is not just a title, but a duty as well. This is my friend, Haskell."

"It is a pleasure to meet you," Archelaus said with a bow. "It delighted me to hear of Gustave's failure in the village due to your appearance."

'I'm happy to be of service,' Haskell told Archelaus.

"He is beautiful," Riva commented.

Bryant was glad to see the smile on Archelaus' face, but Charles was still looking nervous. The women seemed unafraid of Haskell.

"Very soon these caves will be full of dragons," Riva said.

Bryant could hear Haskell chuckling as Charles turned a shade paler.

"Yes," Bryant acknowledged. "When these eggs hatch, the caves will again be filled with dragons."

Bryant put his hand on Charles' shoulder as the man stared at the lumps in the sand.

"Now you see why putting Archelaus on the throne of Burton was so important to Dracona," Bryant told him. "Without the people of Glynis arriving safely, I would have no way to care for all of the baby dragons when they hatched."

'Just as your life has been in service to the king of Burton, Bryant's life has been in service to Dracona's people and dragons,' Haskell told Charles.

Charles looked at Haskell and then at Bryant.

"I had not realized how you came to become Lord Dracona," Charles said.

"Perhaps a brief lesson on the history of Dracona might help," Bryant said. "Let's go where we can sit down."

They followed Bryant to the sitting room of his office. While he was telling them the history of Dracona, Sonje and Auberon were in the courtyard greeting more guests.

* * * * *

Lady Miranda arrived driving a wagon with Brenndah and Bethesda seated next to her.

"Sonje, you look like a queen already," Lady Miranda said as she hugged Sonje. "I bet you can't wait to get through tomorrow."

"The last two weeks have been very difficult for Bryant and me," Sonje replied after hugging Brenndah. "Being able to speak through thought has made it very hard on us."

"I can imagine," Lady Miranda said with a smile. "But it could be a great advantage for both of you tomorrow night."

Sonje blushed at the thought as they started up the stairs. She said nothing until reaching her apartment.

"Father and Hoyt had a talk with Bryant yesterday," Sonje said as she opened the door. "He seems more relaxed now, but he said he is still nervous."

"That is normal," Lady Miranda said. "I remember how nervous I was before the ceremony. But I was even more nervous that night."

"That's what I'm afraid of," Sonje admitted.

"Remember these two things," Lady Miranda said as she took Sonje's hands in hers. "First, you mean everything to Bryant. Second, follow your heart. Let what you have been trying to keep hidden come to the surface."

"I'll remember," Sonje said.

"I've watched both of you. There is no mistaking the love between you. You will be very happy together. And I will be happy having you as a daughter."

That made Sonje feel better somehow. The rest of the morning was spent getting the guests settled into their rooms. Sonje didn't see Bryant again until lunch time. After lunch, Hoyt gathered everyone participating in the wedding in the courtyard. They walked through the wedding ceremony so everyone would know what to do. She felt Bryant's hands trembling as he took hers during the practice. After the practice, Sonje took Brenndah to the tailor's shop for a final fitting.

"You look great!" Sonje exclaimed as Brenndah came out in the pale blue dress she would wear as maid of honor.

Brenndah held the skirt out and turned around as if dancing. Sonje laughed.

"Hoyt said there would be a dance tomorrow night," Sonje acknowledged. "You will probably have a line waiting to dance with you."

Brenndah smiled and went to change. As they were walking back to the castle, Brenndah put her hand on Sonje's arm. She then gestured for them to turn before reaching the castle.

"Isn't the healer's cottage that way?" Sonje asked.

Brenndah nodded. She started down the street. Sonje went with her. At the next corner, they met Bethesda and Raphello.

"We were hoping to find you, Brenndah," Bethesda said.

"Bethesda has told me so much about what you taught her that I can hardly wait to go to Merton with you," Raphello said.

Brenndah smiled and glanced at Sonje. She touched Sonje's arm and gestured to the others before holding out her skirt.

"She wants to know if you have heard about the dance tomorrow night," Sonje said as Brenndah gestured towards the castle. "And are you going to it?"

"Of course," Raphello said. "If you don't mind, Brenndah, I wanted to ask you to save a dance for me."

Brenndah's hand went to her cheek as she began to blush. She nodded her head and looked at Sonje. Sonje understood the look in Brenndah's eye.

"Brenndah would be happy to save a dance or two for you," Sonje said.

Raphello took Brenndah's hand and kissed it.

"I had better get back to the castle now," Sonje said.

Brenndah waved to Raphello and Bethesda before following Sonje.

"I thought that was what you had been hoping for when we were at the tailor's shop."

Brenndah nodded and sighed. Sonje laughed and put her arm across Brenndah's shoulders.

"I've wondered if you had any boyfriends."

Brenndah shook her head.

"I think that is going to change. I thought that the day you first met Raphello."

Brenndah just smiled. When they entered the castle, they found Riva and Xylia talking in the great hall. When Riva saw Brenndah, she fell silent. Brenndah looked at Sonje with concern.

"The heart bound in flame shall be free to bloom as springtime and joyful shall be its voice," Riva said as she stared through Brenndah. "Flame will burn again before the heart can be free."

Sonje saw Riva's eyes close as she began to sway. Sonje stepped to Riva's side and helped Xylia lower her to the floor. Riva sat without moving for a few minutes before opening her eyes again.

"Are you alright?" Sonje asked.

Brenndah knelt next to Riva and took her hand.

"I think so," Riva said. "Sometimes the vision is powerful enough to summon itself. That is when it takes the most out of me."

Brenndah put her hand to her head and winced.

"Yes," Riva replied. "My head hurts a bit."

Brenndah moved behind Riva and put her hands on each side of Riva's head. After a moment, Riva's face relaxed.

"Thank you," Riva said. "That feels much better."

"This is Merton's healer Brenndah," Sonje said after Riva was back on her feet.

"Xylia told me how you made her see again," Riva said. "Thank you."

Brenndah nodded. She and Sonje went up to Sonje's room. They found Lady Miranda putting Sonje's wedding dress into the closet.

"Your gown is beautiful," she told Sonje. "I can't wait to see you in it."

Brenndah nodded in agreement.

"I can't wait until Bryant sees it."

"Not until the wedding. Tomorrow morning we take you outside of town. There will be a tent set up for you to put on your dress," Lady Miranda said. "Olvan and Hoyt will keep Bryant in his room until it is time for the ceremony."

"Then there is one last thing that should be done tonight," Sonje said. "Supper will be served soon. Go ahead and I will meet you there."

When they had gone, she opened the drawer in the night stand next to the bed and drew out the bundle she had stored there when she moved into the apartment. She put her cape over her arm and went down to the dining hall.

* * * * *

Bryant saw Sonje enter the dining hall with her cape over her arm and a bundle in her hand. There was a somber look on her face. Auberon quickly went to her side. He glanced at Bryant and she shook her head.

'What is going on?' Bryant asked Haskell silently.

'I don't know,' Haskell replied in a confused tone. 'But they are both very anxious about something. I am unable to tell you anything more. Whatever it is, they have been keeping it so secret that they don't even refer to it directly in their thoughts.'

'You are impossible to keep secrets from,' Bryant said. 'Whatever it is, I will just have to wait and see.'

Sonje hung her cape over the back of her chair before sitting down. She placed the bundle on her lap under the table.

"I hope you're not thinking of running away," he said to her.

"No," she responded. "Stay with Father after the meal. I, we have something that you must see before the wedding. I will understand if it changes your mind."

"You've had to accept a lot about me that could have made you want to leave," he said sensing how important this was to her. "I can trust you. Whatever it is, we will work it out."

She looked deep into his eyes as if searching for answers to unasked questions.

"Eat," Auberon interrupted. "You both will need the strength."

Sonje nodded and began to eat. Bryant ate, but did not even taste what he was eating. He wished he knew what was bothering Sonje. As soon as she finished her meal, Sonje silently left. The dining hall slowly cleared out until Bryant was left alone with Auberon.

"Elva showed me this same thing the night before our wedding," Auberon said breaking the silence. "You have learned so much in such a short time. We are blessed to have a leader as patient and understanding as you are. Sonje will show you something that only she, Cherie and I know about. It is something out of Glynis' past."

Bryant did not know what to say. He could see that same searching look in Auberon's eyes that he had seen in Sonje's. Whatever was in that bundle seemed much bigger now than its physical size.

"I trust you and Sonje," Bryant said at last. "You two have cared for me when I could not care for myself. You have accepted my past, my present and my future. If I can't trust you two, then I can't trust anyone."

Auberon nodded and seemed satisfied.

'Tell Father I am ready,' Sonje's voice sounded nervous.

"She said she is ready," Bryant told Auberon.

"Come with me, Son," Auberon said. "If you get through this alright, tomorrow will be easy."

Bryant swallowed before following Auberon. The doors to the cavern were open just enough for them to slip through. Sonje stood as still as a white stone statue on the edge of the ledge in front of Haskell's cave. Her cape hung straight down from her shoulders and covered her completely.

Sonje unclasped the dragon clasp on the cape and pulled the cape from her shoulders. Bryant drew a quick breath when he saw what she was wearing. The silver-gray dress was very close fitting and covered from her neck to her wrists. The skirt came only to her knees, revealing tight pants or leggings beneath. He barely noticed Auberon's hand on his shoulder. Sonje turned her back to them revealing two vertical slits in the back of the bodice. Sonje began to glow and something began to protrude from the slits. Bryant gasped again as a pair of wings took shape. Sonje turned and leapt from the ledge with wings outstretched. Bryant watched with amazement as she circled the cavern. He looked at Auberon.

"No one else?" he asked.

"No one," Auberon answered. "Not even Hoyt and Ruth."

Suddenly he recalled Evelina's dream.

"Of course," Bryant said as Sonje landed nearby. "The red cliffs."

He put his hands on her shoulders. Sonje had a puzzled look on her face.

"If the cliffs in Evelina's dream are to become our home, we must adapt," Bryant explained. "Wings would be a perfect solution."

He hugged her, wings and all, before kissing her.

"Oh, Bryant!" she exclaimed when he released her. "I was so afraid that you would not want to marry me when you found out about the wings."

"If you could accept dragons, then wings are no big deal. Actually I wish I had wings myself," Bryant said. "Knowing that we will be married tomorrow, I feel like I could fly."

"Welcome to the family, Son," Auberon said as he patted Bryant on the back. "I'll walk you to your room."

Bryant kissed Sonje once more before following Auberon out.

"You took that much better than I did," Auberon said.

"I think that it will soon be the time to let others in on that secret," Bryant said.

"Let's get you two married first. Glynis has been long enough without a Regis and Regina."

"I can't believe that the day has finally come," Bryant said as they reached the top of the stairs. "By this time tomorrow, Sonje will be my wife."

"Sounds good, doesn't it?" Auberon said with a grin. "It will feel even better."

* * * * *

'May I see your wings?' Haskell asked Sonje.

'Of course,' Sonje replied. 'I know there's no keeping secrets from you.'

She heard Haskell laugh as he stepped out of his cave. She spread out her wings for him to see.

'Beautiful,' Haskell said as he leaned closer.

Sonje could see her reflection in his large eye. The wings were similar to dragon wings.

'You should be going to sleep soon,' Haskell reminded her after a moment.

'Tomorrow I will marry Bryant,' she replied as the wings shrank until they disappeared into her back.

'He did notice more than just the wings,' Haskell said.

Sonje began to blush and said, 'I suppose he would be blind not to in this dress.'

She put her cape back on and gathered up the rest of her things.

'Sleep well,' Haskell said as she left the cavern.

Chapter 22 – In Front of All of Glynis

Bryant awoke just after dawn to a knock at his door.

"Come," he said as he sat up in bed.

Olvan and Hoyt entered followed by Archelaus and Charles. They brought in a large tray of food and set it on the table.

"The first thing you need today is a good breakfast," Olvan announced as Bryant stood up.

He took a seat at the table while Olvan dished up a plate of food for him. Soon everyone had a plate and was eating. As he ate, Bryant looked at each of the men. He was glad they were here. As they finished eating, Olvan looked at the others with a mischievous smile.

"Everyone ready?" Olvan asked.

"Ready for what?" Bryant asked as he heard Haskell laughing.

"I must warn you," Olvan replied. "You're not leaving here until it is time for the wedding. We are here to get you ready."

Bryant could see that Olvan was serious and so were the others. He thought about trying to get to Haskell's cave, but realized it would be futile.

"Alright," Bryant said as he raised both hands in surrender. "I'll cooperate. It looks as if I have no choice."

"You're right," Hoyt said with a laugh. "And if you try to leave early, Edgard and three other men waiting outside that door will make certain you don't."

'Don't feel too bad,' Haskell told him. 'Sonje is getting similar treatment.'

That made Bryant smile. He let them shave, bathe and dress him. As he stood in front of the polished shield, he wondered what Sonje's dress looked like.

"You look perfect," Hoyt said.

"I hope I look that good when I get married," Archelaus said in agreement.

"Now there is just enough time for a few words of advice," Olvan said.

"My father always told me to stand straight and never show fear to the people," Archelaus said.

"Always be faithful in all that you do," Charles said.

"Remember one thing," Hoyt said. "You may be king everywhere else, but in your bedroom your wife is the one who is in charge. If you remember that, your marriage will last for the rest of your life."

Olvan put his arm around Bryant's shoulders and said, "Today is one of the most important days in your life. Don't be in a hurry. Just enjoy the day."

"I want to thank all of you," Bryant said as he looked around the group. "Within the past few months, I have gone from complete solitude to having new friends, new family, and a town full of citizens. Each of you has become an important friend to me. Thank you for being here for me today."

Edgard opened the door and bowed. Olvan led Bryant down to the doors at the back of the great hall.

"I now deliver you to Haskell. The rest of us need to take our places," Olvan told him.

Bryant went through the doors. He was not surprised when the doors closed behind him. Haskell was waiting on the ledge in front of his cave.

'You look very good,' Haskell said.

'You look like you've been bathed as well,' Bryant said with a laugh.

'As a matter of fact, I have,' Haskell responded smugly. 'Come on now, you don't want to be late for your own wedding.'

Bryant took the stairs two at a time and was soon mounted. Haskell took him high above the castle. From there he could see how many people had come for the wedding. He could see many people had been camping in the fields outside of town.

'I told you it would be big,' Haskell said as he circled down to the castle.

When Haskell had landed on the castle wall, Bryant dismounted and walked slowly to the platform. The courtyard and city streets were packed with people. Olvan smiled at him when he stepped on the platform. He crossed to where Olvan was standing. Hoyt stood beside what looked like a low chair with two seats back to back. He heard the hoof beats of Sonje's carriage approaching. He glanced at the others on the platform. His mother smiled as she caught his eye. He could see a tear on her cheek. Everyone turned to the stairs as Sonje and Auberon approached the top of the stairs.

He drew a quick breath as he saw Sonje. Her dress sparkled in the sun from hundreds of tiny gems sewed to it. A piece of white lace covered her face. More of the lace trailed down her back in a bridal veil. The train on her dress trailed to the stairs as she stopped opposite of Bryant. Auberon lifted the veil from her face and kissed her cheek. When Hoyt nodded, they knelt on the chair and clasped hands over the back that stood between them.

"We are here today to witness the wedding of Gwladys Sonje and Lord Bryant Donley," Hoyt began. "They have overcome incredible obstacles to come to this day. They have proven their love for each other and now declare it to the world."

Hoyt turned to Bryant.

"Lord Bryant Donley, do you take this woman to be your wife, to love, honor, and cherish until the end of your time?"

Bryant took a deep breath and looked into Sonje's eyes before saying, "I do."

"Gwladys Sonje, do you take this man to be your husband to love, honor, and cherish until the end of your time?"

His heart beat faster as she returned his gaze and said, "I do."

"Then let no barrier stand between these two," Hoyt announced as he pulled on the chair back and it folded down. "Let it be known to all that from this moment on they are husband and wife. The rings?"

Olvan stepped forward and held out the rings to Bryant and Sonje. Bryant took the dragon ring from her finger and slipped the diamond ring in place before returning it to her finger. Sonje placed a ring with a large diamond held by two dragons on his finger.

"You may now kiss your bride," Hoyt told him with a smile.

She lifted her face to meet his kiss. He kissed her tenderly. She returned his kiss, but more demanding. He released her hands and put his to her waist to pull her closer. When their lips parted, he gasped for air as he felt his heart racing. Her gaze held his eyes as they rose to their feet. He barely noticed the noise of the crowd as they descended the stairs.

The crowd parted as they reached the bottom of the stairs followed by the rest who were on the platform. They went to the dining hall where a delicious smelling lunch was laid out. As they took their seats at the head table, Bryant noticed there was only one plate between Sonje and him.

'To symbolize that we are now as one,' Sonje silently answered his unasked question. 'We are to feed each other at this first meal as husband and wife.'

As they ate, Bryant realized that he was indeed hungry.

'I like this idea,' he told her silently as she took the food from the fork he held. 'I enjoy taking care of you.'

She smiled as she held the fork for him to eat from. When the meal was finished, they went out to the great hall. Along the walls were tables laden with gifts. On one of the tables was the chair Bryant had made. He led her to that table.

"This is what made me miss lunch the other day," Bryant told her as he laid a hand on the seat. "I made this as a wedding gift for you."

"Oh, Bryant! It's beautiful," Sonje replied. "I made a sleeveless jacket for you. It is in my... our room."

"Our room," Bryant repeated. "I can't tell you how good it sounds to hear you say that."

"I think I know," she said with a smile.

They spent several hours looking over the gifts and talking to their guests. Bryant caught occasional glimpses of Auberon and his mother talking. They both looked happier than Bryant had seen his mother look in a long time. As supper time was drawing near, Auberon and Mother came out of the crowd.

"You look so handsome, Bryant," Mother said. "I wish your father could have seen this day. He would be so proud of you."

"I think he is watching," Bryant replied as he hugged her.

"It would please your mother to see how happy you are," Auberon told Sonje as he hugged her. "It's time for you two to go upstairs. Agatha says there is a tray of food for you in your room. Now come cut the cake so you can leave."

Sonje and Bryant followed to where the enormous cake had been set in front of the doors at the back of the great hall. Together they held the knife and cut two small slices. Bryant held one piece while Sonje took a bite from it. She then held a piece for him. It tasted sweet coming from her hand. They were handed a napkin to wipe their hands on when they had finished. The crowd parted as they made their way to the stairs.

Bryant was relieved to be away from the crowds of people. Bryant opened the door and followed Sonje into the room. The room was lit by candle light. They sat down at the table and ate. Bryant could not take his eyes off Sonje. He had never seen her so beautiful.

"Could you help me with this?" Sonje asked as she began to unfasten the veil from her hair.

Bryant quickly stood and went to her side. He helped her lift the veil from her head. He put the veil on the chair next to the door. He could see a long row of buttons down the back of the dress. He placed his jacket next to the veil before helping her unbutton the dress. When the last button was undone, she turned to him. He leaned down and kissed her lips. A chill went up his spine as he felt her hands unbutton his shirt.

No words were exchanged as they helped each other undress. He kissed her along her bare shoulder until reaching her ear as he felt her hands on his skin and her breath hot on his chest. They moved closer to the bed. Sonje put her hand in a bowl on the night stand and drew it out covered with sweet smelling oil which she spread on his skin before following her hand with her lips. He began to spread the oil on her skin and found it to taste as sweet as it smelled. As they explored each other's bodies, their long buried desires began to surface. As they opened their minds to one another, Bryant found that she wanted the same things that he wanted. No words were needed as thought became action.

Down in the darkness of his den, an old dragon was very pleased. His duty to Lord Eamon was at last fulfilled.

* * * * *

Sonje awoke to find Bryant's arms still around her. She smiled as she recalled the night before. She had never thought that she could be this happy and content. She turned over when Bryant began to stir. She kissed his cheek as she put her hand on his chest.

"Good morning, My Husband," Sonje said as his eyes opened.

"So it wasn't just a dream," Bryant replied with a smile.

"A dream come true."

Sonje raised up and kissed his lips. Her heart began to race as she felt him lift her on top of him. She drew a quick breath before kissing him again.

"We should be getting bathed and dressed," Bryant told her. "Our coronation is today."

"So, let's go bathe," she said with a laugh.

* * * * *

'They're up,' Haskell told Hoyt.

'Thank you,' Hoyt said as he turned to Lady Miranda and Regis Auberon. "They are finally awake."

"Let's give them an hour before taking up the tray of food," Regis Auberon said as Lady Miranda nodded in agreement.

When they took the tray of food up, they found Lord Bryant and Gwladys Sonje were nearly ready.

"Did you sleep well?" Regis Auberon asked as Bryant and Sonje began to eat.

Gwladys Sonje nodded while Lord Bryant flashed a smile. When they had finished eating, Ruth and Lady Miranda helped Sonje finish getting ready while Regis Auberon and Hoyt helped Lord Bryant.

"Where is the box you brought from Burton?" Regis Auberon asked.

"Down in my office," Lord Bryant answered with a questioning look. "Fanchon's Sword is there too."

"The box contains your crowns," Regis Auberon explained. "That is why we hid it from Gustave."

"But it is too small isn't it?" Lord Bryant asked.

"You'll see. Let's go get it opened up," Regis Auberon said as he opened the door.

As they walked down the hall, the people they passed bowed low or curtsied. Lord Bryant sighed.

"You'll just have to get used to that," Hoyt told him.

* * * * *

When they reached his office, Bryant brought the two boxes out of the jewel chamber. While Auberon opened the box he had brought from Burton, Bryant belted on Fanchon's sword. Auberon drew two metal spheres from the open box. The smaller one was silver and the larger one was gold. Bryant looked up to see Auberon smile at his puzzled expression.

"Two crowns," Auberon said. "When they are placed in the hands of the rulers of Glynis, they will transform. As the new regis, your crown will be different than mine was."

"There are still things for you to learn about Glynis," Hoyt said with a smile.

"Even so, I like the way things are now better than when I was alone," Bryant admitted.

"And now you won't ever be alone again," Auberon said with a laugh, "not even at night."

"And that is the best part of all of this," Bryant agreed with a grin.

A knock at the door interrupted them. Hoyt opened the door at Bryant's nod. Archelaus and Charles entered. Charles bowed to Bryant.

"Even without a crown, you look every bit a king," Archelaus told him.

"Thank you," Bryant said. "I think I am finally ready to formally accept the leadership of Glynis."

"From the stories I've heard from your people, I can only strive to be as good of a king as you already are," Archelaus said. "I hope you don't mind if I occasionally ask you for advice."

"Not if you don't mind if I ask for your advice in return," Bryant said as he extended his hand.

"I'd be happy to," Archelaus said as he shook Bryant's hand.

"The coronation will take place after supper," Hoyt said. "We can meet the ladies in the library to go over a few last minute details."

"I will meet you there," Bryant replied. "I want to see Haskell first."

Hoyt bowed in acknowledgment. Bryant left the room followed by the others. He paused before opening the doors to the caverns.

'Sonje,' Bryant called out in his mind.

'Yes, Bryant?'

'Meet me in Haskell's den before going to the library.'

'I'll be there in a few minutes.'

Bryant smiled as he opened the doors. It felt good to not have to worry about hiding his thoughts from her. Haskell was waiting for him.

'You look very dignified,' Haskell told him as he put his head down for a closer look. 'And very happy.'

'My life has changed so much.'

'It will change even more. You are taking on a lot of responsibility.'

'I am finding that I like taking care of the people of Glynis.'

Sonje joined them in the cave. Bryant bowed to her and kissed her hand.

"You are the most beautiful regina I have ever seen," Bryant told her.

"I am the only regina you have ever seen," Sonje replied.

"Does that really matter?" he asked. "What matters to me is that you are my regina."

'I am proud of both of you,' Haskell said in a satisfied tone.

"I don't know how we could have done it without you," Sonje said placing a hand on Haskell's cheek. "Thank you."

"You kept me going when I felt there was little reason to go on," Bryant added.

'Your father knew how you would take his death,' Haskell replied. 'And so did I. To some extent, I needed you as much as you needed me. You two had better go now. Hoyt is getting impatient and supper is almost ready.'

Bryant and Sonje hurried to the library. The others fell silent as they entered.

"Lord Bryant, you have been briefed on the traditional coronation ceremony," Hoyt said. "Are there any changes you would like to make?"

"Actually there is one thing I want to add," Bryant replied. "You know by now that I am not fond of addressing large crowds, but I have a few things I would like to say."

Hoyt's face showed his surprise. Auberon and Mother looked pleased.

"Archelaus' coronation inspired this idea. I would like a few moments to speak while I hold the crown in my hands."

"Alright," Hoyt agreed. "I think that might work well. What is it you will say?"

"You can find out when everyone else does," Bryant answered with a straight face which was difficult because he could hear both Sonje and Haskell laughing in his mind.

Hoyt bowed and said, "As you wish, My Lord."

"Let's go eat," Sonje suggested.

Bryant and Sonje led the others down to the dining hall. As they entered, all of the people bowed low as they walked to the head table. Bryant glanced at Auberon who smiled in return. He noticed that the room was much quieter than usual. Several people began to bring the food in for the head table. Bryant found his plate and goblet filled before he could do it himself.

When the meal was finished, Bryant and Sonje left the dining hall. A large crowd had already gathered as the large front doors were opened. A pathway opened as they made their way to the stairs to the platform. The sun was barely visible above the forest when they reached the platform. The crowd was silent as Auberon and Ruth held the spheres of metal above their heads.

"Today it is presented to you, the people of Glynis, of Merton, of the village, to join together here at Dracona," Hoyt began as he stood between Auberon and Ruth. "It is presented to you, the people, that Lord Bryant Donley and Gwladys Sonje be designated Regis Bryant and Regina Sonje to rule over and protect Dracona. It is presented to you, the people, that they be given crowns as symbols of their duties."

"So be it," the people said as one.

Bryant found his hands trembling as he held them out to receive the sphere of gold. Auberon smiled as he met Bryant's gaze. Bryant took a deep breath as he felt the cool metal in his hands. As he began to glow, the shape of the metal began to change. He watched in awe as the crown took shape. To his surprise, there had been gems of different size and color hidden within the sphere. A dragon formed with the largest diamond over its head and a large diamond over each wing. On one side of the dragon stood a winged man and on the other side stood a winged woman. The base of the crown was decorated with the remaining gems. Bryant glanced at Sonje and saw that her silver crown was identical, but smaller.

"I see you were right about not keeping that secret any longer," Auberon said quietly to Bryant.

Hoyt and Ruth seemed stunned by the crowns. That pleased Bryant. Hoyt was not easily surprised. He turned and stepped forward to the edge of the platform.

"I want to thank you for the faith that you have shown me," Bryant said as he began to address the people gathered. "Looking back on my life, I can see that it was in preparation for the responsibilities that you are entrusting to me. Regina Sonje and I will strive to serve you well. This day marks a new beginning for all of us. Our future lies ahead. We must all have the courage to face the changes that are before us. We have forged an alliance with Burton's King Archelaus. We thank him and all of Burton for the generous gift of food that will feed us until the next harvest."

Bryant did not have to look to know that Sonje was now beside him. He held the crown high above his head.

"We accept these crowns which we will wear as a symbol of our commitment to serve all of Dracona and Glynis," Bryant and Sonje said in unison.

As they placed the crowns upon their heads, a cheer rose from the people and those from Glynis began to glow.

Although the sun had set, there was no darkness left in Dracona as the cheers of the people shattered the silence forever.

Tales of Asculum and Map

A group of refugees stranded in the hostile snow covered north divide up hoping to find shelter on this world they call Asculum. All of the dragons and some of the people fly south in search of warmer climates while the rest of the people face a journey they are ill prepared for. They are lost and freezing as their leader urges them forward through the blizzard into the mountains for as a seer she knows that they will find temporary shelter there. They manage to stumble out of the snows into a paradise created by a ring of active volcanoes. Their magical talents become vital in building a city they name Glynis.

As they begin to settle into their new home their leader sends out small scouting parties to discover who inhabits this world. They find that while the people of Asculum look very much like them, they are a short lived primitive people. The people of Glynis learn what they can from these people without revealing that their past and magical abilities. They begin to make wagons and carriages for cargo and people. They even learn to make and use swords along with bows and arrows they've seen the people of Asculum using. As the people of Glynis search for a new home away from the volcanoes that could destroy their valley their past is forgotten.

It is in this environment that the **Tales of Asculum** are set. Each book is meant to be a standalone book involving a particular region of the planet and the characters that inhabit that region.

You would think the life of a prince would be great, but for the crown prince of Brinley that's far from the truth. The only others near his age in the palace are children of the servants who all tease him for having no name. When he goes into the military he must conceal his identity but finally gains some friends. When he is sent to deliver a message to the overthrown tyrant King Burkhart he falls in love with the one woman he knows he can't have.

Aurita knows everyone hates her and her father but everyone is forbidden to tell her why. What she does know is that for her and her father the village is their prison and to leave seals their deaths. King Langward controls their lives including who she will marry when she is of age but he is kind to her. When King Langward's son sends her a gift her father teaches her to read and write so she can send him a note to thank him. They begin to exchange letters. As the years pass she looks forward to the letters she gets from the prince but doesn't dare admit she has fallen in love with him. When she meets the handsome corporal sent to deliver a message to her father her heart is torn between him and the prince.

The last Lord of Dracona is a lonely man with a dark past who is thrust into unexpected responsibilities. He lives alone in an empty castle in the center of the deserted town of Dracona. He faces tasks that he has no hope of accomplishing on his own and no one to turn to for help. Lord Dracona's story includes a nation in search of the answer to an ancient riddle and another nation in the grip of a tyrant king. When he falls in love with a mysterious woman he goes from desperate for companionship and purpose to overwhelmed by new responsibilities as new citizens begin to arrive.

The new King of Burton is in search of a wife but is dissatisfied with the spoiled princesses sent by neighboring kingdoms to court him. At a dear friend's funeral he falls in love with a beautiful servant girl that had a life of slavery and abuse. Through their love and perseverance they are able to unite several kingdoms in peace.

In the dying kingdom of Mannton women are not treated as people. They work for scraps of food and sleep on woven mats that will become their burial wrappings. This all changes after Li is purchased by the king to provide him an heir. He soon finds that she is no ordinary woman.

For more information and social links see www.vjogardner.com

Asculum

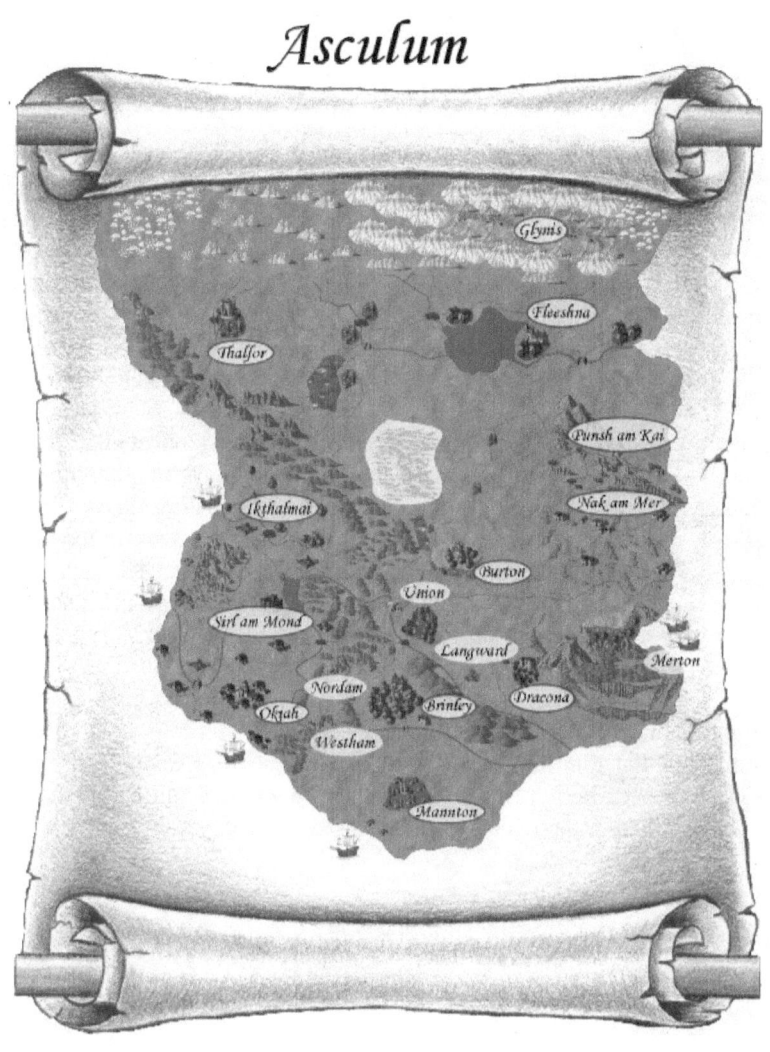

About The Author

Writing under the pen name V.J.O. Gardner, Valerie is an award winning author of full length fractured fairy tale fantasy novels. She has self published *Blood of Ancient Kings* which won an award in the very first contest she had ever entered. Her second book, *Dracona's Rebirth,* is published by Ink Smith Publishing.

Always fastinated by both medieval times and sci-fi she was an avid reader and enjoyed a wide variety of literature and authors. She began writing in in the late 1980's after graduating from Dixie State University in St. George, Utah, where she studied Fantasy Lit and Writing. Valerie is a member of the League of Utah Writers. Although she thought she was writing a short story when she began *Dracona's Rebirth* it blossomed into the full novel it is today.

The good values Valerie was brought up with she instilled both in her children and in her writing. One of her first professional reviews commented that the story reminded him of the Boy Scout Law. While Valerie has been both a Boy Scout leader and a Girl Scout leader the story was written before then. You can visit her at www.vjogardner.com.

www.ingramcontent.com/pod-product-compliance
Lightning Source LLC
Chambersburg PA
CBHW032026240626
47154CB00003B/802